ATTENTION: ORGANIZATIONS AND CORPORATIONS
Most Eos paperbacks are available at special quantity discounts
for bulk purchases for sales promotions, premiums, or fund-
raising. For information, please call or write:

Special Markets Department, HarperCollins Publishers Inc.,
10 East 53rd Street, New York, N.Y. 10022–5299.
Telephone: (212) 207–7528. Fax: (212) 207-7222.

JAMES ALAN GARDNER

ASCENDING

An Imprint of HarperCollins*Publishers*

*This one is to all the gang
from Clarion West '89:*

*I'm a lousy correspondent,
but I still remember.*

EOS
An Imprint of HarperCollins*Publishers*
10 East 53rd Street
New York, New York 10022-5299

Copyright © 2001 by James Alan Gardner
Excerpt from *The Gambler's Fortune* copyright © 2000 by Juliet E. McKenna
Excerpt from *Sky of Swords* copyright © 2000 by Dave Duncan
Excerpt from *Law of Survival* copyright © 2001 by Kristine Smith
Excerpt from *Wheel of the Infinite* copyright © 2000 by Martha Wells
ISBN: 0-380-81329-7
www.eosbooks.com

First Eos paperback printing: November 2001

Eos Trademark Reg. U.S. Pat. Off. and in Other Countries, Marca Registrada, Hecho en U.S.A.
HarperCollins® is a trademark of HarperCollins Publishers Inc.

Printed in the U.S.A.

10 9 8 7 6 5 4 3 2 1

A WORD ABOUT OAR

Oar, the narrator of this story, first appeared in the novel *Expendable*. At the end of that book, she was left for dead after she grabbed an enemy and plunged with him from a window on the eightieth floor of a building.

To human eyes, Oar is as clear and transparent as glass. Although she actually has bones, muscles, and an assortment of internal organs, these were bioengineered to be indiscernible when humans look through her skin.

Oar's ancestors were humans themselves, born on Earth around 2000 B.C. At that time, a collection of *Homo sapiens* were removed by aliens to the planet Melaquin, where the aliens gave these people a new home. The aliens didn't explain why they did this, but they built the humans beautiful glass cities with self-repairing robotic systems designed to provide all the comforts of life.

The aliens gave these humans one additional gift: the people's children were born as strong, intelligent glasslike humanoids who never grew old or sick, and who were tough enough to withstand damage that would kill normal flesh and blood. Only later did it become apparent that these glass offspring had a flaw: although their bodies could survive for millennia, their minds were not so long-lasting. Around the age of fifty, these people succumbed to so-called "Tired Brains"—they lost interest in all aspects of existence, often just lying down and never bothering to get up again. They could still stir themselves if something remarkable happened, but for the most part, they remained catatonic down through the centuries.

Glass parents continued to have glass children, but in decreasing numbers. The population declined in cities, towns, and villages all over Melaquin—gradual extinction from pure ennui. By the time of the events in *Expendable* (the Earth year 2452 A.D.), almost the entire species had fallen into apathetic hibernation. Only a few were still young enough to have active brains.

In *Expendable,* Oar was forty-five . . . on the verge of her race's customary "senility."

Now she's four years older.

1

WHEREIN I AM NOT
DEAD AFTER ALL

My Story

This is my story, the Story of Oar. It is a wonderful story. I was in another story once, but it was not so wonderful, as I died in the end. That was very most sad indeed. But it turns out I am not such a one as stays dead forever, especially when I only fell eighty floors to the pavement. I am made of sterner stuff than that.

Actually, I am made of glass: clear, see-through glass. I am therefore extremely beautiful . . . more beautiful than you, but you should not feel bad about that, because you cannot help being opaque. People who are not beautiful—or strong and clever and wise, as I also am—should take comfort from being ugly and boring, because you will never be Called By Fate to undertake Difficult Adventures. Fate does not invite ugly boring people to save the world; and if you *do* try to save the world (without being beautiful, strong, clever, or wise), you will soon die pointlessly and how much adventure is there in that?

I do not die in this story. Those of you who have looked at the last page—which is only sensible, because you wish to make sure I do not make a long speech telling what lessons I have learned—those who have looked at the end will know that instead of dying, I win *everything*. I defeat the bad people, am adored by the good people, and get to say, "I told you so," as freely as I wish.

That is the whole point of being in stories: to have a Happy Ending.

My Technique

When I decided to present my story to opaque persons, I endeavored to learn what chronicling techniques are popular with your kind. My research methods were most diligent . . . which is to say, I waited for my friend Festina to leave the room, then instructed her computer to show me any documents she had written of a narrative nature.

Therefore, I have discovered that the proper way to write for Earthlings is to divide one's tale into modestly brief sections with titles at the top, such as *My Technique*. This is certainly an Effective Literary Device, especially when addressing persons with a short attention span. The technique also helps one skim ahead for sections whose titles seem more exciting than the passage one is supposed to read next. Thus one can jump forward to read *Facing A Hellish Maw* before coming back to *Conversing With A Little Man Whose Sole Amusing Quality Is That He Is Colored Orange*.

Most importantly, putting many titles into a story makes it easier to find your place if you happen to use your book to smash an irksome buzzing fly, and you hit the fly so hard that pieces of metal and plastic go shooting out of the book mechanism, so then you are forced to put the story chip into a new reader and you cannot remember where you were.

That happens more often than you might expect.

My Resting Place After I Died

When I woke after my eighty-story plunge, I felt most horrible indeed. Many things inside me hurt worse than they had ever hurt before . . . which is not saying much, because this was the first time I had been seriously injured, but pain is more dreadful when one is unaccustomed to physical suffering. If I took a deep breath, sharp aches erupted all across my ribs, as if a dozen axes were chopping at me. And behold, I *did* have an ax pressed against my flesh: a beautiful silver one I have always carried as both weapon and wood-cutting tool. However, the ax was not attacking me in any way; it simply lay on my chest, as if someone had put it there after I fell.

To be honest, I was glad to have the ax with me—it provided a sense of protection. For a brief moment, I tried to cuddle the blade more snugly to me as if it were a pet or a toy . . . but the pain of moving my arms made my vision blur with tears. Every muscle felt bruised to a pulp; I wondered what bruised glass looked like, but knew if I lifted my head to see, the agony would be more than I could bear.

Therefore, I just lay where I was. It happened to be a hot pleasant place to lie, with an abundance of soothing light. I am such a one as absorbs many wavelengths outside the visible spectrum. Radio waves, X rays, and gamma particles are like vitamins to me, while infrared and ultraviolet are basic food groups. (I also eat real food, as produced by the synthesizing machines found in every community of my world. But when I am not having Adventures, I can survive quite well on nothing but sunshine, provided I get a little rain as well.)

Where I was lying, I felt a light spray of water from time to time. I opened my mouth and let the drops trickle down my throat. The water tasted slightly of minerals that were probably good for me.

The light and water and minerals indicated I was in a Home for Ancestors. There are many such Homes on my planet Melaquin, though I did not know this before I became a world traveler. These Homes are designed to contain persons with Tired Brains: persons who have lost interest in life and simply want to lie someplace warm. To keep them happy, every town has skyscraping towers where Ancestors can lie all day, getting plenty of light and squirts of enriched water. It is a boring way to spend the time, and I had promised myself I would never get so sad and lonely that I surrendered to languishing numbness . . . but when one is damaged from falling a long way, it is not so very cowardly to rest for a while in the bright quiet.

So that is what I did.

Clear-Cutting

Now and then, I told myself, "Oar, you must arise, you must find something to do." But there *was* nothing to do. The Home took care of my physical needs, and beyond that, I could think of no goals I wished to accomplish.

There was a time when my world was full of great people doing great deeds. We had a Thriving Culture, creating lovely music and art and literature—the teaching machines in my home village had taught me all about the splendid achievements of our past. I would gladly recite some of our excellent poetry for you, but it does not translate so very well into Earthling languages and anyway, I confess there are gaps in my grasp of human vocabulary: I have worked hard to memorize your *best* words, but I cannot be bothered to learn the second-rate ones (which is to say, the ones with no counterparts in my native tongue).

Besides, I have no great ambition to be a poet . . . or an artist or even musician. In my whole life, I have only embraced one useful occupation—using my ax to cut down trees. I did this because a human Explorer told me that deforestation was how cultured persons tended their planets: clearing land in preparation for constructing farms and roads and cities. I did not know how to construct things, but I was excellent at chopping down timber, so that is what I did.

It turns out I destroyed so much woodland, the results were noticeable from space . . . which became a source of much pride once an Explorer informed me of my achievement.

That Explorer had been an opaque human named Festina Ramos. When I first met Festina, she was lost and frantic, marooned on my planet with no means of escape. I therefore embarked on my first great Adventure: to return Festina to her own people. I did not quite know how that Adventure had turned out, since I suffered my terrible fall before Festina went home; but my friend was not here now, so I assumed we had triumphed in all particulars. Through selfless heroism, I had helped Festina leave Melaquin . . . and I could congratulate myself on a Glowing Success.

But as I lay inside the Tower of Ancestors, drowsily reflecting on My Life So Far, I felt no thrill of achievement. Festina was gone, as if she had never been here at all—what did I have to show for my time with her? I had chopped down vast stands of trees, but to what end? No farms or roads would ever be built on the cleared land, for my people were almost extinct. To be sure, millions were still alive all around the globe; but they did nothing except breathe and soak up light. They had no goals or purpose . . . and what purpose could *I* find alone in a world of the dead?

Of course, there was always the chance a new group of Explorers would visit my planet. Earthling Explorers tended to be repugnantly opaque, not to mention uncouth and slow to understand the simplest things, but at least they could supply me with acclamatory feedback: "Oar, you cut down trees more prettily than anyone else in the universe!" (Except they would put this sentiment in their own words to achieve the effect of sincerity.) Then I would once more feel joy in changing the face of my planet, and would know that my life had Direction.

All I required was someone to assure me I was not wasting my existence on meaningless busywork.

I waited for someone like that to come along. And eventually, he did.

Being Roused By A Small Orange Alien

One day, I awoke to find an alien creature shouting into my face. "Are you Oar?" it yelled in the language of Explorers. "Come on, baby, wake up. Tell me if you're Oar."

"I am not a baby," I answered. "I am forty-five years old."

"If you're Oar, you're older than that. You should be forty-nine by now. *Are* you Oar?"

"Who wants to know?"

The creature leaning over me was neither glass nor human. However, it *was* approximately human-shaped, with two arms, two legs, and a head. The head did not have normal ears; instead, there were two bulgy balls on top of the skull, like puffy mushrooms growing from the scalp. For clothes, the alien wore a white short-sleeved shirt, gray short-legged pants, and tan sandals, all of them stained with spills of unknown origin. The creature's scaly flesh was not transparent like mine, nor anywhere on the pink-to-brown-to-black spectrum of Earthlings. Instead, the skin was a shade of orange that grew darker as I watched: from tangerine to pumpkin to an extremely burnt ocher.

This struck me as thoroughly foolish—an alien who can change color should endeavor to become clear and beautiful, not more opaque and unattractive. But the universe is full of beings with Different Views Of Life. Often these views are stupid and wrong, but a wise-minded one (such as I) always practices tolerance in the company of irrational persons.

Conversing With A Little Man Whose Sole Amusing Quality Is That He Is Colored Orange

"The name's Uclodda Unorr," said the darkening orange creature, "but everybody calls me Uclod. As in, 'Get off my foot, Uclod!' "

The alien grinned as if it had just told a joke. I decided this creature must be male; only a man could believe I might be charmed by such a feeble witticism. I also concluded he must be a *young* man—perhaps in his early twenties. An older person would not gaze at me quite so eagerly hoping for approval.

When the alien saw I merely stared at him without amusement, he harrumphed in his throat and went back to his former line of questioning. "So spill it, missy—are you Oar or not? I was told you'd be lying here starkers with an ax cuddled against your wallabies; but I was also told you'd be dead, so there's obviously something out of whack."

Clutching my ax, I sat up and glared at this Uclod person. Though I was seated on the floor, he was not so much taller than I. If I stood, his head would only come to the level of my wallabies. (You will notice how quickly I pick up words from foreign languages.) "I am Oar," I told him frostily. "An oar is an implement used to propel boats."[1]

"That's exactly the phrase I wanted to hear," Uclod said. "And you're an acquaintance of Festina Ramos?"

"I am Festina's dearest friend. We went on a great Adventure recently; she is my Faithful Sidekick."

"Your adventure wasn't so recent, toots," Uclod replied. "It was four Terran years ago. What've you been doing with yourself? Just letting your brain go to mush?"

"No," I told him, "I have been resting to recuperate from grievous wounds." But it was most disturbing to hear that four whole years had gone by. One less courageous than I might be scared she had let so much time pass in a daze. She might worry most acutely that her brain was getting Tired like the elderly persons around her.

Fortunately, I am not such a one as gets the shivers over a little thing like aging. My brain was not Tired. My brain was *just fine*.

Proving I Am Just Fine

"Are you all right?" Uclod asked.

"Yes. I am superb."

To demonstrate, I rose to my feet with fluid grace . . . and if I chose to lean on my ax, I did not need a crutch, I was merely taking a Sensible Precaution. This was the first time

---

[1] It is a custom of my people to suggest how others may remember our names: since our older citizens have Tired Brains, they need all the memory aids they can get. I was not actually named after a paddle—that would be very foolish, because I am a person, not a stick of wood—but the English word "oar" sounds much like my real name. (For those who wonder what Oar means in my own language, it translates to "extremely clever and beautiful person whom everyone envies even if they are too small-minded to admit it." At least, that is what it means *now*.)

I had roused myself to stand since my calamitous fall; perhaps I would be wobbly or infirm. But I felt no pain or stiffness—my ribs did not ache when I took a breath, and my battered bruised muscles had healed to their usual perfection.

Perhaps I really *had* been lying in a doze for four whole years—long enough to recover from all my injuries. But the time for dozing was over.

"There," I said, feeling better now that I was taller than the little orange man with balls on his head. "You see how well I am."

"Can't argue with that," he replied, staring up at my wallabies. "You got definite photogenic appeal. Pity you look so much like a computer-generated effect."

I did not understand him, so I assumed he was talking nonsense. Many people do. "Why are you here?" I asked. "Did Festina Ramos send you?"

"Nope, a friend of hers. Well, not exactly a friend—a fellow admiral. Alexander York."

Uclod leered as though he believed the name would shock me. It did not. "Who is this Alexander York person? And why should I care about him even a little bit?"

The small man's grin faded. "Missy, you *have* been out of touch, haven't you?"

"I have been right here. It is everyone else who has been out of touch."

"You got me there." Uclod wiped sweat from his forehead. "Can we talk about this outside? My skin blocks most of the radiation in here, but I'm still getting my gizzards cooked."

"There is no radiation in this tower," I told him, "there is simply an abundant supply of light. But I do not want your gizzards to cook, for then you might smell even worse than you do already. Let us go."

A Clear Path To The Exit

Together we headed for the exit. The route was unobstructed, which I found most odd: usually Ancestral Homes have dozens of elderly persons littering the floor, particularly near the front entrance. Those with brains on the verge of exhaustion have a deplorable habit of walking in from the street and flumping straight down on the closest patch of unoccupied ground. After several generations, there is no space at all in the first few rooms.

But here, the clutter had been partly cleared. Though many senile persons still sprawled about, they were all shoved against the glass walls to make an open path up the middle.

The path led straight to where I had lain.

"Did you do that?" I asked Uclod. "Did you move these people out of the way?"

"Not me, toots. It was like this when I got here."

"Then it is a Mystery," I told him. "I enjoy solving mysteries. I am excellent at rational deduction."

"I can see that," Uclod replied . . . though his gaze was directed at a part of my person that is seldom associated with intelligent thought.

"Wait," I told him. "Observe my methods." Then I walked to the side of the path and kicked an old man so hard he flew off the floor and smashed into the wall.

The secret is to get your toe underneath the body. Use a strong scooping action.

"Whoa, missy!" Uclod cried. "Are you trying to kill that guy?"

"Do not be foolish," I answered. "My people cannot be killed. They seldom even feel pain—especially those whose brains are Tired. Look."

I pointed to the man I had kicked. Though he now lay awkwardly against the wall, he showed no sign of being roused from his stupor; he had slept through the whole thing. On the other hand, my kick had propelled him onto an old woman, and she was not nearly so lethargic. Indeed, she embarked upon a Storm Of Invective wherein she claimed to know all about my parentage, particularly how my mother became pregnant and what unusual measures she took thereafter. The woman was wrong in almost every respect, but her ill-informed harangue proved her brain was not so Tired as those around her.

"Hush, old woman," I told her in our own language. *"I wish to ask you a question."*

"Who are you calling old?" the woman grumbled. *"You're likely older than I am."*

"I am not!" I snapped.

"What'd she say?" Uclod asked. He had not understood our words, but he must have recognized the anger in my tone.

"She said I was old," I told him. "Whereas, in fact, it is *she* who is elderly."

"How can you tell?" Uclod asked. "You look the same age to me."

"Of course, we *look* the same—my species ceases to change physically after the age of twenty. But mentally this woman must be older than I; she lives in an Ancestral Home."

"You've lived in this same home for the past four years. How do you know that lady didn't come in after you?"

"Because . . ." I stopped. I was going to say I would have noticed if someone new arrived; but perhaps that was not so certain. Especially if the woman had arrived while I was sleeping.

But no, she could not be younger than I. I was Mentally Alert, whereas the woman before me was already starting to lapse back into slumber. Her gaze was losing intensity; the fire that had flared up while she cursed me was now turning to ash. I tucked my hands under the woman's armpits, lifted her up, and slammed her back against the tower's glass wall. Uclod grimaced at the crack of glass bones on glass bricks . . . but I knew the wall would break long before this woman suffered the least bit of damage.

My people are more sturdy than walls.

"Wake up!" I shouted in the woman's face. *"Do not go to sleep again."*

"Why not?" Her collision with the wall had brought back the focus in her eyes, but her voice was sullen—like a cranky child who wants to remain in bed.

"Because if you stay awake," I told the woman, *"you will be able to lead a rich life wherein you accomplish great things."*

"Like what?"

"Like . . ." I looked about me for inspiration; seeing the open path down the center of the room, I remembered why I had awakened her in the first place. *"We shall solve a mystery, you and I. We can discover who cleared the space from me to the door."*

"Oh, I saw that," the woman said. *"It was interesting. Sort of. I think . . ."*

Her voice was fading. *"Wake up!"* I cried. *"Stay awake and talk to me."* With a burst of fierceness, I thrust my silver ax close to the woman's face. *"Stay awake or I shall cut off your wallabies."*

"Missy!" Uclod said, staring at the ax. "What the hell are you doing?"

"I am attempting to make a friend." Without letting him interrupt further, I turned back to the woman. *"Talk to me. Talk to me about . . . about this interesting thing you saw."*

"There was an alien," the woman replied with grumpy ill will. *"A big white thing—like some animal, but bigger than a buffalo and it didn't have a head."*

"Then where did it put its ears?" I asked.

"It didn't have ears. Or eyes or a nose or a mouth. Because it didn't have a fucking head. Have you heard a word I'm saying?"

"I am listening most attentively. This headless beast picked you up to clear a path to me?"

"It didn't touch us," the woman answered, *"but we moved anyway. Everybody. We floated off the floor and out to the sides. Then the creature took away your body and when it brought you back, you were alive again."*

"But I was always alive. I am not so weak as to die from a little tumble."

"You didn't look alive," the woman said. *"But you got taken away and when you came back . . ."*

Her voice faded again. I gave her another smack against the wall. *"Wake up! Is it not interesting that I appeared dead but then was alive? Do you not wish to find this headless beast and learn the reasons for its actions? I am clearly enmeshed in Portentous Events and if you accompany me, we shall both . . . wake up! Wake up! Wake up!"*

I slapped her hard. She did not react. I lifted my hand to slap her again, but Uclod seized my wrist.

"Enough, missy," he said. "You've knocked her out cold."

I looked at the woman before me. She was beginning to slump to the floor—but not because I had battered her unconscious. I had not hit her hard enough to cause injury; in fact, I had not hit her hard enough to keep her awake.

And through all this, none of the others within hearing had opened an eye to watch. Too lost to care. The woman had been the most awake of them all; but she had not been awake enough.

Perhaps no one in this tower was. No one in this city. No one in the world.

Uclod eased his grip on my wrist and took me by the hand instead. "Come on. Let's get out of here."

I let him lead me away.

2

WHEREIN I BECOME
AN IMPORTANT WITNESS

Subterranean Snow

Outside the tower, it was snowing. Only a few flakes trickled directly onto my shoulders, but many more were falling three blocks over.

The snow came through a great hole in the roof. This city—and I do not know the city's true name, so I shall call it Oarville—was built within a gigantic cavern dug deep under a mighty mountain. The place seemed empty and abandoned now, except for thousands or even millions of Ancestors who slept in their great bright towers. Apart from those towers, all other lights had been damped down by the supervising machines that concern themselves with power consumption. The result was a permanent dusk, illuminated only by Ancestral Towers shining amidst the underground blackness.

At one time, the whole cavern had been completely sealed off from the outside world; but then my friend Festina used Science to blow a great fissure in the stony roof so she could fly inside with an aeroplane. Although that happened four years before, the city's repair machines had not yet patched up the damage . . . which disturbed me very much indeed. The purpose of machines is to work automatically: to mend breakage and to shield people from the Harsh Cruel World.

13

Here in Oarville, the Harsh Cruel World was enjoying free rein—a blizzard gusted with arctic ferocity through the mountains outside, and its thick showers of white spilled in through the roof's hole.

Why had the damage not been fixed? Unless perhaps the city's repair machines were becoming as Tired as the people: lapsing into torpor like the woman in the tower. But I did not want to think such a thing—I did not want to think about my whole world guttering out like a candle. Therefore, I tried to empty my mind of mournful thoughts, concentrating only on the here and now.

Standing in the open air. Snowflakes falling down.

The hole in the roof was high above us, higher than the city's glass towers. Wind whistled across the gap, but did not reach all the way to the street; the gale sent snow swirling madly as it entered the cavern, but the furious spinning whiteness lost energy as it fell. By the time the snow brushed past my face, it had resigned itself to perfect calm. Even over by the central square, directly under the rupture in the roof, the snow floated quietly as it settled onto the pavement.

"Whoa!" Uclod said, staring at the soft white tumble pouring onto the city. "Where did that come from?"

"It is snow," I told him. "Snow is a weather phenomenon."

"It wasn't a weather phenomenon ten minutes ago," he said. "But I guess things change fast in the mountains. Give me a sticky-hot beach any day."

"I will not give you anything," I said. "I have heard about you aliens trying to obtain other people's land. If you offer me beads and trinkets, I shall punch you in the nose."

"You got the wrong idea, missy. I'm not here to give you grief." The little man grinned. "But maybe together, we can give grief to other people."

"Are these other people evil?"

"Utter bastards."

"Then they deserve trouble. I feel no pity for bastards, especially utter ones."

I started toward the central square, where the snow drifted down the thickest. Snow is a fine thing indeed: it is pleasantly cool as it falls on your arms, and when the flakes melt against your skin, they leave attractive droplets of water. I am not such a one as wears clothes even in winter, but snowflake sprinkle is an excellent look for me.

The short Uclod man trudged at my side, muttering about the snow; he was obviously a Warm-Weather Creature, unprepared for a Melaquin winter. His skin, which had darkened in the tower, was now growing light again: turning from umber to orange, and onward to a bleached yellow jaundice reminiscent of dead grass. It could not have been that he was sickening from the cold, for the city was well-heated despite the hole in the roof. (All around us, the snow melted as soon as it touched the pavement.) But Uclod's skin seemed intent on reacting in exaggerated fashion to every tiny change in the environment.

"You were telling me about utter bastards," I said, "and why you have come to Melaquin if you are not after our land. Are you another fucking Explorer, marooned against your will?"

"Not me, missy," he replied. "I'm what you might call a private entrepreneur. Working at the moment for Alexander York."

"Who is a friend of Festina's."

"Friend isn't exactly the right word."

"What *is* the right word?"

"Uh. Victim."

Uclod's tone suggested there might be an excellent story in how this York person became Festina's victim. I asked him to disclose everything . . . and he did.

The Sinister Admiral York

Alexander York had been a very bad man. He was a high-ranking admiral in the Technocracy's Outward Fleet, where he did many awful things to humans and a race called the Mandasars. York's greatest villainy, however, was trying to kill my Faithful Sidekick, Festina. She tried to kill him right back, and with the help of some alien moss, she *won*. (I did not quite follow how that worked, but I believe she stuffed moss into the bad man's stomach until he exploded. That is not how Uclod told the story, but his version was so strange and implausible that I chose to reconstruct his tale in a way that made more sense.)

At any rate, Alexander York died horribly as all base villains should. Soon everyone in the human Technocracy learned of the admiral's reprehensible deeds. It was a top-of-the-broadcast story for many days, and the Most Famous Actor In The Galaxy played York's role in the news dramatizations. The producers even got a Reasonably Famous Actress to play Festina. Apparently, the actress invented a delightful accent in lieu of characterization . . . and even though Festina does not actually have an unusual accent, the critics unanimously agreed it was what a Fringe-Worlder named Ramos *should* sound like.

In this way, York's wickedness provided much wholesome family entertainment; but unbeknownst to the public, there was more to come.

The Unscrupulous York's Protection Policy

The evil Mr. York had always suspected he might suffer violence from his enemies on the High Council of Admirals. (The council is a place where everyone schemes against everyone else, and people talk incessantly about Power with a capital "Pow.") For insurance against his council colleagues, York kept meticulous records of every scandalous thing the high admirals did, individually and as a group: every foul trick, every breach of the law, every secret betrayal. In fact, Uclod said, "York collected enough dirt to send the whole damned council to jail till the next millennium. Enough to get them chopped into giblets and fed to ugly dogs."

(I asked if that was the type of thing one could watch. Uclod told me it was only a metaphor.)

As York accumulated this damning evidence, he placed it in the keeping of a family named Unorr: Uclod's relatives. According to the small orange man, his uncles and aunts and cousins were reputably disreputable . . . which meant they were dreadful criminals who would do many dishonest things for a price, but once you bought them, they stayed bought.

"It's quite the profitable market niche," Uclod explained. "You'd be amazed how few crooks actually keep their word . . . and the same with so-called honest people, lawyers and banks and all. Lawyers will always buckle under to something, whether it's bribes, violence, court orders, or the weight of their own bullshit. Same with banks—they turn tail and run the instant something upsets the stockholders. But we Unorrs do what we're paid to do, even when things get hot. *Especially* when things get hot. Which is why York hired us to take the High Council down."

As soon as the Unorrs heard York was dead, they assembled the information they had received from the admiral and prepared to deliver it to the most irresponsible journalists they could find. But they also delegated junior family members (such as Uclod) to collect extra evidence of misdeeds that were not perfectly documented.

Therefore the small orange man had come to Melaquin. Until four years ago, my planet was used as a dumping ground for individuals the Admiralty wished to make disappear—Persons Who Knew Too Much, Persons Who Broke The Unwritten Code, and Persons Who Did Not Do Anything Specifically Wrong But Were Strongly Disliked Anyway. My clever Festina had forced a stop to this practice, but part of her agreement with the High Council was that she would keep the matter a secret. Everything had been hushed up and nobody breathed a word . . . except Alexander York, who wrote down the story and passed it to the Unorrs.

"The sticky point," said Uclod, "is that York's only evidence about Melaquin was Festina Ramos's statement. He didn't bother getting substantiation—no footage of folks actually marooned here, no outside corroboration, no smoking gun . . ."

"The gun did not smoke," I said, "it whirred."

"What gun?"

"The one with which I was shot. Repeatedly. By a wicked

man." (This was the same wicked man whom I later killed—he had a Pistol Of Inaudible Sound that wreaked hypersonic mayhem on the crystalline parts of my body. He thought his weapon would shatter me, but I am not *real* glass, so I survived. Shortly thereafter, I shattered *him*. Hah!)

"Right," Uclod said, "I read about that in Ramos's report—the one she gave the High Council. But that report was the only documentation we ever got on Melaquin, and our family didn't think it was enough. Even as we speak, my Grandma Yulai is back on New Earth, revealing the dirt York gave us. Next thing you know, the Admiralty and the media will send crews blasting toward Melaquin; but the navy flies faster, and by the time reporters arrive, there'll be nothing to see. This place'll be swept cleaner than the prick on a long-tongued dog. That'll damage the credibility of the Melaquin story, which'll damage the credibility of everything else in York's exposé." He gave me a grin. "So, missy, my grandma decided we needed more evidence *before* the navy had a chance to mop up. And that's why I'm here."

Evidence Lying All Over The Place

Uclod had come to Oarville with something called an Honest Camera, a complicated recording device invented by an advanced race called the Shaddill. The camera used clever scientific tricks to prevent people from tampering with the pictures it took; it also had built-in clocks and locator devices for proving exactly when and where its pictures had been taken. Lesser species like humans had not yet pierced the complexity of most Shaddill technology. In particular, they did not know how to circumvent the Shaddill's protective measures, so the camera's photographs would be accepted in Technocracy courts as Unfalsified Truth.

The little orange criminal had taken many photos to establish that human Explorers were once marooned here. When we reached the central square, I could see for myself the evidence those Explorers left—bits of navy equipment scat-

tered all over, little tools and machine parts and backpacks.
During their stay, the humans had worked to build a spaceship as a means of escape . . . and when they finally left,
they departed so hurriedly they had not picked up after
themselves.

If you want the truth, the square was a Scandalous Mess.
Moreover, the litter was opaque—metal and canvas and colored plastic. The clutter had sat where it was since the humans left four years ago . . . and because it lay directly
under the opening in the roof, it got snowed on in winter and
rained on in summer, till it was very quite disgusting indeed:
covered with molds of vivid fuzzy colors. When I picked up
a discarded wad of clothing, I even saw speck-sized holes
that must have been chewed by *insects*.

"That's an Explorer jacket," Uclod said, pointing to the
garment I held.

I nodded. Most of the humans exiled on Melaquin had belonged to the navy's Explorer Corps. I did not like Explorers
so much—the worst of them could make you feel awkward
and stupid, because you did not Know Science or how to Act
Like A God-Damned Adult, For Christ's Sake. At night they
pleaded with you to play bed games, yet when morning
came, they were Too Busy, Go Away and would not look
you in the eye. Explorers could make you feel lonesome and
bad . . . but my friend Festina was also an Explorer and she
was always most kind, so Explorers were not all horrible.

I hugged the jacket to my chest. It was made of thick
black cloth; snowflakes speckled the cloth like stars in the
night sky.

"Did that belong to someone you knew?" Uclod asked.

"I do not think so. But Festina spoke most fondly of the
Explorer's black uniform. It was a Valuable Important
Thing; she felt quite sad she had not thought to pack a spare
outfit when she came to this planet."

"I guess she had other concerns to worry about," Uclod
said. "Considering how she thought Melaquin would be a
suicide mission."

"But many other Explorers thought to pack uniforms.
They were warned they might be marooned here, so they

brought important equipment and valuable personal treasures." I looked at the trash strewn about the square. "It
seems those treasures were not so valuable after all. When
the Explorers were ready to go, they did not care what they
left behind. They just tossed everything away to rot in the
street . . . to get cold and wet and snowed on, because they
did not *really* care about anything except themselves."

I stared up into the cold wet snow, suddenly feeling sad.
"Even Festina went away," I whispered.

Uclod patted my hand. "Hey," he said in a soft voice, "I
read your friend's statement about what happened here.
Ramos didn't leave your planet willingly; and anyway, she
thought you were dead."

"But I told her I could not die! I told her my people go on
and on—"

"Oar," Uclod interrupted, "you looked dead. Ramos
couldn't find a heartbeat, not even with topnotch Explorer
sensing equipment. She decided to leave you among your
own people, because that's what she thought you'd want."

"But I was not dead! Not even a little bit!"

"Yeah, okay," the wee orange man said, "Ramos got it
wrong. But even so, she didn't just desert you—she took
you back to that tower and laid you out all pretty. Hands
folded, eyes closed, ax across your chest." He gave a little
smile. "That's what I thought I'd find when I came looking
for you: a nice glass corpse I could photograph. I was even
debating whether to lug your remains back to New Earth,
so's the lawyers could use you as Exhibit One. But when I
got to where Ramos said you'd be, lo and behold, you were
breathing. That's why I asked if you were really Oar."

"Which I am!" I told him, suddenly feeling bright again.
"You may rejoice, for I am not deceased after all."

The little man shrugged. "I'm thrilled for you, toots, I really am; but I gotta say, you were worth more to me as dead
meat. A good-lookin' gal, all battered and broken—that
would have played big-time with the viewing public. But if
you're still alive and kicking, what can I sell to the network
news?" He kicked at a rusty hunk of debris lying in the
street. "You think they want pictures of this boring old junk?

They'll flash it on the screen for five seconds, tops; then they'll move on to some *interesting* story, like a dachshund who juggles goldfish."

"But it is *better* me being alive," I said. "I will play with the viewing public very big-time indeed, for I shall describe all the awful things that were done to me. I am excellent at Sensationalized Descriptions Of Emotional Trauma."

"Uh huh." He looked me over from head to toe. "I have to admit, toots, you'd wow 'em on the news. And the nets will be *much* happier putting your face in the headlines than Festina Ramos."

I nodded sympathetically. Festina is a very nice person, but she does not have a Dazzling Regal Beauty.

"The more I think about it," Uclod said, still gazing at me, "this could work. It really could. I've got the footage I need from this world—pictures of the city, the Explorer equipment, the missile crater in the roof. That'll be fine for the courts. But for the media, you'd add that extra level of authenticity to make this story *zing*."

"I am most zingfully authentic," I assured him. "I am an extremely credible witness."

"Yeah, I can imagine Mr. and Mrs. Slack-jawed Viewer saying, *Look at the credibility on that babe!*"

He paused and his face grew more somber. "Now, toots, I gotta warn you: this could get pretty ugly. Those buggers on the High Council are vicious bags of shit—that's damned obvious from reading York's files—and if they decide murdering you will solve more problems than it creates, they'll hire some dirt-wad to shatter your glass caboose."

"Hah! I am not the type of glass that shatters into cabooses. If any dirt-wads try, I shall make them very sorry."

Uclod scowled. "You gotta take this serious, missy. Bad people will want you dead. And no matter how unbreakable you think you are, those navy shits can dream up something to put you in a coffin. Blow you up, crush you under a dozen steam-hammers, then dump whatever's left in an acid bath. If you treat this like a game, you'll die . . . and maybe take other folks with you. Me and my family, for instance." He peered sharply into my eyes. "If I let you come to New

Earth, are you going to be smart? Because if you aren't, to hell with you. I'm taking enough risks already, and I don't need someone who's just a liability. For all I care, you can go straight back to that tower and let your brain rot to tapioca."

I attempted to return his gaze with righteous indignation—I truly did my best. But I will tell you a thing: there are times I am not so strong as I want to be. When humans or other aliens tell me, "Oar, you must behave the way we say," I am not always wholly defiant. I am, after all, perfectly able to conform with Conventional Rules Of Propriety; under the tutelage of human Explorers, I learned Earthling modes of conduct as quickly as I learned the Earthling language.

But I am not an Earthling. I do not wish to be one. I do not wish to be *mistaken* for one. As the last of my kind, I refuse to betray my species by submitting to alien dictates. When I am strong, I therefore comport myself in a defiant fashion of my own choosing.

At that moment, however, I was not strong. If Uclod went away, perhaps no one would ever come to my planet again—except navy persons endeavoring to eradicate evidence of humans on my world, and I knew better than to approach *them.* I would end up forever alone . . . and in time, I might go back to the Tower of Ancestors, and I might lie down, and I might not get up.

"I know this is not a game," I mumbled to the little man. "I know there is much at stake. *Much.* I will not act crazed and irresponsible."

Uclod stared into my eyes a moment longer, then nodded. "This way," he said. "The spaceship is down here."

The Jacket

He started along one of the streets leading off the square. I threw away the Explorer jacket I had been holding and followed him a few steps . . . then went back and picked up the jacket again. It was damp and smelly and pierced with insect nibbles; but I knew certain people in the Technocracy thought you were stupid and disgusting if you Walked Around All Day With Your Bare Ass Hanging Out.

I am not such a one as cares about surly people's opinions; but as I have said, at that particular moment I was not possessed with great strength of spirit. And perhaps, I thought, there were important Science reasons why one had to wear clothes on other planets. Perhaps there were dangerous cosmic rays or poisonous atmospheric substances, so one had to don jackets to protect oneself from peril.

Wearing clothes might not be a cowardly concession to the small-minded prejudice of hateful persons. It might be a sensible precaution.

Yes.

Clutching the jacket, I took a deep breath. Then I hurried along behind Uclod, following his tracks through the light sheen of melting snow.

3

WHEREIN I AM SWALLOWED BY A LARGE CREATURE

The Diversity Of Spaceships

The spaceship was three blocks away, still well within the snow zone. Uclod had set it down in a wide intersection where two streets met; there was not so much landing room as if he had chosen the central square, but I suppose he had not wished to disturb the Explorer evidence back there.

Uclod's vessel was nothing like the spaceship the Explorers had been working on when I arrived in the city. The Explorers' ship had been shaped like a large glass fish . . . except Festina told me it was not a fish at all but a mammal called an orca, or killer whale. The whale shape was not the Explorers' choice—many of them thought it barbaric for a starship to look like an animal instead of an abstract geometric object—but the Explorers were using the hull of an old space vessel built by ancient inhabitants of Oarville, and beggars cannot be choosers.

As for me, I thought a fish was an excellent form for a spaceship; one could picture it diving into the great blackness and plunging past whirlpool galaxies. Also it would be very good at orbiting, for fish are constantly swimming in mindless circles. Uclod's ship, on the other hand, was not so easy to imagine speeding through The Void—it was nothing more than a huge gray ball, five stories high and powdered with snow. One could picture such a thing avalanching down a mountain, but it certainly did not fit the image of a Graceful Nomad Of The Space Lanes.

"Isn't she a beauty?" Uclod said as we walked toward the ship. "Isn't she the loveliest little girl you've ever seen?"

"It is quite spherical," I answered with tact. "You do not think the snow on top will cause problems, do you? Sometimes when machines get damp, the electric bits go fizz."

"Lucky for us," Uclod said, "she doesn't *have* electric bits. Bioneural all the way."

I had not made the acquaintance of the word "bioneural," but I assumed it was a boring Science concept that would only vex me if Uclod tried to explain. Besides, I had greater concerns on my mind. The closer we got to the ship, the more I saw it was not just a plain gray sphere; it was, in fact, a *whitish* sphere, covered with snarled-up threads of gray string. As for the white undersurface, it looked all wet and gooey, glistening as damply as the snow falling around it. To get the exact picture, imagine the egg of some slimy creature that breeds in stagnant water, then wrap gray spiderwebs all over the egg's jelly so the strands sink into the goo.

In short, the ship was very most icky . . . so when I got close enough, I touched it to see if it felt icky too. It felt quite appalling indeed—like bird poop just after it falls from the sky.

"What are you doing?" Uclod asked.

"I wished to see if your craft feels as vile as it looks. Which it does."

"Hey!" he said sharply, "don't insult Starbiter!"

"If you have named your ship Starbiter," I said, "there is little more I can do in the way of insults."

The Nature Of A Creature Which Bites At Stars

I began to circle the ship's exterior, wondering why alien races always make their machinery unattractive. Surely the universe does not *require* space vehicles to be large gooey balls wrapped in string; a sensible universe would not even *approve* of such a design. If you constructed your starship out of nice sleek glass, I believe the universe would let you fly much faster, just because you had made an effort to look presentable. But one cannot suggest such things to Science people—they will laugh at you in a very mean fashion, and make you feel foolish even when you know you have an Astute Perspective On Life.

"Why is it like this?" I asked Uclod, who was following at my heels. "Why is it all stringy and damp? The spaceships of the human navy are not so awful—I have heard they are big long batons, covered with pleasantly dry ceramics. They are also white . . . which is not as good as being clear, but much better than a sodden gray."

"Well, missy," he said, "when humans joined the League of Peoples, they were given a different FTL technology than my ancestors. Humans got baton-ships; we Divians got Zaretts."

"This is a Zarett?"

"It is indeed." He reached up to pat the ball's gluppy exterior. "A sweet little filly, only thirty years old . . . but smart as a whip and twice as frisky."

I stepped back a pace. "It is alive?"

"Absolutely. The daughter of Precious Solar Wind and Whispering Nebula III . . . which would impress the nads off you if you knew anything about thoroughbred Zaretts. This baby is worth more than a minor star system; I'd be the squealing envy of rich men and gorgeous women, if only I could tell the world what I've got. Which I can't: Starbiter wasn't exactly born with the blessing of the Bloodline Registry Office. A slight irregularity in the breeding procedure."

"In other words, you did something criminal to procure her."

"Not me personally," he replied. "Someone else pulled the actual heist: a load of fertilized ova went missing under unconventional circumstances. My family simply acted as go-betweens, finding buyers who'd provide good homes for the misplaced little tykes . . . and we took several ova off the top as our consulting fee." He patted the ship again. "You can't imagine how long I had to suck up to Grandma Yulai before she let me have this one."

I continued to stare at the Starbiter creature. Uclod called it smart and frisky, but I could see neither quality in evidence. It did not frisk *at all*; and one does not display much intelligence by sitting in the middle of an intersection. "If this is an animal," I said, "what does it eat?"

"Oh, this and that. We feed her a mix of simple hydrocarbons, calcium nitrate, small quantities of heavier elements. She doesn't have much of a digestive system for breaking down complex nutrients, so you need to keep the diet pretty basic."

"I am not so much interested in what she can *digest* as what she might *swallow*."

"Well, as to that . . ."

Uclod walked farther around the base of the Zarett, then reached up to touch a bleached-out spot on the creature's skin. He planted his palm firmly and began to rub with strong circular motions, the way one scours hard at one's body when one has slipped and got grass stains. The goop beneath Uclod's fingers made soft slurpy sounds as his hand moved; slowly, the sounds grew louder, until he pulled back and the slurping continued without him. The skin bulged in and out, like a person's jaw as she chews. Moments later, an enormous patch of the Zarett's gooey exterior opened wide to reveal a dark throat leading into a darker gullet.

A giant mouth loomed before me, big enough to gobble me up!

Facing A Hellish Maw

The Zarett's breath smelled exactly like the breath of an animal that eats simple hydrocarbons, calcium nitrate, and small quantities of heavier elements. It was particularly hydrocarbony . . . and I suspect many of those hydrocarbons had not been sufficiently fresh. Starbiter's breath was, in short, quite the Fetid Reek. My stomach lurched at the odor, and the only thing that prevented a regurgitory incident was that I had not eaten solid food in the past four years.

Uclod gestured to the creature's mouth. "After you, toots."

"You wish me to go inside?"

"There's plenty of room. A big girl like you should scrunch down going past the epiglottis; but it'll be clear sailing after that."

As far as I could see, he was telling the truth: the Zarett's mouth was big enough for me to enter, provided I ducked under the lips. The throat was very large too—pink and gummy-looking, but with ample room to let me pass. On the other hand, I was not such a one as would calmly proceed into a large creature's stomach on the invitation of a man who admitted to being a criminal.

"You first," I said.

Uclod shrugged. "If you want." He moved to the creature's lower lip, which was level with his own waist. Planting his hands on the edge, he hopped up and half-twisted, so that he ended sitting on Starbiter's bottom palate with his legs dangling out of the mouth. The little man swung his feet around and stood up; his backside was damp with saliva. He held out his hand to me. "Coming?"

"To be consumed by this creature?" I asked. "I am not such a fool as you think."

"Look, missy," he said, squatting on the Zarett's lip so his eyes were on my level, "there's no way my sweet baby can hurt you. She's engineered to the last little enzyme, perfectly safe and harmless. Here on Melaquin, I guess you're used to gadgets being electronic or mechanical; but we Divians have a long history of going the organic route. Back where I live, my home is a macro vegetable pod, kind of like a big Terran cucumber; its lighting comes from fireflies and its air-conditioning comes from a friendly old worm the size of a tree trunk, whose innards are designed to exhale cool air into the house and fart out hot through a hole in the wall.

"So you see," he continued, "riding in Starbiter is perfectly natural to me. She's a lovable little gal who won't hurt a hair on your head. And if you don't believe me, believe the League of Peoples. They let her come to your planet, didn't they? Which means she can't be dangerous. And even if she *was* dangerous, I'd be crazy to feed you to her . . . because if I deliberately tricked you into becoming dinner, the League would get after *me*."

I stared at him as I thought very hard. Festina had spoken of this League of Peoples: a group of aliens millions of years advanced beyond human technology. These aliens were too lofty to bother themselves with the affairs of lesser species, but they did enforce a single law throughout the galaxy. They never let murderous beings travel from one star system to another; if any such creature made the attempt, it simply died as soon as it left its home system. Festina did not know how the League managed such executions, but she assured me no one ever avoided this death sentence when it was deserved.

Since the League infallibly exterminated "pests" trying to spread into other people's homes, this small Uclod person (who had just traveled through space without dying) might be an awful lawbreaker, but he was not so wicked as to kill me in cold blood.

"Very well," I told him. "I shall see what this Zarett looks like inside. But if she does not behave, I shall kick her hard in the stomach. Or wherever I happen to be."

"Starbiter is always a perfect lady," Uclod said. He gave me a look that implied he could not say the same about me.

Hmph!

A Question Of Sentience

I was still carrying the Explorer jacket and my lovely silver ax. I laid them inside the Zarett's mouth, preparing to jump in myself . . . but Uclod said, "Leave the ax behind."

"I do not wish to leave the ax behind. I wish to bring it with me, in case there are trees to clear or evil persons to behead."

The little man sucked in his breath. "You can't take a lethal weapon into space—the League of Peoples will fricassee us both as soon we go interstellar."

"My ax is not a lethal weapon. It is a useful tool for chopping wood."

Uclod made a face. "If you truly thought that, you could probably keep it: the League are such bloody great mind-readers, they can tell peaceful intentions from nasty ones. Good thing, too—otherwise, nobody could take so much as a toothpick from one system to another. A weapon is only a weapon if you *think* it's a weapon." His eyes narrowed. "And since you just mentioned beheading evildoers, we all know what's on your mind." With the annoying air of someone taking the role of your mother, Uclod pointed sternly toward the pavement at my feet. "Sorry, toots. You gotta leave the hatchet."

I wanted to argue with the little man; but it occurred to me, this was not just about my ax. This was a pivotal test of my civilizationhood. The League of Peoples would not want me venturing into space if I was such a one as enjoyed hacking others into small screaming pieces . . . and if I *was* prone to fits of violence, Uclod would get into serious trouble for transporting a person possessed of homicidal impulses.

Therefore, this small orange criminal was waiting to see whether I was moral enough to set my ax aside. If not, he would consider me a Dangerous Non-Sentient, unfit to mingle with more polite species. He would say, "Oar, I have reconsidered, and have decided you would be happier remaining on Melaquin."

But I Would Not Be Happier

I did not wish to remain on Melaquin.

My planet was the most beautiful place in the universe, but it had become exceedingly lonely. There was nobody here except Tired-Brain sleepyheads, and not one of them would be your friend, no matter how desperately you begged them.

In my whole life, I had only known two awake persons of my own kind. One was my mother, who forced dozy men to couple with her until she got pregnant, in the hope that children would keep her from Fading Into Indifference . . . but her stratagem did not work. By the time I reached my teens, Mother spent all her days in an Ancestral Tower, impossible to rouse with any, "Mommy, please look, please listen to me!" The last time she had stirred was many years ago, when the first Explorers arrived at our village; and even the appearance of aliens only held her interest for a few hours. Then she went back into hibernation.

The other person I had known on Melaquin was my sister, Eel. She was several years older than I, born from another of my mother's desperate attempts to keep her brain from the Glassy Sleep. Eel was my best friend, my teacher and my second mother . . . until the Explorers came. Then she became my rival, always clamoring for their attention and ignoring me.

It is strange how the presence of additional people can make you feel more alone.

But Eel was gone now, murdered by a wicked Explorer— so there was nothing to keep me on Melaquin. Why should I not accompany Uclod to opaque lands, where I could astonish those worlds with my crystalline beauty? And what about my dear friend Festina? She must have been devastated believing me to be dead. Should I not go to her and lift her from the depths of despair?

Yet it was still very hard to leave my home . . . and to leave my ax as well. It was only an object, but it was *mine*: my sole possession, the thing I had held in my hands through many solitary nights of chopping trees, hoping someone would notice how I cleared land in the manner of civilized persons.

Now the test of civilization was not *using* my ax but *abandoning* it. This sounded very much like what humans call "irony" . . . and I do not like irony *at all*.

With great reluctance, I removed my ax from Starbiter's mouth and laid it on the pavement. A snowflake fell on the blade. I did not brush it off.

"There," I said . . . speaking loudly and firmly, so no one could claim my voice trembled. "I am going now; and I shall

willingly leave behind my ax, though it is my sole belonging—because I am a person of peace and never kill others
unless they really truly deserve it."

Uclod rubbed his eyes as if they pained him. "You scare
me, toots. You honestly do." Then he reached to help me into
the ship.

Fondling The Inner Cheek

Since my skin was already damp with snow, I could not
feel the wetness of the Zarett's mouth. However, I could see
it glistening moistly beneath my feet—and it looked very
slippery indeed. I resolved to walk most carefully, for fear of
sliding on a slick patch and Falling Precipitously. (The fall
would not damage me, but it might make Uclod think I was
clumsy. I did not want that, not even a little bit.)

So I stood unmoving on the ribbed floor of Starbiter's
mouth, staring forward at the creature's yawning throat.[2]
Since we had entered the Zarett at ground level, the throat
ran upward, further into the center of the ball. Proceeding
forward would require a difficult ascent, all slippy and slidy
like scrabbling up a muddy riverbank; but the throat was too
dark to see how steep the slope might truly be.

"What do we do now?" I asked Uclod.

I turned and saw the little man had gone to the side of
Starbiter's mouth, where he was rubbing a patch of the
Zarett's inner cheek. Most of the tissue around us was pale
pink, but the patch he touched showed a redder tinge. I remembered the way he had massaged the creature to get it to
open its lips; apparently, one communicated with Zaretts
through fondling.

---

[2]I do not mean Starbiter was yawning as a bored person does. She could not
have been bored at all—it must be very interesting to have a beautiful glass
woman enter your mouth. But it is a time-honored figure of English speech
to say that darkened cavities "yawn" . . . and I am *excellent* at reproducing
others' clichés.

This struck me as most inefficient. "When a machine has buttons," I told Uclod, "you press a button and something happens right away. That is how machines *ought* to work. I do not think much of a spaceship you must rub to get its attention."

"Not to get her attention," the little man replied. "Sweet baby girl is checking out my taste: making sure I'm her real daddy. Can't be too careful with a Zarett this valuable. So the cells in this part of her mouth can do a complete DNA analysis on my hand, not to mention verifying my palmprint and fingerprints—all to make sure she doesn't open up to strangers."

"That is foolish," I told him. "If criminals wished to impersonate you, they could simply cut off your hand. Then they could rub the detached member against the wall—"

"Whoa!" Uclod interrupted. "Just whoa." He swallowed hard. "What is *wrong* with you, missy? How can such grisly ideas pop into such a pretty head?"

"I am simply practical," I said. "Unlike your Zarett's security precautions, which seem to encourage villains to amputate—"

"Hush! Right now. Not a word."

I hushed. He was clearly a *squeamish* alien.

A moment later he muttered, "You left your ax behind, right?"

I did not dignify that with an answer.

Past The Teeth And Over The Gums

The little man stepped back from rubbing the Zarett's mouth. "She's recognized me," he said, quickly putting his hands behind his back. "We're ready to go."

I looked at the shadowy throat slanting upward. "It appears to be a difficult climb."

"Climb?" he said. "We don't have to climb."

"Then how—"

I did not finish my question, because two distractions occurred. First, Uclod dropped to his stomach, lying flat on Starbiter's lower palate. Second, the Zarett's lips clamped shut and sealed themselves, plunging us into blackness.

"Get down, toots," Uclod said.

I did not obey. "Why?"

Without the slightest warning, Starbiter lurched. I had time to think, *Oh, it is a big ball and it is rolling along the street:* then the floor beneath me tipped to the vertical and I fell down hard.

Down

The impact of my fall made a splash in the Zarett's spittle. Though I could not see, I had the impression the creature's mouth was flooding with saliva. I did not have long to think about that, because the rolling soon reached the point where the throat was no longer up but down. With nothing to hold on to, and nothing but slippery oral tissue under my body, I slid helplessly forward, tobogganing headfirst: bouncing blindly off the walls of the mouth, until I was funneled into the throat and hurled downward.

Zoom.

Saliva whooshed me on my way, like a stream of mucousy water, very slick and oily. I could not slow myself at all; when I flailed my arms, I only managed to roll onto my side. Then onto my back. Then onto my side again. But of all the positions, it felt the most pleasing to whiz along on my front, so I worked over to that.

At one point, something brushed against my spine—a thinning in Starbiter's throat, perhaps the epiglottis Uclod had mentioned. I did not have time to grab it; anyway, it felt as slippery as everything else around me, so I doubt that I could have managed to stop myself.

The ride continued, but not in a direct line down. Soon after the epiglottis, the path veered to the right, rolling me high up on the throat wall before the route straightened again. That sent me seesawing back and forth, up the left wall, down to the bottom, up the right . . . which would have been

most enjoyable, except that the slide leveled out quickly after that and my motion began to slow. Apparently, the Zarett
had come to rest in a position that left this part of the throat
horizontal. I saw light glimmering ahead; and with my last
momentum, I slid into a small room whose walls shone as
yellow as buttercups. Uclod was there, already on his feet.
As I came to a stop, he bent over and asked, "How're you
doing, missy?"

How I Was Doing

"I am exceedingly vexed," I said, elbow-deep in spittle.
Though the fluid was rapidly seeping away through the
porous tissues around me, I was still soaking wet in every
particular. That is not a nice feeling, especially when one
does not know if Zarett saliva is the type of liquid that leaves
stains or crusty patches when it dries. Therefore, when
Uclod offered me his hand as an aid to standing up, I
scowled and did not take it; I rose on my own (with magnif-
icent grace) and told him, "It was very most rude not to warn
me what would happen."

"You weren't keen on being swallowed," he said. "I figured
it would cause less fuss if I didn't explain ahead of time."

"Because you thought I might flee? Or make trouble?" I
glared at him. "From now on, you can best avoid trouble by
keeping me well-informed. Do you understand?"

The only answer I received was a slight shudder under my
feet. "Starbiter doesn't like it," Uclod said, "when people
threaten her dad. You might remember that, missy, if you
want to avoid trouble."

"What will she do? Eat me? She has already succeeded in
that."

"We didn't get eaten," Uclod replied, "we got inhaled.
Back where the throat curved, we got shunted away from the
stomach and into the lungs . . . which are set up as living
quarters. There's eighteen rooms in here, bedrooms, bath,
the works, all made from enlarged alveoli: cells for air stor-
age. The old gal's got real alveoli too, tiny little buggers like

the ones in your own lungs, but these special eighteen cells were engineered big enough for people our size to live in."

"So we were not swallowed but instead Went Down The Wrong Way. When that happens to me, I cough."

"Starbiter's not going to cough!" Uclod answered most snappishly. "Just . . ." He glared at me. "Just forget she's alive, okay? Think of her as a normal spaceship, nothing fancy, nothing strange. Now come with me down this bronchial tube to the bridge."

He walked to the far end of the room and stomped his foot once on the floor. A section of the wall opened like a sphincter to reveal a passageway leading onward. The passage was lit with the same buttercup-yellow as the room we were in.

"If you can have light down here," I said, "why not in the throat too?"

"That'd be nice," Uclod admitted, "but it's not practical. The light here comes from a phosphorescent fungus growing on the alveolar membrane—a symbiote that absorbs nutrients from Starbiter's bloodstream. You can't get the fungus to root in the throat: the saliva tends to dissolve . . . umm . . . well, saliva is like water, right, and fungus won't grow under water."

He could not fool me—he had intended to say the saliva would dissolve items passing into the digestive system. And here I was, still damp with spittle, and beginning to get unpleasant runnel trails where the liquid was drying.

Fortunately, my Explorer jacket had washed down the same route as Uclod and me. It was soaking wet too, but I picked it up and began to mop myself as I followed the little man forward.

4

WHEREIN I TERRIFY A GIANT

The Soul Of Timidity

The corridor was long and round like the inside of a worm.
The ceiling hung just low enough that I had to duck, which
meant I trudged along with my head bent over. In that position
I could only see the floor, which was most unattractive—the
floor's surface was corduroyed with riblike ridges spaced a
fingerwidth apart, and in the gaps you could see icky bluish-
white skin with snaky purple veins. One walked up on the
ridges, with one's feet never touching the skin beneath . . .
but I could tell the skin would feel soft and weak and distressingly *pulpy*. It reminded me of dead birds and animals I
had sometimes found while cutting wood: half-eaten, bloody,
wet with dew, withered in some parts and bloated in others.

Ugly, ugly death.

But the skin below my feet was not dead, though it looked
most revoltingly corpselike. I tried to ignore it and continued
to walk, head down, Uclod's feet padding in front of me, until we passed through another sphincter and entered a second
yellow-lit room.

Two more orange feet stepped in beside Uclod's. I lifted
my head and saw a creature much like the little man but with
important differences. First, this was obviously a female;
she wore short gray pants and a white shirt of the same style
as Uclod's, but under the woman's shirt lurked a sizable pair
of wallabies. Also lurking under her clothes were massive

muscles packed exorbitantly onto every bone in her body: huge arms, huger legs, and such an ostentatious set of shoulders they made one furious just to look at them. She was not much taller than I—well, perhaps she was two hands taller, but I do not call that a lot—yet compared to Uclod, she was an absolute giant. At the same time, she shared enough physical attributes with the little man to show she was definitely the same species: spherical globes atop her head, a similar facial structure, and the same scaly orange skin.

The woman said nothing for several seconds—she simply gazed at me with wide-open eyes. Her body pressed tight against Uclod's back, as if she were trying to hide behind him . . . which was like a full-sized bear taking cover behind a woodchuck. She placed her hands on Uclod's shoulders and gripped him tensely, balling up the cloth of his shirt in her fingers.

Still she did not speak. Uclod reached up, placing his hands gently over hers. "Don't worry," he told her. "Everything's fine. This is a friend."

The woman did not move. She kept staring at me with her mouth shut, her eyes unblinking. At last, I lowered my voice and asked Uclod, "What is *wrong* with her? Is she simply crazed, or is there something chemically wrong with her brain?"

"There's nothing wrong at all," the little man said. He moved to one side so he could put his arm around the woman's back and propel her a shuffle-step forward. "Honey?" he addressed her in a soft low voice. "Honey, this is Oar."

"Oar?" the giant woman whispered. "Oar?"

"Yes," I told her. "An oar is an implement used to propel boats."

"But . . ." She closed her mouth so quickly, it made a clopping sound.

"I know," Uclod said, "we were told Oar had died. The reports must have been wrong."

"Yes," I agreed, "I have never truly been dead. Not even once. You should not fear I am a moldering corpse, risen from the grave to ravage mortal souls."

My words of reassurance showed no sign of comforting

her. Uclod had to nudge her forward another step and ask, "Are you going to say hello to Oar, honey?"

"Hello, Oar," the woman said softly. There was something odd about her voice—as if it was actually quite low but she was forcing it higher, like a male pretending to be female. I wondered if this person might truly *be* a man, despite the wallabies looming under her shirt; perhaps some types of alien men had prominent wallabies. Then again, perhaps some types of alien women had low voices they forced higher for foolish alien reasons . . . and it was all very boring to think about, so I stopped immediately.

I am excellent at putting a stop to moments of introspection.

"Well done," Uclod told the woman beside him, apparently believing that saying hello took great courage. "Oar, this is my wife, U. C. Lajoolie."

The woman half-whispered, "A lajoolie is a small glass bottle used for holding *paprikaab*."

Uclod gave her a smiling squeeze. "Isn't that nice, Oar? Lajoolie told you what her name means."

I said, "I do not know what *paprikaab* is."

When Lajoolie did not answer, Uclod leaned his head toward me. "Damned if I know either. The little woman comes from a different planet than me—she's a Tye-Tye, I'm a Freep. We're newlyweds, and still kind of sketchy about each other's cultures."

"Oh," I said. Then I stared straight into the woman's eyes and spoke with the clear enunciation one uses to address the mentally unfit. "I am most glad a lajoolie is a *glass* bottle. I am sure it is very pretty."

The big woman stared at me in silence for a moment. Then she touched my arm and gave a timid smile.

Scanning Starbiter's Bridge

"Okay, great!" Uclod said in the over-hearty way of males who wish to pretend all problems have been solved forever. "Enough blathering—it's time for work. Sooner or later, the navy will show up . . . and by then, we want to be gone."

He moved a tiny distance away from Lajoolie, who still had an arm wrapped tightly around him. This led to a dainty tug-of-war between the two . . . not that the woman was truly trying to keep hold of the little man, but even her unthinking strength was enough that Uclod could not break her grip. He had to pull away slightly, wait for her arm to ease, then detach himself a bit more. I could not understand why he did not say, "Release me!" or why she made him wriggle free in such a manner rather than just letting go; but there is no comprehending aliens unless you try, and it is seldom worth the effort. Instead, I averted my gaze from their antics and took my first good look at my surroundings.

The previous chamber had been completely empty except for glowing wall-fungus. This new room, however, had Mysterious Protrusions jutting from the floor, the ceiling, and the single round wall that encircled the place. The floor protrusions were obviously chairs . . . provided one did not mind sitting on great ugly lumps that appeared to be bone and cartilage upholstered with half-dried jellyfish. Normally, I would not be distressed by such jellyfish—at least they were transparent, which is why I could see the chair's bony frame underneath—but their shriveled outer surfaces were starting to flake off, while the inner parts retained enough of their juices to wobble with shivery abandon. When you sat on them, I suspected they might *squirm* like things alive.

As for other protrusions in the room, I had no idea what they were. For example, above each chair hung long cords dangling from the roof: cords that resembled the intestines of a groundhog after it has been partly consumed by a coyote. This is not the sort of thing I would suspend from *my* ceiling, especially not above where people might sit; the intestines would sweep back and forth across a person's hair with agitating gooeyness. If this is what amused Uclod and Lajoolie, I would not enjoy their company . . . but then, I would not enjoy remaining on Melaquin either—especially if navy humans arrived with the intention of eradicating evidence of Explorer habitation.

After all, *I* was such evidence myself: a firsthand witness to everything that happened. Wicked navy persons could not murder me on sight or the League of Peoples would never let them leave Melaquin. However, there was no League law against abducting me to parts unknown: to *isolated* parts unknown, where one would be devoid of sufficient stimulation to keep one's brain from becoming Tired.

I turned sharply back to Uclod and Lajoolie. "Hurry now. Let us leave before malicious Earthlings arrive."

Appropriate Restraints

"Right you are, missy." Uclod finished detaching himself from his wife (or rather she let him go when she saw I was ready to pry him loose myself). "Find yourself a chair," he said, moving to a seat of his own. He chose a place in front of the largest collection of bulges swelling from Starbiter's wall. Lajoolie fairly ran to the position on his left . . . and since the chairs were arranged like a circle of toadstools all facing the wall, I took the seat on Uclod's right.

No sooner had I settled down than a number of leathery tendrils sprouted from the chair and wrapped about my person. Some sprang from the seat and belted across my thighs, while others snaked from the chair-back to tie down my arms and torso. It happened so quickly, I did not have time to fight . . . and one good heave of my muscles proved the straps too sturdy to break.

Instead, I turned toward Uclod, intending to demand he release me; but he too was tethered to his seat with bindings like mine, as was his wife. Somehow they had contrived to keep their arms free, but that was all: they were well and truly webbed in.

Neither of them looked concerned at such confinement, not even the fainthearted Lajoolie. Therefore this must be standard operating procedure for spaceships—nothing at all to fret over.

When I recovered from my initial surprise, I remembered flying with Festina in an aeroplane. Aeroplanes also have straps, used as safety devices to prevent Calamitous Injuries during flight. That made me feel better about the tendrils clutched around my body. After a moment, I decided it would not be so bad if the restraints were even tighter in certain locations; but I could not see how to cinch them up myself, and Uclod was busy rubbing his hands against the bulges on the wall in front of him. I resolved to ask about adjusting the straps later . . . but that thought immediately vanished when something swallowed my head.

Intestines With Mouths

I had forgotten about the intestines dangling from the ceiling. When I first got seated, I had ducked low enough to keep the things clear of my head. Now, however, they descended to grab me, first making slimy contact with my scalp, then creeping quickly downward. I had not noticed the intestines possessed mouths, but obviously they did— mouths that could open as wide as a snake's, stretching without difficulty to envelop my hair, brow, and eyes. Writhing could not shake the mouth off me . . . and my arms were locked under the straps that held me to the chair. At most, I might have screamed; but I refused to do that, for fear Uclod and Lajoolie would think I was a coward.

After all, this might be another procedure of alien Science: if I howled and moaned, Uclod might dismiss me as an ignorant savage who did not understand the requisites of space travel. Perhaps the intestine was actually an Important Safety Mask designed to keep one alive in the depths of The Void. It might provide air that was necessary for survival, and only a Childish Numskull would fuss over a simple life support system.

That is the nature of Science—it is often confusing and terrible, but you must pretend you are not troubled or else Science People will call you names.

So I sat there trembling as the intestines swallowed my face. Just before they covered my mouth, I took a deep breath; then I attempted to inhale more air through my nose, which was already sealed over. If I had not been able to breathe, I would have tried to break the seat-straps, no matter how strong they were . . . but I could inhale without effort despite the guts closed over my nostrils.

It was all very strange indeed—I could feel the stretchy intestines pressed tight against my face, yet when I breathed, there was not the least hindrance to normal air flow. I stuck out my tongue to touch the membrane; it felt solid and rubbery, as though it should be impermeable . . . yet when I blew out hard, I could not feel the tiniest backwash against my face.

In one way, the membrane *was* impermeable: I could not see. My eyes were open, but all was in blackness. All was silent too—the intestines had plastered themselves tight enough over my ears to muffle outward sound. Gradually, though, I became aware of a vague hum and a small patch of light, only visible with my left eye . . . a swath of colors like a rainbow. The colors slowly became brighter, but still only in my left eye; and it did not seem to matter whether my eye was open or closed, because I continued to perceive the rainbow even when I shut my eyes tight.

Then my left ear came awake, hearing a pure musical note that began as a whisper and gradually increased to moderate volume. Its tone did not quaver, not even a little bit. The sound continued for ten seconds . . . then it suddenly split in two, one half rising quickly in pitch while the other half plunged, high up and low down until both notes disappeared.

The rainbow in my left eye vanished almost as soon as the sounds stopped. A moment later, it reappeared in my right eye, brightening quickly this time and soon accompanied by a musical note in my right ear. The sound split to extremes again, the rainbow blinked out . . .

. . . and suddenly I could see perfectly, except that I was not inside the Zarett but out on the city street.

Seeing Through New Eyes

Snow still fell through the hole in the roof, accompanied by a distant roar of wind scouring through the mountains overhead. When I turned my neck, I could see in any direction, even far back to the central square—much farther than I had actually been able to see when I was outside the Zarett. My viewpoint was centered at a level considerably higher than the ground; so I peeked down and saw not my own body but Starbiter's.

This was very odd indeed. I appeared to have become a Zarett. It was most unpleasant to see myself all stringy and awful, but if I was now a spaceship, perhaps there would be entertaining compensations. In a spirit of experiment, I willed myself to roll forward along the street; and I managed to move a quarter rotation before Uclod's voice cried, "Whoa!"

"Do not address me as if I were a horse," I told him. "I am now a Zarett."

"Wrong," the little man said. His voice came out of nowhere, all around me at once. "Sorry to disappoint you, toots, but you're not Starbiter—you're just linked to her nervous system. You can see what she sees, hear what she hears, feel what she feels . . ."

"I cannot feel anything," I said. And it was true. Though snow still fell all around, I could not feel its cold dampness, nor could I sense the solidity of the street beneath the Zarett's body.

"Don't worry," Uclod said, "you'll likely feel something in time. It's just a matter of the dear girl analyzing the structure of your brain: where to send which impulses to make you experience the proper input. You shouldn't be hard to figure out—you're likely similar to *Homo sapiens*, and Zaretts can link with humans. I'll just check . . ." He paused, then muttered, "No, I'm wrong. I'm looking at your neural readouts, and you got some major deviations from normal Earthling configurations. Vision and hearing are close to *Homo sap*, but your touch and body kinetics are totally alien. Starbiter can't even find your basic pain centers."

"That is good," I said. "I do not wish to feel basic pain."

"Can't blame you," Uclod replied, "but it means you'll miss the full experience. Speaking of which, I'll let you drive once we get into empty space where you won't hit anything . . . but in the meantime, don't give Starbiter orders, okay? That bit where you rolled her along the street—you could get us all killed if *you* tell her one thing while *I* say something different. She knows I'm her daddy, and she'll always listen to me over you; but she can still get confused with two folks shouting at once."

"I shall not shout," I said, "provided you drive wisely. Or at least amusingly. May we fly into the sun?"

Lajoolie responded with a Gasp Of Horror. Uclod too seemed upset, for he cried, "Are you out of your mind?"

"It is not insane to solicit information through polite inquiries," I said with wounded dignity. "I would find it most agreeable to fly through the sun—I am such a one as derives pleasant nourishment from sunlight, and it would be delightfully invigorating to be bathed in such light from all sides. But if you choose not to gratify me, I am sure you have your own small-minded reasons."

"Missy," Uclod said, "you clearly don't understand suns. Or solar radiation. Or big fucking gravitational forces. Not to mention the solar wind, the electromagnetic field, and God knows what else. Hell, on sheer density alone, we'd have an easier time flying through the core of Melaquin than the heart of your sun."

"We do not have to fly through the core of Melaquin," I told him. "I have already seen Melaquin. And we would not have to fly through the *heart* of the sun if it frightens you. We could just venture in a short distance. At least to begin with. Until you grew comfortable with the idea."

"Not today," Uclod said, in the tone people use when they mean *Not ever.* "Our first concern is hightailing it out of this system before the navy shows up. Now be a good girl, and shut your trap while I finish preparing for takeoff."

He was a lucky little man. My arms were still strapped to the chair.

5

WHEREIN I BECOME A STAR PILOT

Up

Three minutes passed in silence. The snow continued to fall through my field of vision, but I could not feel its touch. Now and then, odd twinges erupted in random parts of my body—a bite of cold behind my left knee, something brushing my right shoulder, the strange sensation of lifting heavy objects with both hands—but nothing lasted more than a heartbeat. Apparently, Starbiter was still trying to understand the tactile centers of my brain, but my intellect was too complex to yield to the Zarett's comprehension.

Hah!

"We're ready," Uclod finally announced. "Takeoff in five, four, three, two, one."

We lifted slowly from the street . . . which is to say, my point of view rose upward, higher and higher as if riding the elevator in an Ancestral Tower. I could not, however, feel the movement in my body: according to my muscles, I was still sitting flat and level in a motionless chair. It was most strange indeed, and disturbing too—especially when Starbiter rolled in midair so that we faced straight up at the hole in the roof. From this angle, I should have felt I was tipped back on my spine; yet it still seemed as if I were comfortably upright, the way one might sit in the chair of a teaching machine.

I wondered if the starship had finally discovered how to make me feel sensations that were not actually so: sitting up straight instead of lying on my back. Then I decided the opposite must be true—Starbiter did not know how to make me feel the correct experiences, so she simply kept me in the one state she understood, leaving me "sitting up" until she learned how to simulate something else. That would become most annoying in time . . . but perhaps it was not so bad to begin my journey this way, especially if the Zarett were to embark upon dizzying maneuvers that could provoke Stomach Upset in one unaccustomed to aerobatic gyrations.

The ship climbed face upward into snow, the blizzard thickening around us by the second. Sounds grew muted, even the howling storm—its wind threw snowflakes at us in a constant whirl, but the noise had faded to a soft and sandy blur. Soon I could see nothing but buffeting white; I did not know how Uclod would ever find the hole we were aiming for. I dearly hoped Starbiter possessed Technical Features that could see more than I could, or there was an excellent chance we would smash against the stone ceiling instead of our intended exit.

Suddenly the blizzard disappeared, leaving nothing but starry night above us. I looked around perplexed, wondering where the snow had gone. There was nothing in sight, no buildings, no roof, not even mountains; but when I turned my attention downward, I saw dark billowy clouds receding swiftly below us.

"We are up in the sky!" I said. "We are high above the clouds!"

"Yes," answered Uclod's disembodied voice.

"We are up so high, one cannot see the ground!"

"You'll see it again once we get more altitude," Uclod said. "You'll see the land, the ocean, the polar ice-caps . . ."

"Husband," Lajoolie interrupted. Her voice possessed a sharp edge I had never heard before. "An object on long-range sensors," she said. "It's huge."

I looked around but saw nothing. Lajoolie's "long-range sensors" must be special devices for perceiving great distances. Perhaps as Uclod drove, his wife scanned the depths in search of potential danger.

"When you say 'huge,'" Uclod said, "how big are we talking? Asteroid? Comet? A fucking navy cruiser?"

"Bigger than the navy's largest dreadnought," Lajoolie answered, her voice a bare whisper, "but it's not a natural phenomenon. I'm detecting a coherent electric field. Internal power generation."

"What does that mean?" I asked.

"That we're in for a crapfest," Uclod replied. "It must be a starship . . . but if it's bigger than anything in the human navy, it doesn't belong to any alien race we usually meet. Gotta be a heavy hitter from higher up in the League. Somehow we've caught the interest of the big boys." He growled something under his breath, then told Lajoolie, "Honey, chart me an evasion course while I fire up the drive. Oar!"

"Yes?"

"You've spent time with Explorers. You remember that phrase they use? *Greetings, I am a sentient citizen . . .*"

"Of course I remember. They say it incessantly."

"Then you're our new communications officer. I'll set you up for broadcast, and you keep repeating that *Greetings* crap till I tell you to stop."

I did not appreciate the way he barked orders at me . . . but I liked the idea of becoming communications officer. I am *excellent* at communications.

"Okay, toots," Uclod said, "you're on the air. And no matter what, keep talking till we're ready to go FTL."

I took a deep breath. "Greetings," I said in my most winsome voice, "I am a sentient citizen of the League of Peoples. I beg your Hospitality."

This was an Important Message Of Goodwill, supposed to be Universally Recognized. At least, I had been told so by human Explorers. I did not know how the speech could impress alien beings who did not comprehend Earthling English . . . and surely the galaxy must be full of such creatures. Therefore, as soon as I had recited the phrases in human words, I repeated them in my own language, which is more beautiful and therefore more apt to be used by highly advanced cultures. After that I switched back to English, then my native tongue, then English again, and so on at least three times—by which point I was sure the aliens must be as bored as I was. I had begun to ponder ways to "spice up my delivery" with heightened emotive inflection and perhaps some very funny jokes I invented with my sister, when a Large Inexplicable Object materialized in our path.

Chased By A Bundle Of Sticks

One moment, there was nothing ahead of us but empty black sky. The next, my field of vision was filled with what looked like a tangle of bracken: sticks woven together randomly, with twigs jutting out at all angles. I could not guess how huge it might be—with no reference points, I could not even tell if the stick-thing was close at hand or far away—but it easily dwarfed our Zarett and appeared to grow ever more enormous by the second. The twigs sticking out so haphazardly might be the size of full trees or even gigantic towers: as if someone had torn up the buildings of a great city and tossed them into a loose heap straight in front of us.

"Waaaahhh!" Uclod screamed. Starbiter veered sideways so fast my eyes blurred. For a moment, it seemed we could zip around the stick-thing's edge, and perhaps get past it; but then the great bundle of twigs shifted in the same direction, blocking us off again. Uclod said something guttural in a language I did not understand, and our Zarett began a furious zigzag.

"Not to worry," the little man called, "another few seconds and our FTL will be ready. *Then* let's see those bastards block us."

"They may manage it," Lajoolie said in a weak voice. "Do you know what that is, husband?"

"Not a clue."

"It's a Shaddill ship. I've seen drawings in the Tikuun Archive."

"Shaddill?" Uclod repeated. "Here and now? Fuck, fuck, fuck, fuckity-fuck."

"Are these the same Shaddills who created your camera?" I asked. "What do they want?"

"Your guess is as good as mine. Just keep up the *Greetings*, okay? Make sure they know we're sentient."

I scowled at him, though he could not see my face. Why should I waste time on a foolish message when the words had no effect? The stick-thing was playing the bully, hindering us whenever we tried to go around. Such behavior deserved a punch in the nose, not *Please, may we be your friends*.

"Greetings, you churlish Shaddills!" I said. "I am a sentient person named Oar. I no longer want your Hospitality; I just want you out of the way, you big poop-heads."

"Oh lovely," Uclod muttered. "Top marks for diplomacy, toots."

But even as he spoke, a second voice whispered in my ear. "Oar?" it said. "Oar?"

"Yes," I answered. "An oar is an implement used to propel boats."

"Oar," the voice whispered. "Died . . . died . . . dead."

"Do not be foolish!" I snapped. "I am not dead at all, you crazed Shaddill ones!"

"Interference," the whisperer said. "Someone has interfered with our plan . . ."

"What plan?" I asked.

"Shut up!" Uclod yelled. "We don't want to hear about the plan. We don't want to *know* there's a plan. We weren't here, we didn't see a thing, we're gone."

"Oar . . . died, died, die—"

Something milky oozed out of Starbiter's skin: like wispy smoke, thin enough to see through. I had no trouble peering at the stick-ship past the rippling white veil, but the unknown voice cut off midwhisper.

"Good baby Starbiter," Uclod cooed. "Charged her FTL field in record time. Hang on, folks, we're going to—"

A flash of blue-white light exploded from a stick jutting out of the Shaddill ship's belly: a short sizzling burst like a lightning bolt. It made no sound, no thunder; but Uclod gave a surprised grunt and Lajoolie a gasping sigh. I too could not suppress a yelp . . . but the light disappeared as quickly as it came, not even leaving a burnt afterimage in my eyes.

"What was that?" I asked.

No one answered.

"Uclod?" I said. "Lajoolie? Speak now!"

Silence.

"This is a foolish game," I said. "Especially at a time when one is in a state of consternation."

But the only sound was my own breathing.

Finally Taking Command

What had happened? I could only assume the lightning was a weapon that had killed or disabled my companions. With luck, they were only unconscious—a fate I had been spared because of my superlative constitution. Perhaps too, I should be grateful that the tactile centers of my brain had not been linked with the Zarett; whatever bludgeoning force had been transmitted to Uclod and Lajoolie, the effect had not got through to me.

I wished I could see my two comrades and evaluate their health. However, my eyes still perceived nothing but the world outside Starbiter: the black sky above, eclipsed by the looming stick-ship. The sticks were moving closer now, while our own craft merely drifted—sailing sideways in the direction we had last been heading. I could see sparks of light arcing between spindly projections on the alien ship, like fireflies flickering in the heart of a bramble patch. Something about them made me doubt they were harmless insects; perhaps the alien ship was a single gigantic brain, and the sparks were evil thoughts crackling through its consciousness.

A stick on the ship's belly stretched lazily toward us: a great long tube telescoping outward, with a gaping mouth on the end. *No, no,* I thought, *I have already been swallowed twice today, by a Zarett and by dangling intestines gobbling up my head. I shall not be eaten a third time . . . especially not by a stick.*

Reaching out with my mind, I tried to re-create how I directed Starbiter to roll down the city street. Whatever I had

done then, the Zarett obeyed willingly enough; surely she
would be happy to listen to me again, especially since Uclod
had fallen silent. Our ship was a mare who had lost her
rider—would she not be thankful if a trustworthy person
took over the reins?

I opened my mouth to say soothing things to the dis-
traught Zarett . . . but quickly I changed my mind. As far as I
knew, I was still hooked up for broadcasting; if I spoke
aloud to Starbiter, the aliens would hear and I would lose
the element of surprise. Therefore, I resolved to address the
Zarett only with my thoughts; and to do it swiftly too, for the
great stick-mouth was drawing near.

Starbiter, good and friendly one, I thought, squinching up
my concentration very hard, *you thought you were alone, but
behold! I am Oar and I am here. We must now escape the
evil sticks. Are you ready?*

An answer did not come in words . . . but I thought the
milky veil surrounding our craft rippled with relief. The
Zarett had obviously been frightened; now she could rejoice
she was not on her own, all sad and abandoned by people
she trusted. *All will be well,* I told her, *but we must fly very
fast. As fast as you possibly can. Will you do that?*

The veil rippled again. I got the impression our ship rel-
ished the chance to travel at top speed. If you viewed her as
a racehorse with ancestors bred for competition, perhaps she
felt *underused* by one such as Uclod: a mere errand-boy for
his Grandma Yulai, cruising from place to place on tedious
assignments that probably did not require sufficiently many
daring escapes.

Do not worry, Starbiter, I thought, *now that I am your pi-
lot, life will become more exciting. Let us fly!*

Flying At Break-Light Speeds

Zoom!

The stick-mouth was almost upon us . . . but in the blink
of an eye it was gone. And *we* were gone: nothing in front of
us but stars. When I looked behind, I could not see the stick-

ship at all—just a half-moon object whose color was mist-faded blue. In less than a second, it dwindled to nothing more than a bright point of light. Only later did I realize it was not a half-moon at all but my planet Melaquin, blue with oceans; and now it was far behind us, scarcely different from anything else in the blackness.

But there was one object which stood out from everything else in The Void—the sun, hot and flaming, a ball of fire blazing fiercely in the night. Its glare was so brilliant, I could have been blinded if I stared into it with my real eyes; but Starbiter was projecting the image straight into my head, by-passing the tender retinas that would have melted under such withering intensity.

In that moment, I had only one decision to make—should we fly toward or away from the sun? All other questions of navigation could not be answered: I did not know the way to New Earth, if that was where Uclod intended to go; I did not have any other destination in mind (except to find Festina, and who knew where she might be?); I did not know if the stick ship could track us, and I could not guess what artful tricks of evasion I might employ to make us harder to pursue. My only meaningful decision was whether to go toward the light, or to flee in some random direction through the blackness.

I am such a one as enjoys bright sunshine.

Starbiter seemed perfectly content to change course to-ward the sun. The moment the idea passed through my head, we started in that direction . . . and we moved most exceed-ingly fast, as if falling from a great height into the giant ball of fire. Indeed, we moved faster than the speed of light, thanks to the milky smoke surrounding us. Uclod had called that smoke our FTL field, and Explorers had told me FTL was a scientific effect allowing starships to defy the Laws Of Physics.[3] Law-breaking or not, we reached our goal in less

---

[3]Personally, I would not use the word "law" for any principle that breaks so easily. However, Science People like to believe in laws, even when such laws can be circumvented by their own Science. They become most dis-pleased if you suggest it would be more accurate to speak of the Generally Good Idea Of Gravity or the Three Useful Guidelines Of Thermodynamics.

than a second and a half: hovering motionless in space before the sun's blazing immensity.

Here is a thing you may not know about suns—they are large and bright. By this I mean that no matter how large and bright you believe suns to be, they are larger and brighter than that. I had certainly expected my planet's sun to prove impressive, but I had not known how utterly imposing it would be. *Perhaps,* I thought to myself, *Uclod was not entirely wrong, deeming it foolhardy to enter such an inferno.*

Starbiter had chosen to halt when we got sufficiently close, like a horse reluctant to venture too near a fire. I too was beginning to think we had approached to an acceptable distance—near enough to see great curling streamers of flame shooting into the void, and mysterious darknesses drifting across the brighter surface like icebergs on a burning sea—when I caught a flicker of motion out the corner of my eye.

Materializing beside us, lit by the searing light of the sun, there was the stick-ship again.

Retreating Starward

I do not know if I unconsciously gave an order to Starbiter, or if she moved on her own—bolting from something that frightened her. Either way, we took a big hop up and over the sun, as if we were jumping a small rock in the middle of a path.

Hah! I thought, *now find us*; for even if the stick-people had uncanny viewing devices that perceived great distances, I did not believe they could see us straight through the sun. Alas, I was mistaken—almost immediately, the alien craft appeared again and this time directly behind our ship, like a massive brush barrier walling us off from open space, penning us against the sun itself. All around the outer edge, sticks began sprouting outward, growing at a prodigious rate . . . until the whole alien vessel resembled a hand with hundreds of outstretched fingers, and we were almost cupped in the palm.

What to do? Starbiter was certainly swift enough to zip around those fingers and out to freedom; but the stick-ship seemed able to track us no matter where we went, and if we headed for open space, could we outrun the alien in a straight contest of speed? I did not know. Even if Starbiter was faster in a short sprint, could she stay ahead of the big ship hour after hour, as we blundered through space in search of safe haven? I did not know that either . . . but I disliked trusting to luck.

Back! I ordered. *Back into the sun!*

The Zarett retreated reluctantly, halving the distance between us and the roiling ball of fury at our backs. For a split second, the stick-ship fell out of sight . . . but then it appeared closer than ever, a monstrous hand reaching out to grab us. *Back!* I ordered. *Back all the way!* Because I thought to myself, which is more likely to catch fire first: a damp Zarett ball, or a great bundle of sticks? It was simple logic that the stick-folk would be in greater danger than Starbiter; if they insisted on chasing us all the way into the flames, they were fools who could suffer the consequences.

We skipped backward in a series of hiccupy motions, zipping a short distance, stopping to see if the stick-ship followed, then retreating farther when our pursuer reappeared. I could not tell if the aliens were truly teleporting after us, or just moving so quickly they seemed to come from nowhere. Starbiter and I traveled quickly ourselves, each backward hop so fast I could not perceive the transition: the sun simply ballooned a little larger with each jump, its prominences wilder and more threatening, its dark spots looming ever nearer.

With every jump, I sensed greater fear in the Zarett. She showed no damage from the heat—looking down at her body, I could see no sign she was burning or even turning the slightest bit crispy—but like most lower animals, Starbiter seemed cowed by the very presence of fire. Each time I ordered her to retreat, I felt her reluctance growing. *There,*

there, I thought in my most soothing way, *it is all right, good girl, do not worry you will be burned to a cinder and disintegrate into howling ash* . . . but there came a time when even such encouragements could not overcome her terror: when I said, *Jump,* she did not move.

Move now! I thought again. It had no effect. She stayed where she was, trembling, as the stick-ship shot into view. *We must move,* I told her desperately, *or we shall be captured.*

Starbiter did not budge. Perhaps she did not care if we were captured . . . or killed, or whatever these Shaddills wished to do with us. To be honest, I was not sure what we feared from them; but they had shot Uclod and Lajoolie despite my pleasant message of friendship, so I assumed they were most awful villains, intent on doing us harm.

We had been stationary long enough that the other ship was nearly on top of us. Once again, the long tube-stick began telescoping outward, its mouth open wide enough to swallow Starbiter whole. I could see absolutely nothing inside: complete blackness, more inky than the darkest night sky. All around, the sun cast its blazing light, washing out every possible shadow on the alien ship, even the shadow Starbiter should have cast against the ship's belly . . . but in the mouth that wanted to eat us, the darkness was stronger than light.

"You foolish Zarett!" I yelled aloud. "Do you wish to be gobbled by the enemy? You must run now. You must fly straight into the sun. Go!"

Still Starbiter refused; and in my ear, I heard a whispery voice, nearly lost amidst crackle and hiss. "Oar . . . wait . . . you will die . . ."

It spoke to me in my own language, not the English it had used before. For some reason, I found that unsettling—as if these Shaddill ones were my personal foes, not aliens whose grudge was against Uclod.

"Go away!" I yelled at the whisperer. "Go away, or I *shall* fly into the sun." An idea struck me. "If we burn up," I said, "it will be your fault for chasing us. You will be branded as Callous Murderers, pursuing us to our deaths. What will the

League of Peoples think about *that,* you poop-heads? Will you enjoy their wrath?"

"Oar . . ." the voice whispered.

"Go away," I said. "Go far away and leave us alone. Otherwise, I shall fly into the sun and the League will know you as killers."

For several seconds, nothing happened . . . except that the stick-mouth slowed its approach, as if it were no longer quite so confident about swallowing us. *Be wary,* I thought to Starbiter. *They may wish to lull us into a false sense of safety. If anything happens, fly into the sun immediately. No more mulish hesitation!*

I could feel my heart beating in my chest. Thud . . . thud . . . thud . . . then two things happened almost simultaneously.

First, the stick-ship vanished like a bubble going pop.

Second, Starbiter reacted. More precisely, she leapt in total startlement . . . being a creature of limited brain, and not aware that we *wanted* the stick-ship to vanish.

So we jumped straight into the sun.

6

WHEREIN I DEFEAT
THE ENTIRE HUMAN NAVY

Not Burning Up At All

It is very very bright inside a sun. There is brightness in all directions. It must also be quite hot, but I did not feel any unusual warmth. I felt nothing except the straps binding me to my chair and the never-changing sense that I was sitting up straight.

Still, I am certain such a largish fire must be an Inferno Of Hellish Proportions—except that when I looked at Starbiter's body, she did not display the tiniest ill effect. Indeed, she appeared much as ever: strings mired in goo, with the goo glistening brilliant and wet in the sunshine. It was a shame the sun did not dry her icky surface even a little bit, for it would have improved the Zarett's complexion; but some skin conditions are beyond all help (as my friend Festina bemoans most frequently).

So Starbiter herself did not seem touched by the sun's scorching heat. There was, however, a visible change in the milky envelope surrounding us—it seemed to be *thickening*, like a fog at dusk. Mist rolled around our ship; the blaze outside was still strong enough to see, but the light had grown hazy and smeared over, gentled and damped down.

Hah! I thought. *We have tamed the sun.*

I could think of only one explanation. The smoky FTL

field surrounding Starbiter must possess the same nature as myself: drawing nutrition from light. During the past few minutes, skipping back jump by jump from the stick-ship, the envelope had absorbed great quantities of luminous energy—enough that when we entered the sun itself, the field was sufficiently strong to protect us.

Now that we were inside, the field was growing even thicker and more insulatory; but perhaps it was not wise to remain too long. Uclod had been so afraid of entering the sun, it might be that a Zarett could gorge itself too fully on light . . . like a fox eating so much dead rabbit it grew bloated and sick. Perhaps it was even possible for our protective FTL envelope to burst in an explosive Too Much Of A Good Thing. I did not understand FTL fields, but I did not trust them to limit their diet wisely in the presence of overwhelming quantities of tasty tasty sun.

Therefore I thought, *Good excellent Starbiter, you were a fine brave Zarett to enter this frightful place. Now here is our new plan: you must swim through the shallows of the sun, around and out the other side, where perhaps we will not be seen as we exit. Be careful not to go into the very heart of the sun; on sheer density alone, Uclod mentioned some foolish problem I do not understand, but perhaps this is not the time to press our luck.*

We began to advance through the great fire. I did not feel the motion, but I could tell we were moving because enigmatic darknesses drifted past my view. Quite likely those darknesses were the mysterious Spots I saw earlier crossing the sun's surface; but perhaps they were even more puzzling entities never before glimpsed by outside eyes.

It occurred to me there might be uncanny beings who dwelt their entire lives within stars, sailing the solar winds and farming the electromagnetic fields. Such beings could possess fabulous cities hidden in the Great Brightness. With all this nourishing light, perhaps the sun-folks' brains never became Tired; perhaps they were happy all day and never got scared or lonely, nor did they feel guilt that they were not Doing Something With Their Lives. I decided such creatures must look like large butterflies, with gentle eyes and kindly smiles. They would be made from glass, and sing beautiful songs—the type of songs that can only be sung by creatures who have never been afraid of the dark.

I held my breath and listened in the hope I might hear such a song . . . but if there was any sound outside, Starbiter did not transmit it to me. No doubt, there should have been the crackling of flames and the gusting of wind, maybe the boom of solar storms sweeping overhead across the sun's surface; but all I heard was silence as we soared through the fire and out the other side.

Solar Vision

We emerged from the sun surrounded by a fogbank of creamy smoke. Our FTL field had grown so fat on the banquet of solar energy, it was too thick to see through—there was only a great brightness at our backs and murky darkness everywhere else. If the stick-ship returned, the murk would blind me to its presence . . . so I projected my thoughts to Starbiter, asking if I might be connected to the special devices for perceiving long distances, particularly if they could see past the smog around us.

Within seconds, something went click inside my head; and suddenly, the milkiness occluding my eyes was gone. So was the color—the sun at my back had gone white with mottles of gray, and grainy too, as if the image were painted on sand. Apparently, the special devices for perceiving long distances did not experience color in the same way as real eyes . . . but then, there must be esoteric Science processes at work and I was not seeing real light at all. In a ship that travels FTL, you need a better-than-light way to see your surroundings; otherwise, you do not know when you are about to smash into something.

Also you do not know when you have company. The moment I turned my attention away from the sun, I saw four newcomer starships mustering in formation around me.

Out Of The Frying Pan, Into The Fliers

The newly arrived craft were not nearly so large as the stick-ship—not the size of a forest, but merely single trees. Or rather single towers, such as the eighty-story building where I supposedly died. These ships were long and thin with a bulb on one end, like the cattails one finds in a marsh. Each vessel was surrounded by its own smoky FTL field, but the fields were vapor-thin and extended far past the ships themselves, making long dangly tails that swished languidly through space. From descriptions given me by Explorers, I concluded these were baton-ships of the human Technocracy's Outward Fleet.

This was a Ghastly Predicament, coming face-to-face with the very people Uclod wished to avoid. It made me wonder if perhaps the stick-ship had wished to avoid them as well. Perhaps the stick-folk, the Shaddills, had not broken off their pursuit because of my threats and persuasion, but because they perceived Earthling vessels entering the star system. The stick-ship had fled, leaving me to face the entire human navy on my own.

Those Shaddills were very great poop-heads indeed.

In the blink of an eye, the navy ships arranged themselves into a four-pointed pyramid with Starbiter in the middle. This was clearly a military tactic intended to intimidate me . . . and to place me in the middle of a crossfire if the navy chose to apply armed force. It made me angry, the way humans arrived in my home system and immediately began acting like bullies. Especially when I had done nothing wrong, and the stick-people were the true villains.

"Greetings," I said aloud, assuming my words would still be broadcast to anyone listening. "I am a sentient citizen of the League of Peoples. It is most nonsensical to gang up on me when there is a genuinely hostile vessel nearby. Seek it out and ask why it fired on us."

"You had a ship fire on you?" a voice asked. The voice was female and haughty . . . as if I were some vile creature who could not possibly be believed.

"Yes," I replied. "It was a ship made of sticks."

"What a shame—we must have missed the ship made of straw and the ship made of bricks." The navy woman gave a sniff of great disdain. "What kind of idiots do you think we are, Unorr? There's nothing on our sensors, not the slightest trace of tachyon residue anywhere in this system . . . except the stuff from your Zarett looping around the sun. Did you think flying close to the star would hide your tracks? If so, you're even dumber than the rest of your family."

"I am not one of the Unorrs," I said, "and I was not flying *close* to the sun. I was inside the sun, fleeing from the stick-ship."

"Oh for Christ's sake," the navy woman growled, "if you're going to tell lies, be believable. *Inside* the sun? So you've magically overcome Sperm-field breakdown? We'll have to award you the Galaxy Prize for Physics . . . after we finish arresting you."

She took in a deep breath—the way some people do, not because they need air, but because they want you to know they intend to deliver a momentous oration. "All right, for the record: Unorr ship, I am Captain Prope of Technocracy Cruiser *Jacaranda*, and I order you to stand down. You are under arrest for entering a star system that was lawfully placed under total quarantine . . ."

She continued to speak, but I did not listen. I was too startled by the revelation that she was Festina's foul enemy, Captain Prope. It was Prope who marooned my friend on Melaquin . . . and Prope whom Festina cursed on a regular basis, adding many picturesque phrases to my English vocabulary. If Prope was here, there was indeed villainy afoot. But how could I foil Prope's dastardly schemes?

I decided to run. It angered me to act so craven—I should have liked to punch Prope in the nose, while chiding her for past evil deeds—but there were four navy ships against one small Zarett, and as far as I knew, Starbiter had no weapons with which to resist arrest. Anyway, according to Uclod, these humans must have come to conceal what happened on Melaquin. Therefore, I could best defeat them by escaping to tell my story.

When I *did* tell my story, I would be sure to mention

Prope was a most utter scoundrel who had tried to Suppress The Truth.

Starbiter, I thought, *once again we must fly.* I decided it was not wise to flee back into the sun—with four ships, the humans could space themselves around the star and catch us wherever we came out. Besides, I did not know how much more fiery energy our FTL field could absorb.

On the other hand, we had sopped up so much power, perhaps we could fly faster and farther than usual, like a bird who has fed well all summer and is in peak condition for migrating south. (Alternatively, we might resemble a great fat beast who had eaten so much it was only fit for sleeping off its meal . . . but I am such a one as prefers positive thoughts.)

Are you ready, Starbiter? I asked. I picked a direction that would take us away from the sun, scooting out through the gap between two of the navy vessels. *That is our heading,* I thought. *Now go, go, go!*

We shot forward like lightning. The humans surely must have been ready in case we made a break for it, but they were not prepared for our speed. Beams of gray-white light lanced from the navy ships toward our craft, but in the strange monochrome vision of Starbiter's long-range sensors, the light beams traveled in slow motion. Snaky snares of energy reached out sluggishly from the bellies of all four baton-ships, but we dodged past as easily as ducking under the branches of a tree.

In a heartbeat, Starbiter darted out of the trap the humans had built around us. Something big flashed past my eyes almost too swiftly to notice . . . possibly Melaquin or some other planet, maybe even the stick-ship, still present but invisible to the arrogantly blind navy folk. Then there was nothing but stars; and even the sun at our back dwindled in seconds to nothing but a pinprick.

I directed Starbiter to change course five times at random to make us harder to follow—I did not know how easily the navy might track us, but surely keeping to a single straight line was imprudent. Then again, perhaps it did not matter; the four ships vanished from sight in the first instant of our escape, and I never saw them again.

7

WHEREIN I AM OFFERED
A DEAL WITH THE DEVIL

**You Would Not Think Annoying Persons
Could Find You In Outer Space, But You
Would Be Wrong**

Here is a fact about space travel: it is very very boring. I greatly enjoyed the excitement of escaping implacable foes . . . but once I got away, there was nothing to see but stars, stars, stars. Some of the stars were no doubt galaxies; others might have been planets, or comets, or incandescent space butterflies singing of life in the sun; but they all looked like stars, *and I have seen stars before.*

I wondered whether the journey would be more interesting if we slowed down—perhaps we were passing all manner of appealing space objects, but so quickly they could not be seen. However, with the human navy pursuing us, it did not seem wise to ease up even a little bit. Therefore, we hurtled through the tedious black for hour after frustrating hour, while the untwinkling stars went on and on without meaning, like one's life when one is devoid of lofty goals . . . until suddenly, I heard a man clearing his throat.

"Uclod?" I called. All this time my eyes had been linked with the Zarett, unable to see my companions sitting in the chairs beside me. I had not known if they were alive or dead; and to tell the truth, I had mostly forgotten about them. The great starry sameness tended to blank my thoughts . . . which is not to say my brain grew *Tired*. I was fatigued, nothing more—and perhaps in need of solid food now that I had left the sustaining light of my Ancestral Tower. One must not let one's heart become choked with panic over simple weariness and hunger. "Uclod?" I said much louder. "Are you finally awake, you churlish little man?"

"Nope, not Uclod. Guess again."

The voice was definitely not Uclod's. It sounded male but had a raspy nasal quality to it: the type of voice one's sister might adopt when saying, "Nyah, nyah, look whose bed is wet!" The words were spoken in Explorer English with a quick flat accent that cut rapidly through syllables and left them sliced in pieces on the ground.

"Who are you?" I asked. "*Where* are you?"

"Ooo, direct questions!" the voice said. "That's what I like about primitive organisms: no wasting time with social niceties. No throwing yourself into postures of abject worship and offering infant sacrifices like *some* races I could mention. You come right out and say, 'Who the hell are you, pal?' "

"You are not my pal," I said. "And despite your admiration for direct questions, you have not answered mine."

"Absolutely right. That's cuz I'm an asshole."

"Do you have a name, Mr. Asshole? Do you have a location?"

"Yes and yes. See? I can answer questions with the best of 'em. And before you get your knickers in a knot, let me reveal myself in a tiny fraction of my eye-popping glory."

One second I was looking at starry space, unable to see my own body; the next, I was standing in the flesh on a fiery red plain that was definitely *not* inside Starbiter.

The Fiery Red Plain

Less than a stone's throw away, chunky pools of lava hissed up thin streams of smoke, making the air ripple with their heat. Small black things swam in the crimson-hot pools, two-headed slugs that slithered short distances along the surface, then buried their noses into the magma and dived out of sight. There were insects too, buzzing loudly enough to be heard over the molten sizzle, flying from one smoke streamer to another and pausing briefly inside each, as if sipping from flowers.

As soon as I thought of flowers, a garden sprang up around me: a garden that had not been present two seconds before. I did not recognize the plants—they were scarlet and black, with huge limpid blooms hanging heavily at the level of my thighs, their petals the color of human blood. They rustled restlessly against my legs and against each other, though I could feel no wind. I felt no heat either, nor the ground beneath my feet, nor the touch of the flowers, though I could see them brushing my skin . . . and suddenly I realized the truth.

"This is a simulation!" I cried. "Nothing more than a trick. You are transmitting sights and sounds to Starbiter, who is transmitting them to me; but I cannot feel anything, because the Zarett is unable to send me such sensations."

"Ooo, aren't you the smarty-pants!" said the voice. "Except for the pants. Doesn't your backside get breezy?"

I looked around. There was no sign of anyone else in the bubbly volcanic landscape—nothing but the garden and the lava, plus some peaky black mountains on the farthest horizon. The sky was empty too: an ashy maroon with no clouds or stars. "Are you hiding, Mr. Asshole?" I called. "Or are you preparing an extravagant entrance you think will impress me?"

"Bright girl," the voice chuckled. "You're obviously miles ahead of my feeble brain."

With a surging explosion of smoke, something erupted from the depths of the closest lava pool. It was big and white, with fizzing droplets of molten rock running off its hide. Where the drips spilled onto the blood-red flowers, the plants sprouted brand-new blossoms that appeared with a soft screaming sound. The screams were an excellent touch—if one intends to simulate a volcanic garden, there is admirable showmanship in flowers that howl as they grow.

But the white thing continued to rise from the magma, as if it were standing on a submerged platform being lifted by an elevator mechanism. I could see now the beast was exceedingly leathery, the approximate size and pebbly texture of a rhinoceros.[4] It had four massive legs and even a fuzzy tail tucked between the armorlike slabs of hide covering its haunches . . . but unlike a rhinoceros, this creature had no horn. It had no nose at all, and no eyes or mouth either, because the animal completely lacked a head—its neck simply stopped at the throat, where an open hole led back into the chest cavity.

As I watched, the headless creature leaned forward so the hole in its neck tilted downward. A thick gout of lava poured out of the gap, as if the beast were emptying unwanted fillage that had flowed into the opening while submerged. "God, that itches," the animal said in a gargly voice. It made a hawking sound in its throat the way a crude person does before spitting; then a wad of lava spurted out the neckhole and splashed back into the pool.

"That's better," it said in a much clearer tone. "How 'bout you? Not too intimidated by seeing the real me?"

"Why should I believe I am seeing the real you? Since this is just a projected image, you may look nothing like a headless rhinoceros. You could be something small and *squishy,* attempting to make yourself look more impressive."

"If I wanted to make myself look impressive, I'd pick something better than a headless fucking rhino." The beast stepped from the surface of the lava onto the solid ground of the garden; the flowers he tread upon gave high-pitched squeals and dragged themselves out of the way, ripping their roots from the soil and replanting themselves at a safe distance. I stared at them . . . and the beast noticed me looking. He glanced at the fleeing plants, then up at me. "Too much?"

---

[4]Although I had never seen a living rhinoceros, the teaching machines in my village had shown me many excellent pictures of them. Also elephants. And kangaroos. And many other creatures who did not make their homes in my part of the world but had endearing qualities such as being eaten by their mates or spitting lethal venoms.

"Yes. You are trying too hard to dazzle me."

"Fair enough," he said. "Screw the special effects."

He slopped across the garden toward me, now moving *through* the flowers as if they were not even there. They did not screech or pull away; they did not even quiver as his body passed through leaves and blossoms that were no more solid than smoke. Or perhaps it was the beast himself who had become insubstantial—large and white and unnatural, coming toward me like a decapitated ghost.

As the creature drew nearer, I got an unobstructed view of the gaping hole where his head should have been. The sky's dim red light did not pierce far into the beast's inner blackness; yet down his open throat, as deep as his heart and lungs, two crimson orbs glowed like the dying coals of a campfire. I suspected these were Baleful Burning Eyes, buried in the recesses of the creature's body . . . but if so, it was a most foolish place to locate one's sight, because one's view would be greatly restricted by the sides of one's own neck.

I myself would not enjoy that type of tunnel vision; but then, we must not expect aliens to see things our way.

Introductions

"So," the beast said, "let's deal with formalities." He took a deep breath, then rattled off quickly, "Greetings-I-am-a-sentient-citizen-of-the-League-of-Peoples-I-beg-your-Hospitality-what-a-load-of-horseshit."

"Oh yes," I replied. "Me too. Except for the horseshit."

I was vexed I had not been the first to speak the required phrase. As official communications officer, I should have been faster; but this creature had deliberately distracted me with ostentatious spectacle, so that was my excuse.

"And it's time to introduce myself," the creature said. "I'm called the Pollisand. Does that ring any bells?"

Searching my memory, I could not recall hearing the name; but suddenly I remembered my conversation with the woman in the Tower of Ancestors. She claimed I had been visited by a big white thing *like some animal, except without a head.* "Your name is unfamiliar," I said, "but you came to me on Melaquin, after I fell."

"Give the glass lady a transparent cigar!" the Pollisand cried. "I brought you back from the dead."

"You did not! I am not such a creature as can die."

"Oh, you can die, *cheri*," the Pollisand said. "You are more than capable of that little feat. The only reason your species doesn't kick the bucket more often is because you're a bunch of preindustrial hayseeds—so damned Paleolithic, you've never invented weapons more lethal than pointy sticks. As if those could pierce your hard glass heinies!

"But," he went on, "you've left your world behind now, sweetums. You've entered the hostile high-tech universe, and there's many a method to make you a corpse. Monofilament garrotes that can saw through your jugular. Hypersonic pistols to shatter your glass guts. Plain old dynamite or plastique. And that's not to mention alien microbes or toxins—you may be immune to the diseases and poisons on Melaquin, but I guarantee you weren't built to handle every damned biochemical compound in the galaxy. Bump against the wrong kind of leaf, and you might keel over like a poleaxed steer."

I looked down at the flowers brushing my legs. It would be most cowardly to back away from them, and anyhow they were unreal mental projections; so I stayed where I was. "Perhaps it is true I now have a heightened risk of decease," I said, "but it is most unlikely you came just to warn me of such dangers. What do you want?"

Before he could answer or at least before he *did* answer—a patch of scarlet flowers rustled behind me. I turned quickly, expecting attack; all this time, the Pollisand might have been a devious villain whose only goal was to provide distraction while a confederate stole up on me from behind. After being forced to flee from the stick-ship and the human navy, it was pleasant to have the prospect of a solid enemy I could punch in the nose . . . but when a creature leapt from concealment, I was dismayed to see it *had* no nose.

It was a round gray ball the size of my own head; and as it

sped toward me, I recognized its texture: gray strings on white goo. Furthermore, the creature was not attacking so much as *bouncing*—a small gray animal jumping up and down with excitement, scrambling around my ankles as it made happy little cheeps. It seemed to take pleasure from hopping against my calves, rebounding back, and skipping around to try the same thing at a new angle.

"Is this what it appears to be?" I asked the Pollisand.

"Yes ma'am," he answered, "that's the one and only Starbiter."

"The real Starbiter is much larger."

"Clearly, she *thinks* of herself as smaller. I'm not creating her image, she is. In fact, I didn't expect her to show up at all; but since I'm using her to project bumpf into your brain, she must have decided to get in on the act. And this is how she sees herself."

The Pollisand tilted his neckhole downward as if he wanted to look more closely at the little Star-bouncer. She must have noticed the red glowing eyes in his chest cavity, and found them a source of allure; skittering away from me she bounced toward those eyes, squashing flowers as she went. I could see the Pollisand's eyes blaze more brightly . . . just before Starbiter made a tremendous leap and jumped straight down the Pollisand's throat.

Starbiter, The Cannonball

It is most amusing to see a haughty alien with a small energetic creature stuffed into his neck. Starbiter made happy squeaky sounds as if she were proud of her mischievous accomplishment; she wobbled back and forth inside the throat cavity, thudding against the sides and giggling each time she bounced off.

As for the Pollisand, he seemed frozen in astonishment: he did not move for a full count of five. Then with a great shudder, he raised his shoulders and filled his lungs full of air. His breath made tempestuous sucking sounds as he in-

haled around the Zarett crammed down his throat; I could
see his ribs expand wider and wider, until suddenly he blew
out with all his strength.

Starbiter shot from his neckhole like a cannonball. She
squealed something that sounded like "Wheeeeee!" as she
flew in a perfect arc, hurtling far across the garden and landing precipitously in a patch of blood-flowers. For a moment,
I worried she might be hurt; but almost as soon as she
splashed down she bounced up again, making joyful peeps
and whistles.

"Look," I told the Pollisand. "She wants to do it again."

"Tough titty," he said. "Do you know what would happen
if certain folks saw me with a Zarett down my maw? I'm
supposed to retain my dignity, for Christ's sake—some
species worship me like unto a god. A fat lot of good it
would do my reputation if people knew I'd been used as a
basketball hoop."

"Perhaps it would *help* your reputation. Perhaps you
would not be considered an asshole if it were known you
played cheerfully with others."

"What do you mean, cheerfully? I'm not cheerful—I've
got Zarett guck in my mouth."

He made another loud hawking sound and spat out a blob
of stringy gray and white. "Besides," he continued, "I *like*
people thinking I'm an asshole. Being an asshole is my life's
vocation; I'm a goddamned asshole professional. When
other people act like assholes, they're doing it on their own
time, but me, it's my *job*."

"Is that why you have come then? Someone is paying you
to annoy me? Because you are very most irritating indeed,
and I do not wish to spend time with you unless you
promptly explain what you want."

The glowing eyes in his throat burned brighter. Before
speaking, he glanced toward Starbiter; but the little Zarett
had got herself distracted with the two-headed slugs that
swam in the lava pools. It appeared she was *bouncing* on the
vermin with great delight, splashing up fierce hissing splut-
ters of magma each time she smacked the boiling surface.

The heat did not bother her a bit . . . but then, she had already traveled through a sun, so how could she be harmed by mere molten minerals?

"All right," the Pollisand said, turning back to me, "let's talk business. I don't often make deals with lesser species, but you're in a unique position, even if you don't know it." The Pollisand's eyes flared brightly. "Oar, my sweet, my sugar, my sucrose-based carbohydrate, suppose I had a way that your brain would never get Tired? Would that interest you? Hmm?"

Temptations

I stared at him speechless for several heartbeats. More out of reflex than conviction, I said, "My brain never *will* get Tired, you foolish beast. I am not such a one as succumbs to mind-numbing ennui."

"Unlike your mother?" the Pollisand asked. "And the hundred generations before her? They all swore they wouldn't turn into mental rutabagas, but now they're cluttering up a thousand glass towers."

He stomped his foot and suddenly the world changed. There was no garden, no lava, no scarlet-ash sky; we were back in Oarville with mute snow swirling through the air.

The Pollisand and I stood atop the Tower of Ancestors where I had suffered my great fall. Some distance off, near the edge of the roof, the small figure of Starbiter gave a surprised yelp, then bounced speedily toward us. Within seconds, she was pressed fearfully against my leg, clearly disturbed by the sudden change of scenery.

I knelt and gave her a reassuring pat. A tiny amount of goo came off onto my hand, but I could not feel it—this was still a simulation, giving me sight and sound but not touch. Continuing to stroke the worried Starbiter, I glared at the Pollisand. "Why are we here?"

"Just a visual demonstration, lass." He stomped his foot again, and the city changed. Instead of the many different buildings it had held before, now it was filled with Ancestral

Towers exactly like the one beneath my feet: tens of thousands of them, shining brightly but somehow not illuminating the cavern around us.

"Oar," the Pollisand said, "this is your world and your people. Damned near comatose—as good as dead. Only a few dozen of your species haven't gone zombie; and how soon before they give in? How soon before *you* do?"

He lifted one foot and waved it casually at the vista: tower after tower, stretching back as far as I could see, much farther than the actual wall of the cavern. "Up till now," he said, "there's only been one way to keep your gray cells from turning to zucchini—throw yourself over and go KERSPLAT. Smash your body to mush before your brain mushes out on its own. You've taken the high dive once, Oar; it's still there for you. Cast your cares to the wind and die a decent death. This time I promise I won't sew you back together. Nor will angels appear to bear you up safely."

I stared at him. "Why would I imagine angels should appear? That is a most absurd notion."

The Pollisand gave an ostentatious sigh. "Classical allusions are just lost on you, aren't they? I suppose there's no point my even *suggesting* you turn stones into bread."

"You may suggest such a thing, but I cannot do it. Can you? I would be most happy if you did, for I have not eaten in quite some time. But if you do bake bread from stones, make sure it is *good* bread—not the horrid opaque substance Explorers are so proud of cooking."

"Okay," the Pollisand muttered to himself, "scratch the three-temptations scenario. Didn't work the last time I tried it either. On to Plan B."

He stomped his foot more forcefully than ever, and in the blink of an eye, we were back where we started: in the garden, surrounded by steaming lava. Starbiter bleated with excitement and bounced off to bother the wildlife. Meanwhile, the Pollisand kicked the heads off a couple flowers and ground the blooms under his heel. "All right," he said. "We were talking business. *Deals*." He gave the plants one more whack, then turned back to me. "I was proposing you could avoid rampaging senility, if only you play ball with me."

"What sort of ball do you wish to play?"

"It was only a metaphor, damn it!" The Pollisand squashed another patch of flowers, leaving his foot red with their juices. "I'm suggesting a simple agreement. An exchange of favors. My favor is I'll ensure your brain doesn't go Tired."

"And what do you wish in return?"

"I wish . . ." He took a deep breath. "I want . . . well, to put it in terms you'll understand, I want you to tell the League of Peoples it's okay if I accidentally get you killed."

The Deal

"It is *not* okay if you get me killed! That is very much not okay at all!" I glared at him in outrage; he had red flower sap all over his foot and I hoped it would stain *forever.*

"Why isn't it okay?" he demanded. "Point one, you've already died once and I was the one who brought you back to life; you owe me big-time, lady. Point two, your brain's almost curdled to gorgonzola, and when it goes, you're as good as dead anyway. Point three, I'm so far above you on the ladder of sentience my IQ can only be measured with transfinite numbers, and I promise there's only the teeniest-tiniest-eensiest-weensiest chance my plan will go wrong enough to get you killed."

"Hmph," I said. "Tell me your plan and let me judge for myself."

"Tell you my plan? I can't tell you my plan. My plan is so complex, your brain doesn't have the capacity to comprehend it. This entire *universe* doesn't have the capacity to comprehend my plan—there aren't enough quarks to encode the simplest overview. I've got fifty-five million backup universes grinding away at figuring out what I have to do next, and that's just the underlying logic, not the user interface. No way I can tell you my plan."

"In other words," I said, "you do not *have* a plan."

"Well, I've got a few rough ideas. My greatest strength is improvising."

One of the red eyes in his throat disappeared for a moment, then blazed back to life; I had an eerie feeling the Pollisand had just winked at me. "Seriously, kiddo," he said, "I have plans upon plans upon plans, reaching all the way down to the end of time. I have agendas both social and temporal, I have schemes both simple and ornate; I create conspiracies and tear them apart; my name is a byword for foresight and I have honed the blade of strategy to a razor's edge."

"If you always talk this much," I said, "it is a wonder you have time for planning at all."

"Damn, but you're a stick-in-the-mud," he grumbled. "All right, I do have a plan, okay? It's a good plan, aimed at a noble purpose . . . but there's a teeny-tiny-eensy-weensy chance that at a particular point as events unfold you'll die rather permanently. Under circumstances where I won't be able to patch you up like the last time. And that's where I run afoul of the League of Peoples: cuz if I have this foreknowledge, which I do, of a lethal danger, which there is, to a sentient creature, which you are—borderline sentient, but you're still on the civilized side of the ledger—then I'm morally obliged to ask if it's okay I might get you murdered. Basically, you have to agree you want to achieve the same lofty goal I do . . . at which point it ceases to be *me* putting your life at risk, but *you* accepting the risk yourself because you're so doggone eager to do the right thing."

"And what is this right thing I so recklessly wish to do?"

"Um. Well." The Pollisand stubbed his toe bashfully into the dirt, a gesture no doubt intended to appear winningly ingenuous. "Do I really have to tell you? Couldn't you just take my word, as a being seventy-five trillion rungs higher than you on the evolutionary ladder, that I'm honestly pursuing the greatest good for the greatest number?"

"I do not care about the greatest good for the greatest number," I said. "Most people are poop-heads; I do not care about them *at all*. And I have no confidence you are as clever and advanced as you claim to be—all I have seen you do is simulate visions using Starbiter."

The Zarett heard her name and began bouncing toward me . . . until she became distracted by a bug flying by, and bounced after it instead. I turned back to the Pollisand. "Zaretts do not seem so high on the evolutionary ladder. I have seen no evidence that you are either."

"Ah," the Pollisand said, "but perhaps my facade is an act. A truly advanced being might realize it's best to approach lesser species in a nonthreatening way—as a ridiculous-looking creature who comes across as a pompous jerk barely able to keep his foot out of his mouth. It puts you at ease, doesn't it, when you say, *This Pollisand guy isn't so scary; he's not the swaggering staggering supergenius the rest of the universe thinks he is.* You catch me making a few goofs, you throw my words back in my face, and after a while, you relax cuz you think I'm not smart enough to pull the wool over your eyes."

If this was an attempt to disconcert me, it nearly worked. A vastly intelligent beast who controlled what I saw and heard might indeed present himself as a silly buffoon so as not to be taken too seriously. On the other hand, a silly buffoon might boast of himself as a vastly intelligent beast who was merely play-acting. Which was more likely?

"The most important point," I said, "is that I wish to know the direction of your plan. What is your goal? What is your purpose?"

The Pollisand shuffled his feet. "All right. The part of the plan that concerns you—the *immediate* part of the plan—is related to the race you call the Shaddill."

"Are you *for* them or *against* them?" I asked.

"I fervently want," the Pollisand said, "to wipe them off the face of this galaxy. And your part in the plan will help accomplish that."

"Why did you not say so?" I reached out and laid my arm across the alien's back in a comradely manner. "Of course I shall help you defeat the Shaddill . . . especially if you fix my Tired Brain too. You should have known I would say yes if you put it like that."

"I *did* know," the Pollisand said in a soft voice totally unlike his previous obnoxious tone.

Suddenly, I realized I could *feel* my arm lying on the Pollisand's hide . . . and as soon as I realized that, I could feel the ground beneath my feet too. A hot stinking wind blew around me, and the crimson flowers brushing my legs felt scratchy against my calves. Nearby, little Starbiter yelped in fright and bounced fearfully toward me, leaping high at the last and jumping straight into my arms. I caught her and held her; when she pressed her gooey body against my chest, I felt her warm trembling stickiness.

The Pollisand turned toward me and the fire of his deep-buried eyes blazed hotter than all the lava pools around us. A wave of scorching heat struck me square in the face, a blistering slap so fierce I feared my cheeks would melt . . . and suddenly, I had the terrifying suspicion this was all *real*, that the Pollisand had truly transported me across untold light-years to this lava world, and shrunk Starbiter to the size of a puppy, and kept me from feeling the boiling temperatures so I would believe it was only an illusion . . .

Then everything went black: black with lonely stars. My body was back in its former position, seated rigidly upright. When I looked around, all I saw was Starbiter's stringy physique, returned to its normal size: big enough that she could hold me in a tiny corner of her lungs, instead of being cradled in my arms.

One might think it had all been a dream; but my face still burned as if it had been shoved into searing flame.

8

WHEREIN I CANNOT FIND A GOOD PLACE TO BE

Back To The Mundane

A few minutes later, someone groaned beside me. "Uclod?" I whispered. "Pollisand?"

A voice muttered garbled words. I did not recognize the language, nor did I recognize the voice—it was too deep for Uclod, too guttural for the Pollisand. "Lajoolie?" I whispered. Perhaps this growling baritone was what she sounded like when not putting on her false soprano. I strongly hoped that was the explanation, because I did not want to deal with another unknown visitor. "Lajoolie, is that you?"

"Unh . . . unh . . ." Unfocused moans came out in the same baritone. Then the voice forced itself to a higher pitch: "What happened? What did you do to me?"

It *was* Lajoolie—past her initial grogginess, and now remembering to feign more missish tones. More missish questions too: when she said, "What did you do to me?" she did not sound like someone who truly believed I had worked some devilish trick on her. I got the feeling she spoke as she thought a certain type of woman would; a flighty *helpless* woman, not a woman whose body was covered with more muscles than a dead squirrel has flies. Clearly, Lajoolie possessed a confused self-image I would have to investigate when I had the time . . . but for now, I was simply happy not to be alone anymore.

"There was a terrible stick-thing," I told her. "What you called a Shaddill ship. It shot you with a Diabolical Weapon Ray, leaving me to effect an escape single-handed. Which I did most proficiently. Since then, I have flown through the sun and defeated the human navy, not to mention meeting . . ."

I stopped myself. Perhaps it would not be so prudent to disclose my encounter with the Pollisand. Someone like Lajoolie (or even worse, Uclod) might chide me most scathingly for entering into a poorly defined pact with a powerful alien of dubious motives. Therefore I resolved not to speak of the Pollisand until I had time to ponder the ramifications on my own.

The Vexation Of Newlywed Sentiments

Off to my left, a noise went click. The next moment, something crawled up my face—the icky intestine covering my head. It had been in place so many hours, I had forgotten it was there. My vision went black for a moment, then returned; only now I was seeing with my own eyes, where Uclod sat slumped in his chair and Lajoolie was just straightening up from the bumpy controls in front of her seat. Obviously, she had pressed a release that withdrew the linkage attached to our heads . . . and had also disengaged the straps holding us to our chairs. I felt myself being freed as the straps slithered back into the chair's jellyfish upholstery; and it was a good thing I was not such a one as stiffened from periods of inactivity, or I would now be a Solid Mass Of Discomfort.

The straps around Uclod unclasped too. He would have toppled onto his nose if Lajoolie had not leapt to catch him. In that instant, I could see she was extremely fast as well as strong—especially for one who had just lain unconscious many hours. She eased Uclod back into his seat and spent an inordinate amount of fuss arranging him: positioning his body just so, with his head propped up instead of lolling to one side, his hands folded neatly in his lap, and so on . . . whereas *I* might have started by checking his pulse to see if other actions were worth the effort. It took at least a minute to convince myself Uclod was even breathing; but at last, when Lajoolie stopped fretting with him, I saw a definite rise and fall in his chest.

Once Lajoolie had composed her husband to her satisfaction, she seated herself on the floor at his feet and leaned against his legs. I believe she would have liked to lay her head on his knee or rest it in his lap—she was just the type to seek the most submissive posture available. However, she was too tall for either of those positions, so she contented herself with settling her arm across his thighs and huddling tight to his body. I watched her for a count of five, then said, "Should we not try to wake him?"

She lifted her head, meeting my gaze with large brown eyes. "How?" she asked.

"In stories," I answered, "it is customary to slap the face. Beginning lightly, then with increasing force."

"I don't want to do that," Lajoolie said.

"You would rather he stayed unconscious?"

"I'd rather he woke on his own. There's no hurry, is there? You said we've escaped from the Shaddill. And Starbiter doesn't need to be piloted—once you stopped giving her direct orders, she automatically adjusted her course toward New Earth. The heading was preprogrammed: I checked. So we're going home and we can take our time."

"But waiting is irksomely tedious. It is better when you make the next thing happen *right away*."

Lajoolie stared at me a moment, then shook her head. With a slight smile, she hugged herself tighter to the unconscious little criminal and closed her eyes.

She was obviously doing this to vex me. Rather than stay and watch her pretend to be patient, I stomped out of the room to explore the ship.

Obstinate Doors

I did not do so well as an Explorer. There was only one way to leave the bridge: down the long tubular corridor whose floor had those corduroy ridges over bluish-white skin. The corridor led back to the room where I had landed after sliding down the throat . . . and I could see no other direction to go from there. Uclod said the Zarett had eighteen rooms, but I did not know where they were.

"Starbiter," I said aloud, "we are friends now, are we not? We have ventured together into the sun . . . and far from home, in a place of lava, we nestled together for comfort. Therefore you know I am trustworthy, and you may safely open concealed doors to reveal your hidden depths."

Silence.

"You may open them any time now, Starbiter. My comrade. My ally in times of distress."

But nothing happened. I did not think my bouncing bleating friend would completely ignore me so soon after we had shared precious moments of closeness on an alien plain; more likely, she just could not hear me speaking. Few of us, after all, have ears in our lungs. If I wanted the Zarett to admit me to her inner recesses, I would have to find the proper places to rub my hand or tap my foot.

Therefore I experimented with rubbing the walls at random: palpating the soft mushiness, leaving fingerprints all over the yellow fungus that lit the room. From the first, I felt most foolish . . . but as time went on without success, I could not help a sense of betrayal—as if Starbiter was deliberately shutting me out like some unwanted cast off.

That made me very sad. Besides the standoffish Zarett, the only people within light-years were in the other room, deliberately being husband and wife together . . . which was a most appalling spectacle of Married Sentimentality, and I would never want a person to sit at *my* feet, nor would I willingly sit at someone else's. But I did not enjoy being all by myself inside a large creature's lung. I did not even have the Explorer jacket I had brought from Melaquin; it was back in the bridge, and I refused to go get it. What would I say as I entered the room? "Excuse me, I wish something to hug for I am feeling glum?"

So I seated myself in the middle of the floor and squeezed my legs tight to my chest. I did not cry, not even a single tear; but I kept my eyes tight shut. My eyelids are a lovely silver, almost the only parts of my body that are opaque . . . and at that moment, with my face pressed against my knees, I did not wish to see *anything*.

(My legs act as distorting lenses. Sometimes, when I look through them, the world appears most strange and threatening indeed.)

One Does Not Expect Hauntings To Occur Inside Lungs

Something brushed my shoulder. I jerked in surprise—I had heard nobody approach. When I turned, I expected to see Uclod or Lajoolie, or perhaps some icky polyp protruding from the wall and trying to attach itself to me for unknown alien purposes.

I did not expect to see a ghost.

It was a thing made of mist, like the spooky patches of fog that form in hollows at sundown. Unlike our milky-white FTL field, this mist had no color: clear as a spray of water, and thin enough for me to see right through to the wall on the far side. But this was no random vapor wafting through Starbiter's lungs like breath on a winter's day; it had a vaguely human shape, with legs and arms and head. Nothing was distinct—the feet had no toes, the hands had no fingers, the face had no features at all—but this was definitely a coherent entity leaning over me. It had touched my shoulder with its barely substantial hand . . . and I could not help flinching, swatting the hand away.

My swat passed through the thing's arm with no resistance: like sweeping my fingers through smoke. Though the mist looked like fog, it felt dry, and neither cold nor hot— just a tiny bit gritty, like dust.

"Go away, ghost," I told it. "Go haunt someone else." I waved my hand through its chest, trying to scatter it to bits. The particles of its body, droplets or ashes or soot, swirled on the wind of my movements, but did not fly apart. As soon as I stopped stirring up breeze, the thing drifted back to its original shape, a person leaning over me.

"Sad woman . . . sad woman . . ."

The words were a whisper, coming from the entity's entire body: not just from its mouth area, but resonating completely from head to foot. "What is wrong, sad woman?" the creature whispered. "What hurts you?"

"Nothing hurts me," I answered. "But I am easily annoyed by intrusive beings of unknown origin. What are you?"

"The ship's mate . . ."

"What?" I said in outrage. "I was forced to drive this ship myself when there was a high-ranking crew member aboard? Were you incapacitated by the stick-ship's weapon?"

"No," the entity replied, "but I know nothing about . . . flying Starbiter. She would surely . . . not obey me . . . if I tried. I am not . . . a crew member; I am . . . the ship's *mate.*"

For a moment I just glowered at him. Then I realized what he was saying: that he was Starbiter's *spouse.* The male of her species. Her *lover.* Which suggested that some or all of the tiny particles making up his body were Zarett *seed*—designed to fertilize whatever eggs Starbiter produced.

Quickly, I wiped my hands off on the floor.

Conversing With A Cloud

"What are you doing here?" I demanded. "We are in the lungs. Should you not be in another organ altogether? Doing whatever foul things a cloud man does to make babies?"

"I visit every organ on a regular basis," the ghostly entity answered. "In addition to my . . . husbandly duties . . ." (he sounded most amused) ". . . I am also what you might call . . . a veterinarian. Or perhaps the ship's engineer. I patrol my mate's airways and bloodstream in search of . . .

metabolic imbalances . . ." The misty figure gestured in my direction. "Which led me to you."

"I am not a metabolic imbalance!"

The cloud man pointed to the place I was sitting. "You're creating a hot spot," came the whisper. "And I sensed the presence of . . . unfamiliar chemicals . . ."

"My chemicals are very familiar! Have you never heard of glass?"

"There are many kinds of glass," the cloud said, "and you're none of them. Your skin is . . . an amalgam of transparent polymers, serviced by an army of . . . sophisticated agent-cells . . . that perform general maintenance and . . . ward off external microbes. There are also . . . trace fluids on your exterior, the purpose of which I can't identify. Not conventional perspiration—possibly just a light body wash to prevent you from caking with dust . . . possibly something more complicated. All such . . . biochemical compounds are cause for concern, given the slight but real chance they may have a detrimental effect on my . . . patroness."

"Do not be foolish," I told him. "You can see I have had no detrimental effect—Starbiter is healthy and happy."

"At the moment, yes," he answered. "But you're a stranger with an alien biochemistry, and I find that troubling."

"I am not a stranger," I said, "I am Oar. An oar is an implement used to propel boats. Who are you, you poop-head cloud?"

"Nimbus," he replied. "Or if you want the complete mouthful from the Bloodline Registry books, *Capella's Coronal Nimbus of Lee-Thee Five*." His mist suddenly went blurry . . . as if every particle of him was shuddering with distaste. "In my grandfather's day," he said, "Zarett males were called *Lucky* or *Fogbank* or *Rain Cloud*; but then our owners made contact with *Homo sapiens* and picked up the Earthling fondness for giving thoroughbreds ridiculous names. My previous mate was called *Princess Fly-in-Amber Heliopause,* whatever that means. The person who chris-

tened her didn't speak a word of any Terran language, but
he gave her a gobbledygook title to impress human buyers."

The cloud man's voice had gradually risen from a whisper
to normal speaking volume. His new tone sounded a good
deal like Uclod . . . as if Mr. Zarett had taken the little orange criminal's voice as a model. I also noticed Nimbus was
no longer hesitating between phrases. When he spoke his
first words, *Sad woman,* it seemed he knew almost no English; now he spoke it overfluently. Perhaps Starbiter carried
Ingenious Language Devices such as a mist man might employ to learn a new tongue within seconds. If so, it was most
unfair—I put in weeks of diligent work to acquire my English, and disapproved of persons who bypassed the whole-
somely tedious education process by using mechanical aids.

"I do not care about Zarett names," I told him, "but if you
dislike what people call you, choose something else."

"It doesn't work that way," he answered. "We Zaretts
have an unshakable instinct to defer to our masters, even
when we'd dearly love to do otherwise. The compulsion is
too strong to overcome, no matter what the rational part of
us thinks about it. Being a good and obedient slave is hard-
wired into my genes."

"You are not good and obedient if you complain about
your master to someone you have just met. Do you think I
will now go to Uclod and say, 'Please change Nimbus's
name to Fluffy'?"

"It wouldn't matter," the mist man replied. "Uclod isn't
my owner. He's just renting me . . . for stud purposes."

I suspect he added that last part just to provoke a reaction
in me. His tactic succeeded; I stood up angrily and said,
"This is not the type of talk I enjoy. I cannot tell if you are
deliberately trying to appall me, or if you are just a foolish
creature who knows no better. Perhaps if I were compelled
to follow the sordid profession of gigolo, I too would speak
lightly of foul things. But I do not."

Turning sharply away from him, I headed for the corridor
back to the bridge. I glared at him over my shoulder when I
reached the doorway . . . and to my surprise, I found myself

saying, "I am not a virgin, you know." Then I stormed away, feeling that my face had become very hot.

No One Ever Congratulates One On Her Daring

I did not wish to return to the bridge—it was not nice seeing Lajoolie snuggled up to Uclod, as if no one else in the world mattered. I feared, however, that if I sat on my own in the corridor, Nimbus would come after me again, claiming I had provoked more metabolic imbalance. "I am not an imbalance," I muttered. "I am, in fact, the only one on this ship who knows How To Behave."

Dawdling most slowly, I walked down the corridor, hoping some diverting event would occur before I reached my destination . . . but it did not, and I was forced to enter the bridge after all.

Lajoolie had not budged from her previous position, but Uclod was now awake. The two were talking quietly, nose to nose. I stomped my feet hard as I walked in, to make sure they knew I was there. It would have been gratifying if they had jumped up guiltily at being caught . . . but they merely turned to face me, moving in exasperating unison.

Their cheeks were almost touching. That was exasperating too.

"So I see you are conscious," I said loudly to Uclod. "It is high time—I grew most bored flying this ship on my own."

Uclod's face looked grim. "What did the Shaddill want, missy?"

"I believe they wanted to capture us. But we escaped."

The little man's eyes narrowed. "How?"

"I flew into the sun."

"*Into* the sun?"

"Yes. And the stick-ship did not follow, for those Shaddill were not as daring as I. Unless," I added, "they ran away, not because of the sun but because of the human navy."

"The human navy," Uclod repeated.

"The entire human navy," I said, "and perhaps *they* were the ones who scared off the stick-ship. But the humans were not so formidable after all. Starbiter outran them most easily . . . which might be because her FTL field had absorbed invigorating energies from the interior of the sun. By the way, are there creatures who live inside stars? Giant glass butterflies who sing? Because this would be a highly pleasant universe if such creatures existed."

Uclod blinked several times. Then he turned away and pushed forward in his seat, tapping the bumps in front of his chair. Unlike machines on Melaquin, Starbiter did not possess an obvious display screen; but the Zarett must have been furnished with some means to convey information to Uclod because the little man slumped back from his console in utterish amazement. "Holy shit," he whispered, "we *did* fly into the sun."

"Yes," I said. "It was very bright."

"I can imagine."

"But it was safe and peaceful. No harm came to us. You were wrong when you thought we would burn."

"Look," he said quietly, "I wasn't concerned about the heat so much as everything else. The gravity. The magnetics. Every damned particle in the subatomic bestiary, plowing into us at fusion intensities. I can show you solid mathematical equations proving an FTL field can't survive more than a nanosecond . . ."

"Do not be foolish," I said. "Mathematical equations are not solid—they are just scribbles someone writes down. And whoever wrote your equations must have made a mistake, because we are all *just fine*."

Lajoolie leaned closer to her husband . . . if that were possible. She told him, "The FTL field integrity equations were given to us by the Shaddill."

Uclod looked at her. His eyes widened. "Holy shit. Holy *shit*!"

"The Shaddills?" I said. "The monstrous villains who tried to eat us with sticks? I would never believe their equations, ever."

"But . . . but . . ." Uclod broke into a series of spluttery noises before he could achieve full words again. "The Shaddill *invented* Zaretts. And FTL fields. We've been using their equations for centuries and not once . . . not once . . . damn." He looked at Lajoolie. "This is bigger than some piddly-shit exposé on the human navy. We've gotta get home at top speed, and . . ." He glanced at the control bumps in front of him. "Bloody hell! Do you know how *fast* we're going?"

"Very most fast," I said. "We were strengthened by entering the sun. That is how we escaped from the Earthlings and the stick-people."

"Bloody hell," Uclod said. He swept his hand over his brow, as if wiping off sweat. "Finding a secret like this—it's like dynamite, missy. Worse than dynamite: pure antimatter. If hopping into a star doesn't destroy FTL fields but actually makes them stronger . . . if the Shaddill have deliberately misled us for centuries about the limitations on our FTL envelopes . . ." He shook his head. "But how could they get away with it? Our people must have run tests—experiments to measure FTL field collapse. That's the sort of thing engineers do! And if the Shaddill *still* managed to fool everybody down through the centuries . . . hell, the Shads will go ape-shit that we've discovered the truth. They're probably after us already. What are we going to do?"

Lajoolie stood, her movement not making a sound. "Whatever you decide," she said, "I'm sure it will be wise. We'll leave you to think in peace; when you want, I'll bring you food."

She bent over him, cupping her hands gently around the globes of his ears and touching her lips to his bald scalp. It was a most intimate gesture—the kind that makes a watcher embarrassed and angry and lonesome, all at the same time. Then she turned and walked silently away.

As she passed, Lajoolie took my hand in a firm grip. She led me from the room . . . and I felt so subdued, I went without argument.

9

WHEREIN I LEARN ABOUT OUR ENEMIES

Bone Appétit

Lajoolie's hand felt cold holding mine—so cold her blood must have been the temperature of slush. It irks me that aliens never have the *correct* body heat: they are always too warm or too cool, and too hard or too soft, too dry or too damp, too hasty or too slow, too stupid or too annoying. Sometimes, they are also too strong . . . which is why I had no choice but to hasten behind the orange woman as she dragged me away from the bridge.

Partway down the corridor, Lajoolie stopped and placed her free hand on the glowing yellow wall. I did not see anything special about the spot she touched, but after a count of three, the opposite wall opened with a faint sucking sound. It revealed another corridor, taller and narrower than the one we currently occupied. When Lajoolie moved forward, there was no room to walk beside her; therefore, I trailed along behind, trying not to feel like a little girl being pulled to the place of teaching machines by her older sister.[5]

---

[5]The teaching machines in my home village were not the advanced Science kind that plant education straight into your brain. We only had *crude* teaching machines that made you recite your elevenses tables until you wanted to scream. They were very most stupid machines; alas, they were also unbreakable, even for such a one as happens to possess an excellent silver ax.

We soon came to a branch, a pair of even narrower bronchial tubes forking left and right. Lajoolie escorted me to the left where the corridor spiraled upward into a wee cubbyhole of a room. Bony ridges jutted from the room's side wall, making flat surfaces with curved-up lips at the front. Clearly, these were shelves . . . although if I were a Zarett, I would not go to the inconvenience of growing bones in my lungs, just so people had someplace to put their belongings. The shelves held bowls which appeared to be bone too—suggesting that someone had chopped off parts of Starbiter's skeleton in order to obtain containers for soup.

That was quite icky indeed. Even worse, there were cups on the shelves too: big bone cups, which reminded me of skulls. They did not have facial features, but they were almost exactly the size and shape of a half-rotted wolf's head I found in the woods when I was twelve. There were also bone utensils of recognizable types—spoons, spatulas, and so on—plus a variety of objects whose purpose I could not divine. Some were long and thin, others were boxy, and a few were so oddly shaped (all curlicues and spikes and knobs) that one suspected they had no actual use at all; they were either abstract sculptures, or objects left lying about simply to convey an alien ambiance.

Lajoolie took a bone-knife from a bone-shelf and laid out three bone-bowls on the bone-counter. I could not tell where the food synthesizer was in this small room, but I assumed obtaining dinner was simply a matter of pressing more bumps on the wall. There was an especially noticeable protrusion just beside the water spigot—a greenish-colored bulge the size of a cabbage, budding from Starbiter's tissues. I thought there might be small indentations in the bulge, buttons that you pushed in order to specify what sort of meal you wished . . . so it did not surprise me when Lajoolie reached out to take hold of the protuberance.

It *did* surprise me when she used the knife to cut the bulge right off the wall. Then she chopped the material into equal-sized portions and placed the chunks into the bowls.

"What are you doing?" I asked in horror.

"Making supper." She sniffed one of the lumps of green.

"It smells like *choilappa*; that's glazed ort-breast baked with several kinds of Divian vegetables. Of course, this is really just a mixture of simple amino acids and minerals—very basic, digestible by any DNA-based life-form we've ever encountered."

"It is not digestible by me!" I said. "It is a piece of my friend Starbiter!"

"Yes."

"You cut it right off her body!"

"Yes."

"It is Zarett meat!"

Lajoolie looked at me, then at the greenish matter in the bowls. "It's not exactly *meat*; it's a specialized skin tissue, purposely produced to be cut off and consumed by a Zarett's passengers. It grows fast enough to feed eight people three meals a day . . . which we feed right back to Starbiter if we don't eat it all. Each meal is artificially scented and flavored to taste like a different dish: it's Divian cuisine, but humans really enjoy most of our food. There are a few things we eat that make *Homo sapiens* nauseous—things that hit your taste buds the wrong way—but if you wait half an hour, the artificial flavoring dissipates and the food turns completely bland. Not very appealing, but it's still got nutritional content."

With a false smile of encouragement, she handed me one of the bowls. The green mound in it had the color of raw vegetation and the texture of a dead rabbit half-devoured by cougars. "It is a part of my friend," I said. "It is also opaque."

I set the bowl back on the counter.

"Oh dear," Lajoolie murmured. Her gaze shifted guiltily to my belly; I hoped she was imagining what my beautifully clear glass body would look like if I consumed a substance of hideous green. She would see it in my mouth as I chewed and in my throat when I swallowed. It would hang like a weedy blob as it churned in my belly. Then it would proceed quite visibly through the remaining stages of digestion and disposal. This would not be at all nice to witness—neither for Lajoolie nor for me. The food turning in my stomach would turn my stomach.

On Melaquin, we did not have such problems. Our synthesizers only created transparent foods . . . and the chemical composition of each dish was cunningly designed to remain invisible while the food was in our bodies, from one end of the alimentary canal to the other. Science People have told me the biochemistry of such a process must be most complex; but I do not see why there should be any great difficulty. Avoid opaque meals, and everything else follows.

"I don't know what to say," Lajoolie told me. "This is the only food on the ship. It really won't hurt you . . ."

"It will just make me look ugly and foolish."

"You could wear clothes," she suggested. "To cover what happens inside you." She took a step toward the door. "I didn't bring a big wardrobe with me, but there must be something we could make fit. You and I are, uhh, close to the same height."

"But we are not the same width *at all*. I am pleasantly slender; you are unnecessarily broad. Fortunately," I said, "I do not need your cast-off garments. Thanks to admirable foresight and planning, I have an excellent jacket of my own. It is a perfect fit . . . and I shall wear it when I deem necessary. But for now I have no appetite."

This was not strictly true. For one thing, I had not yet tried on the jacket; and I was not precisely certain what it meant for clothes to be a perfect fit, since I had never worn clothes before. Nevertheless, I was closer in size to human Explorers than to the muscle-bound woman before me. The jacket back on the bridge would fit better than any of Lajoolie's apparel.

As for what I said about having no appetite—I was not yet so ravenous as to consume a part of Starbiter (especially not a *green* part of Starbiter), but I could feel hunger gnawing with growing insistence. During my four years of basking in the Ancestral Tower, I had built up a modest energy reserve . . . but that reserve would drain quickly now that I was up and moving. I certainly could not sustain myself with the dim phosphorescent glow from Starbiter's wall fungus; therefore, I would need solid food soon or I would drop into a coma of starvation.

But I refused to eat immediately. Not until I retrieved my jacket and covered my digestive tract.

Lajoolie waited another moment to see if I would tuck into the food. Then she shrugged, picked up the green wad from her bowl and took a bite. "It's quite good," she said. "Really."

"I am not interested in eating," I lied. "I am more interested in understanding recent occurrences. Who are the stick-people? The ones you call Shaddill. Why did they treat us as enemies?"

The big woman chewed for an irritatingly placid period of time before she swallowed. "Until today, I would have said the Shaddill were the most benevolent race in the universe. Now . . ."

She sighed. Then, with many an annoying pause to eat, she told me what she knew.

The Divians Divided

Lajoolie's race (the Tye-Tyes) and Uclod's race (the Freeps) were both offshoots of a species called the Divians. Some one thousand years ago—I do not know if those are Earth years, Divian years, or years of the solar butterflies, because I did not care to ask—the Divians were a single species occupying a single star system. Back then, they did not have Zaretts with FTL fields; they only had primitive rocket-beasts that puttered between their birthworld and a handful of crude colonies on nearby planets and moons. The Divians were totally ignorant of the universe at large . . . until the Shaddill showed up.

No Divian saw a Shaddill in person; all communication was conducted through robotic go-betweens who looked exactly like the Divians themselves. No one even saw the Shaddills' spaceship except three people from an outpost on a remote moon. By sheer chance, this outpost suffered an accident involving a poorly designed something that was supposed to keep a second thing properly fueled, so that the second thing could prevent a third thing from catching fire, but then the third thing *did* catch fire and even though the fire was put out, the smoke suffocated a beetlelike creature that served as some sort of safeguard for the outpost's life

support systems ... and in short, disastrous events transpired, threatening death to all concerned. Since no poky Divian vessel could reach the outpost in time, the Shaddill
were prevailed upon to sail to the rescue. Their ship
swooped in, picked up the Divian personnel, and sent them
back to safety inside the first Zarett ever—but not before the
people from the outpost had seen that the Shaddill drove a
ship made of sticks.

Such a chivalrous rescue put the Shaddill in an excellent
light ... and the Divians were already inclined to regard the
Shaddill as visitors of wondrous philanthropy. The Shaddill
had introduced themselves as emissaries from the League of
Peoples, ready to induct "acceptable" Divians into the
League. In order to be acceptable, persons had to agree to
the League's only rule: never to slay another sentient being,
either by deliberate deed or willful negligence. Creatures
who obeyed this law were considered sentient themselves
and were guaranteed protection; everyone else was considered non-sentient, possibly a dangerous threat to the universe. The League did not actively seek to destroy dangerous
non-sentient beings, but they never *ever* allowed dangerous
non-sentients to move from one star system to another.

The Shaddill offered Lajoolie's ancestors a choice: to
abide by the League's law (in which case the Divians would
be granted the means to venture into the galaxy at large) or
to reject the law (in which case they would be killed if they
tried to leave home).

In the abstract, this sounds like an easy decision—few persons would openly say, "I must decline the chance to see the
galaxy; I prefer the option of slaughtering whomever I
choose." But in concrete terms, the situation was more contro-
versial ... because the Divians would be required to leave all
lethal weapons on their homeworld, thus traveling to the stars
unarmed. The Shaddill claimed that consciously equipping
yourself with the means to kill other beings was direct evidence you were *not* sentient; those who refused to lay down
their guns were not "civilized" enough to join the League.

(At this point, I asked Lajoolie what was wrong with carrying, say, a shiny silver ax, if one only intended to use it on bad

people who truly deserved what they got? But she told me the League did not view it that way . . . and the League did not engage in debate, they simply executed those who did not Play Along. That is the problem with aliens—their heads are so full of alien thought processes, they will not see reason.)

So each Divian of those long-ago days had to make a decision: either to hold on to his or her weapons and stay home, or to lay down arms and go to the stars. The Shaddill promised that those who chose disarmament would be granted pleasant tracts of land in another star system, on a planet specially prepared to mimic the Divian homeworld. The Shaddill also offered excellent enticements as "Welcome to the League" gifts: breeding seeds for Zarett spaceships, making it possible to fly from one star to another; a chemical called YouthBoost that helped people live twice their normal lifespan, without growing weak or shriveled; and new tricks of gene-splicing that allowed the Divians to engineer their offspring into specialized forms—huge muscular women, for example, or talkative little men whose skin automatically turned dark to block out radiation.

Despite these incentives, many Divians were not eager to accept the Shaddill offer. They did not trust aliens who said, "We will take you someplace nice, except you must leave behind all means to resist us." Indeed, the only ones who embraced the deal were wild optimists or people with nothing to lose—those trapped in terrible poverty or under murderous regimes, not to mention persons afflicted with fatal illnesses who threw themselves at the mercy of the Shaddill's superior medical technology. Oddly enough, Lajoolie told me, there were many many people enduring precisely such desperate conditions: living in fear of war, facing death by famine, or growing sick from poisons in the air, water, and soil.

Anyone wanting to escape simply had to call upon the Shaddill. A few soft words would do . . . and even if there were killers breaking down your door or you were locked in a hideous torture chamber, you would be teleported instantly to the safety of a Shaddill carrier ship. In some regions of the Divian homeworld, this possibility of escape only *increased* the local brutality, as ruling authorities attempted to purge Unwanted Elements by scaring them into flight. Terrifying people into leaving the solar system was virtually as good as killing them . . .

. . . except that a few years later, many of those people came back. Looking healthy and prosperous. Flying wonderful Zaretts. Showing off gene-spliced babies who were more beautiful and intelligent than anyone who stayed behind, not to mention that these children were expected to live hundreds of years without suffering the infirmities of age.

That is when a number of stay-at-homes said, "Holy shit indeed!"

For one thing, most who had stayed on the Divian homeworld were suffering difficult times. Their planet had lost a goodly percentage of its underclass—the poor who worked at unappealing jobs for a pittance a day, the sick who fueled the economy by requiring expensive medical treatments, and the persons of despised background who served as scapegoats for those in power. With these people gone, the economy tottered, and the rich had to cast around for new underlings to grease the wheels of industry with their life-blood . . . but the new underlings were just as likely to jump ship as the old ones. The Shaddill were still around; their offer was still open. At the end of a bad day, anyone could decide that her boss was a fool, her lovers unworthy, her family more trouble than it was worth, and poof! Away she went to a new life, in a place where no one was hungry and no one had guns.

When the first wave of emigrants came back to say how wonderful their life was, a second wave of departures went flooding out. Those who were bored. Those whose lives had grown harder since the first wave left. Those who would have gone the first time but feared the Shaddill would butcher them for meat. Young people who could not get jobs, old people who despised the jobs they had, curiosity seekers, petty criminals running from the law, faithless paramours abandoning unwanted commitments, unappreciated homemakers storming out of the house, scientists wishing to learn advanced Science things, farmers who could not face one more drought, women cornered by would-be rapists, teenagers whose parents could not understand True Love, get-rich-quick gamblers who were certain they could Make It Big if only they got a fresh start on a planet where the system did not work against you . . . all of them called or screamed or whispered to the Shaddill, and were swept off to a place of second chances.

The more people who left, the more chaos for those who stayed behind—and the more incentive for the hangers-on to get out too. Lajoolie said her own ancestors had lived in a large city on a tropical coast, a major port and shipment center. One summer ten years after the Shaddill arrived, a hurricane struck the city, killing or crippling many car-creatures and house-creatures. By the time the storm passed, half the populace had decided rebuilding would be too much trouble, so they disappeared into space. Within a week, eighty percent of the remainder had also flown away: the half-empty city was turning dangerous with gangs and looters, not to mention that hundreds of businesses were forced to close due to lack of customers.

Then, after all those people departed, there were not enough workers to unload the boats docked in the harbor. Far inland, other cities began to suffer because they did not receive shipments of food and imported goods. People of the inland cities also called on the Shaddill when the hardships grew too severe, making further breaks in the chain of production and supply.

For twenty years then, the Shaddill left their offer open: twenty years during which the old Divian economy collapsed. (Scientific civilizations are so spindly and weak, if you take away too many people, the whole system breaks down. Hah!) The homeworld became a dog-eat-dog ruin, abandoned by everyone except those who were too stubborn to leave or too fond of violence to accept the League's law.

"So it seems," said I, "the Shaddill were great villains who used divisive handouts to destroy your cultural infrastructure."

"No, no," Lajoolie protested, "they *helped* us. They *improved* us . . . not just by giving us Zaretts and all, but by weeding out the most vicious elements of our species. Those who left the homeworld were the peaceful, intelligent members of society—not perfect, of course, but we're much better off, now that a big strain of brutality has been removed from our breeding pool."

"But what will you do if an occasion arises when you *need* to be brutal?"

"That won't happen," Lajoolie said. "The League makes sure no one can hurt anyone else."

"No. The League kills certain people under certain conditions; that is all they do. They still permit a great deal of hurting to take place: I can attest to that. You can attest to it too—where was the League when the Shaddill shot you with their weapon ray?"

She had no answer . . . perhaps because she was descended from people who had been insufficiently suspicious of gifts that were too good to be true. Mistrust did not come naturally to persons of her ancestry; I wondered if that was pure accident, or if the Shaddill had deliberately created a situation where people would breed for gullibility.

Hmm . . .

The Shaddill Spread More Bounty

At the end of twenty years, the Shaddill left the Divian homeworld, never to return. Presumably, they went to help other races on the verge of space travel—because according to Lajoolie, Cultural Improvement was the Shaddill's chief occupation. In the same way they uplifted the Divians, the Shaddill had visited many other species throughout the galaxy . . . including *Homo sapiens*, which is how the human Technocracy got its start four hundred years ago.

My friend Festina had told me that story: how aliens visited Old Earth in the twenty-first century. And she claimed the same aliens had approached some portion of the human race one other time before, in a year she called 2000 B.C. Way back then, the aliens scooped up humans and carried them off to the planet Melaquin . . . where those humans became my ancient ancestors. The gifts the Shaddill gave my forebears were pleasant underground cities that supplied all their needs, and virtual immortality for their children—which is to say, the children were engineered to be beautiful, clever creatures of indestructible glass.

Like me.

Beware Of Aliens Bearing Gifts

Lajoolie told me that "Shaddill" was a name invented by Divians, meaning "Our Mentors." The Shaddill themselves never used any special title, preferring just to call themselves "Citizens of the League of Peoples"—telling everyone they were good and noble envoys, bringing happy enlightenment to lesser species out of pure gracious generosity.

Hah! I thought. These supposedly nice Shaddill shot us with a Sinister Unconsciousness Ray. They chased Starbiter most mercilessly. They had lied to the Divians about what a Zarett could do, and perhaps they had run from the human navy, like thieves fleeing the scene of a crime. Above all, they had placed a most terrible curse on my people . . . and our Ancestral Towers were full of the comatose results.

Of course, Tired Brains were supposed to be a lamentable accident due to unforeseen genetic complications. The more I heard about the Shaddill, however, the less I believed in their beneficence.

I said as much to Lajoolie. "These Shaddill are not so kindly as you think. They did you a great disservice."

The big woman did not answer. She pensively chewed her Zarett meat.

"Did they not unbalance your homeworld?" I asked. "Did they not deliberately drive a wedge between those who stayed loyal to their planet and those who were cut off from their roots by leaving home? Why, for example, did the Shaddill only give YouthBoost to those who agreed to leave? Should they not give it to *all* Divians, so everyone could live a longer life? Is it not wicked to let many die young, if they could be saved?"

Lajoolie finally swallowed her mouthful. "Not according

to the League of Peoples. The League doesn't require you to take extraordinary measures to save a creature who's reached the end of its span. The League's version of sentience is all about your *own* actions—you're forbidden to do something that would hasten another sentient's demise, either through direct action or carelessness . . . but you aren't obliged to lift a finger if someone's dying for reasons unrelated to you." She shrugged. "It can be a tricky call. Suppose right now I start choking on my food. Are you justified in letting me die because it's my own fault for trying to eat and talk at the same time? Or do you deserve some blame because I wouldn't be talking if you weren't here?"

"It does not matter who is to blame. If you start to choke, I shall squeeze you hard about the middle to make you cough up the blockage. Civilized persons help one another."

Lajoolie smiled. "Thank you . . . but that's not required by League law. If you don't cause my predicament, you don't have to save me. Which is why the Shaddill weren't obliged to offer YouthBoost to the people who stayed on our homeworld. It isn't the Shaddill's fault that Divians get old and die at a certain age; therefore the Shaddill didn't have to give YouthBoost to anyone."

"But they *did* give it to you. For unknown reasons of their own. Your ancestors were very foolish if no one asked, *Why are these aliens so generous?*"

"Of course they asked. The Shaddill only answered, *It's our way.*" The big woman stared broodingly at her food. "A lot of people assumed the Shaddill simply believed in helping others. Religious altruism. Cynics preferred to think it was a status thing: the Shaddill made themselves feel important by tossing handouts to others.

"Of course," Lajoolie continued, "there's always the chance the Shaddill were motivated by thought processes too alien for us to understand. We Divians and humans spend so much time together, we forget we're rarities in the universe: intelligent species who are physically, mentally, and socially similar. We have comparable biological needs, we share the same range of emotions . . . but most other races have much less in common. Aliens aren't always motivated by desires we can comprehend."

"I comprehend the Shaddill perfectly," I said. "They are villainous tempters who enjoy disrupting the lives of others: the type of people who come from the sky, fill your head with talk of Wondrous Science, and make you think you are respected . . . then they toy with you and laugh behind your back that you are a foolish savage. The presents they give are not nearly so fine as you first believe. Either the gifts turn out to be mere trinkets, or they are secretly intended to make you weak and dependent." My face had suddenly become hot, and my eyes all stinging and watery. "Even if such tempters are not outright villains, they still want you to change, to be like them. They want you ashamed of what you are, and afraid of saying the tiniest thing for fear it will prove you are ignorant."

Lajoolie stared at me a long moment, then lowered her gaze. "You're really talking about the Technocracy, aren't you? I've read the report of what happened on Melaquin. What the Explorers did to you. But those were mere humans, one of whom went murderously insane. The Shaddill are very different: more highly evolved, and really, truly benevolent. They aren't just well-meaning idiots who bungle their attempts to help; they've shown themselves to be decent, caring, nonexploitive—"

"We've got company!" The shout came from the wall, but the voice was Uclod's. Apparently, Starbiter had ways for someone to project sounds through the tissues surrounding us. "Back to the bridge," Uclod yelled, "on the double!"

Lajoolie threw her bowl onto the counter and was out the door in a split-second. She moved very fast; I could barely keep up with her as she bounded through the bronchial tubes. Without slowing, she called, "Husband, do you know who it is?"

"Shaddill," the walls answered in Uclod's voice. "Bloody bastards still want a piece of us."

I tried to say, "I told you so." But we were running so fast, the words came out as mere gasps.

10

WHEREIN I EXPERIENCE GREAT FRUSTRATION

Pursuit

Back on the bridge, Uclod was strapped into his seat, with an icky pink intestine plastered over his face. It was not an appealing look—perhaps even *I* do not look so attractive wearing a major piece of bowel on my head—but I was beginning to get used to the constant presence of Starbiter's internal organs. I did not even flinch as I threw myself into the jellyfish seat . . . but this time I lifted my arms high so they would not be trapped when the safety straps wrapped around me.

My strategy worked most excellently: the tendrils snaked up from the chair almost as soon as I touched down, weaving tight around my body but leaving my arms free. Then I had to lower my hands quickly as the intestine dropped from the ceiling—kissing the top of my head, then creeping down over my face with an itchy tickle. This time Starbiter did not have to test my vision or hearing: as soon as the hood was in place, I could see the star-speckled blackness of the void.

"Go to long-range scan," Uclod's disembodied voice said. I do not know if the instruction was aimed at Lajoolie or Starbiter; either way, the starry view jumped and shimmered for a moment. When it stabilized again, I realized I was viewing the world in the monochrome I had experienced before—seeing through the special devices for perceiving great distances.

Even with this new perspective, I had difficulty picking out the Shaddill vessel; there was so much sky to survey, all around us, above and below. No doubt the stick-ship was pursuing from our rear, but with nothing to see but unmoving stars, I had no sense of which direction we were heading. At last I discerned a bristly dust mote just visible against the bleak constellations—definitely the stick-ship, though Uclod must have had very good eyes to spot it at such a distance.

"It's gaining on us," he said. "Not quickly, but it's definitely gaining."

"Then we must go faster," I told him. "Encourage Starbiter to put on more speed."

"Missy," he answered, "my sweet little girl is already ripping along ten times faster than any Zarett before her. It doesn't seem to hurt her, but I'll be damned if I risk her life trying to speed up."

"She is a good and willing Zarett. She will try to go faster if you ask."

"I'm not going to ask! There's no reason to drive her till she drops. Even if the Shaddill catch us, they won't kill us, will they? They're afraid of the League, just like anyone else."

"But they can lock us in prison forever! The League does not care about kidnapping or enslavement; they only object to murder."

"I know," Uclod said. "That's why we're running, toots."

We were not running fast enough: little by little, the image of the stick ship grew. That was all I saw—the background stars did not shift, and I had no sense of motion in my body. It felt as if we were standing still, while the Shaddill approached us as slow as squinch-bugs.

This is not good at all, I thought. It appeared as if the Pollisand's teeny-tiny-eensy-weensy chance of disaster befalling me was not so minuscule as he implied. How long ago had I talked with him? Less than an hour. And already catastrophe clutched at my throat.

No wonder the Pollisand arrived when he did; and no

wonder he so blithely promised to cure my Tired Brain. He must have known, even as we spoke, that the Shaddill were chasing us . . . and if he knew that, he must have guessed the Shaddill would commit horrid deeds on my person once they caught us. That is the whole reason Mr. Asshole Pollisand had tricked me into saying, "Oh no, the League should not hold *you* to blame if awful things transpire; I will assume responsibility myself."

It seems I had been taken for a Sucker. Sometimes, even I can be a most grievous poop-head.

A Brilliant Idea

I desperately wanted to *do* something—to run on my own two feet, or throw stones at the incoming ship; but that was pure foolishness. We had no way to fight or intimidate the stick-people.

Unless . . .

"Uclod!" I called. "As official communications officer, I should like to broadcast a message."

"What kind of message?" he asked.

"A loud one. Can you arrange for it to be heard at long distances?"

"Sure—Starbiter can broadcast in deep ether. God knows she's brimming with enough power, we can probably cover fifteen cubic parsecs in a single burst."

"Good. I want everyone to hear me."

"We'll hit all the public bands. Give me a second."

I could hear soft noises nearby—Uclod working the Zarett's controls. Then he murmured, "Okay, toots: you're on the air. Can't wait to hear you persuade the Shaddill to back off."

But I had no intention of speaking to the evil stick-people. "Attention Technocracy navy!" I said. "Especially the foolish Captain Prope. Here we are. Come and get us!"

Silence. Seconds slipped by with no answer. Then Uclod let out his breath in a long sigh. "You think the Shaddill will run away if the human navy shows up?"

"Yes," I answered, attempting humility despite the brilliance of my idea.

"Toots," said Uclod, "you got two problems with that. First, the navy ships are way the hell back in the Melaquin system; we're traveling light-years too fast for them to catch up with us. Until a few minutes ago, I didn't think *any* ship could make the speed we're going . . . but it seems a suncharged Zarett can, and a Shaddill ship is even faster. The navy are goddamned snails in comparison. By the time they get here, we'll be long gone—probably swallowed by the Shaddill ship. And that's if the navy even heard us. The other problem with your tactic is that half a second into your broadcast, the Shaddill jammed our signal. The most anyone heard was a hiccup."

"I did not hiccup!"

"Whatever you did, no one heard past the first two syllables. Granted, the navy was probably listening on all bands, hoping we'd break radio silence; good chance they caught the blip. They may even have got a location fix. But they're just too far away, missy—we've been zipping along for hours at a speed they can't possibly match. They're out of the picture, and we're on our own."

Of course, the navy *could* speed up their ships . . . if they ventured into the sun and energized their FTL fields. But the insolent Captain Prope would never be brave enough to attempt such a stratagem—not when she believed going into the sun meant death.

Perhaps one of the other captains would try, but even that seemed unlikely. These fools had possessed starships for centuries, yet none had experimented with venturing into a star. No sense of curiosity . . . nor any other sense I could discern. Had no rich wastrel ever sent a ship into the sun just to see it burn? Had no crazed person ever tried to commit suicide by solar immolation? Humans had been driving starships for four hundred years; Divians had ridden Zaretts for a thousand. In all that time, had no one ever swooped close to a star? How could that possibly be?

But I had no answers; I only had the image of the stickship coming slowly toward us, like a tumbleweed blowing in from the horizon. It was still far off, no bigger than a bumblebee against the blackness; yet second by second, it grew perceptibly.

"Maybe I *should* ask Starbiter for more speed," Uclod muttered nervously. "But what would be the point? The Shaddill are sure to have the edge on us, no matter how fast we go. If they gave us Zaretts for free, you can be damned sure they kept something better for themselves. Like handing your frumpy old *zigrim* to your kid brother, after you get a snappy new *lentz*."

I did not know what those things were; but I had lived beneath the thumb of an older sister, and I understood the principle quite well. The Shaddill would not give away Zaretts unless they had something at least slightly superior. "Perhaps," I said, "if we flew into another sun, we could charge Starbiter to even greater speeds."

"We're in open space now, toots—nowhere near a sun." The little man grunted. "Nothing to do but keep going, and hope for a lucky break. Maybe the Shaddill will have a malfunction . . . or shut off their engines for a holy day of rest."

"Is that likely?" I asked.

"No. But when my back is to the wall, I always like to pretend there's a way to dodge the bullet. Maybe the Shaddill captain will keel over from a heart attack and his crew will run away, thinking we have some fancy cardiac weapon."

"Maybe," Lajoolie murmured, "the captain will let us go because he falls in love with Oar."

"I do not think that is funny," I said.

Uclod tsked his tongue. "Don't be such a party-pooper, missy—when you're well and truly screwed, either you just sit pissing yourself or you invent some reason to hope. Maybe we'll get sucked into a wormhole and pop out halfway across the universe."

"Maybe," said Lajoolie, "my talented husband will discover he has telekinetic powers that can hold the Shaddill at bay."

"Maybe our enemies will get eaten by giant glass butterflies," I said sharply. "This game is a waste of time! We should take evasive action."

"We will," Uclod said, "as soon as it'll do us any good. When the Shaddill get close enough to grab us, we'll stay out of their clutches as long as possible." He laughed without humor. "It's not like I want to get caught, missy . . . but we're bare-ass in space with nowhere to hide for a few trillion klicks in any direction. We don't have weapons, we don't have friends, and we don't have a lot of options. Run or surrender: pick one."

"Hmmph," I said. "I made a very bad choice when I decided to accompany you."

"Do you think so?" Lajoolie asked. "On Melaquin, the Shaddill ship appeared right above your city. They recognized your name; they knew you were supposed to be dead. When they heard you were alive, they said someone had interfered with their plan. It sounds like they wanted to use you for something. Or at least use your corpse. If they'd landed and found you still breathing, what do you think they would do?"

I had not considered the situation in such a light . . . but Lajoolie was correct. It seemed quite plausible the Shaddill had been heading for Oarville to carry out some plan involving my dead body. Perhaps that explained why the Pollisand took me from the Tower of Ancestors and gave me medical attention after my fall: as the Shaddill's enemy, he could somehow foil their plans by keeping me alive.

I should have asked about that. I should have asked him many questions. But he rudely terminated our conversation as soon as I agreed to his proposal, so I did not have time to inquire about topics of personal relevance. If the Pollisand returned now, I would ask how my life and/or death concerned the Shaddill . . . and why he was not helping us in our current predicament. The Pollisand had bragged of his superiority to other species, yet he was conspicuously absent now that the Shaddill were at close range.

As for the Shaddill themselves—if they had arrived on Melaquin and discovered I was not yet a corpse, would they have endeavored to make me one? I did not know . . . but however they reacted, I probably would not have enjoyed it. Perhaps it *was* better I had boarded Starbiter, rather than getting caught on the ground. At least I was still alive and free.

And perhaps the Shaddill captain would fall in love with me. It was high time *somebody* did.

Cat And Mouse . . . And Another Cat

We flew on. The stick-ship edged ever closer.

It was very most frustrating not to do anything. From the odd perspective of the far-seeing devices, we seemed to be sitting still, just waiting for our doom. But could we shoot at the enemy? No. Could we call for help? No. Could we even scream at our pursuers, cursing them with vile obscenities? Yes we could, but the Shaddill would not hear; they were jamming our broadcasts, so they would not receive any taunts I might transmit.

All I could do was glare at the alien ship, hoping if I hated them strongly enough, they would explode. This never works, but one must try it anyway—one feels it *ought* to work if your loathing is sufficiently sincere.

After several minutes of the enemy closing upon us, I decided the trick might lie in *not* looking at them. If I turned my eyes away and refused the tiniest glance in their direction, maybe the Shaddill would simply cease to exist. This was no more plausible than my previous plan, but I was weary of staring at sticks; so I aimed my gaze directly opposite, toward blank blackness and stars . . . only to find that the blackness was not completely blank.

Far off in the distance, I could see a small object—not like a star but a minuscule bone, a tiny knuckle from a baby mouse's toe. I held my breath, not daring to speak for fear it would vanish . . . but it remained in sight as my heart pounded out a beat of ten. The distant object might even have grown by a hair. Another ten count, and I knew it *was* growing. I also knew what it was: a ship from the human navy, one of those long white batons I had last seen under the blaze of Melaquin's sun.

Apparently, the four ships which had accosted us earlier were not the only ones sent to Melaquin. One more ship must have been dispatched hours behind its companions, on its way from New Earth to my planet. Since Starbiter was headed for New Earth now, we must be traveling in the same space lane . . . or at least close enough that the navy ship had heard our attempt at sending a message. They could have detected our "hiccup" and shifted to a course that would let them check the source of the broadcast.

"We are saved," I announced.

"What do you mean?" Uclod asked.

"There is a navy baton-ship coming straight for us. The Shaddill will flee again, for they are terrible cowards . . . and since we are faster than human vessels, we can outrun the baton anytime we choose."

"You're a hell of an optimist." But Uclod did not sound as gloomy as his words suggested—he too must have welcomed any prospect of eluding the stick-ship. Given a choice between our Shaddill pursuers and the Technocracy navy, who would not prefer the humans? Better the villain you know than the one you do not . . . and also I was smarter than humans, which allowed us more chance of escape.

"Oar's right," said Lajoolie, "there *is* an Outward Fleet ship. Calculating coordinates . . ."

"I don't need numbers," Uclod interrupted. "Just tell me who gets to us first."

"Almost a dead heat," Lajoolie answered. "The human ship is coming straight at us, and we're aiming straight at them. The gap will close fast. But the Shaddill are right on our tails."

Without thinking, I checked on the stick-ship. It was very most close indeed; in the minutes since I made up my mind not to look at them, they had crept steadily nearer. Now they loomed directly behind us—a great wall of bramble blocking our entire rear view.

"Beware," I said to my companions. "This is the distance at which you were flashed unconscious."

"Not true, toots," Uclod replied. "You're seeing through long-range scanners now—the Shaddill are still a million klicks away, and I'm hoping their weapon can't shoot that far. Even so, I've decoupled the wife and me from Starbiter's neural feedback. We can still see, but we aren't feeling anything. Let's hope that keeps us awake."

I turned to the front once more and saw the navy ship had grown considerably since my last peek at them. If they possessed long-range scanners like Starbiter, they must see both us and the stick-ship . . . which meant the stick-ship could also see them. Any moment now, the Shaddill would flee like the cowards they were.

But they did not. They kept coming, lumbering up slowly; and one of the sticks began to reach for us, the same long mouth that had tried to swallow us before.

"They are attempting to snatch us!" I cried.

"They can't," Uclod said, "they're still too far away. Long-range scanners, remember? Things appear closer than they really are. But," he continued, "the Shaddill are getting ready for something. Maybe they think they can swoop in and gobble us before the navy ship can react."

"Maybe they intend to seize the navy ship too," Lajoolie said.

"Ooo, that's an unpleasant thought," Uclod said. "It'd mean they're so desperate to keep us quiet, they don't mind antagonizing the entire Technocracy."

"The Technocracy would never find out," Lajoolie told him. "The Shaddill are still jamming all signals in the region, so the navy can't report what's happening. If we both get grabbed, we'll disappear without a peep."

"Ouch," Uclod said. "And by the time the fleet sends another ship to investigate what happened to this one, the Shaddill will be long gone—dragging us with them."

"Is there nothing we can do?" I asked in outrage.

"If you've got ideas, I'd love to hear them."

"Do we not have some means of attack? A weighty object we could hurl at the stick-ship?"

"Only ourselves," Uclod replied dryly. "If you're aching to be a martyr, we could ram the Shaddill at top speed. We might even take out something critical: their computers maybe, or their engines. That'd let the navy ship get away."

I did not care for such a plan. Perhaps it could be reversed: the human vessel might volunteer to smash the Shaddill, thereby allowing Starbiter to escape. But with our transmissions jammed, there was no way to suggest this scheme to the navy ship . . . and I did not believe they would spontaneously choose to destroy themselves for our benefit.

"Husband," Lajoolie said in a soft voice, "there *is* some potential in what you suggest."

Uclod snorted. "I didn't suggest anything. Do you think I want to splash ourselves all over space on the off-chance—"

She interrupted, "Starbiter has emergency ejection procedures. And the human ship is right here to pick us up afterward."

"Aww, no, sweetheart . . ." The little man's voice filled with horror. "We can't."

"We cannot what?" I asked.

"We can't!" Uclod repeated.

Lajoolie said nothing.

I opened my mouth to demand an explanation; but before I could speak, Starbiter shuddered and everything went black.

A Noble Sacrifice

At first, I thought we were under attack — perhaps the stick-ship had assaulted us with a sinister Blinding Weapon, robbing us of our sight. I had seen no beam or missile shoot in our direction, but I had been listening to my companions rather than paying attention to the Shaddill. It would be just like those villains to commit an atrocity while I was distracted.

But moments later, the intestinal hood jerked off my face and I could see again. The ship's bridge showed no sign of damage . . . though I noticed the mouth of the exit corridor had sealed itself. Beside me, the hoods came snapping off Uclod and Lajoolie too: a fierce yanking motion as if Starbiter were pulling the guts away with all her strength.

Uclod cried to his wife, "Did you do that? Did you disengage the controls?"

"It wasn't Madame Lajoolie," said a voice beside me. "Starbiter is taking independent action."

I was still strapped tightly in my chair, but I could turn my head far enough to see who was speaking: Nimbus, the infuriating cloud man. His ghostly mist was clotted thick and murky around the chair to my right.

"What do you mean," Uclod asked, "independent action?"

"Starbiter was linked with your mind," Nimbus said. "She saw the idea that flashed through your head . . . and she knew you'd never go through with it on your own. She informed me she was taking the initiative herself."

"Aww, no," Uclod groaned. "Aww, baby, no."

The bridge shuddered again. From beyond the closest wall came a fierce ripping noise, wet and gooey. Uclod covered his face with his hands.

"What is happening?" I asked.

"When a Zarett is in mortal danger," Nimbus said, "she can eject her passengers to save their lives."

Another ripping sound tore across the room, this time from the opposite wall.

"But the passengers are housed in the Zarett's lungs," Nimbus said. "For us to escape, Starbiter has to expel a sizable wad of pulmonary tissue. She can't survive such an injury."

"You mean she will . . ." I did not finish my sentence. Starbiter would die? My fine bouncy Starbiter? But I did not *want* her to die.

"She thinks she can save us," Uclod said, tears trickling down his cheeks. "Rip herself apart. Send us shooting to safety, then ram the main mass of her body into the Shaddill like a cannonball." He caught his breath. "Oh, my crazy little girl . . ."

The entire bridge chamber jerked twice to the right, as if there was some stubborn attachment on the left that refused to pull free. One more lurch, and I heard something snap. Then we were moving, pushed off sideways by muscles that must exist for this purpose alone—to let my friend Starbiter commit suicide.

O Starbiter! You foolish one!

Rips And Tears

Our journey outward was not smooth, but a series of jerky jumps: ramming against a blockage of tissue, bouncing back, then bashing through the barrier. Things squished and popped all around us. I did not wish to imagine what internal organs were being crushed by our passage, what long strands of meat were left bloodily behind . . . but never once did Starbiter falter. Though she was ripping a portion of lung from her body, she did it with all her strength.

In addition to the terrible rending and gurgling, the light had begun to fade. The great fuzzy beds of fungus on the wall were dimming their phosphorescence like a grass fire burning itself out. Uclod had said the fungus derived sustenance from Starbiter's own tissues; now, as my friend disemboweled herself, perhaps the fungus's nutrition supply had been cut off. Either the icky fuzz was dying of starvation, or it had some instinct to go dark as a way to conserve energy when its food supply was interrupted.

Meanwhile, the banging and bumping of our trip was loosening the fungus's grip on the wall. Off to my right, a sheet of the stuff peeled away with a whispering sigh, its yellow glow snuffed in an instant as it toppled heavily to the floor. The bare wall behind was nothing but a clear membrane, transparent except for three big splotches of pinkish fluid: Starbiter's blood. As we jerked forward again, I could see fierce shivers beyond the membrane, unknown organs shuddering with pain as we passed.

Another patch of fungus slumped off, this one from the ceiling over Lajoolie's head. The big woman batted it away with one arm; it hit the floor beside her with a thud. More thuds sounded all over the room, as other clumps of fungus

fell . . . until the floor was heaped with crumples of butter-
cup yellow, and the walls and ceilings were nothing but bare
membrane. Any patch of wall I looked at, I could see
straight through into Starbiter's guts. Gouts of fluid slapped
against the outer tissues; strands of connecting fiber snapped
as we barreled forward, bashing our way through. Closing
my eyes I could shut out the sight, but I still heard the
splashing and splitting of gristle . . .

. . . then it all went silent. A deep deep quiet. And I felt
myself shift under the straps that bound me to my chair, as if
my own weight no longer held me down.

"Artificial gravity's gone," Uclod said in a whisper. "We
just passed the edge of the field."

I opened my eyes. Through the clear membrane, I saw we
were not quite separate from Starbiter: we poised half-in,
half-out of a great rupture in her side, as if we were an egg
she was trying to lay. In one direction was the blackness of
space, with stars smearily visible through vacuum-dried
smudges of Zarett blood. In the other direction was noble
Starbiter herself, her damaged body straining for one last
push to shove us free. I could see muscles bunch and contract . . . then with a great heave, we were hurled tumbling
away.

My friend Starbiter vanished in a heartbeat—an FTL cannonball shooting through the night. Seeing with my naked
eyes rather than long-range scanners, I could barely make
out the stick-ship . . . but there was no way to miss the flash
of blazing light that reached us thirty seconds later. For a
moment, I feared the Shaddill had fired their unconsciousness ray again; then I realized I had just seen Starbiter's
death as she bravely struck our enemies.

Whatever she had hit, it made a fine explosion.

Grief And New Burdens

The stick-ship was not obliterated, but it did not come any
closer—it simply remained hanging in space, an image no

bigger than my thumbnail.[6] From this range, there was no way to guess the extent of the damage . . . but I had faith Starbiter would have aimed for the most vulnerable spot she could find.

She was an excellent Zarett.

Beside me, Uclod snuffled into his hands. Lajoolie did not weep; but she rested her fingers on her husband's shoulder and stared at him with sympathy. At last, the little man took a shuddering breath. "She died alone."

"She did it for us," Lajoolie told him. "She did it gladly."

"But she died alone!" He pounded one hand on his chair, then turned around sharply to glare at Nimbus. "She was your mate, for God's sake. Why didn't you go with her?"

A ripple passed through the cloud man's body. "I offered to," Nimbus replied, "but she wouldn't permit it. She said I had a higher responsibility."

All this time, the cloud man had been clotted around the chair beside me. Now he oozed away from it, revealing what he had shielded with his body during our bouncing passage through Starbiter's guts.

Nestled on the seat was a tiny ball half the size of my fist. Its exterior had the same stringy gray texture as Starbiter herself . . . but very delicate, the strings as thin as hairs and the gray more fragile than frost.

"She's very young to be separated from her mother," Nimbus said. "But Starbiter insisted; and I swear I will take good care of our daughter."

The fog of his body billowed back around the chair, swaddling the baby Zarett like a protective blanket.

---

[6]For examining distant objects, it is very convenient to be able to see through your thumb, nail and all. The curve of my nail gives a slight magnification; if I line up my thumbs at the right distance in front of my eye, I can get a telescope effect.

11

WHEREIN I MAKE FIRST CONTACT WITH THE HUMAN RACE

Snared

One second, there was only blackness in front of us; then there was the slim white baton of a Technocracy vessel, stretched across the stars. Its FTL field wagged out behind it in a long milky tail, like a well-fed eel drifting lazily in a starry river's currents.

"We should speak greetings to the humans," I said. "We should assure them we are sentient citizens."

"Can't," Uclod answered, wiping his nose with his bare wrist.

"Without Starbiter," Lajoolie told me, "we have no communication system. We can't transmit or receive."

Uclod gave a snort that threatened to degenerate once again into weeping . . . so I said nothing more.

Slowly, the navy ship came about—the knobby ball on its nose swung away from us, until all we could see was the round cross-section of the ship's hind end. The FTL field swished its tail in our faces like an ill-mannered cat. Then a bright red beam shot toward us, shining pinkish light through the clear membranes that served as our "windows."

"That's it then," Uclod said in a hoarse voice. "They've grabbed us."

"Better them than the Shaddill," I told him—hoping my words were true.

"Yeah, well . . . I won't be the first Unorr sent to a prison planet."

"We can survive it," Lajoolie said. "And thanks to Admiral York, your family knows all the places the High Council hides political prisoners. Your cousins will rescue us eventually."

Uclod's lips tilted up in the ghost of a smile. "There is that." Then he turned his gaze back to the ship outside.

Coming Aboard

The red beam worked like a rope, reeling us toward the navy ship. I wondered if we would feel anything as we passed through the edge of the milky FTL field . . . but there was only the softest jerk forward, and a tiny bit of dizziness wherein my toes felt momentarily tingly.

Ahead of us, a great round door opened in the rear of the ship—almost big enough to have swallowed Starbiter whole, so our single section of lung slipped inside easily. The instant we crossed the threshold, gravity returned; we slammed down hard onto a metal floor, bounced once, and juddered forward until we jolted to a stop against the far wall. *Hmmph*, I thought, *these navy humans are clumsy. Either that, or they are intentionally treating us coarsely because they are great arrogant bullies.*

Uclod let out his breath. "Okay . . . okay . . . okay . . ." He was talking to himself more than the rest of us. "Okay, we're here." He glanced at me. "And we're going to mind our P's and Q's, right, missy?"

"I am always most courteous. Except to fools and crazed people."

"Damn it, toots, you aren't filling me with confidence."

He reached behind himself and did something to the back of his chair. The straps holding him went slack, but did not withdraw into the chair as they had done before; I suppose the retraction mechanisms would not work now that we had been disconnected from Starbiter. With straps sagging around him, Uclod leaned toward my seat and loosened my bonds too. He said, "You're on your own, sweet-knees," then turned to untie Lajoolie.

While I worked to free myself, the navy ship closed its hatch behind us, sealing us in completely. My view through the membrane walls was smudged with pinkish Zarett blood; but I could see we had been deposited in a large chamber with multicolored trees painted on the walls. The walls themselves appeared to be white plastic with a glossy sheen . . . all except a section high up on the back, which was rose-tinted glass. I assumed there were important navy people on the other side of that window, staring down and discussing our fates. From my current angle, however, I could see nothing up there but a bank of metal machines.

Lights on the navy ship's ceiling suddenly grew brighter, and the membrane walls around us made ominous crinkling sounds. "Our hosts are pressurizing the transport bay," Uclod said. "Any second now, the place'll be swarming with Security mooks."

Apparently, a mook was a humorless person wearing olive body armor and brandishing a truncheon or stun-pistol with great officiousness. A troop of such persons clattered into the chamber with bustling self-importance, racing to take up positions around our little chunk of Starbiter and training their weapons upon us in a most aggressive manner.

Their leader (of a gender I could not identify, thanks to the armor and a voice more howl than human) shouted something that did not sound like words. One of the others jumped forward, pistol at the ready; the mook fired directly at our outer wall, and a splooge of noxious green splatted from the gun barrel. The substance must have been some Chemical—the instant it struck our chamber's membrane, the tissue began hissing and spitting, bubbling up clouds of vile smoke. In less than ten seconds, a ragged hole had burned itself open, letting air from the human ship gust into our little chamber. The air smelled most foul indeed, tainted with a piercing coppery odor that must have been vaporized Zarett flesh.

"Harout!" cried the mookish leader. "How, how, how!"

"What language is that person speaking?" I whispered to Uclod.

"Soldierese," he replied. "Start with English, then skip any consonants that sound too effeminate."

"Hout!" shouted the mook. "How!"

"Yeah, yeah," Uclod said. "We're coming."

He took a step toward the gash in the wall. I put my hand on his shoulder to stop him. "Wait—we must do this correctly."

I glanced around the room and saw what I wanted, lying against one wall: the black Explorer jacket I had brought from Melaquin. Snatching it up, I pushed my arms into it, discovering the fit was very fine indeed. The coat was not so heavy, and not at all tight; it also hung down to the middle of my thighs, quite long enough to cover my digestive bits if and when I finally forced myself to eat opaque foods. I took another moment to straighten the garment and fasten the strip down the front, just as I had seen Explorers do. Then I stepped out through the hole and historically made First Contact.

"Greetings," I said in a loud clear voice. "I am a sentient citizen of the League of Peoples. I beg your Hospitality."

For a long moment, nobody spoke. I could see the mooks' faces through their clear visors; several appeared disconcerted to be confronted by someone dressed as one of their own Explorers. "I come in peace," I said. "My name is Oar. An oar is an implement used to propel boats."

Someone gasped at the far end of the room. I turned and saw an unarmored person standing in the doorway.

"Oar? *Oar?*"

Festina Ramos hurled herself across the floor and wrapped her arms around me.

A Fervent Reunion

I myself am not given to spontaneous displays of emotion (at least not the happy hugging emotions), but I embraced her gladly with all my strength. When you think you have been captured by dire navy villains, then are unexpectedly reunited with your very best friend . . . well, of course, you are filled with boundless joy. You want to enfold her and squeeze her and say foolish things, thinking all the while what a mistake it was to don a jacket that is now just a stuffy barrier between the two of you.

But it is odd how quickly boundless joy acquires bounds again: suddenly you remember you are being watched by little orange criminals and large-muscled women, by hard-eyed mooks and a cloud shaped like a man. In a single heartbeat, you become most clumsy and feigned—you find yourself wondering how you look in the spectators' eyes, and you worry it is not quite *proper* to be all happy and hugging and open, for fear they will think you are an ignorant simple-head. Your body stance feels all wrong: your friend is so short and you are so tall that perhaps you look un-gainly bending over her, like a great oafish giant stooping over a delicate flower. You tell yourself, *No, I will not push away my friend just because I have grown self-conscious* . . . but you *are* self-conscious, and whether you choose to back off mumbling or to continue clinging with stubborn determination, it has now become a show for other people.

Which makes you feel an unworthy friend for letting such thoughts enter your mind. You become most angry with yourself; and the next thing you know, you have stepped back abruptly, and you fear you might even be scowling.

Why does one behave like that? It is a great infuriating mystery. But perhaps I should blame the Shaddill who cre-ated my race. They gave us defective brains, not only prone to becoming Tired, but also subject to floods of embarrass-ment at times we should not be embarrassed at all. I am sure persons of natural origin do not turn shy and standoffish dur-ing hugs with old friends.

But I did. Perhaps I had even upset poor Festina by pulling abruptly out of her arms . . . so I forced myself to squeeze close again, then lowered my lips to the top of her head and kissed her hair. "I told you," I said in a voice that sounded overloud, "I am not such a one as can die. You were very most foolish to believe I could be killed by a silly little fall."

Festina made a noise that might have been either laughter or weeping—I could not tell because she had buried her face in my coat. A moment later she stepped back, wiped her sleeve across her eyes, and gave a beaming smile. "You're right. I should have known better."

It was pleasant to see her smile so happily, though Festina was exceedingly ugly, even for an opaque person. She had a large violet blemish on her right cheek: what she called a port-wine birthmark. When last I saw her, she had concealed the blemish under a patch of artificial skin . . . but now the great blotch was open to the world again, exposed for all to see. Perhaps she had removed the patch in mourning for me—which made me feel proud and *throbby* inside, though it also brought tears to my eyes.

She was such a good friend.

See No Evil

"So, Oar," Festina said with a laugh, "you're alive and causing trouble again. Do you mind explaining what you're doing in the middle of nowhere? And why your Zarett self-destructed a few minutes ago?"

"We were fleeing the evil stick-people," I said, hurriedly wiping my tears. "Starbiter died with great heroism, striking the enemy vessel and rendering it impotent."

"Enemy vessel? We haven't seen any other ships." Festina raised her eyes to the window at the rear of the room. "Lieutenant, did we register anything like that?"

A disembodied voice answered, "Negative, Admiral."[7]

Behind me, Uclod snorted. "It's time to repair your scan-

---

[7]Since I had seen her last, Festina had apparently risen from lowly Explorer to lofty Admiral—but she assured me this did not mean she was evil like Alexander York, because her admiralship was more a legal fiction than an actual Rank Of Power.

ner, folks. The damned ship was hard to miss. Just before you showed, it was close enough to see with the naked eye."

"There's the problem," Festina said. "Our navy ships can't see *anything* with the naked eye—we're limited to cameras and sensor arrays. I once asked a navy construction contractor if it would really be impossible to build a nice simple porthole into every ship. She nearly had a stroke, laughing at the dimwit Explorer who knew nothing about preserving hull integrity."

"So you didn't see the Shaddill ship?" Uclod asked.

"We saw your Zarett whizzing along at the most godawful speed ever clocked. The bridge crew couldn't believe their readings; they decided your beast must be suffering some cataclysmic flame-out, burning energy way beyond safety limits. They predicted she'd explode any second . . . and sure enough, she expelled your escape pod, then zipped away and blew herself to space dust."

"You didn't see her hit anything?"

"She exploded in empty space," Festina said. "I was watching the vidscreen myself."

Uclod rolled his eyes. "We are so fucked." He looked to Lajoolie as if waiting for her to agree, but she barely responded. The big Tye-Tye woman was attempting to hide behind foggy Nimbus, as timidly fearful as when she first met *me*.

Apparently, Lajoolie was poor at dealing with strangers.

"What's wrong?" Festina asked.

I did not know if she was asking why Lajoolie was frightened or why Uclod looked dubious about Starbiter exploding on her own. Since Lajoolie would not enjoy a discussion of her cowardice, I decided to take charge of the conversation. "Your Science devices are blind," I told Festina. "The evil stick-people can obviously deceive your machines . . . and if Starbiter did not completely incapacitate the villains, they may be creeping up on us even now."

My friend called to the back window, "Still nothing on the sensors?"

The unseen lieutenant answered, "Negative, Admiral."

"What about communications?" Uclod said. "The Shaddill were jamming all signals in the neighborhood. Did you detect that?"

Festina's eyes narrowed. "We *are* having problems—we lost contact with the Admiralty navigation grid a few minutes ago. The techies are looking into it." She glanced at the window. "Do we have communications back, Lieutenant?"

The voice from above answered, "Not yet, Admiral. Still running diagnostics."

"Shit." Festina peered sidelong at Uclod and Lajoolie. "You're saying there's a ship our scanners can't pick up, and your Zarett smashed into it at some outrageous speed. We don't know how much damage the impact did . . . but since our communications are still being jammed, the enemy wasn't completely annihilated. Just fucking wonderful." She turned back to the window. "Lieutenant—my compliments to the captain, and could we get the hell out of here at maximum speed?"

"What heading, Admiral?"

Festina glanced at me. "No point in going to Melaquin now," she said, "and it's a long way back to New Earth." She turned to the window. "Aim for the closest inhabited planet—doesn't have to be human. If we end up facing an invisible ship, let's surround ourselves with witnesses."

A Christening

We left the receiving bay with the horde of mooks clattering behind us. Festina apologized, but said it was now official fleet policy for outsiders to be watched at all times.

"And I'm afraid," she added, "the ship has dispatched nanotech defense clouds to keep an eye on your Zarett." She turned toward Nimbus. "If any of your component cells go wandering, they'll be imprisoned immediately." She gave an apologetic shrug. "The High Council has recently developed a phobia about unsanctioned microbes aboard navy vessels."

"I don't intend to spread myself thin," Nimbus assured her. "I have to concentrate on my responsibilities."

"He has a child," I whispered to Festina. "A baby girl."

My friend's eyes went wide. "An egg? A living egg?"

Nimbus rippled the mists of his belly, revealing the little ball nestled inside. "Not an egg," he said. "A very young child." His misty hands reached in to caress the baby. "As soon as possible, we should discuss her care. Nutrition, immunization treatments, optimal environmental conditions— it would be best if we could find an adoptive mother, but I can bring up a child on my own if necessary . . ."

Festina was not listening. She knelt in front of the baby, her eyes shining. The front two mooks were also gazing at the infant with dewy sentimentality, though they endeavored not to show it.

"She's beautiful," Festina said in a hushed voice.

"She is stringy and gooey," I clarified. "No doubt she is an excellent Zarett, but she is most unattractive, Festina. Is there something wrong with your eyes, or have you been crazed by an uprush of hormones?"

Festina chuckled and got to her feet. "Don't be jealous, Oar; I'm not going dizzy with maternal urges. But I like eggs—I *adore* eggs—and a little creature who resembles an egg, even if she's already hatched . . ." Festina turned her eyes toward Nimbus's foggy head. "What's the baby's name?"

Nimbus quivered. His stomach closed, wrapping around and around the infant until he completely lost his humanoid form: becoming a thing like an egg himself, with the child swaddled in the middle. "Her name?" he said. "Don't ask me, I'm just the father. I have nothing to do with my *own* name, let alone my daughter's."

"She should be named Oar," I said. "Then she would be admired and respected by all the world."

"No," Uclod said, "I'm calling her Starbiter. That's final."

He glared around, daring us to challenge him. Lajoolie laid her hand approvingly on his arm. Nimbus kept silent and I decided to hold my tongue too—it would be pleasant to think of a small young person growing up to carry on my name . . . but there are always things one cannot have, are there not? And having a new Starbiter was almost as good as having a new Oar.

Almost.

The Tale Of A Tainted Tree

We proceeded down a hallway, passing many closed doors with trees painted on them. Festina explained these trees were hemlocks, because the name of the ship was *Royal Hemlock*.

Not long ago, this had been the flagship of Admiral Alexander York himself, the awful villain whom Festina had slain. I wondered if she had received this ship as the spoils of conquest, like gaining ownership of an enemy's possessions once you had killed him . . . but apparently the navy did not work that way.

Festina explained there had been a Purge after York died, wherein *Royal Hemlock*'s former crew members got dispatched to unappealing posts because they were tainted by association with the late admiral. This left the ship almost empty . . . and the remaining high admirals quickly attempted to restaff the vessel with their own toadies. This was a perennial game amongst members of the Admiralty, each one endeavoring to expand his or her power by creating ships whose crews were loyal to a single admiral rather than to the navy as a whole. In this way, the admirals created ships that could be called upon for private errands—like the ones I had met near Melaquin's sun. They had been sent to my homeworld to suppress the truth, even though their "official" duties required them to be someplace else.

With *Royal Hemlock*, however, no admiral succeeded in gaining an upper hand. Indeed, the new crew had a handful of people from each high admiral's camp, making the ship totally unsuitable for covert villainies: whatever secret scheme one admiral might attempt, all the other lackeys would immediately report to their own masters. *Royal Hemlock* became useless for Corrupt Intrigues . . . so the council assigned the ship to Lieutenant-Admiral Festina Ramos. If nothing else, all those spies would keep watch on my friend's activities.

"So we are surrounded by sinister infiltrators?" I whispered, peeking surreptitiously at the mooks behind us.

"Absolutely," Festina said. Turning to the mooks' leader, she asked, "Sergeant, whose payroll are you on?"

"Admiral Wang, ma'am." The sergeant favored her with a quick salute.

Festina smiled and glanced back to me. "He gives a different name every time. It's become a little joke between us." She turned back to the mook-man. "A good way to put me at my ease, right, Sergeant? Makes it simpler to stab me in the back later on."

"Whatever you say, Admiral." The mook saluted again.

The Lassitude Of Traitors

A door opened ahead of us; Festina waved us inside. "Conference room," she said. "We have a lot to discuss." As our group and the mooks filed past her, she called to no one in particular, "Ship-soul, attend. Captain Kapoor, please."

A moment later, a man's voice sounded from the ceiling. "Yes, Admiral?"

"Are you free to join us in the conference room?" Festina asked.

"If there's an enemy ship nearby, I'd prefer to stay on the bridge."

"Very well, Captain . . . but please listen in, and offer your opinion whenever you like."

"Thank you, Admiral. Do you want the meeting secured?"

Festina thought for a moment, then answered, "No. If we keep our talk too hush-hush, we'll have all the spies on board trying to find out what's happening . . . which means they'll ignore their real jobs." She sighed and glanced at the rest of us. "I swear, sometimes I want to grab the intercom and announce, 'Attention all spies, the secret meeting in Conference Room C will be broadcast on Circuit Five.' Or record every word I say and sell video-chips: proceeds to go to the fleet's Memorial Fund. Maybe that'd stop our secret snoops from hacking the ship's computers with peek-and-pry viruses. One of these days, someone's going to make a programming error while trying to crack our security and it'll crash some vital system."

Uclod snorted. "Conducting everything in the open won't prevent that, missy. If I were a spy and everything you did was fully public, I'd be convinced you were hiding something *really* juicy. I'd tear the place apart looking for it."

"*You'd* do that," my friend said, "but that's because Un-orrs have a genuine work ethic. I doubt if the *Hemlock*'s spies are that keen—almost no one in our pampered Technocracy has a sense of enterprise these days. Certainly not the toadies who spy for high admirals."

"Hmmph," I said. "It sounds like your spies have Tired Brains."

Festina cocked her head and looked at me with her garishly green eyes. "Speaking of Tired Brains . . ." She stared at me keenly for several moments without finishing her sentence. I stared back, attempting to look as Un-Tired as possible. Finally my friend shrugged and said, "Let's talk."

12

WHEREIN I GATHER
CRUCIAL INFORMATION

Ticking Bombs

The conference room had chairs that swiveled. This was
most excellent indeed—if you sat with your knees tucked up
to your chest, you could keep spinning round until you got
dizzy. Even better, one whole wall of the room was a great
panel showing a blizzard of stars; the panel pretended to be
a window, but Festina said it was actually a computer simulation. Either way, when you spun on your chair, you saw
stars whizzing past like white streaks . . . which just goes to
show Science is not totally bad, if it can make highly advanced chairs for Personal Amusement.

While I spun, Festina revealed how *Royal Hemlock* came
to be in this region of space. Apparently, it was due to
Uclod's great-great-uncle, an elderly person named Oh-
God. Like all Unorrs, Uncle Oh-God was a terrible criminal—one who happened to specialize in an offense called
smuggling. (I did not quite understand why smuggling was
such an odious crime, nor why humans gave it the cozy
name "smuggling," which sounds like a pleasant bed game,
not a felony at all; but my head was reeling in circles, so that
is my excuse for not following the logic.)

This Oh-God had not always been a professional lawbreaker—in younger days, he belonged to the Technocracy's

Explorer Corps, though he was not human.[8] Ex-Explorer Oh-God still kept in touch with his friends from the corps . . . which is why he contacted Festina when he heard the Unorrs intended to release Admiral York's secret files. He had warned Festina that trouble was brewing—there was no telling what the High Council might do to prevent the full truth from coming out. Therefore, Oh-God advised Festina to protect herself.

As soon as my friend received Oh-God's message, she realized the Admiralty would try to erase all signs of what had happened on Melaquin. Accordingly, she raced for my planet to preserve what evidence she could. Festina did not know that four navy ships had several hours headstart on her; nor had Oh-God mentioned that his great-grandnephew Uclod had set out for Melaquin even earlier. Therefore, Festina hastened through The Void, thinking she had a chance of reaching Oarville first . . . and she would have flown all the way to my planet, if her ship had not detected the brief transmission I made before the Shaddill jammed our communications. Since it was not far off her intended route, she ordered her crew to check the source of the signal. That is how my Faithful Sidekick found me in the infinite depths of space; and I was only a tiny bit angered she had not been searching for me, and had never visited Melaquin in the years since I supposedly died.

"But the planet was off-limits," Festina protested—as if that were sufficient excuse for not coming to weep on my grave. "I'd forced the Admiralty to agree no one would ever land on Melaquin again: not the council, not me, not anyone associated with the Technocracy. It was the best way to keep the League of Peoples happy. That's why nobody had cleaned up the evidence before; the top admirals didn't want to risk upsetting the League. Now, of course, with their asses on the line, the council will do *anything* to stay out of

---

[8]Apparently, the Technocracy welcomed Freeps, Tye-Tyes, and other Divian subspecies as citizens. Many Divian planets had even joined the Technocracy as Fringe Worlds . . . which I believe means they served as Faithful Sidekicks to *real* worlds.

jail . . . which means they're like rabid dogs, biting anyone who gets in the way."

"Including us?" Uclod asked.

"You, me, and their own dear mothers . . . not to mention," Festina raised her voice slightly, "anyone who's managed to hack into the ship's internal intercoms to eavesdrop on this meeting."

"You think we are being spied upon?" I whispered.

"On this damned ship, it's a certainty. The ship-soul computers are constantly listening . . . which means other ears could be listening too."

Uclod snorted. "Hell of a security system you got if any Tom, Dick, or Harry can hack into your hardware."

Festina glared at him. "The fleet's computer security is nigh well unbeatable against outsiders; the problems only come from insider spies. The spies work for admirals, and admirals all have backdoor access codes that circumvent our regular safeguards." Her fierce expression melted to a rueful smile. "Basically, this meeting is shielded against everyone except the bastards who are most likely to eavesdrop on us. And if anybody *is* eavesdropping," she said, raising her voice again, "you now know too much for the High Council's comfort. If I happened to be a spy, I'd think long and hard about my own personal safety. If, for example, I received a secret order like, 'Sabotage *Royal Hemlock*,' I'd wonder what would happen if I obeyed. Suppose I disabled the *Hemlock* so it could be captured by the council. Would the Admiralty really reward me for devotion to duty? Or would I end up with everyone else on a thousand-year sleep-ship to Andromeda?"

She let the question hang in the air. Finally, it was the mook sergeant who broke the silence. "The admiral realizes," he said, "how unlikely it is that *every* spy on board will accept your reasoning?"

"Certainly," Festina told him. "There'll always be idiots who dream of big payoffs, even when they know they're working for treacherous bastards. But I'm hoping there'll also be sensible people to stop them. People who'd rather not fall off the map, thank you very much, and who'll blow the whistle to me or the captain."

"The admiral is an optimist," Sergeant Mook said, though he was smiling behind his visor.

"The admiral likes people to know where their best interests lie," Festina replied. "She also likes taking every possible precaution. For example, Sergeant, I would never tell you your job, but do we really need this huge contingent to guard unarmed civilians? Aren't there better places your people could be?"

The sergeant's eyes flickered. "Does the admiral vouch for these guests being trustworthy?"

Festina looked at us a moment—Uclod, Lajoolie, Nimbus, and me—then laughed out loud. "Of course not. All four are ticking bombs, for Christ's sake. But compared to *some* members of the crew, these folks are absolute saints. Why not leave a few of your guards here, and send the rest to . . . oh, wherever you think a not-too-smart spy might stir up mischief."

The sergeant said nothing for a count of three, then nodded. "The admiral's suggestion is well taken." He tapped a button on his wrist, then began speaking rapidly—which is to say his lips moved at high speed, though I could not hear a sound coming out of his helmet. I assume his words were transmitted privately to the troops around him . . . because in a few seconds, all but two of the mooks saluted and clattered out of the room. As for the sergeant himself, he and the two remaining Security persons took up a position in front of the door: all three of them in exactly the same stance, hands folded below their waists, feet slightly spread apart.

"Lovely," Festina said, turning back to the rest of us. "Now let's get caught up, shall we? What's been going on?"

When I told her my story, she screamed.

The Gawker

Festina did not scream loudly, nor in one continuous howl . . . but at key points in my tale, she yelped or winced or muttered most engaging profanities. She was not at all happy about the Shaddill hovering over Melaquin; she became all growls when I told how they shot us with a sinister unconsciousness beam; she was eyes-wide astonished when I described flying into the sun with no ill effects; but her most violent reaction came at the end, when Uclod rudely took it upon himself to fill in the "gaps" of my narrative.

I had chosen not to provide overmany details about my so-called death and the four years thereafter—if Festina learned I had lain in one place for month after month, she might mistakenly think my brain was becoming Tired. Furthermore, I omitted all mention of the Pollisand, including the description I got from the woman in the tower. Unfortunately, I had already told Uclod what the woman said; therefore, he cheekily thrust himself forward to reveal that information to my friend. This caused Festina to splutter with oaths most vile.

"A big white thing like a headless animal?" she asked.

"That's what we were told," Uclod answered. "Right, Oar?"

"Yes," said I, most reluctantly. "Is this creature known to you, Festina?"

One of the mooks by the door laughed under his breath. The sergeant glared at him. So did Festina. Without taking her eyes off the mook, my friend said, "He's known, all right."

"Who is he?" Uclod asked.

Festina did not answer right away; instead, she pressed a button on the conference table's surface. A section of table in front of her rolled open to reveal a vidscreen and keypad. She tapped on the keys a moment, then turned to face the false window that had been showing all those pleasant stars.

The window had changed. Now it displayed a picture of a beast I recognized all too well—a headless white rhinoceros with eyes down his throat. "That," Festina said, "is an alien who calls himself the Pollisand. Possibly the most frightening creature in the entire galaxy."

Cleverly feigning ignorance, I said, "This Pollisand is a wicked villain?"

"No. Not in the usual sense. But if the Pollisand is in the area, consider me officially terrified."

"Why?"

"Because he's a gawker. A disaster junkie. Someone who loves showing up at a certain kind of catastrophe."

Festina pressed more keys. The picture screen shifted to a different view of the Pollisand: this time standing inside a poorly lit room filled with machinery. In front of him sat a human woman wearing a baggy green outfit of the type called overalls. She was not looking at the Pollisand, but he was definitely looking at her.

"This," said Festina, "shows the Pollisand's first appearance in human space. The year 2108 on the planet Meecks, in the control room of the Debba colony's fusion reactor. Surveillance cameras recorded this headless white alien materializing behind the command console at the very moment a technician finished entering a manual override on a safety mechanism that was supposedly malfunctioning."

Festina rose from the table, strode to the display screen, and glared at the baggy green woman. "The techie was an utter numskull. She'd misdiagnosed the problem, botched the solution, disabled a warning alarm so no one would know she'd screwed up . . . then kept hot-dogging with moronic attempts to stop cascading system failures throughout the installation. Result? Total reactor meltdown. Not a big boom, but the entire power generation system got slagged. Considering the outside temperature was ninety degrees below zero, it looked like the colony would freeze to death in a matter of days.

"And that's when the Pollisand showed up." Festina pointed to Mr. Headless Asshole on the display screen. "Right in the control room, at the precise moment meltdown became inevitable. He pranced up to the woman and began to ask questions. *Why did you do that? Why didn't you call for help? Why did you ignore the expert systems? Is there some disturbance in your personal life that's rendered you mentally incompetent?* It's hard to feel sorry for a techie so stupid, but it must be rough getting badgered with questions right after you've doomed a hundred thousand people to become icicles."

"Did the colony die?" Lajoolie asked softly.

"The colony did; the colonists didn't. They sent out an SOS and got evacuated before they came down with terminal frostbite. Unlucky for them, they were picked up by a Cashling outreach crusade . . . which means nothing to you, Oar, but suffice it to say, the colonists became indentured servants for ten years to pay off the cost of their rescue. After a decade of grunt work and listening to Cashling sermons on Godly Greed, those people must have wished they'd frozen."

Uclod wore a large frown. "You're sure the reactors melted because of that technician?"

Festina nodded. "There was a thorough investigation. Why do you ask?"

"Because it's awful damned convenient this Pollisand just happened to be in the right place at the right time."

"Isn't it though," Festina agreed. "And since his first visit, he's showed up in human space over and over again: always right after someone has made a disastrous mistake."

She moved back to the table and reached toward the keypad . . . then withdrew her hand. "I've got pictures of other Pollisand sightings, but they aren't pretty. He's particularly drawn to the Explorer Corps. Whenever someone has body parts bitten off, gets impaled on a poisonous plant thorn, or steps in something that explodes, there's a chance the Pollisand will appear out of nowhere and ask, *Why did you think that was safe? Why didn't you walk around? What was going through your head . . . besides that big wooden spike?*"

Uclod snorted. "You're sure he isn't to blame for these socalled accidents?"

"No one's sure of anything. But we've never found a shred of evidence that he sets up these scenarios himself. It's always people going about their normal business, making their own catastrophic decisions."

"Could he not have a Sinister Ray," I said, "that compels one to commit foolish deeds?"

"Theories like that have been suggested," Festina replied, "especially by the people caught acting like imbeciles. But investigations don't bear it out; almost always, these folks have a history of similar stunts before the one that really cooks their goose. Coworkers are likely to say, *It's exactly the kind of stupidity we expect from that idiot* . . . which begs the question why the idiot didn't get fired long before, but incompetence is the norm in our beloved Technocracy." She turned back toward the screen and scowled at the baggy-suited woman.

"So if the Pollisand doesn't cause these accidents," Uclod said, "how can he tell they'll happen? You think he can see the future? He knows someone's going to mess up, and gets a kick out of calling you a dope?"

"He doesn't call people dopes," Festina said. "I could play you recordings of his conversations with Explorers—Explorers who've just got themselves or their partners maimed through bonehead mistakes. Judging by the Pollisand's tone of voice, he truly wants to know why they made such bad choices: like he's trying to get some insight into the human decision-making process."

"You mean he can tell in advance when someone's going to flip the wrong switch," Uclod said, "but he has no idea why? What is he, some sort of time traveler? When he hears that someone screwed the pooch, he goes back into the past so he can find out the details?"

"That's one possible explanation," Festina replied. "We've never got solid evidence of an alien practicing time travel . . . but the top echelons of the League do so many hard-to-believe things, why not that too?"

"You think the Pollisand belongs to the top echelons of the League?" Nimbus asked. The cloud man had clustered himself around one of the other swivel chairs at the conference table, but he was not making it spin or *anything*. He had placed his baby on the seat and was taking great care not to jostle the child . . . even though a small Zarett person might enjoy a little controlled rotation under an adult's cautious guidance.

Festina told Nimbus, "Whether or not the Pollisand ranks high in the League, he definitely has technology better than our own. For one thing, he always appears out of nowhere: teleportation, or maybe turning off an invisibility field."

"Perhaps he is only projecting his appearance," I suggested. "Perhaps he is actually far away on some planet known for its lava pools, and he simply sends out *images* of himself to ask these questions."

Festina looked at me most curiously . . . but Uclod waved away my words as if they had no bearing on the subject. "What if there's more than one Pollisand?" he asked. "Maybe there are hundreds of these bozos wandering around, just waiting for people to get in trouble."

"Another valid possibility," Festina said, "and I could give you a dozen more. Navy Intelligence has plenty of hypotheses . . . but no real facts except that this headless white alien occasionally shows up at the precise moment of a disaster and begins to ask infuriating questions. Since the aliens always look and act the same, our NAVINT folks are inclined to regard the Pollisand as the only one of his kind; but who knows?"

Uclod made an ungenteel noise in his throat. "And your gurus think this Pollisand ranks high in the League? A super-evolved creature should have better things to do than thumbing his nose at people who screw up."

Festina shrugged. "In Explorer Academy, we studied all the advanced species known to humanity . . . and we came to the conclusion no one knows why *any* of them do what they do. Hell, in most cases, we have no idea how up-ladder aliens spend their time. Do they sit around contemplating their navels? Indulge in arts and sciences we don't comprehend? Project themselves into higher dimensions and play chess with otherworldly powers?"

"If *I* were an otherworldly power," I said, "I would not play chess. It is a most boring game. Except for the little horses. If I were an otherworldly power, I would create a new game that *only* had the little horses. And the winner would receive excellent prizes, instead of that nonsense about the thrill of intellectual achievement."

Uclod gave me a look. "Try to stay focused, missy. Real live aliens don't play board games with fictitious deities. Presumably," he said, turning back to Festina, "real live aliens have to eat and reproduce and gather raw materials for whatever gadgets they manufacture . . ."

"Don't be too sure," Festina said. "From what we've seen

of highly advanced races, they engineer themselves to transcend mundane needs. At the Academy, one of our professors theorized that to get past a certain point of evolution, species have to jettison almost all their natural drives. You can't go forward till you dump the primitive crap that's holding you back. And not just stuff like eating and breeding, but mental attitudes too. Territoriality, for example—humans, Divians, and other races of our approximate intelligence level all have at least some expansionist tendencies. We build colonies, terraform planets, try to keep our economies growing. But species above us on the ladder aren't interested in such things. *None* of them has any known planetary holdings. They just . . . well, have you heard of Las Fuentes?"

She was looking at Uclod. When he shook his head, she went back to the keypad and typed for several seconds. The display screen changed to show a bright desert landscape of hard-baked dirt, punctuated in places with scrubby weeds that looked like tiny orange balloons glued onto twigs. A white-surfaced road ran diagonally across the picture—a road pocked with holes where the pavement had turned to rubble. It looked most ancient and crumbling, stretching toward the horizon . . . until it suddenly disappeared over the edge of a large drop-off.

The view zoomed forward, closer and closer to the drop-off. Soon I could see this was the lip of a great crater, a huge round bowl sunk deep into the land. I had heard of such craters being made from the impact of cosmic objects hurtling out of the sky . . . but the one on the screen looked more like an artificial feature dug by an alien culture. The road continued forward down the side of the crater, fading now and then due to erosion but always resuming again, traveling in a straight line until it reached the bottom of the bowl.

There, in the center of the crater, stood a simple fountain made of bleached gray stone. No water bubbled from the central pillar and the basin was dry as salt; however, I could tell that long ago this fountain must have gushed as cheerfully as the two fountains in the central plaza of my home village.

"This," Festina said, "is the legacy of Las Fuentes—a race

who once occupied most of the worlds now belonging to the Technocracy . . . including my home planet of Agua." She waved at the screen. "This particular fountain is in an Aguan high desert called Otavalo. There are other fountains all over my world: in rainforests, in the mountains, on the prairies, even a few underwater. Always at the bottom of great whopping craters dozens of klicks across, with one or more access highways leading in. And the fountains aren't just on Agua; they're on every planet Las Fuentes colonized."

"Religious shrines?" Uclod asked.

"Perhaps. People on Agua thought so—my nana used to take me to one in the deep jungle so we could light candles." She paused for a moment, staring off into the distance; then she shook her head briskly and went on. "Anyhow, Las Fuentes dominated ninety-two star systems till five thousand years ago: a total population estimated to be at least a hundred billion.

"Then," she continued, "they just gave it all up. Peacefully, as far as we can tell—no signs of war or other disaster. And Las Fuentes are still around nowadays . . . or at least a race that claims to be the successors of the crater makers."

She pressed a key and the screen changed once more— this time showing the interior of a room that was plushly appointed according to human standards. By this, I mean it had a number of big fat chairs that might have been very handsome if they had been clear instead of an ugly opaque brown. There were also grumpy paintings of humans on the walls, surrounded by tall shelves of objects that were probably books: the ancient type of book that always tells the same story and has no push-buttons. The scene looked most opulent indeed . . . except that one of the chairs was filled with a mound of vivid purple jelly.

Festina pointed to the jelly. "That's what Las Fuentes look like today."

I stared. It did not look like a living creature at all; it had no structure, no orifices, no notable physical features—nothing but purple goo coagulated on the seat of the chair and heaped halfway up the backrest. If placed on the floor, the pile might reach to my knees.

"This creature does not look advanced," I said. "It is nothing but ooze."

"But *smart* ooze," Festina replied. "The picture was taken in the study of Admiral Vincence, current president of the navy's High Council. Vincence found the ooze one night when he got home; it had somehow sneaked past the most sophisticated security system our navy ever assembled. The jelly introduced itself as official ambassador of Las Fuentes, gave a comm number where it could be reached, then disappeared—sank straight through a leather armchair and into the floor."

"Were the Fuentes purple jelly before?" Lajoolie asked softly. "When they were building the fountains?"

"Not according to archaeologists. Las Fuentes were big into cremation, so we don't have any physical remains . . . but we've found a few tools, broken furniture, things that suggest they had conventional bodies. Flesh, blood, bone, the usual. When you ask the jelly ambassador what caused the big change, he'll only say, *We grew up.*"

Festina turned to look at the purple blob picture once more. "So now," she said, "Las Fuentes don't have a home planet that we know of . . . just a single ambassador on New Earth. He won't talk about trade, refuses to advise on scientific matters, and ignores requests for cultural exchange. Once in a while, he arbitrates disputes or clarifies the League of Peoples' views on tricky legal questions—what we have to do to stay sentient—but he never seems to *want* anything from us. He isn't interested in our labor, our data, our resources, our manufactured goods . . . so whatever goals jelly-people have, we humans are too primitive to be useful."

"And yet," Nimbus said pensively, "Las Fuentes maintain that embassy."

"I'll bet they want to keep an eye on us savages," Uclod answered. "We lesser species may not be smart enough to contribute to these guys' lofty existence, but there are probably ways we could screw them up. If we suddenly invented a way to mutate ourselves into the same kind of goo, Las Fuentes would damned sure want to know. Overnight, we'd change from harmless yahoos into direct competitors."

"That's one obvious explanation," Festina agreed, "but it's never smart to assume aliens think the way we do. Maybe there's no such thing as 'competition' once you reach a certain stage of development. Maybe it's nothing but sweetness and light: one big happy melting pot of cosmic love."

We all stared at her.

"Hey," she said, "it was a *joke.*"

Plans Within Plans

"So what've we got?" Uclod said. "The Pollisand spends most of his time badgering people about being idiots. But four years ago he broke with his usual modus operandi: he showed up on Melaquin, and instead of asking Oar why she jumped out a window, he simply patched her up."

"Is that unusual for him?" Nimbus asked Festina. "Providing medical aid in a crisis?"

"He's never done anything like it," she replied, "and he's been present at plenty of crises. I don't think he's ever showed up at a lethal accident—he seems to avoid fatalities. But he's watched plenty of people crippled or bleeding, and he's never tried to help a single one."

"All right," Uclod said, "so the Pollisand broke his pattern for Oar. We've also got the Shaddill getting upset when they find out Oar's not dead. They say someone's interfered with their plan. Obviously, the person who interfered was the Pollisand; he's the one who took Oar away and brought her back to life. Do you think the Pollisand did that deliberately to screw the Shaddill?"

"Who knows?" Festina answered . . . but I thought I *did* know. The Pollisand told me he wanted to wipe the Shaddill off the face of the universe; if ministering to my health was a way to foil some Shaddill-ish scheme, he would gladly do so.

"I believe," I said, "that he helped me as a means of frustrating the Shaddill . . . though I do not know what role I play in all this."

Festina was looking in my direction, but her gaze was distant. "If the Shaddill thought you had died," she said, "and they *still* came to Melaquin . . . they might have been interested in your corpse." A light sparked in her eyes. "And why did they show up when they did? They must have known the navy was on its way to clean up evidence. Either the Shaddill wanted to examine your body before the navy took it away . . ."

"Or," Uclod finished her thought, "they wanted to remove missy's body so the navy *couldn't* check it out."

Festina nodded. "Both possibilities suggest there's something special about you, Oar. Something that sets you apart from the rest of your people."

"Of course. I am more clever and beautiful."

Festina gave me a look. "It would be nice to find something even *more* distinctive."

"They thought she was dead," Lajoolie said softly. "That's quite a distinction in itself." She looked at me with her mild eyes. "Isn't it almost impossible for your people to die? You don't age, you don't get sick, you can't drown or suffocate . . . short of falling off an eighty-story building, not much can hurt you. And if the Shaddill wanted a glass cadaver for some purpose, they couldn't just kill one of your people; the League would never let them get away with outright murder."

Uclod smiled at Lajoolie. "My darling wife has put her finger on a fascinating possibility. If the Shaddill wanted your body to dissect or something . . ."

His voice trailed off as he caught sight of Festina shaking her head. "The Shaddill wouldn't need to dissect Oar. They *designed* her race; they built her whole genome down to the last little nucleotide. What could a dissection tell them they don't already know?"

"Perhaps," said Nimbus, "we should perform our own dissection to find out."

I glared at him and swept my fist through the place where his nose would have been.

"Settle down," Festina told me. "I assume Nimbus means we should give you a medical exam. See if there's anything unusual."

"There is nothing unusual about me," I protested. "I am more healthy than anyone else on this ship."

"Then you're unusual, aren't you?" my friend said with a smile. "Anyway, I want you examined. If nothing else, we should know what the Pollisand did to you. Did he just fix your injuries, or did he do something else while he had you on the operating table?"

"What might he have done?" I asked.

"I don't know. That's why we're going to check you out."

"I do not wish to be checked out," I grumbled. "Such treatment is only for damaged people."

"Humor me," Festina said, "it's important. Your friends can keep you company . . . unless you'd rather be examined in private?"

"No," I told her. "I have had a good deal of privacy in my life. If you think I enjoy being alone, you are much mistaken."

Festina's breath caught in her throat. She let it out slowly. "I'm sorry. But you aren't alone now, Oar. I promise." She gave a small smile. "Go to sick bay, all of you—the sergeant will show the way." She glanced toward the door; the mook man nodded. Festina turned back to me. "I'll join you as soon as I can, but I have to look into a few things. Okay?"

"Okay," I answered, using her own vernacular. Then, most bravely, I asked, "Do doctors hurt?"

"If he hurts you," Festina said, "you have my permission to punch him in the nose."

This made me very happy . . . but I still looked back with a lump in my throat as I went out the door.

Festina sat at the table, her eyes staring off into space as if she were thinking very great thoughts. I decided it would be pleasant to think great thoughts of my own; but the only thing in my mind was that I was walking away from my friend.

13

WHEREIN I AM
THOROUGHLY EXAMINED

More Tiny Things Invading My Person

Sick bay did not hurt, but it tickled. I could not see what did the tickling, so I blamed Nimbus—I thought he was sending specks of himself to brush against me, making my nose itchy and causing awkward irritations all over my body. But the cloud man swore he had nothing to do with it; he claimed to be suffering personal disturbances of his own, because the air of the infirmary was filled with Analysis Nano.

I did not know what Analysis Nano was, but the navy physician was delighted to explain. He was, in fact, delighted about every conceivable aspect of existence: the opportunity to examine me was "fabulous"; my personal transparency was "amazing"; and the chance to carry out a task for Festina was "a great, great honor." His name was Havel, a paunchy watery-eyed human who seemed to perceive more reasons to laugh than anyone else in the room. Dr. Havel was constantly chuckling or giggling or snickering over things that seemed quite ordinary indeed. He also displayed much hearty enthusiasm about anything that passed before his eyes . . . which meant when he said, "Ho, ho, you're a stunner, the most gorgeous woman I've ever seen," I was not so gratified as I might have wished.

Some men are too easy to impress. When they praise your

ethereal crystalline beauty, you get the feeling they would be just as ecstatic over a glittery red pebble or a potato shaped like a fish.

On the other hand, Dr. Ha-Ha-Havel was a good person to approach for clarifications of important Scientific topics—he was so enchanted with the glories of the universe, he would gladly tell you whatever he could, and never suggest you were ignorant for not knowing. Therefore he explained that Analysis Nano was a swarm of millions and billions of tiny machines, so small they could not be seen. They buzzed around patients in sick bay, reading your pulse, your body temperature, and the composition of your sweat. At instructions from the physician, the little bugs could also delve beneath your skin, digging for blood samples or flying down your throat to examine the workings of your stomach.

I did not want tiny machines journeying through my digestive system; but Dr. Havel said a number of them had already gone down my esophagus, and it did not hurt a bit, did it?

He was correct. It did not hurt, so I could not punch him. But everything itched a great deal, as I have already said, and some of the nanos ventured into places they were not welcome. Though I wore my Explorer jacket, the coat did not seem sufficiently skilled at protecting the parts of me that needed safekeeping.

Myself Exposed

After five minutes of such indignities, Dr. Havel clapped his hands together with Anticipatory Zeal. "Well then, let's see what my clever little helpers have discovered."

He scurried to a table in the middle of the room: the sort of table one might lie upon when being examined by a *real* physician.[9] However, Dr. Havel never once asked me to lie down; and when I looked at the table, I saw why not.

---

[9] I am familiar with physicians because there were excellent medical machines in my home village. Once every month, I was required to recline on

The entire table-top was a viewing screen . . . and there on the screen, life-size, was the exposed anatomy of a woman who could only be me. I do not say I recognized myself—instead of a face, there was an opaque rendering of my skull, not to mention whitish versions of other bones in my body, laid over internal organs depicted in ugly unnatural colors—but the general outline matched my own, so who else could it be?

"I do not look like that," I said. "My bones are not white; they are pleasingly transparent."

Dr. Havel laughed the way he laughed at everything. "Quite right, Ms. Oar, quite right, ha-ha. I got the computer to colorize your lovely insides so we could see everything better. You're clearly designed to be clear, ha-ha, at least to human eyes; but once we scan you on IR and UV, not to mention X rays, ultrasound, MRI, bioelectrics and so on, we get a lovely picture of what we can't discern in the visible spectrum."

He proudly waved his hand toward the image—which I found most disconcerting to look at. When I breathed in, the picture's lungs inflated; when I exhaled, the picture's lungs did the same. I tried taking breaths in quick little gasps, hoping the machine would be thrown off and unable to match my rhythm . . . but no matter what I did, the image on the table imitated it exactly.

If I held myself quiet, I could feel my heart beating in perfect unison with the ugly crimson heart shown on the screen. Just noticing that made my heart beat faster. The picture's heart beat faster too. I had the most disquieting sensation the image controlled my pulse instead of the other way around; so I looked at the floor until the sensation went away.

Meanwhile, Dr. Havel went around the table and placed his finger against the screen—not on my picture, but off to one side, where there was nothing but blank blackness. A host of squiggles appeared where his finger touched: print-

---

a proper examination table and submit to Necessary Regimens Of Health. These entailed *authentic* poking and prodding, not annoying little itches that lacked the courage of their convictions.

ing in four different colors of light, and little diagrams that probably revealed vital facets of my health.

"Hmm!" Dr. Havel announced. "Ms. Oar, it turns out you're yourself."

"This is not a clever machine if that is its best observation."

"Oh," said he, "you think it's reporting the obvious? Not at all, ha-ha, ha-ha. Before you got here, Admiral Ramos called to brief me . . . and when I heard your story, I bet the good admiral a modest sum you'd turn out to be a clone of the original Oar. But you aren't."

"How can you tell?" Uclod asked.

The doctor must have been hoping for that question. "See here?" he said most gleefully. He patted his fingers against the screen, right on the picture of my ribs. The image expanded to show a magnified view, twice as big as before. Havel patted again and the picture expanded a second time; several more pats, and all you could see was one little patch of bone, blown up to fill the body-sized screen.

"All right," the doctor said, "fourth rib, right side: look at this area here." He circled his pudgy hand above the center of the picture, where there was an obvious line etched into the bone. "See this ridge running up the middle? And the bump at the top: one side of the ridge is a bit higher than the other. That's a fracture site. The bone broke and didn't quite knit cleanly. It's only a microscopic discrepancy—whoever set the fracture did a fantastic job, better than any human surgeon. And the healing was more complete than anything I've seen in *Homo sapiens*. But magnify the image a few hundred times, and ta-da! The glitch is there, plain as day."

I stared at the picture. I did not like thinking my rib had a flaw in it, no matter how small.

"And," the doctor went on, "there are dozens of similar breaks throughout the skeletal system: the chest, the arms, the front of the face. Ms. Oar, you definitely suffered massive trauma at some point in the past—consistent with falling from a tall building, and your upper torso taking the brunt of the impact. Since I don't know your species' rate of recovery, I can't tell how long ago the damage happened; but it's safe to conclude you're the same Oar who plummeted off the tower four years back."

"I *know* that," I told him. "I suffered Grievous Wounds and it took me time to heal."

"You didn't heal by yourself," Havel said. "If the bones had knit on their own, the fracture sites would be a million times worse. A lot wouldn't heal at all—the bone ends would be too apart to grow back together again. Someone damned good at orthopedics set each little break so it would fuse as good as new . . . and the surgery was performed within a few hours of the damage.

"On top of that," the doctor continued, "here's the real telltale sign you got high-class medical attention." He pointed to a series of squiggles written in bright red on the table screen. They were not an alphabet I recognized; I assumed they were some hateful Scientific Notation describing tedious Chemicals.

"Your spinal fluid," Havel said, "contains the residue of a nifty little drug called Webbalin: developed on the planet Troyen several decades back, when the Mandasars were the best medical researchers in our sector. Webbalin prevents cerebral degradation after your neurons stop getting fresh blood; without it, a human suffers irreversible brain damage within five to ten minutes of coronary arrest. Even if someone gets your heart pumping again later on, you won't be the same person. Your old brain architecture has fallen apart— the trillions of linkages that make you unique get erased by neuron decay. Even if we grow you new neurons, they won't link together in the same way. Without Webbalin to keep your original gray matter from rotting, your body might get brought back to life, but your memories and personality sure won't."

"And you found this Webbalin stuff in Oar's spinal fluid?" Uclod asked.

"She obviously received a massive dose," Havel replied. "Enough to leave traces four years after the fact."

"Doctor," Nimbus said, "how soon does Webbalin have to be administered after death? In order to be effective."

"It's usually given *before* death," Havel answered. "If a

trauma victim's in danger of dying, you want Webbalin in the patient's bloodstream as soon as possible. Get it circulating while the heart is still working; then when the crash comes, ha-ha, the brain will be safe for ten hours instead of ten minutes. Gives you a lot more leeway for patching up the poor bastard."

"But suppose the patient has already died. Does that mean you only have ten minutes to inject the drug?"

"Worse than that," Havel told him. "Ten minutes to get the drug saturating the brain. Which is damned difficult if you don't have blood circulation. You can force-pump a dose inside the cranium and hope it soaks into the cells . . . but that's just farting around to mollify the next-of-kin. It seldom works at all, and it never works completely. If you're lucky, you salvage thirty percent of the brain, tops. That's rarely enough to keep the patient alive, let alone, ha-ha, help him remember the password to his bank account—which is often the family's prime concern."

"So if Oar's brain survived . . ." Nimbus said thoughtfully.

"It *did* survive," I told him. "It survived *just fine*. I am quite as clever as I have ever been."

"Maybe," Uclod said, "that's because you ain't human, toots. Your brain cells might not rot as fast as the average *Homo sap*. Maybe that's how you stayed intact till the Pollisand picked you up."

"Or maybe," Nimbus suggested, "the drug was injected ahead of time. While you were still alive. *Before* you took the fall."

"No one injected me with drugs! I would know!"

But I was not so certain as I pretended. Only a short time before my fall, I had been lying unwatched in a state of unconsciousness. This was the result of being shot repeatedly with a whirring noise-gun, causing such horrendous damage that I blacked out. When I eventually awoke, I located the villain who shot me and plunged with him from the tower . . . but during the period I was insensate, there was no way to tell what someone might have done to me.

"It does seem far-fetched," Dr. Havel said, "that the Pollisand injected Ms. Oar with Webbalin in advance. There'd be no reason to do that unless he knew she was going to take a swan-dive, ha-ha, onto bare cement. And the only way he could know that is by . . ."

"Foreseeing the future?" Nimbus said. "Isn't that what the Pollisand is noted for? Being in exactly the right place when things go wrong?"

No one spoke for a moment. Then Uclod muttered, "Bloody hell."

Unpruned Anomalies

A time passed without conversation . . . which is to say, Dr. Havel talked and nobody paid attention. What he talked about was me as a "specimen"—his first "marvelous chance" to examine an "alien life-form never before seen by medical science," and he was "thrilled, absolutely thrilled" to have the opportunity.

But the foolish thing was, he did not examine me at all: he examined my picture on the table, while I stood bored at his elbow. And instead of praising my beauty or grace, he was forever blathering about *Chemicals:* substances with long complex names that my body contained, in lieu of *other* substances with long complex names that it did not. For example, it was apparently most remarkable that my blood did not include Hemogoblins (which I believe are little trolls that live in human veins); in place of those, I had Transparent Silicate Platelets (which, as the name suggests, are miniature plates that carry food from one cell to another).

Moreover, though I appeared visually similar to *Homo sapiens,* my composition was entirely different. I had numerous glands not found in humans; my basic internal organs (heart, lungs, and stomach) were arranged differently from Earthlings; even my bones were unique, and their attachments to various muscles deviated greatly from the Terran standard. I was, Havel said, a vastly different species from humans, structurally as well as chemically . . . but my nonhuman parts were assembled in such a way that I looked "morphologically human" on the outside. "Like a cat," said the doctor, "who's been engineered to resemble a dog. Except that cats and dogs have a lot more in common with each other than you do with humans—your body chemistry is utterly extraterrestrial."

Finally, it seemed my brain had never undergone a process the doctor called *pruning*. He said this was something that happens to all known intelligent races by mid-adolescence: a large number of existing connections between mental neurons wither away in the interest of "efficiency." The theory goes that during childhood, the brain has many surplus linkages between neighboring nerve cells, because there is no telling which will eventually prove necessary. By adolescence, however, a person's day-to-day experiences have established which connections are actually used and which are superfluous fripperies—links that never get activated in everyday life. The brain therefore discontinues low-use links as a means of streamlining the most common thought processes . . . making sure that essential mental activity is not slowed by extraneous clutter.

The doctor claimed pruning is good and desirable: a pruned brain is more quickly decisive, less plagued by needless doubts and uncertainties. After pruning, your brain knows conclusively that objects always fall down instead of up, that it is a poor idea to stick your hand into fire, and that mere animals never really talk; indeed, a pruned brain is resistant to, and even threatened by, any notion it has come to regard as absurd. The "mature" mind shuts the door on the impossible, so it can concentrate on The Real.

Or at least, that is what Havel claimed.

For myself, I did not think The Real deserved such drastic sacrifice. If pruning is the price of adulthood, is it not more courageous to remain a child? Of course one knows animals speak infrequently (and it is hard to believe ugly animals such as lizards will ever become engaging conversationalists); but it seems most high-handed to reject the possibility entirely. I tried to argue this point with the doctor, but because his brain had been pruned, he exhibited nothing but galling condescension toward my "naïve" views . . . which meant I was close to choking him when Festina entered the room.

This was indeed a welcome interruption. "Hello, hello!" I said in great happiness. I wondered if she would want to hug again, and if I would be so foolishly self-conscious as before, and if maybe *I* should start the hugging this time to prove I was not standoffish . . . and none of that happened, because I saw my friend's face was grave.

"Uclod," Festina said quietly, "our communications came back on-line: either the Shaddill have stopped jamming or we're out of their range. Anyway," she took a deep breath, "I received a message from my staff on New Earth—your Grandma Yulai has been killed."

What Expendable Means

In a quiet voice, Uclod asked, "How?"

"Electrocuted by a faulty VR/brain connection. Several thousand volts to the cerebellum. Supposedly an accident." Festina rolled her eyes in disgust. "And the rest of your family is missing. I hope to God it means they've gone into hiding; my people haven't collected enough details to know if that's what happened, or if somebody got them too . . ." Her voice trailed off. "I'm sorry."

Uclod appeared frozen. Lajoolie had moved in behind him as soon as Festina began speaking; the big woman's arms wrapped around her husband, holding him tight. She seemed made of stone . . . but Uclod was made of ice.

"What is that phrase you Explorers say?" he asked Festina. "Uncle Oh-God told me once—when somebody dies in the line of duty. What is it?"

Festina pursed her lips. "We say, *That's what 'expendable' means.* Because the navy has always treated Explorers as expendable baggage."

Uclod stared at her a moment, then shook his head. "No. I can't say that. Not for my own grandmother."

He turned around and buried his face against Lajoolie's strong body.

The Utter Truth Of Death

Through all of this, I had not said a word. Indeed, I could not speak.

I did not know this Grandma Yulai personally, and the few things I had heard about her were bad. She was a criminal who dominated a family of other criminals.

And yet.

She was dead. She had *died*. She was no different now from the animal corpses one finds in the forest, the fresh ones covered with flies or the old ones as dried and withered as bread crusts.

Let me tell you a thing: my mother taught me death was holy, a blessing bestowed only on natural creatures. Rabbits and squirrels and fishes could die, but my own glass people could not. We were artificial beings; the Hallowed Ones refused to take us to the Place Beyond because we were not worthy of progressing to the life after life. Our species was cursed, spurned by death . . . or so my mother said.

It turned out my mother was wrong. My sister had died, died forever. Perhaps I had died for a short time too . . . though it does not count if someone brings you back.

But when I first met Festina, I got most angry with her when she claimed Earth humans could achieve death. I believed she was putting on airs, pretending to be holy herself. The ability to die seemed too wondrous and special to be true.

However, I did not feel that way anymore. Starbiter had died. Grandma Yulai had died. Even villains like Admiral York and the man who killed my sister had died. For the very first time—there in the infirmary, watching Uclod weep and Lajoolie comfort him—for the first time, I realized just how un-special Death was. How *common*. It was not the exception, it was the rule: a ubiquitous poison infesting the universe, and those of us from Melaquin were total simple-heads to think death was a blessed gift we had been denied.

Starbiter: disemboweled and smashed at high speed into the Shaddill ship. Grandma Yulai: her brain burned to smoke by some mysterious device. My sister: shot with invisible sound, churned up and blasted until her insides shattered, then buried to rot in the dirt.

What did that bode for anyone else?

Festina could die. Truly die. At any time. Perhaps as a no-ble sacrifice, perhaps as the foolish result of blind bad luck. The same for Uclod and Lajoolie. The same for me as well—the Pollisand had promised I was not immune to death, and had warned that a time of danger was imminent.

I could die. *Anyone* could die. The doctor, the cloud man, baby Starbiter, they were no more permanent than leaves on an autumn tree; one day their winter would come and then they would be trampled in the dirt.

How could these people stand it? Did they not know? Did they not *realize*? Why did they not scream and scream at the thought their lives would end?

But I did not scream either. The utter truth of death had taken my breath away.

Don't Die Stupid

"Are you all right?"

Festina stood by my shoulder, her face filled with concern.

"I am not all right," I whispered. "I am not all right at all."

"What's wrong?"

I steeled myself, then told her the truth. "Things die."

"Yes."

"*People* die."

"Yes."

"You and I, Festina—we could die."

"We *will* die, Oar. Sooner or later. Maybe in the next sec-ond, maybe years from now; but we *will* die."

I looked at her. Was this not a good time for my friend to

offer an embrace, a comfort, a reassurance? Lajoolie had en-
folded Uclod in her arms, but Festina was only watching
me—as if she did not want to make the moment go away. As
if she wished the thought of death to impress itself on my
brain, deeply, deeply, deeply.

I fought back tears. "How can you stand it?" I asked.
"Why do you not scream and scream?"

"Because screaming doesn't do any good. *Nothing* does
any good in the long run. Death will come." Festina locked
my gaze with her blazing green eyes. "But we have choices,
Oar. There are some deaths we don't need to accept. If a
blood clot hits my brain right here, right now, there's nothing I can do about it, so no regrets. But if I die from something I could have prevented if I'd just thought ahead . . ."

She shook her head fiercely. "We Explorers have a saying,
Oar—*don't die stupid*. It's got a double meaning: don't die
because of your own stupidity, and don't die in a *state* of stupidity. Learn things; learn everything you can. Keep your
eyes open. Prepare, prepare, prepare. You'll still die eventually, but by God, in the final second you can tell yourself you
didn't just throw the fight."

"And yet," I whispered, "one still dies."

"Yes. One still dies." She glanced at the weeping Uclod.
"It seems you've just recognized your own mortality, Oar.
Everyone does sooner or later . . . then most people immediately try to put it out of their minds. They go into denial, except when the grim truth strikes so close to home it can't be
ignored." She turned back to me. "Don't do that, Oar. Stay
mindful of death. Stay constantly mindful."

She held my gaze a moment, then lowered her eyes with
shy chagrin. "Of course, some people say you should also
stay mindful of life. I'm still working on that one. C'mere."

Festina opened her arms to me and I finally, gratefully,
slid into her embrace.

More Pressing Matters

We did not stay that way long. Behind my back, someone made the sound that humans call a Polite Cough . . . but I did not think it polite at all, for it caused Festina to release me. "Yes?" she asked.

I turned. Dr. Havel stood there in the company of the cloud man, Nimbus . . . who was now not shaped like a man but a featureless ball of mist. At the center of the ball lay the delicate silvery Starbiter; and do not ask me how a ball of mist can support a ball of baby for I do not know. Some mysteries are too pleasing to be questioned.

"Uhh," said the doctor, all shamefaced, "sorry to interrupt you, Admiral, but uhh, ha-ha, Nimbus has been saying some things I think we should, uhh, discuss."

"What sort of things?" Festina asked.

The doctor gestured for the cloud man to answer. "Well," Nimbus said, particles of mist roiling within him, "I'm sure you realize Grandma Yulai won't be the last. She's only the first casualty in a much larger campaign to keep York's exposé hushed up. If someone on the High Council was desperate enough to murder her—"

"Wait," Havel interrupted. "Does it *have* to be someone on the High Council?" He turned to Festina with his big watery eyes . . . as if, ha-ha, the admiral would reassure him the universe was not truly cruel. "Maybe it was just someone misguided," Havel suggested. "A lowly ensign perhaps, who thought killing this woman would make the admirals happy. That could be how it was, couldn't it?"

"The council will try to make it look that way if this business ever gets out." Festina curled her lip. "They'll find some gung-ho hotshot who'll confess to doing it unasked . . . and the admirals will howl with horror that anyone could believe they'd approve of such a deed. For all I know, maybe it *was* some lousy lieutenant who wanted to impress the High Council. But we have to assume the worst: one or more admirals have gone bug-fuck and they're ready to out-and-out murder folks who pose a threat." She gave a grim little smile. "I'm afraid I fall into the threat category. So does Oar. So does everyone on this ship."

"But even if the admirals *are* on the warpath," Havel said, "they can't do anything, can they? They're all on New Earth. They can't send execution squads to murder us in space— the League would never allow killers to leave New Earth's system."

"The admirals don't have to *send* killers. Every planet in the Technocracy has locals who don't mind slitting throats for a price. And our beloved high admirals know who those people are. Wherever we dock, someone will be waiting for us."

"Then we don't dock," Havel said. "We're a navy starship, for heaven's sake—we can survive in deep space for three full years. Even longer if we sneak into uninhabited star systems every so often and mine a few asteroids."

"And in the meantime, we let the killers run free?" Festina scowled. "I wasn't the only Explorer marooned on Melaquin—there were dozens of others, and they're all at risk. Most are still serving in the fleet; the next time their ships dock, there'll be assassins waiting in port. As soon as my fellow Explorers go on shore leave, they'll get their throats sliced. Do you think I'll sit back and let that happen?"

"Then let us confront the Admiralty," I said. "Let us make them stop killing. Let us make them know how awful death is."

Festina shook her head. "The admirals are all on New Earth, and it's way too dangerous for us to go anywhere near there. I don't just mean New Earth itself—just entering the system may be a risk. Entering *any* Technocracy system. The council could spread word that *Royal Hemlock* has turned renegade: non-sentient. Every navy ship might have orders to manufacture missiles and put us down."

"Missiles?" Nimbus said. "You mean *bombs*? I thought the League of Peoples wouldn't let ships carry lethal weapons."

Festina gave the cloud man a weary smile. "The League won't let us carry weapons from one star system to another . . . but they certainly *do* let us kill dangerous non-sentients. Sometimes it's nigh on mandatory. How do you think we handle pirates or terrorists? Plenty of nasty folk arm their ships and cause trouble for passers-by. If killers like that leave their home star system, the League takes care of them; but if the bad guys stay in one place, hiding in a handy asteroid belt and popping out from time to time to hijack local shipping, our navy has to declare a police action. A squadron goes in, sets up a secure base, then manufactures warheads from standard ship supplies. The warheads attach to normal probe missiles, and voilà, you're ready to shoot non-sentients. Once the enemy has been blown to smithereens, you dismantle your leftover warheads and go home with your pockets full of danger pay."

Dr. Havel muttered under his breath, "If the League lets you."

Festina nodded. "True. The biggest danger isn't fighting a scruffy bunch of outlaws; it's afterward, when you find out whether the League accepts your actions. The bad guys damned near always have innocent hostages aboard their ships, so the navy can't just leap into an indiscriminate firefight. You try to negotiate, which seldom works, then you try blockading, then maybe a sneak attack to grab the enemy with your ship's tractors . . . and nine times out of ten it still comes down to a shoot-out where you blast the bastards to bat-shit.

"Afterward, you ask yourself scary questions: did we really do our best to save sentient lives, or is the League going to hand us a death sentence when we reach deep space? Even worse, did we really clean up a nest of homicidal maniacs, or were those so-called terrorists actually high-minded dissenters against some corrupt local regime . . . and the fat-assed generalissimos fed our navy a pack of lies so we'd wipe out their squeaky clean opposition." Festina shrugged. "You can never be sure. The only way to learn if you did the right thing is to head home; if the League doesn't kill you, you're a *bona fide* hero."

"But even if the League doesn't kill *you*," Dr. Havel said, "they may kill the person next to you." He dropped his gaze. "Admiral Ramos hasn't mentioned what usually happens af-

ter our navy blows some ship from the sky. Even if you think
you've pulled off a textbook operation, the League still exe-
cutes a few people in your crew. Maybe those folks liked the
killing too much—or maybe they didn't do their best to encourage a peaceful surrender. Maybe the League are secretly
sadists and they kill a couple crew members at random to
keep everyone else nervous. You never know: God forbid the
League should explain its actions. All you can say for sure is
that the nice woman who always ate lunch with you, and the
funny guy from engineering who had a new joke every
day . . . they both got executed by the League and you're
still alive."

His voice carried such bitterness, we all stared at him. The
doctor did not say more. It occurred to me that a man who
laughs at the least opportunity may not be half so jolly as he
seems.

Avoidance

"Well," said Festina in a quiet voice, "we won't give anyone the chance to shoot us. *Royal Hemlock* will stay far
away from Technocracy star systems; even if the council orders the rest of the fleet to vaporize us on sight, we'll never
come within target range."

"Then how shall we defeat the villains?" I asked.

"We'll go public," Festina said. "Loud, brash, and the
sooner the better. Before I came down here, I asked Captain
Kapoor to contact news agencies on the closest planet to us:
a Cashling world named Jalmut. We'll record our testimony
here on *Hemlock*, transmit everything to the Cashlings, and
let them blare it across the galaxy." She smiled grimly. "I
like the idea of putting out the news through nonhumans; it's
less likely the fleet will be able to get to them."

"Get to them?" Havel gulped. "What do you mean?"

"Bribe them, intimidate them, tie them up in red tape.
Every human news agency has a few people who've been secretly bought by the navy." She glanced over at Uclod, still
huddled against Lajoolie. "That must be how the Admiralty

learned what Grandma Yulai was planning: she approached some reporter and the snitches got wind of it. But nonhuman media services are less subject to fleet interference; and once our statements hit general broadcast, the High Council won't be able to keep things quiet. Even better, they won't dare bump off the other Explorers who can testify about Melaquin—it'll be too obvious.

"On top of that," she continued, "the whole council will likely get tossed in the clink as soon as we tell our tale, so they'll find it hard to arrange assassinations. The government on New Earth will go berserk at what's been happening behind their backs . . . especially the murder of Uclod's grandmother. The top echelons of the Technocracy have never cared how the fleet handles its own people, but when admirals start killing civilians—even disreputable civilians like Yulai Unorr—every politician in human space will howl for blood."

"They might get it," Nimbus said. "Blood running in the streets. If the civilian government tries to crack down on the Admiralty, the admirals may crack back. Next thing you know, there's a civil war."

Festina shook her head. "If our statements get out into public broadcast, the admirals' own people will turn against them. That's the problem with hiring opportunist scum to do your dirty work; they won't stick by you when the wind turns. A few admirals may hole up in their mansions with squadrons of hired goons, but the police can deal with that. There's absolutely no chance the navy itself will stick by the council once the truth gets out—honest folks in the fleet will be outraged, and dishonest ones will leap at the chance to eliminate the people above them."

"Then we must disseminate the truth immediately," I said. "Let us broadcast our messages *right now*."

Festina glanced at Uclod again. Lajoolie had dropped to her knees, the better to hug her little orange husband. They looked most ridiculous like that, the woman so big and the man so small; yet I thought how comforting it must be to have someone who did not mind looking ridiculous when you needed to be held.

"Uclod is a key witness," Festina said softly. "We'll give him a few more minutes. Anyway, we can't do much till the captain makes arrangements with some news agency. Then," she continued, "we'll put a whole lot of nails in the Admiralty's coffin."

"I am excellent at using a hammer," I said.

14

WHEREIN I PREPARE FOR FAME

The Insides Of Aliens

As we waited for Uclod to recover his composure, I inquired about this race who would be handling our broadcast: the Cashlings of Jalmut. I confess I was not truly interested in them, but I did not wish to brood any more about Death so I needed something to occupy my mind.

The moment I asked, Dr. Havel rushed to locate a picture of the Cashling species. He did not succeed immediately . . . or rather, he *did* succeed, but the first images he found were anatomical diagrams wherein the skin was omitted, in order to reveal internal organs.

I can tell you a Cashling has many internal organs indeed. Cashlings are, in fact, *distributed* creatures, which means they have more than one of almost everything. They do not, for example, have a single heart: they have several small hearts spread throughout their bodies, and the number varies with age. Babies begin with five working hearts, but develop additional ones as life goes on; by the time they reach puberty, they have twenty hearts pumping day and night, which makes them most energetic and a trial to their parents. From this circulatory peak, the hearts begin to shut down again, an average of one ceasing to beat every seven and a half years. When the last heart stops, so does the Cashling.

But hearts are not the only things Cashlings have in abundance—they also have numerous mouths. Some of these are attached to digestive systems, others to lungs, and still more to *stibbek* . . . long thin organs the size of one's little finger, designed to test what gases are currently in the air and to induce metabolic changes in response. Apparently, the Cashlings evolved on a world with great atmospheric variability: volcanoes belching sulfur, algae producing unusual effluvia, and plants exuding poisonous vapors in order to kill passing animals and thereby fertilize the soil with corpses. To cope with this, Cashlings developed *stibbek* as little chemical factories, constantly tasting the wind for threats and producing hormones to counteract the danger.

"Marvelously complex, ha-ha," said Dr. Havel . . . and he began to enthuse about Chemicals again.

Hmph!

The Outsides Of Aliens

While the doctor prattled, I examined the skinless anatomy pictures of the Cashlings. In one diagram, the creature looked squat and rounded like a toad; but in another, it was stretched tall and thin, like a pole with a multieyed head on top; and in a third, the Cashling appeared almost humanoid, with two fat arms and two fatter legs, though the legs were long and the torso short, so the hips were only a hand's breadth below the shoulders.

When I asked how there could be so much difference in one species, Festina explained their skeletal structure could shift into three distinct configurations. In the all-crouched-down position, most of the bones lay above the vital organs, shielding the body; it was a Defense Posture which made the Cashling much harder to injure than in other positions. The polelike configuration was nicknamed The Periscope—stretching twice as high as a human, the Cashling could raise its head above brush and other obstacles, in order to scan for danger or tasty things to eat. The drawback of both these arrangements was that the bones locked in place against each other, making it difficult for the Cashling to walk or even crawl. Therefore the third configuration, the high-waisted humanoid one, was most commonly used for every-day purposes. In this form, the Cashlings strutted about like Daddy Long-Legs, taking exaggerated strides that could cover distance quite speedily.

"Ha-ha, here we are," called Dr. Havel. He clicked a but-ton that changed the examination table's screen from the picture of me to a filmed panorama of several dozen Cash-lings. They looked quite different with their skins on . . . for their skins were every color of the rainbow, plus many other colors no self-respecting rainbow would dare exhibit.

Bright violets. Florid reds. Piercing blues.

Some were a single solid hue, and always fiercely eye-catching: flashing gold, burnished silver, gleaming bronze. Others were mottled with high-contrast tones, like orange and blue, or yellow and black. A few had stripes like tigers, but in garish colors a true tiger would consider beneath its dignity. Then there were others with swirling circular pat-terns starting as colored rings around their heads and twirling all the way down their bodies to end in fussy little curlicues on their toes. Only one figure in the picture showed any restraint, a creature who seemed snow white; but when Festina noticed me looking at that one, she said, "He's sure to be just as strongly colored as the rest, but in a frequency of light our eyes can't see. Infrared or ultravio-let—Cashling eyes perceive the widest visible spectrum of any race we know."

"But these Cashling ones are so *foolish*!" I said. "Hostile beings could see them from far far away."

Festina shrugged. "What hostile beings? Cashlings have tamed all the worlds they live on. No dangerous animals ex-cept in zoos . . . and of course, with the League of Peoples, no one has to worry about attacks from off-planet. Cashlings have no need to be circumspect, and they definitely don't want to." She waved a hand at the garish picture. "Some pri-mordial circuit in the Cashling brain is attracted to bright colors. Flashy is beautiful. Sexy. The same instinct as a lot of Terran birds. So for several dozen centuries, the most desirable mates have been the ones who look like a laser show. Over time, selective breeding, bioengineering, and cosmetic injections have made the whole damned populace fluorescent."

"But they are so ugly!" I said. "They are practically obscene."

"Don't say that to their faces. Cashlings are stupendously vain; if you insult them, they may decide not to broadcast our story."

"Then I will charm them most graciously," I answered. "I am excellent at winning the hearts of aliens, even when they are thoroughly repugnant."

Festina looked at me a moment, then broke into a grin. "You do have the knack," she said. "Come on, let's get ready for the broadcast."

A Temporary Nursery

We left Uclod and Lajoolie in the infirmary. They were talking to each other in low voices, Uclod sounding most trembly while Lajoolie spoke with soft calmness. The rest of us had no desire to interrupt such a conversation, and I for one was glad to get away. Each glance in their direction brought home the terrible reality of bereavement; and I did not wish to be reminded of that at all.

The place we went first was a room for Nimbus. He said he had nothing to contribute to our testimony against the High Council, and more importantly, he needed to minister unto baby Starbiter's needs. Therefore Festina took him to a passenger cabin which was tiny and cramped and blemished with hideous blue paint on the walls, but which had a full-service synthesizer that would let Nimbus obtain food and other necessities for the child. We tarried a moment to make sure he was properly settled in, then left him to his fatherly work.

Departing through the cabin door, we were forced to pass through a gritty black dust cloud swirling silently in the corridor. Festina said the cloud was a swarm of fierce microscopic machines, cousins to the Analysis Nano back in sick bay but designed to keep watch on Nimbus. If any speck of the mist man tried to sneak away from his body, tiny robots in the black cloud would swoop in, grab hold of the speck, and carry it off. The robots had been programmed not to damage Nimbus's component bits, for he was a sentient creature and therefore not to be killed . . . but apparently, the League of Peoples would not raise a fuss if all of Nimbus's individual particles were dissipated like fine dust throughout the ship, thereby preventing them from working together and doing harm.

Festina told me additional sentinel robots lurked in the ventilation ducts of Nimbus's cabin, and even in the plumbing and electrical outlets. This proved the cloud man was a closely watched prisoner, much less trusted than I . . . for I only had a single mook chaperoning me whereas Nimbus had *billions*. Hah!

My Mook

My mook was the sergeant, and he showed excellent taste—he left his two lesser mooks in the infirmary to watch Uclod and Lajoolie, but he went with me himself. That must be the chief reason to become sergeant: so you can assign yourself to monitor the most beautiful security risk.

The sergeant's name was Aarhus. When he finally took off his helmet, he proved to be a bearded man with hair the color of stone . . . by which I mean the yellow type of stone, not the gray, white, red, or brown types of stone which are also quite common, so perhaps I should have said he had hair like a goldfinch, except it was not that color at all. It was *exactly* the color of a pebble my sister once found on the beach, and *close* to the color of certain leaves in autumn, but not the sort of leaves that turn scarlet. So this tells all you need to know about Aarhus, except that he was tall, and he occasionally said odd things which might have been jokes but one never knew for sure.

The sergeant accompanied Festina and me as we pro-

ceeded toward the room where we would record our broadcast; and although he was not discourteous, his presence was
still a Burden. This was my first time alone with Festina
since we had been reunited, and there were many personal
subjects we might speak of . . . but not with a stranger dog-
ging our steps. In addition, I could not reveal my conversation with the Pollisand: bargaining with aliens is just the sort
of thing a keen-edged Security person might take amiss, believing me to have become a Tool Of Hostile Powers.

Festina clearly felt the same inhibitions as I, stifled under
the sergeant's gaze. Instead of relating how she had grieved
while believing me to be dead, or describing the joy she felt
to have me back, she seemed at a loss for words; after an
awkward silence, she simply began to name the rooms we
were passing. "Main Engine Room. Secondary Engine
Room. Hydroponics. Gravity generators . . ."

The lack of conversation might have been more tolerable
if I had been allowed to look into any of the rooms as we
passed. After all, the engines of a starship must be quite a
sight: great fiery furnaces tended by muscular persons with
sweat glistening over their rippling torsos. But every door
we passed remained shut and unwelcoming . . . until finally
one hissed open just ahead of us.

Festina and Aarhus halted—they must have assumed
someone was coming out into the corridor. When no one did,
they simply shrugged and started forward again; but I remained frozen where I was, for I had heard a familiar voice.

The voice was distressingly nasal, coming through the
open doorway. When the door began to hiss shut again, I
dashed forward and grabbed the edge of the sliding panel.
The door fought against me for a moment; then it grudgingly slid back into the wall.

"Hey," Aarhus said, "that's the main computer room. Off-
limits to civilians."

I ignored him. Striding into the room, I searched for the
source of the voice. It was coming from behind an array of
computers so tall and wide I could not see past them. I
could, however, hear the voice's words quite plainly: "What
did you think you were doing? Why didn't you test the code

first? Did you really think an undebugged program would work perfectly the first time?"

Festina grabbed my arm. "Oar, where are you going? What's wrong?"

"That is the Pollisand!" I whispered.

My friend's eyes grew wide. "Oh *fuck*!"

Then she and the sergeant sprinted forward.

15

WHEREIN I TAKE CHARGE OF OPENING DOORS

Logic Scum

We rounded the bank of computers at a run . . . then stopped in the face of chaos.

First, there was the Pollisand: exactly as I had seen him in the lava garden. Indeed, I could still detect reddish stains on his feet, obtained when he peevishly stomped the scarlet flowers. This was definitely the same creature I had met hours earlier . . . or else such a perfect copy I could not tell the difference.

The Pollisand was not the only one with crimson stains on his skin. In front of him stood a human dressed in dark brown attire: a woman whose flesh was dark brown too, except for the fingers of both hands. Those fingers were smeared a vivid red—not blood, but a scarlet dust that sifted off flakes whenever she moved. Speckles of that dust lay scattered across the floor at her feet . . . and red chalky fingerprints glowed on the access panels of the computer in front of·her.

Though those panels were shut, something bubbly leaked out around their edges: a charcoal gray foam, forcing itself through the seams of the computer's casing, trickling down the machine's exterior, and pattering onto the floor tiles. The glup had a musty smell, like human feet enclosed too long in stockings. When a clot of the stuff slopped down near the brown woman's boots, she jumped back fearfully as if the foam could hurt her.

"Bloody hell!" Festina said. Shoving the brown woman aside, my friend drove a kick into the junction between two of the computer's access panels. The kick must have snapped whatever locking mechanism held the panels in place; both doors swung open, propelled by great gouts of foam that had built up inside. Gray bubbles spilled and gushed to the floor, releasing such a wash of musty odor I nearly gagged.

"What is that?" I asked, feeling choked.

"Logic scum," Festina said. "Chunks of the ship's data get encoded in organic molecules: DNA, long chain polymers, stuff like that—then all those chemicals are packaged into a single living cell. A data bacterium. The only problem is that bacteria can be killed."

She nodded toward the red powder on the floor. "That's a chemical called Modig—a bio-poison that rips data bacteria to shit. This foam is the result: a slurry of bacterial corpses. All that's left of the logic circuits."

Festina booted another kick into the left access door, cracking it off its bottom hinge. The impact splashed back a flurry of foam that spattered onto the leg of her trousers. She retreated a quick step and shook her foot, endeavoring to throw off every speck of foam clinging to her pants. As she did so, she said, "Oar, break that panel off. Try to stay clear of the scum."

"Yes, Festina." I pulled down the sleeve of my jacket so it completely covered my hand, then slammed my forearm against the remaining hinge of the access door. The hinge was flimsy indeed—it broke with a <PING>, and the door flew several paces before clattering to the tiles. Sergeant Aarhus ran after it; snatching it up, he hurried back to the computer and began using the panel to shovel foam onto the floor. Although he still wore his armor, Aarhus flinched whenever the froth splashed against him.

"Is logic scum poison too?" I whispered to Festina.

"Not the scum itself," my friend said. "But mixed in with

the dead bacteria are traces of the Modig that killed them; and Modig is an utter bitch."

She glanced toward the woman in brown . . . particularly at the red dust on the woman's hands. The woman was looking at the dust too: lifting her hands in front of her eyes, staring at her crimson fingers. Bits of gray foam had begun to bubble from beneath the woman's fingernails—the same type of foam that was flooding from the computer, only this came from the woman herself. Festina opened her mouth as if to tell the woman something; then she shook her head. Turning away sharply, she headed in the opposite direction, toward a console at the far end of the computer bank.

The Pollisand Follows His Trade

"The circuits are shot," Aarhus said, still scooping foam out of the computer. "Electronics as well as biologicals. Must have been a feedback surge." He glanced at a label on top of the machine. "Unit 4A51," he told Festina. "What is it? Navigation? Engine control?"

Festina had reached the console. She bent over it, tapping buttons. "4A51 is the primary security module. Damn . . . the readout says it's in master mode."

Aarhus growled. "How the hell could she put it in master? Only the captain and the XO know the privileged access codes."

"Not true," Festina told him. "Admirals on the High Council know the codes too . . . or backdoors to get around the usual security. Obviously, some admiral ordered this woman to sabotage us, and gave her the codes to do it."

"But why did she follow such an order?" said a nasal voice. "And why so incompetently?"

We had forgotten about the Pollisand. He stood exactly where we had first seen him . . . but by some disquieting co-incidence, that position was conveniently out of the way of everything we had been doing. He had not been in the flight path of the panel I knocked across the room, nor Aarhus's rush to grab the panel, nor Festina's route to the control console. When the woman in brown stumbled back from the foam, the white headless creature had been just a bit to one side of her retreat.

As I looked around, I could not see a single other spot he could have settled himself without getting in the way of at least one of us. Yet he had put himself in that special location *before* we entered the room.

Deep in the creature's neck, one of his glowing eyes vanished for a moment—a Pollisandish wink. It was almost as if he were acknowledging the thought which had silently gone through my head . . . but I did not want to believe that, so I put it out of my mind.

Meanwhile, the Pollisand's words had drawn Festina's attention. She whirled on him, shouting, "What are you doing here? What do you want?"

"I want answers to my questions," he said, "but do I get them? Not bloody likely. Nobody ever has time to talk: it's always Crisis this and Emergency that, with everyone far too busy for civilized discourse. Bet it would be different if I *had a goddamned head*—but no, you're all so superior, constantly wearing hats and flaunting your peripheral vision, never mind how it eats me up inside, condemned forever to be cranially disadvantaged . . ."

He lifted his large foot and pointed toward the woman in brown, whose hands were now covered in foam that bubbled from her own skin. "Speaking of being eaten up inside," the Pollisand said, "this woman has thirty grams of Modig ripping her apart. You might want to deal with that before she dies of shock."

"Damn!" Festina said. Raising her voice, she called, "Ship-soul, attend. Tell Dr. Havel we have a severe case of Modig poisoning in the main computer room."

"Aye-aye, Admiral," a metallic voice answered from the ceiling.

"Hurray," Aarhus muttered, "the computer is still on-line."

"Don't celebrate too soon," the Pollisand told him.

The sergeant winced. "Why?"

"You'll see in seventy-two seconds."

"God damn it," Festina said, "quit being a know-it-all, and tell us something useful. What did this woman do, and how can we stop it?"

"You can't stop it," the Pollisand replied. "And what this woman did—by the way, her name is Zuni, if you care, which you don't, or you wouldn't need a complete stranger to introduce you to someone who's been under your command since the day you inherited this ship—but no, let's not waste time on civilities which are only the bedrock of society, what this woman, Zuni, that's still her name, even if you don't care about it, did . . ." The Pollisand took a breath. "What Zuni did was write a program she believed would let her override the captain's commands."

"Which explains why she put the system in master mode," Aarhus said. "If her program worked, she could set our course straight back to New Earth . . . and prevent anyone from changing it."

"But the program didn't work," the Pollisand told him. "Zuni didn't test it first: she just wrote it and ran it. Which clearly shows that *possessing* a head isn't the same as *using* it. (Not that I'm bitter.) What kind of programmer is so divorced from reality she thinks she'll get complex software right the first time? Especially when she's hacking the ship's most important security settings—"

"Look," Festina interrupted, "we'll discuss Zuni another time. Just tell us what the program did."

"It went out of control," the Pollisand said. "Romped off on its own, overwriting basic system code. She tried to rein it in from the console, but it had already stomped part of its own control settings; that's when she popped open a tube of Modig powder."

"Why was she carrying a vile red poison?" I asked. "Was she a secret assassin?"

"No," Festina answered, "it's navy policy to have some Modig available—precisely for situations where you've got a runaway computer and can't shut it down."

"It is better to turn off the power switch," I told her, "or to adjust the machine's mechanisms with an ax."

"Zuni didn't have an ax," the Pollisand said, "and the way

to turn off a power switch on this ship is to ask the computer to do it—which doesn't work if the computer is already fucked up the snout. Anyway, Modig is standard issue for last-ditch emergencies, and Zuni had been immunized against tiny exposures . . . but she should have known better than to scoop it up with her hands and smear it into the circuits. No immunization can protect a human from that much contact. Why would my poor Zuni do such a thing?"

"We'll ask her at the court-martial," Festina said. "Right now we have to figure out what's been damaged, what the runaway program did . . ."

The Pollisand's eyes flared brightly. "I can tell you that. It overrode the safeguards on Captain's Last Act."

"Oh shit!" Festina and Aarhus said in unison.

"What is Captain's Last Act?" I asked.

Festina's face looked pained. "If a crew is forced to abandon ship, it's the final command a captain gives . . . to make it impossible for outsiders to learn military secrets if they capture our equipment. Captain's Last Act means—"

The room lights suddenly went out.

"Doing some drastic Science thing that breaks all the ship's machines?" I asked.

"Good guess," Festina said.

Shutdown

The room had not been noisy—the computers operated with quiet hums rather than ventilatory hiss. But when the lights went out, the sound level dropped to complete silence, as soft whirs and purrs faded to nothingness. The gentle breeze caused by the ship's air circulation system grew still. A moment later, within the cores of all the machines, trickles of fluid began to drip, drip, drip, as if the circuits were bleeding.

"Look on the bright side," Aarhus said in the blackness. "At one time, the Admiralty wanted Captain's Last Act to cause a total self-destruct. Fortunately, the League wouldn't let navy ships sail around with their bellies full of explosive."

"So," Festina said, "instead of blowing ourselves up, we get to freeze in the dark. Goody."

A light clicked on from the direction of her voice. My friend held a thin wand that gave off a bright silver shine; the beam reflected off my hands, so that when I moved my arms, little patches of silver flashed across the floors and ceiling.

"I see you came prepared, Admiral," Aarhus said.

"In rank, I'm an admiral," Festina told him, "but at heart, I'm an Explorer. I don't go anywhere without a chemically powered light, a first-aid kit, and twenty meters of rope."

"Same things I carry on a first date." Aarhus dropped his gaze to the floor and asked, "Why do we still have gravity? The Higgs generators are surely off-line."

"They're more than off-line," Festina said. "The whole grav system is now a steaming pile of slag. Why *do* we have gravity?"

"Oh for heaven's sake," the Pollisand grumped. "Don't you know anything about your own ship?"

"Not really," Festina replied. "The navy likes to keep Explorers uninformed about ship operations—otherwise, we might realize how incompetent the regular crew members are."

"Same with Security," Aarhus said. "We only guard the ship, we don't push the buttons."

"And you wonder why your species hasn't evolved farther." The Pollisand raised his eyes heavenward in exasperation. The eyes cast dancing red glows across the dark ceiling. "Listen," he said, turning back to us, "just because your gravity *generators* go poof doesn't mean your gravity *field* does too. The field dissipates gradually—like heat when you turn off a furnace. Ten hours from now, you and your gear will be floating off the floor, but it doesn't happen all at once."

"Thank God for small mercies," Festina muttered. "And speaking of mercy," she said to the Pollisand, "I don't suppose a technically brilliant entity like yourself would help resurrect some of *Hemlock*'s basic ops?"

"Never!" said the Pollisand in shocked tones. "How will you lesser creatures learn to take care of yourselves if you don't face the consequences of your actions? Hardship builds character . . . and I'm sure you'll build a lot in the next few hours. Ta-ta, y'all."

He lifted a front paw high and flipped off a salute from where his forehead would have been if he possessed one. A moment later, his body exploded into a million pinpricks of light; they scattered in all directions, making zings and whistles as they disappeared through the walls. Then the room fell quiet again, with a conspicuous absence of Pollisand where he had just been standing.

"Ooo," said Festina. "Showy."

We all nodded silently.

Knock-Knock

Our contemplative silence was interrupted by a crashing noise from the other side of the computer bank. In the blink of an eye, Festina dived to the ground, rolled along the tiles, and ended on her feet again. Her hands came up clenched into fists. Somewhere during her dive, she had dropped the glow-wand; it lay a short distance from her feet, casting strong upward shadows across her features.

The sound came again: a smash that echoed through the quiet computer room. Festina grabbed up the light and disappeared around the bank of dead machines. The sergeant and I ran after her; we were just turning the corner when we heard a third kaboom. It was someone battering against the closed door to the hallway, an unknown person trying to bash through. Already the door had a conspicuous bend in it, though it was made of metal and appeared to be moderately thick.

One more whump and the top of the door snapped out of its frame. It sagged slightly inward, but not far enough to reveal who was hammering on the other side. I quickly assumed an aggressive stance in case the intruders should prove to be enemies—perhaps the Shaddill had invaded the ship now that we had no defenses. Festina, however, had put down her fists, and Aarhus was making no effort to prepare for attack. They simply stood warily, clear of the doorway, waiting for whoever came through.

Something struck the door with a fierce thud. The mangled metal could not withstand this final impact—it collapsed completely, propelled by a muscular body that fell forward with the door onto the floor tiles.

Lajoolie looked up, blinking in the beam of Festina's light. Behind her, Uclod and Dr. Havel peeked around the edge of the door frame; the watery-eyed physician held a shining wand exactly like Festina's. Smiling down at Lajoolie, Havel said, "Nothing like a Tye-Tye, ha-ha, when you have to make a house call. Someone reported a poisoning?"

Medical Matters

The doctor hurried off to examine the woman in brown . . . or perhaps I should call her Zuni, though I do not know if she deserves to be dignified with a name. This Zuni was a spy and saboteur; I did not quite understand what she had tried to do or what she accomplished instead, but the end result was readily apparent. There was no light in the hallway, and no machinery sounds either. "It appears," said I, "this vessel has slain itself."

"Yes," Havel called from the other side of the computer bank, "the *Hemlock* has taken hemlock, ha-ha."

If that was a joke, no one laughed. I asked, "Do all starships have suicidal tendencies? Because I have only ridden in two such vessels, and both have killed themselves within hours of my coming on board. This constitutes a Disturbing Pattern . . . and I should like to point out *I am not to blame*."

"Don't get defensive," Festina said, patting my shoulder. "If anyone here is a trouble magnet, it's me."

She turned to check on the others. Uclod was helping Lajoolie stand up after bashing the door. He did not provide much practical assistance—since his head only came to her wallabies, he could not actually pull her up to her full height—but she held on to his hand anyway and tried not to look too encumbered by him as she got to her feet.

"Are you okay, sweetie?" Uclod asked. His voice had a ragged edge to it and his eyes were ringed with red, but it seemed he had finished weeping over his grandmother . . . at least for the moment. Lajoolie did not answer the little man's question, but she pressed his hand softly to her stomach.

"All right," Festina said, "let's get to the bridge and see what the captain can do about this mess. Havel," she called, "do you need any help?"

"No, Admiral, not right now," came a reply from the other side of the computer bank. "Eventually we'll have to carry the patient to sick bay . . ."

"I'll send you some stretcher bearers," Festina said, "but I don't know if sick bay is any better than here. Captain's Last Act will have killed all your medical equipment."

"Oh dear, yes," Havel said. "Then maybe, ha-ha, it's best if we stay away from the infirmary. The place is swarming with Analysis Nano, and without the ship-soul controlling them . . . well, the eager little devils may get out of hand. There was a case on Morrikeen where a clinic's power went down and every last nanite decided to give the attending physician a blood test. Sucked the poor fellow dry, ha-ha."

"Ha-ha indeed," Festina said. "And here I thought our only alternatives were freezing to death or starvation. I love it when new options thrust themselves forward." She made a face. "Come on—let's find the captain."

Forging Forward

It turns out a starship has many many doors—which Sergeant Aarhus claimed were not doors at all but *hatches*. Festina said I could still call them doors; she reveled in the use of antinautical terms, because it vexed the ship's normal crew. (She called regular crew members Vac-heads, which may or may not have been because they spent their lives sailing through vacuum.)

Many of the hatch-doors were closed, and most were exceedingly stronger than the one Lajoolie had broken. The biggest doors were designed to remain secure despite vast extremes of air pressure; so thick, even I had no chance of smashing through. Fortunately, such violence was not required—though the doors no longer opened automatically, they contained Cunningly Concealed Mechanisms that allowed manual operation via wheels and cranks. Once Festina showed me how these devices worked, I got to turn *all* the wheels . . . which I did most prettily, ensuring our party's speedy progress toward the bridge.

We were not the only persons desirous of making contact with the captain. As we moved forward through the ship, numerous crew members peeked out of doorways, saw who we were, and joined our company. The newcomers did not speak; I do not know if they were intimidated by my beauty, Festina's rank, or Uclod's orangeness, but they seemed as shy as woodland creatures, keeping their distance yet mutely following.

This muteness struck me as foolish. If I had not already known this darkness was the result of a complicated computer tragedy, I should have been asking, "What happened? What happened?" But then, I was not such a one as greatly revered machines. Perhaps these humans were so cowed by the demise of their ship, they had plunged into grief-stricken mourning.

Or perhaps they were not so much wallowing in sorrow as silently giddy with excitement. It is Eerily Thrilling to walk through soundless corridors when your only illumination is a tiny wand of silver, and the blackness stretches for light-years in all directions. You feel that anything could happen . . . and even if there is danger afoot, it will be vastly preferable to lying on the floor with a Tired Brain.

Having a perilous adventure is always better than comatose safety. Always, always, always, always, always.

In The Halls

I did not know how many hatches stood between us and the bridge . . . but I could tell when I opened the last. As I pushed back the great thick door, I saw light on the other side and heard voices talking in subdued tones. Five crew members had gathered in the corridor to listen to a sixth person: a dark-skinned man in a powder blue suit.

He stood slightly apart from the others as he spoke to them, and he held a glow-wand just like Festina's. At the moment I opened the hatch, he was gesturing with the wand, pointing in our direction. The waving light made shadows leap along the corridor walls in a manner delightfully creepy. However, the man stopped waving as soon as he saw our party.

"Admiral!" he said—in a voice not loud but fervent. "I don't suppose you know what happened?"

"A saboteur," Festina told him. "Hacked the ship-soul into committing Captain's Last Act. I'm afraid the ship is . . ."

"EMP'd to rat-shit from bow to stern," the blue-suited man finished her sentence. "That's what Captain's Last Act means." He gave Festina a rueful smile. "At my court-martial, you'll testify I didn't do it, right, Admiral?"

"Of course, Captain . . . if any of us lives that long."

I looked at the man again. This must be Captain Kapoor, who spoke to us earlier on the intercom. He did not impress me much as a Figure Of Authority: he was shorter than I, with thinning black hair and a poorly shaped mustache. I am not well-informed on the subject of mustaches—my own people do not grow true hair, we merely have the suggestion of hair as part of our solid glass skulls—but if *I* were to possess a mustache, I would endeavor to carve it with bilateral symmetry instead of letting it become an unkempt blob of fur that appears to be sliding off the left edge of one's lips.

Still, this Kapoor man did not seem *totally* foolish. He had happy crinkles around the edges of his eyes as if he must laugh a lot . . . and for all the tension that filled the air, he did not seem snappish or stressed. Indeed, one could argue he was altogether too blasé about the situation, considering that his ship *had* been disastrously incapacitated in the depths of Unforgiving Space.

"I suppose you'll be wanting a status report," he said to Festina. "Well, Admiral . . . the status is that everything's Gone Oh Shit."

Many of the crew members looked confused at his words.

I, however, knew that "Going Oh Shit" was an Explorer expression meaning dead, dead, dead. It derived from the fact that many Explorers blurt out, "Oh shit," just before some terrible calamity befalls them. I suppose Kapoor used the phrase to show Festina he was familiar with Explorer vernacular . . . which means the captain was sucking up to the admiral, but I thought he did it most charmingly.

"Everything's gone?" Festina asked. "What about communications?"

"*Especially* communications," Kapoor answered. "Those systems have all kinds of top-secret crypto built into them: not just for encoding transmissions, but for switching bands a few hundred times a second, so we're never broadcasting in one place very long. And then there's the—" He stopped and threw a reproachful look at those of us who were not navy persons. "Ahem. I'm sure you know, Admiral, *Hemlock* has all kinds of gadgetry for keeping our messages secure, and one hundred percent of it is classified. Captain's Last Act makes certain no such equipment can be salvaged. Nothing but melted plastic and defunct biomass."

"But that can't be your only broadcasting stuff," Uclod said. "At the very least, you must have a Mayday signal, right? Something that runs off batteries and doesn't get vaporized when everything else goes pfft. Civilian vessels have to carry at least three Mayday boxes in case of emergency. So a navy ship must surely . . ." He stopped; his eyes narrowed, glaring at Kapoor. "You don't have a working Mayday?"

"Of course we do," the captain replied defensively. "Just not a *good* one. The Outward Fleet doesn't like distress calls that can be heard by absolutely anybody—it's bad publicity to advertise how often navy ships break down. Even worse, the laws of salvage say the first person to find us gets to claim the whole cruiser. The Admiralty doesn't want a civilian vessel, or even worse an alien, tracking us by our distress signal, taking our ship in tow, and dragging *Royal Hemlock* home to use as a lawn ornament. So . . . our Mayday only broadcasts to other navy ships."

"Ouch," Uclod said.

"*Very* ouch," Festina agreed. "The last thing we want is to tell the Admiralty we're stuck adrift. They'll send one of their dirty-trick ships to pick us up, and that's the last anyone will see of us."

Uclod made a disgusted sound. "So you don't have a single useful signaling device?"

Kapoor shrugged. "The ship's escape modules are perfectly fine. They all have homing beacons . . . but they're old-fashioned radio. From here, it would take five years for transmissions to reach the closest inhabited planet. As for using the escape modules for travel—they don't have FTL capability. They can put you into stasis so you won't feel time passing, but it'll be almost a century before you get back to civilization."

"Fat chance of that," Uclod said. "With the Shaddill still in the neighborhood, we won't get back to civilization at all . . . especially not in rinky-dink emergency capsules with their beacons blaring, *Here I am!*" He leaned back against the wall and closed his eyes. "We are right royally fucked."

Festina stared at him a moment, then turned her gaze to the captain. Kapoor only shrugged. "We can check all the systems to see if anything survived, but Captain's Last Act is intended to be one hundred percent thorough. It even hits the storerooms that contain our spare parts. We can't repair a thing."

"So," Festina said, "how long can we last without life support?"

"I don't know," the captain said. He turned to the crew members around him. "Anyone here ever calculated how long the oxygen in a heavy cruiser lasts with a half-crew breathing it?"

Nobody answered.

"Well, Admiral," Kapoor turned back to Festina, "if this were a VR adventure, the captain would put on a somber face and say we've got twenty-four hours before the oxygen runs out. Damned if I know if that's anywhere close—could be two hours, could be two hundred—but let's go with dramatic tradition till our lungs tell us otherwise."

"Just bloody wonderful," Uclod said. "If twenty-four

hours is anywhere close to correct, we'd better whip off a Mayday now. Even at that, we'll be lucky to find a navy vessel close enough to reach us in time."

"But," I said, "there are many navy ships back at Melaquin, and that is not so far away."

"Missy," Uclod told me, "that is a *whole heap* too far away. When my dear baby Starbiter left Melaquin, she was traveling ten times faster than anything the human navy can do . . . and she held that speed for something like six hours, not to mention however far *Hemlock* has gone since picking us up. Those ships back at Melaquin can't get to us in less than two and a half days; and I doubt if the Outward Fleet has any ships nearer. We're a long way past the Technocracy's usual stomping grounds—it'll be a pure fluke if anyone gets to us in time."

"It's not quite that bad," Festina said. "The escape pods can put us into stasis and keep us alive indefinitely. When we run out of air here in the main ship, we'll turn on our Mayday, ditch into the evac modules, and wait for someone to pick us up. But once we're in stasis, we're *really* sitting ducks . . . so let's hold off on that while we try to solve our problem."

"Festina," I said as softly as I could, "what is our problem exactly? What is our Goal?"

She gazed at me a moment . . . and I wondered if she was mentally phrasing her answer in comprehensible words, or if she was debating why she should bother explaining the situation to such a grossly ignorant person. In many cases, Science-Oriented People respond dismissively toward those not of the Science faith—especially when the Science-Oriented People have decided that only extra special Science can save them.

But Festina was not cruel. After a few seconds, she answered, "We need a way to call for help. But all our equipment is either broken or it calls the wrong people." She smiled. "I don't suppose you have a trans-light communicator in your back pocket, do you?"

I patted the pockets of the Explorer jacket. They all felt

empty. "It seems I do not have such a device; but I know where to get one."

"New Earth," Uclod said gloomily.

"There is one much closer than that," I told him. "In Nimbus's cabin."

"In . . ." Festina stopped as she realized what I meant.

"Zaretts," I said, "have the ability to make long-distance broadcasts. And we have an infant Zarett."

Without waiting for an answer, I headed off. I had been official communications officer on Starbiter Senior; I intended to assume the same role with Starbiter Junior.

16

WHEREIN I ACQUIRE NEW FAMILY

Black Goo

Outside Nimbus's room, there was no sign of the black clouds that had been guarding him. However, the floor was smeared with a black goo that looked exceedingly yucky; I did not want to step in it, for fear it would stick to my feet.

Festina stared down at the gunk on the floor and whistled softly. "Looks like Captain's Last Act cooks defense nano."

"Good thing too," Captain Kapoor said. "The defense clouds are controlled by the ship-soul; with the computers off-line, you'd have billions of hunter-killer nano-bots flying around without supervision. Thank heavens we don't have to worry about that."

"Don't speak too soon," Festina said. "We haven't told you about sick bay. Now stand back if you please, Captain, and let an Explorer put her foot in it."

She stepped carefully onto the awful black deposit, tapping it a few times with her toe before setting down her full weight. "Not sticky," she said. Experimentally, she pushed her foot a short distance across the black surface. "Not slippery either." She glanced back at the rest of us. "Considering my usual luck, this is where the cloud suddenly rises from the floor and chews the meat from my bones."

But no such horror occurred. Instead, Festina moved to the

door of the cabin and smashed the heel of her palm against a little plastic patch in the very middle. I had been told that one touched such patches in order to request admittance; I had not been told one could bash in the cover plate and manipulate the exposed mechanisms so as to open the door manually. It made me wonder if Lajoolie had been wasting her strength when she broke down the door of the computer room . . . but then, Lajoolie was not a navy person and therefore did not know the intricacies of the *Hemlock*'s hatches.

Anyway, I am sure she found it far more satisfying to bludgeon a door out of its frame than to twiddle tiny gears until something went click. There is far too little bludgeoning in the human navy.

A Great Fright

After Festina worked her trick with the lock, she could easily pull the door open. To my surprise, the cabin appeared empty; baby Starbiter nestled securely on a padded chair, but there was no sign of Nimbus. "Where has he gone?" I cried.

"Check if the floor's sticky," Uclod said bitterly. "Maybe whatever zapped the defense nanites took out Nimbus too."

"Is that possible?" I asked in Great Consternation.

Festina shook her head. "I don't think so. Zaretts are made of biological components; nano is mechanical."

"On a microscopic scale," Uclod said, "how much difference does it make? Both Nimbus and the nanites are just fancy organic molecules."

"So are we," Festina replied. "And we're still alive."

"We're natural creatures," Uclod told her. "Nimbus wasn't."

"You're not natural," Festina said. "The whole Freep species was bioengineered."

"We're a minor variation on natural Divian stock—just a few tweaks away from the original. But the Shaddill created Nimbus from scratch. God knows, his components may have been closer to nanites than real living cells. We should check for smears on the rug."

"Husband," said Lajoolie. "Hush." She turned to the rest

of us apologetically. "He's still distressed about his grand-mother. Pay no attention."

She gave a reassuring smile . . . but it had no effect on the butterflies fluttering in my stomach. Until now, I had never quite grasped that Nimbus was an artificial being: built by the Shaddill as a gift to the Divian people, just as my own race had been built as a gift to ancient Earthlings. Surely Nimbus and I possessed similar design features, with many DNAs and other Chemicals in common—were we not both transparent, clear and colorless? So in a way, we were brother and sister by virtue of our Shaddillish origins.

And now my brother might be dead? As lifeless as the black nano-things coating the floor like soot? What was wrong with this universe, that so many people kept dying?

Feeling scared and angry, I strode across the black residue encrusting the carpet, straight into the cloud man's cabin. "Nimbus!" I cried. "Come out right away! Do not make us think you died from some foolish Science not even intended for you. Where have you gone, you poop-head cloud?"

For a moment, I sensed no response. Then, with a great whoosh, mist poured through a ventilator grid high up on one wall. The fog circled me once, a thick stream impossible to feel through my jacket; then it swept toward baby Star-biter and coalesced into the shape of a ghostly man seated on the infant's chair.

"I'm back," said Nimbus. "What's the problem?"

"You went away!" I was most furious with him for the fright he had given us. "You foolishly left; you abandoned your child! Whom you are supposed to take care of, so oth-ers do not have to. We are not such ones as know which hy-drocarbons are best for a Zarett of tender years."

"Sorry to upset you," Nimbus said without sounding sorry *at all*, "but I went to see what was happening. The power died, and I heard a sort of crackle in the ventilator; when I investigated, I found my nanite guards were all settling out of the air, dead as dandruff. I decided I'd try to find someone to ask what was happening, but . . ." A ripple went through his body. "I got lost in the air ducts."

"You got lost?" I asked. "That is most irresponsible, you

foolish cloud, when certain persons might choose to worry about you. Persons such as Uclod and Lajoolie. And little Starbiter. But not me, not even a little bit."

"It was pitch black everywhere," Nimbus said. "I couldn't tell where I was till I heard you hollering."

"I was not hollering!" I cried. "I never ever—"

Festina stopped me by laying her fingers lightly on my arm. "Hush. He's fine. I was worried too."

The Howls Of Infants

"Now, Nimbus," Festina said, turning to the cloud man, "we've been sabotaged. Disabled. And we don't have the right equipment for sending a Mayday. We were wondering if the little girl . . ." She took a moment to smile fondly at the baby snuggled inside Nimbus's body; then her smile faltered. "I was going to ask if Starbiter could send out a Mayday for us. But now that I look at her, she's so small . . . is she old enough to broadcast FTL messages?"

Nimbus did not answer immediately. The mist of his body rolled like steam from a fiercely boiling pot. Finally he said, "The ability to broadcast is present from birth; but she's far too young to control it. The situation is similar to newborn children of your own species—they have well-developed vocal cords, but they certainly can't talk intelligibly."

"Starbiter does not need to talk intelligibly," I said. "All she must do is cry. If we cause her to weep in a plaintive manner, will it not catch the attention of ships traveling nearby? And do not pretend she cannot wail, for it is the nature of babies to make such noises."

Behind me, someone made precisely the type of noise I had just described. The sound did not come from little Starbiter; it came from Lajoolie, who was looking most alarmed. "You don't mean . . ." she said. "But you don't want to hurt her . . . you wouldn't . . ."

"I do not know so much about babies," I told her, "for I have only learned about them from the teaching machines in my village. However, it should not be necessary to cause the child pain—just to frighten her to the point where she cries out."

"Oar," Festina said, "can we think about this a minute?"

"Of course," I replied. "We must think very hard how to produce an appropriate amount of terror. My own suggestion would be to create a large fire and drop the child into the middle . . . for it turns out Zaretts fear blazing infernos but are not at all harmed by the heat. If we are lucky, the flames will actually bestow Starbiter with excellent invigorating energies, so her cries will carry farther. Is that not a clever scheme?"

I looked around proudly, believing I would receive heartfelt congratulations from those assembled . . . but I did not see the expected expressions of approval. Indeed, the Vachead crew members appeared horrorstruck. Meanwhile, Lajoolie had covered her face with her hands and Uclod wore a scowl so fierce, one might think he wished to punch somebody.

"What is it?" I asked. "What?"

Festina took me by the arm and led me from the room.

I Am Ignominiously Berated

It seems humans have a foolish taboo against setting infants on fire. Festina took me down the hall and explained this to me in low but intense tones. It does not even matter whether the flames actually hurt the child; this is simply a thing which must not be done.

I tried to tell her the situation was different on Melaquin. Immersing oneself in fire is actually a pleasant experience: it causes no harm or pain, and surrounds one with tasty toasty light. Moreover, it burns off the dirt and stains one inevitably acquires from daily activities. One can have too much of a good thing—flames tend to dry out the skin—but to anyone of my species, a session of self-immolation combines the virtues of a hot bath with a good meal.

Was it not the same for Starbiter? Who was also a Shaddill creation, and who was also nourished by flame? Though she might initially fear to be immersed in fire, was that not just the fussiness of a baby who did not like to try new foods?

Festina said this might all be true, but there were Lines One Does Not Cross. Therefore I must not suggest my plan again, for fear that persons who did not know me would think me a horrible monster.

I almost said, *I do not care what others think.* But that would not be true. I did not want Festina to consider me a bad person, nor did I wish to be despised by Uclod or Lajoolie. I especially did not want Nimbus believing I intended to harm his child . . . for if he and I were siblings in Shaddillhood, I did not wish to alienate his affections.

In my youth, I had often contemplated how much I would like to have a brother—even when I did not always like having a sister. A brother would be different and *interesting*: a comrade rife with maleness, but with no lustful urges to complicate the friendship and ultimately make one sad. I would, of course, have to persuade the cloud man to view me as a sister . . . but were we not partway there already? Back in Starbiter he had tried to boss me around, and I had responded with instant resentment; therefore we were practically family, and all that remained was for him to acknowledge it.

Besides, if Nimbus was my brother, that would make me young Starbiter's Auntie. The thought of that pleased me most greatly.

Auntie Oar. It had an *excellent* ring.

My Induction

"I shall do as you wish, Festina," I said. "In future, I shall not suggest putting babies into fire—not even a little fire that would make the child stronger and healthier than before. However, we still need Starbiter to cry, do we not? So we must find another method of inducement. What would be more palatable to Earthling tastes? Shaking her fiercely? Jabbing her with pins? Piling weighty objects on top of her?"

Festina glared at me a moment, then broke into a grudging laugh. "All right, Oar, I see your point. I've been letting my human prejudices get in the way of figuring out how to treat an alien. And I should know better—I run around pretending to be a hard-headed Explorer, but you're the one who's unflinchingly practical."

"I am excellent at unflinching practicality," I told her. "I would also be excellent as an Explorer."

As evidence for this statement, I held up the coattails of my jacket. Perhaps there is more to being an Explorer than wearing black clothes, but I have never noticed anything else. And the jacket fit very well.

"You're right," Festina said, "you *would* make a good Explorer. If nothing else, you're bulletproof." She took a deep breath. "By the power vested in me as a duly appointed admiral of the Outward Fleet, I hereby grant you the rank of cadet in the Technocracy Explorer Corps. That is, if you accept the position."

"Of course I accept the position. I have been oppressed and exploited by so many Explorers, it is high time I was empowered to do the same to others. When do I receive my stun-pistol?"

"Uh, later," Festina replied. "Much later. It's time we got back to the others."

So that is what we did.

The Compactification Of A Cloud

When we returned to Nimbus's cabin, the cloud man had shrunk to a shadow of his former self . . . which is to say, he had compressed his little flying bits into a much tighter ball around the baby Starbiter. Father and child combined were now just the size of my fists pressed together; the outer Nimbus-y shell looked as hard and dense as quartz.

"Why is he like that?" I demanded. "What did you do?"

"Nothing," Captain Kapoor replied. "He just suddenly clumped down around the kid as solid as a rock. Maybe to protect his daughter from getting thrown in a bonfire." The frowzy captain gave me an accusatory glare.

"No one is getting thrown into a bonfire," Festina said. "If that's what you're worried about, Nimbus, you can let the little girl go."

We all stared at the rock, waiting for some response. Humans must have slower metabolisms than I, for they were still waiting patiently when I cried, "He is just doing this to vex me! He is acting obnoxiously as a blatant plea for attention!"

"Well, he's got *my* attention," Festina said. "He looks like an egg."

She smiled to show she was joking, then knelt beside the chair that held both Nimbus and Starbiter. "Hey," she said to the condensed cloud man, "we won't hurt your daughter, I promise. But we'd like her to send a distress call, if that's physically possible. The call doesn't have to be loud—the Cashlings on Jalmut have some of the best communications technology in our sector, so they'll hear the tiniest peep."

Festina paused; there was no sign that Nimbus was listening. "You know our situation," she said, still using a soft persuasive voice. "At this second, the Shaddill are out of commission, and unfriendly elements of the navy are far away . . . so we've got a window of opportunity to call for help from someone else. If we leave it too long, though, the Shaddill might get themselves repaired; and you can be damned sure the Admiralty has already dispatched one of their dirty-trick ships to track us down. Then there's the added complication that we'll soon use up all of our oxygen. Baby Starbiter may not care, since she's designed to survive in space, but the rest of us are air-breathing. Including you, Nimbus. Sooner or later, you're going to get woozy . . . which means you'll pass out when your daughter needs you most, unless we call for help *now*."

To me, this was excellent logic; but Nimbus remained stony in the face of Festina's arguments. I wanted to poke him (quite gently, with a finger), but did not know how others would view such an action. Anyway, I doubted if prodding would have much effect—the cloud man appeared to be as unresponsive as granite. At last, Festina grimaced and stepped away from him.

"All right," she said, "we aren't accomplishing much here. Captain, any ideas to propose?"

The captain man, Mr. Kapoor, ran a hand through his almost nonexistent hair. "Just to go through the motions," he said, "we should check ship's stores, in case some spare parts didn't get zapped. There's a minuscule chance we can throw together a makeshift communicator—at least something good enough to send a public SOS."

"Very well," Festina told him, "let's hope we're lucky. And while you're doing that, I'll make a quick run around the ship and gather the rest of the crew. Where's the best place for them to assemble? Down near the storerooms?"

Kapoor nodded. "That's as good as any."

"Fine, Captain, carry on. Oh, and please send two people to Dr. Havel in the main computer room. He's got a casualty who'll need to be transported someplace safe."

"Aye-aye, Admiral."

The captain moved his hand in a manner reminiscent of a salute (provided one had a high capacity for reminiscing). As he and his collection of crew members moved off down the hallway, Festina turned to Uclod, Lajoolie, and me. "One of us should stay with Nimbus," she said. "To talk to him if he decides to come out of his shell."

"I shall do that," I said. As his somewhat-sister, it was my obligation to attend to the cloud man's needs; and of course, to berate him for his churlish behavior as soon as nonfamily persons had departed the room.

"I'll stay too," Lajoolie piped up hastily, speaking with uncharacteristic urgency. She must have believed I might do the cloud man an injury if left alone with him . . . which just goes to show what unjust suspicions arise when one conducts oneself in a Forthright Manner.

Festina turned to Uclod. "What about you? Do you want to stay here or come with me for a once-around-the-ship?"

The little man threw a glance at Lajoolie, then turned back to Festina. "I'll go with you. Uncle Oh-God would rip off my ears if I let you go wandering with no one to watch your back."

He reached out quickly, grabbed Lajoolie's hand, and gave it a quick squeeze. Then he and Festina vanished out the door, leaving the rest of us on our own.

17

WHEREIN I AM SWALLOWED BY DARKNESS

Alone In The Dark

If you have been paying attention—and for your sake, I hope you have, so when persons of High Social Standing accost you in the street, saying, "Have you read Oar's book?" you will be able to answer, "Yes, especially the part where she and Lajoolie were left alone with Nimbus"—if you have been paying attention, you will realize our party had only possessed two glow-wands. One belonged to the captain, the other to my friend Festina; therefore, when the captain departed in one direction and Festina went the other, Lajoolie and I were left with a conspicuous absence of light.

Also a conspicuous absence of food. I *still* had not eaten a bite in the past four years, and being in the dark always makes me famished. Quite literally. Especially an enclosed darkness without even the tiny sustenance of starshine. If I did not get food or light soon, I would lapse into the torpid state that befalls my species when deprived of the necessities of life. It had only happened to me once, when I drowned in a great river and remained stuporous under dark water until the current washed me ashore . . . but I did not enjoy the experience, and was keen not to repeat it.

Therefore, to conserve energy I settled myself onto the

floor and attempted to relax every muscle. Lajoolie must have heard me moving, for she asked, "What are you doing?"

"Saving my strength," I said.

"For what?"

"To avoid enforced hibernation. I do not suppose you have any foodstuffs with you? It could even be opaque if that was all you had."

"Sorry," Lajoolie said. "When the captain or admiral gets back, you can ask them for something. The ship's food synthesizers won't be working, but I understand there's a hydroponics facility; that's a place that grows fresh produce."

"I know what a hydroponics is," I told her untruthfully. "I was taught such things in school. Also the elevenses table."

"You went to school?" Lajoolie asked. "I always thought your planet was . . . well . . ."

"Filled with ignorant savages who knew absolutely nothing?"

"Sorry," Lajoolie said.

It was the second time she had said, "Sorry," in the past minute . . . and she had a most abject manner of saying it. I could not see her in the dark, but the way she spoke, I imagined her dropping her head in a posture of crushed self-esteem. Of course, Lajoolie might actually be making rude gestures at me in the blackness; but I did not think so.

I am not such a one as beats around the bush when a person's behavior puzzles me. "Is there something wrong with you, Lajoolie?" I asked. "Are you psychologically damaged in some way, or do you simply act submissive to put others off their guard? I think it most strange that a muscular woman should constantly quail before the eyes of others, or feign an aura of fragility when she is clearly not fragile at all. Was your spirit broken somehow or is this simply a sham, wherein you pretend to be dainty for some foolish alien reason?"

Off in the darkness, Lajoolie began to cry.

Lajoolie's Tears

I had never imagined I would make her weep. Though I am clever and warm and most well-intentioned, it turns out I am not always adept at saying the right things to people. As you must know by now, I have not had a great deal of experience in social circumstances; I spent much of my early life with no one to talk with but my sister, and she *never* burst into tears. At least not until the Explorers came.

So perhaps there are times when my words have an adverse effect. I do not mean to be upsetting; but sometimes it happens, and then I am upset too. It is quite most dismaying to find you have accidentally hurt someone's feelings. I never intend that *ever*. And it is just too bad that some people (especially alien people) are so unexpectedly *vulnerable*.

I never intend to be cruel.

Though I had wanted to conserve my remaining energy, I rose immediately and let myself be guided by the sound of Lajoolie's whimpers: shuffling blindly through the darkness until I could wrap her in my arms. When I did, the big woman did not push me away. She was seated on the cabin's unused bed, so I sat beside her and let her sob into my jacket.

After a time, when her tears began to ease, I murmured, "Why are you crying, foolish one? Tell me, and I shall try to make it better."

"It's just . . ." Lajoolie whispered. "It's just . . ." She succumbed to more sniffles.

"Come," I said, "let us talk about this. I inquired whether you were mentally disturbed, and then you began all this fuss. Does that mean you *are* emotionally damaged? You have been tormented and abused?"

"No," she answered in a small voice. "I was never abused." Sniffle, sniffle. "By anyone." Sniffle, sniffle. "But you thought . . . you said I was putting on an *act,* pretending to be . . . something I'm not. And I *am* putting on an act, but I must be terrible at it if I can't fool some *alien* who's only known me a few hours."

"Ah, but I am more perceptive than most of the universe.

Especially the parts of the universe that are vacuum." I paused. "What precise type of act are you putting on?"

She did not answer right away. I was beginning to realize Lajoolie never did *anything* right away; she preferred to ruminate at length before committing herself to action. At last, however, she said in a low voice, "Have you heard of arranged marriages?"

"Of course," I told her. "They are a narrative device found in works of fiction—designed to explain why persons who lust after each other cannot consummate their passion until the end of the book."[10]

"Arranged marriages aren't just fictitious, Oar. They're quite popular in some cultures."

"Popular with whom?" I asked. "Those who rent rooms for illicit affairs?"

Lajoolie tried to pull away from me, but I held on. She stopped struggling after a moment, but said most angrily, "This isn't about affairs, Oar! It's not about sex at all."

"Then what is it about?"

"It's about . . . oh, you'll never understand."

"Do you believe me stupid or deficient in some way? Or is it that you think an alien can never comprehend your niceties of emotion?"

"I don't mean that. I just . . ."

"Tell me," I said. "Tell me everything, and I shall be a sympathetic listener. Or if I am not a sympathetic listener, you can say to yourself, *I was right that Oar cannot understand.* Then you will feel better for being correct all along, and you will find you have stopped crying."

---

[10] I hope you are not surprised that I was familiar with Tales of Romantic Longing. Under the tutelage of the teaching machines in my village, I learned much more than arithmetic and the social graces. Indeed, there was a time when my planet had a thriving literature, rife with tales of Star-Crossed Lovers Separated By Fate . . . who either pined in stoic silence their whole lives or else threw caution to the winds and thereby precipitated great social upheavals, but either way ended tragically mere inches from each other in the same Ancestral Tower, with their brains too Tired to realize they were together at last.

Her next sniffle sounded slightly like a laugh . . . and in time, with many Lajoolie-like pauses, she explained her Dire Position.

On Being A Wide Woman

According to Lajoolie, all Divian men (including Tye-Tyes, Freeps, and myriad other sub-breeds) are attracted to females with broad shoulders. There is an evolutionary reason for this liking—in ancient days, muscular bodies indicated good health and breeding potential—but that is not what Divian men think about when they slaver over the width of a woman; they simply think how fine it would be to nuzzle such luxuriant flesh.

Therefore, Tye-Tye women are much in demand on Divian worlds. Tye-Tyes were originally engineered to live on a planet with high gravitation, so they had to be inordinately strong just to keep moving; but after Tye-Tyes were created, Divian men from other breeds took one look at the muscular Tye-Tye women and went most thoroughly goggle-eyed.

Though slavery had been outlawed for centuries, non-Tye-Tye males of wealth and privilege found ways to purchase desirable Tye-Tye girls for purposes of matrimony. Or simply for sex. This practice became a major component of the Tye-Tye economy . . . which led to a thriving industry wherein young girls were put through Diverse Regimens Of Training in order to make them more salable. This meant, for example, that brides produced for the off-world market were educated in useful skills: they learned many languages; they became adept at social graces such as music, witty conversation, and how to berate servants; and of course they lifted heavy weights in all directions so as to increase their natural charms.

Most of the girls sold as brides submitted quite willingly—they were young and impressionable, not to mention they had been told from birth what an honor it was, being purchased by strangers because of one's appearance. These girls Did Not Know Any Better. But after marrying rich husbands (or being sold as mistresses), they seldom remained in the same state of ignorance; inevitably, they met other women who enjoyed very different circumstances, and they also met men who whispered such words as "Freedom" and "Love" and "Meet me behind the house when everyone else is asleep." As time went on, an unquestioning girl-bride became an established woman-wife who was not so naïve and controllable as she once was. The woman's husband/master/owner would try to control her anyway, at which point he would discover an important truth:

These women were very strong.

Not just a little bit strong—they were *prodigiously* strong, with muscles on muscles on muscles. Men lusted after them for that very reason. But these muscles made the women exceedingly dangerous in bed (which is where the men fervently wanted them). A few men endeavored to deal with the situation by resorting to chains, manacles, and other forms of restraint, not to mention embarking on schemes to crush the women psychologically . . . but the logistics of this are fraught with complications when your intended victim is muscular in the extreme, not to mention that it takes a certain kind of male to implement such a program with sufficient ruthlessness. Most men who acquired Tye-Tye brides did not want the women as punching bags; they simply desired wives who looked jaw-droppingly gorgeous and who would competently attend to wifely duties without causing undue fuss.

In many cases, husband and wife resolved their differences through awkward nocturnal discussion: there would be a divorce, or an *arrangement*, or even a reconciliation wherein man and woman decided they could do worse than staying together. But some couples were not so adroit at devising peaceful solutions—some just resorted to violence. Wives dismembered their husbands with greatly exuberant ripping; husbands shot their wives without as much gleeful style, but with equally permanent effect; scenes of domestic horror were played up on the news, and dominated the public consciousness in the form of jokes, catchphrases and urban legends. "So this guy had a Tye-Tye wife . . ."

Such negative publicity agitated the Tye-Tye marriage brokers and seriously threatened their business. Male customers still lusted after wide-shouldered Tye-Tye brides, but buyers demanded that adequate measures be taken to avoid wifely insubordination. Thus began a lengthy period during which Tye-Tye girls were subjected to more than just classes in etiquette, needlepoint, and power-lifting; they were also brainwashed with potent pharmaceuticals so they would submit to their eventual masters.

These measures were kept secret from the men who purchased the women, just as the backroom procedures for carving up cows are hidden from those who purchase meat. However, it turns out that husbands can often tell when their wives have been systematically reduced to emotional cripples . . . and many men prefer to have a partner-in-life who is not a pretty shell wrapped around a festering void of numbness.

The Tye-Tye marriage brokers once again found themselves forced to change tactics. This time, they opted for simplicity—they took hostages.

Lajoolie's Situation

When Lajoolie's parents sold her to a Tye-Tye marriage broker, they also sold her brother Xolip. Xolip did not know this; Lajoolie's parents did not know it either. But a frightening man explained to Lajoolie that little Xolip would be slain in a most brutal fashion if Lajoolie did not conduct herself with acceptable diligence and devotion. If Xolip's murder did not improve Lajoolie's attitude, the frightening man would kill Lajoolie's other brother . . . then her father . . . then her mother . . . then random children off the street, chosen on the basis of youthful beauty and joy-filled radiance.

This man was so frightening, Lajoolie did not doubt he would carry out these threats. If Lajoolie's new husband ever complained to the marriage brokers about her behavior, young Xolip would suffer a freak playground mishap wherein the boy's ear-globes were accidentally cut off and mailed to Lajoolie in a box. The same would occur if Uclod died under suspicious circumstances, if Lajoolie were seen sporting with another man, if certain standards of beauty and hygiene were not maintained . . . in short, if Lajoolie did anything that cast unfavorable light on the marriage agency which sold her to the Unorr family.

"But that is horrible!" I said. "Does Uclod know of this?"

According to Lajoolie, he did not. Customers were not told how marriage brokers kept their "employees" in line, and of course, the women themselves were forbidden to speak of it. Lajoolie would not tell Uclod the truth, even if she swore him to secrecy: he would be outraged, for he was a decent-hearted person, even if he came from a family of criminals who thought purchasing him a wife was a nice birthday present. In the long run, the little orange man might also start asking himself, "Does my wife care for me at all, or is she only *pretending* to like me for fear of injury to her loved ones?" This would hurt the little man's feelings and undermine his faith in the Marital Partnership.

Lajoolie assured me she *did* like Uclod; she liked him a great deal, and thought she was very lucky. For one thing, Uclod turned out to be in a similar position to Lajoolie herself: his criminal Grandma Yulai had told him he had to agree to the marriage *or else*. It was a tradition in the Unorr family that older generations ruled the younger in matters of marital choice. If junior Unorrs did not obey their elders when it came to accepting a spouse, the youngsters were deemed too disloyal to be trusted in anything else. They immediately found themselves out on the street . . . or possibly *under* the street, if one was being paved nearby.

So it was not Uclod's fault that Lajoolie was in this dire situation; indeed, she could readily understand if Uclod resented her, regarding her as an undesired stranger foisted upon him when he would have preferred to make his own choice. But Uclod had been the soul of kindness since their recent wedding—he treated Lajoolie as an equal, he included her in everything he did, and he seemed to like having her around.

In return, Lajoolie played the role that had been drilled into her through constant lessons in wifely deportment. Deference. Meekness. Modesty. A type of retiring femininity wherein she pretended to be small and demure, even though she was big and powerful.

This is why, for example, she spoke in false high-pitched tones. All Tye-Tyes had low voices—they were large people with large throats, and vocal cords like the strings of a bass viol. But the marriage brokers had decided a Tye-Tye's natural voice was apt to remind small men (like Uclod) that the woman was a brawny behemoth who could easily cause grievous bodily harm. Therefore, Lajoolie feigned a falsetto, as well as missish helplessness and delicately modest submission.

"Does Uclod enjoy such displays of quivering frailty?" I asked.

"All men do," she replied. "That's what I was taught."

"Why should you believe the teachings of awful people who threaten your kin? And anyone who says, 'All men enjoy this,' is certainly incorrect, for men are changeable ones who do not like *anything* all the time. In my experience, men get sudden ideas in their heads: that it is weak or unmanly to accept certain types of attention, even if they were happy with identical behavior two days ago. To your great astonishment, what they loved yesterday is the absolute worst thing you can do today . . . and they look upon you with disgust or pity, as if you are some loathsome insect who turns their stomach."

Lajoolie stiffened a bit in my arms. "Uclod isn't like that," she said.

"Perhaps he is not like that yet," I told her. "Someday, however, he will be in a terrible mood because of nothing in particular, and he will glare at you and snap, 'Why do you always talk like that, so goddamned artificial? You could drive a man crazy!' Or perhaps he will not say anything at all . . . but he will think it, and every word that comes out of your mouth will make him angrier. You will not understand why he glares so hatefully, and you will ask, 'What is wrong?' but he will wince at the sound of your voice. There will be nothing you can say to make him love you again, since it is your very voice he despises; but you speak to him anyway because you are crazed and unhappy, and you think there *must* be words to make it all better again, if you can only say them in exactly the right way. You know you are only making it worse, but you cannot help yourself . . ."

All this time I had been holding Lajoolie in the dark. My one arm was wrapped around her back and my other was holding her hand, a position most suitable for giving comfort to a person who has recently been moved to tears. Now she let go of my hand; a moment later, I felt her arms curl around me, pulling me in until my cheek lightly pressed against her shoulder. "All men aren't like that, either," she said softly. "Most of them try to be decent. The man who used you and killed your sister—he was the exception, Oar, you know that."

"He was an utter fucking bastard," I whispered. "And even though he's been dead for years, he still makes me feel most sad."

"Obviously, he affected you deeply," Lajoolie answered with the ghost of a chuckle. "Do you realize you actually used a contraction? You said, 'even though *he's* been dead.' "

I jerked away from her in horror. Then I started to scream. I screamed and I screamed and I screamed and I screamed; then I screamed some more.

Contractions

Here is why I screamed.

My own native tongue has contractions similar to those in English—inelegant short forms created by jamming words together. In the highest literature of my people, you can tell that characters are not well-bred when they use such figures of speech. Cultured persons always speak correctly; it is only the uncultured who treat the language with slovenly lack of enunciation.

This distinction impressed itself deeply on my mother. When my sister and I used contractions—which we did oc-

casionally through carelessness or rebellion—our mother
would chide us and say that good clever *pretty* girls should
not speak sloppily. She herself never used contractions . . .
until one day when I was twelve years old and Mother had a
slip of the tongue.

You can imagine how Eel and I teased her about it.
Mother hotly denied she said any such thing: "You girls
must have dirt in your ears if you cannot hear what I say!"
We had to go wash thoroughly, then do a number of unpleasant chores that were completely unnecessary, since all
chores in our village were handled by automatic devices.

In a day or two, Mother slipped again—another contraction. This time Eel and I prudently did not point it out; but
we caught each other's eye and indulged in a moment of sisterly acknowledgment. We did *not* have dirt in our ears. It
was our mother who had grown lax.

Such slips soon became a common occurrence . . . increasing to several times a day . . . then almost every time
our mother spoke. Once in a while, when we did not feel like
good clever pretty girls—when we felt like *defiant* clever
pretty girls—we would use contractions ourselves, right to
Mother's face, just waiting for her to berate us. We were eager to cry back at her, "You use words like that all the time!"

Alas, our mother had ceased to notice; or more accurately,
she had ceased to care. Her brain was becoming Tired. Indifference to enunciation was an early sign.

When we realized that, my sister and I swore an oath to
the Hallowed Ones: we would never use a contraction again.
We would speak with utmost precision, never letting ourselves get carried away with excitement or emotion. It soon
became fierce superstition—that our brains would never
grow Tired as long as we avoided untidy speech. Deprived
of contractions, Senility had no chink through which it
might enter our heads.

From that day to this, I had kept my oath. I had kept myself safe. I had never said the fatal words.

Now the spell was broken.

Or perhaps it was *I* who was broken. That is why I
screamed.

18

WHEREIN I AM BRIEFLY UNCONSCIOUS

A Short Tussle

I remember Lajoolie holding me in the dark. I also remember fighting her, lashing out as I screamed and screamed. Under other circumstances it might have been an Interesting Struggle, revealing which of us was stronger. The blackness, however, proved the deciding factor—with no food in years and no light for photosynthesis, I rapidly exhausted the last of my energy reserves.

My only warning was a wash of dizziness, strong enough to cut straight through my frenzy. I attempted to say, "I am sorry, Lajoolie," but I do not think the words came out. Then my muscles went limp, and so did my mind.

Awakening

When I regained consciousness, the room was much brighter. The brightness came from dozens of glow-wands laid upon my body; someone had opened my jacket and stacked the wands on my chest, with more wands stuffed down my sleeves and others arranged along both sides of my legs. It was warm where they touched me—the pleasant heat of stones that have been baking under a summer sun.

I closed my eyes and basked. This light was not nearly so filling as the illumination in an Ancestral Tower—the towers were filled with many healthful energies far beyond the visible spectrum—but the glow-wands provided sufficient sustenance that I felt alive again . . . and I would get up very soon, after I had soaked in a bit more nutrition.

Someone said, "Did she move?"

The voice belonged to Sergeant Aarhus. When Festina and Captain Kapoor had headed in opposite directions, I could not remember whom Aarhus had followed. It dawned on me perhaps he had not gone with either party; perhaps he had remained unseen in the blackness, listening to Lajoolie and me speak. Was that not the behavior one expected of a zealous Security mook? Hiding in the dark. Keeping us under Covert Surveillance.

And what did he think we might do if left to our own devices? I asked myself. *Did he fear we would damage a ship that was already broken?* But perhaps Aarhus did not care so much about Lajoolie and me as he wished to guard baby Starbiter. The Zarett might provide our only way to call for help; therefore, the sergeant had posted himself to protect the child.

When I passed out, it must have been Aarhus who obtained these glow-wands. The sergeant would know where such items were stored; he would also be familiar enough with *Royal Hemlock* to find his way in the dark. I could imagine him staggering desperately through the blackness, mumbling to himself, "I must save Oar. I must save Oar. She is too beautiful to die."

I found myself wondering dreamily if Aarhus had fallen in love with me. After all, I was far more attractive than opaque human women . . . and far more charming as well, for I was not a mousy little thing eternally fretting about conformance with the dictates of society. Perhaps the sergeant sensed in me a Tempestuous Beauty who could never be Tamed.

Which is quite enough to make some men fall in love.

For a while.

Until something in the male head goes click and suddenly you are Just Too Much Trouble.

A shudder passed through me and I clenched my face in chagrin. All my life I had been most adept at devising delightful fantasies, pleasant reveries of Love and Romance. Why could I not do that now? As soon as I began inventing a tale of Aarhus in love with me, why did something in my brain bring the fantasy to a crashing halt: *Foolish Oar, real love is not so carefree or so sweet?*

Was this what it meant to have a Tired Brain? To find oneself unable to spin rosy dreams? To be constantly burdened by *It is not so easy* and *You must not ignore certain facts?*

Most frightened, appalled, and desperate, I opened my eyes.

Quite Well Again

"Behold!" I said. I sat up and threw my arms wide, attempting to seem like a person not at all tormented by doubts. "Rejoice, for I have recovered! I am quite well again."

My motion sent several glow-wands tumbling off my body. Sergeant Aarhus rushed over to put them in place again. Sometime since I had fallen unconscious, he had removed his ostentatious mook-armor. Now he was wearing an olive-colored coverall, emblazoned with insignia patches I did not bother to read. My attention was more focused on the fact that he had rolled up his sleeves, revealing nicely muscled arms all covered with yellowish hair.

Though men of my own species do not have hair on their arms, I am not so prejudiced as to disdain extra epidermal embellishment. In the course of my relations with humans, I have discovered that hairy arms can be excellently *cushy*.

Before I could remark upon the sergeant's pleasant pelt, Lajoolie knelt beside me. "Are you sure you're all right? Why don't you lie back down?"

"I do not need to," I told her. "And if I sit up, I can absorb light through my back as well as my front."

To do that, I had to take off my jacket completely. As I did so, Aarhus averted his eyes; and for a moment, I felt a pang of concern, wondering if he was turning away because he did not like the way I looked when I was not covered by clothes. I told myself this could not possibly be—more likely, he suffered from overdelicate modesty, whereby he considered it rude to stare at my unclad flesh. Such a quality would soon vex me if he did not Get Over It . . . but in the short run, I decided to regard it as endearing.

"How are you all?" I asked in hearty bright tones. "Are you as well as I am? What has been happening since I began my perfectly normal nap?"

"Nothing much," Aarhus replied, still looking at the wall rather than me. "You've only been out for an hour. No one's come by with any news, and Nimbus is still locked like a rock around his kid."

He jabbed a thumb at the chair where Nimbus had been sitting. The cloud man was still there, enclosing his daughter in the same quartzlike form as before. "Have you not even poked him," I inquired, "to see if he reacts?"

"No," Aarhus answered. "No poking unless the captain or admiral okays it."

"Hmph!" I said, thinking the sergeant's attitude most mulish. I was halfway tempted to poke the cloud man in sheer defiance . . . but such antics would be most childish, and perhaps would make Aarhus think less of me. The notion of having him love me still played in the back of my mind; and although the rest of my mind derided this notion as a foolish dream idyll—an Infantile Whim—I still found myself desirous of his good favor.

It is truly astonishing how a sane and clever one can be torn by ill-founded impulses.

"Now, Oar," Lajoolie said, "you really should relax." She laid her hand carefully on top of my head, precisely where ear-globes would be attached if I belonged to her species. I suppose that to Divians, this was a comforting gesture—or perhaps a means of determining one's state of health, like feeling for a pulse. "Are you okay now?" she asked. "You went a bit . . . out of control."

"I was not out of control," I answered. "There is nothing wrong with my brain."

"You're perfectly clear-headed," said Aarhus.

"Yes," I said, then realized he had been making a joke about my personal transparency. "But I *am* clear-headed," I insisted. "I am not dizzy, I am not Tired, I am not filled with irrational fantasies . . ."

The ship gave a sudden lurch. I looked at Lajoolie and Aarhus. "You felt that too, correct?"

How We Were Found

Before they could answer, the ship lurched again. This time, there was no possibility of mistake. Aarhus was thrown against the cabin wall, hitting hard with his shoulder. Lajoolie lost her balance and toppled onto me . . . but I was falling sideways myself, striking the hard cabin floor with a resounding crack. (That was, of course, the floor breaking—I am made of sterner stuff than whatever substance underlies the carpets of the human navy.)

I shoved Lajoolie off me just as the ship heaved in the opposite direction. She steadied herself by grabbing Nimbus's chair; the chair was firmly secured to the floor and did not budge, even with Lajoolie's great weight flung against it. I caught hold of the desk, which was also bolted down—in fact, *all* the furniture in the room was fastened in place, except for the desk's chair, which slid on metal railings. This was a Wise Safety Precaution in case of Navigational Upset . . . for when *Royal Hemlock* shifted again, the chair slammed forward as far as its rails would permit, going <WHUNK> at the end like an ax hitting wood.

"What is happening?" I cried.

"Something's grabbed us," Aarhus answered. The ship lurched again. "Something damned clumsy."

"Could it be the Shaddill?" I asked.

"Don't know," Aarhus said. "My X-ray vision isn't working today. If either of *you* can see through the hull, go ahead and have a peek."

I recognized this as sarcasm. However, it reminded me that Festina said this ship had no windows—only exterior cameras which would not be working now. As a result, no one on board could know what had seized us . . . which made me feel better, since I was not the only one waiting in ignorance to see what transpired next.

"It's likely the Shaddill," Lajoolie said, full of fear.

"Or our navy," Aarhus answered. "Captain Kapoor thought we got away from New Earth without being noticed . . . but if anyone spotted us, the Admiralty might have sent a ship chasing close on our tail."

"It's not the Shaddill or your navy. Lucky us."

These words came from Nimbus. With a sudden whoosh, he expanded from hard-rock form to his usual manlike mist, holding the small Starbiter steady as the ship continued to rock. "To be accurate," he continued, "our rescuers don't *look* like Shaddill or the Outward Fleet on long-range scans."

"How could you do a long-range scan?" Aarhus asked.

"I didn't. My daughter did."

Of course, we demanded to know how Nimbus had tapped into Starbiter's powers; but the cloud man was reluctant to explain. He seemed worried we might think he had taken undue liberties, for he kept saying things like, "I'm completely trained to deal with any medical situation," and, "It's my most basic function, testing a female Zarett to make sure her systems are working"—all of which made him sound most guilty, as if he had done something improper to the child. When he finally revealed the truth, however, he had not done anything wicked to Starbiter . . .

He had merely tickled her.

Earlier, when we discussed using the little girl to send a distress signal, Nimbus had recognized the worth of our plan, even if he was not so keen about the suggestion to incinerate the baby until she cried, "Wahh!" Instead, he wrapped around her in a protective shell, then carefully eased microscopic bits of himself inside his daughter's body. The process was similar to the way he moved through Mama Starbiter's tissues, but on a very tiny scale. A few of Nimbus's cells worked their way through the child, found the small knot of glands that permitted FTL broadcasting, and stimulated those glands.

The result was no more than an itch . . . like a scratch in your throat that makes you go, "Ahem!" over and over. Little Starbiter responded to the itch with a sort of irritable clucking—a cranky collection of trans-light noises which could never be mistaken for words but which were apt to attract attention from anyone close enough to hear.

And that is exactly what happened. Somebody had heard the signals and came to investigate. Nimbus watched the newcomers' approach by linking some of his cells to young Starbiter's long-range scan abilities: hiding inside the baby's eyes to see what her scanners could see. This was the activity that had caused him shame. According to a whispered comment from Lajoolie, male Zaretts were highly averse to using the capabilities of females in any way—Nimbus and the rest of his sex attended to their women's health needs, but scrupulously avoided any action which might be construed as Taking Over The Driver's Seat.

What an excellent quality that is! They should preach this philosophy to males everywhere.

"It wasn't wrong tickling the girl to send a Mayday," the cloud man muttered. "Uclod clearly wanted that, and he's her owner. So I was just carrying out the owner's wishes, right? But actually linking myself to her, and seeing through her scanners . . . well, I had to keep watch, didn't I? Uclod would want that too, even if he didn't say so explicitly. He'd want to know if the Shaddill were coming, or the human navy . . ."

"So who is it?" Aarhus interrupted. He had allowed Nimbus to ramble in guilt-laden fashion about linking with his daughter, but the sergeant was obviously impatient for a Situational Report. "You only started sending the signal an hour ago," Aarhus said. "Who was close enough to respond in so little time?"

"I couldn't see exactly," Nimbus replied. "Starbiter doesn't have enough control to focus her scanners on anything in particular. And she doesn't have much attention span either; I tried to keep her looking in one direction, but her gaze kept wandering all over the place." He added defensively, "That's perfectly normal for a child her age."

"Sure, sure," Aarhus said. "But what did you *see*?"

"Mostly a bunch of blurs. Nothing large enough to be the Shaddill or even a navy ship. I think it's a swarm of smaller craft: single-person runabouts or family-sized yachts."

"Hmm," Lajoolie said. "That explains the jostling when they took *Hemlock* in tow. This ship is so big, we'd have to be grappled by a whole pack of smaller vessels. They must have had trouble coordinating who pulled which direction when."

She looked to Aarhus, obviously wondering if he agreed. However, the sergeant had other things on his mind; he was staring upward with an unhappy expression on his face.

"What is it?" I asked.

"Trouble," he said. "Unless I miss my guess, we've just been rescued by an outreach crusade." He grimaced, then looked around at the rest of us. "Hope you haven't got anything planned for the next ten years—we've just become Cashling slaves."

Devising A Suitable Ransom

Lajoolie's face blanched to an unattractive shade of yellow. "Are you sure?" she whispered.

"It's a good guess," Aarhus said. "Before *Hemlock* got zapped, we were headed for the planet Jalmut. That's a Cashling world; most likely, the ships that answered our Mayday are Cashling too. But the Cashlings almost never travel in groups—they're too egotistical. Get a bunch together in separate ships, and five minutes later, they fly off in different directions. The only time Cashling ships stay in a pack is when one of their prophets organizes a crusade."

"And what is a crusade?" I asked. "A religious pilgrimage?"

"They get mad if you use the word 'religious'—most Cashlings are devout atheists, and fly into tantrums at talk of deities or souls. But the truth is that Cashlings are religious as hell. Fanatic believers. They just switch beliefs every other day."

"How can that be?"

"Doesn't make sense to me either," the sergeant replied. "But Cashlings believe in something called *Pu Naram* ... usually translated into English as 'Godly Greed.' Don't ask me to define it, because every time you blink, a new prophet shows up to put a different spin on what Godly Greed means. One week, it's all about taking care of yourself and piss on anyone else; the next week, it's switched to everybody working in harmony so you can all get rich together; then it's about compassion and helping others, because tossing pennies to cripples really boosts your ego." He rolled his eyes. "Cashlings always brag how they have a single unified culture, unlike humans and other species at our level of evolution ... but the only unity I see is them flitting from one prophet to another, like flies trying to find the smelliest heap of manure.

"As for their outreach crusades," he went on, gesturing vaguely at some point beyond the ship's hull, "it's traditional for a prophet to gather his or her followers and wander through space every few years. Mostly they visit other Cashling worlds, picking up new converts at every stop and losing just as many old ones. The turnover in people is substantial: after three stops, a crusade seldom has anyone it started with ... not even the original prophet. Someone new decides he or she is a prophet and takes over the whole flotilla."

Lajoolie favored me with a weak smile. "My husband once told me crusades have nothing to do with belief. They come from a powerful instinct to homogenize the population: to break up communities that are getting too insular and to shuttle around the breeding pool. Uclod says the Cashlings have had mass migrations throughout their entire history; crusades are just the latest excuse."

Aarhus nodded. "I've heard that too. But never say that to a Cashling either, unless you want to drive the bastard into a rage. Let's not do that—we're in enough trouble as it is."

"Because they wish to take us as slaves?" I said. "We should inform them that nice religions do not do such things."

"I told you, *Pu Naram* isn't a religion; the Cashlings call it a 'proven economic doctrine.' " Aarhus made a face. "And even though the working definition of *Pu Naram* changes ten times a year, it always retains one core principle: screwing aliens, especially ones who can't fight back. Over the years, outreach crusades have come across a lot of aliens in distress—the Cashlings don't have a navy like ours, so crusades are the primary source of search-and-rescue. By long-established tradition, a passing crusade won't save your life until you swear ten years of indentured servitude."

"But they *must* save our lives," I said. "Are they not required to do so by the League of Peoples?"

Lajoolie shook her head. "Not unless they caused our predicament in the first place. They aren't obliged to help us, and if they do, they can charge whatever price they want."

"Hmph!" I said. "I do not think much of that policy."

"But the Cashlings love it," Aarhus answered. "They consider it a wonderful omen when a crusade scoops up slaves—it boosts the prophet's prestige. Of course, if we're really lucky, this particular prophet might be liberal enough to take a ransom instead: letting us hand over a bucket of cash instead of ten years' hard labor."

He did not sound cheered by that prospect, but I thought it allowed us an excellent means of emancipation. "Then we shall hand over *Royal Hemlock*," I said. "It is quite large and splendid, even if it is broken. Parts of it even have carpet. The ship must be worth enough to pay all our ransoms."

"Probably," Aarhus agreed, "but we can't use it for that. By Cashling laws of salvage, *Hemlock* already belongs to the crusade—the ship became theirs as soon they took it in tow. They'll claim everything on board: even the clothes on our backs. If they accept a ransom at all, it'll have to come from somewhere else." He gave me a sympathetic look. "Somehow I don't think you have family at home with cash in their pockets." Turning to Lajoolie, he asked, "How about you?"

She bit her lip. "No one on my homeworld would pay a cent. As for my husband's family . . ."

"I know," Aarhus said. "They've gone missing."

"What about you?" Lajoolie asked.

The sergeant shook his head. "My only family is the Outward Fleet; and at the moment, I don't feel like turning to the Admiralty for help. Ten years of slavery is nothing compared to what the High Council intends for us—what they *still* might do if they hear we're being held by the Cashlings. The council will swoop in, pay our ransoms, and take possession of us from the crusade . . . whereupon we'll all disappear down some deep dark well."

"Then we must not let that happen," I said. "We shall battle the Cashlings and . . . and . . ."

Sergeant Aarhus just looked at me. He did not have to explain why we could not fight; if we put up resistance, the Cashlings would just go away, leaving us to drift in space. Perhaps we could merely pretend to submit until we were taken aboard the Cashling ships . . . but by then, they might have locked us in irons. Even worse, the many people of *Royal Hemlock* would be billeted over all the small vessels of the Cashling crusade. I would likely be separated from Festina and Nimbus and little Starbiter and Uclod and Lajoolie and even Aarhus.

That would be Just Awful.

"So what will the Cashlings do first?" I asked Aarhus.

He thought about it. "With our communications dead, they can't just call and ask us to surrender. They'll have to send someone over in person."

"Where will this emissary arrive?"

"The only safe way into the ship is our manual airlock. That's back in the rear transport bay."

"Then we must go there," I said. "We shall meet this Cashling and discuss terms."

I picked up a glow-wand from the heap around me. Getting to my feet, I was still quite woozy . . . so I gathered the other wands too and hugged the whole bundle to my chest. "Lajoolie," I said, "please carry my jacket for me; I do not wish to wear it now, but I shall put it on before we make contact with the Cashlings."

"Are you sure this is a good idea?" Aarhus asked. "Cashlings are quick to take offense, and we really don't want to piss them off. Maybe we should let someone else talk to them."

"If you are afraid to confront them," I said, "you may remain behind. I can find the rear transport bay without your assistance; I have been there once before."

Aarhus made a face. "All I'm saying is that talking to these guys will take tact and diplomacy."

"I am *excellent* at tact and diplomacy. Let us go."

I strode off down the hall with dauntless determination. Lajoolie fell in behind me, and Nimbus drifted along as well, nestling baby Starbiter in the midst of his mist.

With a heavy sigh, Sergeant Aarhus joined our little procession.

19

WHEREIN I ENCOUNTER MORE ALIENS . . . AND THEY ARE NOT NICE

The Drawbacks Of Photosynthesis

Moving through the corridors was a Buoyant Experience. At first, I thought this was simply the result of renewed health and purpose; but then I realized my step was lighter because *I* was lighter. Gravity aboard the ship had begun to diminish . . . and though I could not leap impossibly long distances, I certainly possessed more spring than usual. This was a most interesting experience, and it kept me amused (bounce, bounce, bounce!) all the way to the transport bay.

By the time we got to our destination, Festina had arrived too. This is an excellent trait in a Faithful Sidekick: anticipating where you will be and attending upon you. Of course, Festina feigned surprise to see me, and pretended she had merely come to await the people who had taken *Hemlock* in tow . . . but that is what she had to say, because an important navy admiral cannot admit she feels lost and lonely without her very best friend.

Uclod was in the transport bay too, which meant that he and Lajoolie found it necessary to have a tender reunion. Their whisperings and touchings proved most vexatious, so I turned my back on them in a very pointed manner; but Festina, Aarhus, and Nimbus were no more amusing than the Divians, because Festina wanted to be told how Nimbus had induced baby Starbiter to cry for help. This led to much repetitious talk about outreach crusades and why it was not at all wrong for the cloud man to tickle his daughter . . . which was very quite boring, because I had heard it already.

My only recourse was to walk around the bay on my own, occasionally muttering in the hope someone would ask if I had achieved a brilliant insight. No one took notice *at all*, which made me annoyed and irritable . . . but just as I was about to berate them for their churlish lack of attention, the heat of my anger turned to spinning dizziness and I sat down hard on the floor.

Oof.

Living on light is a fine thing indeed, but it is not enough to sustain substantial activity. This explains why plants do not perform hand-springs. (That and the fact that plants have no hands.) I still carried an armload of glow-wands, but the energy they provided was not enough to keep me going if I persisted in moving about.

"Are you all right, Oar?" Festina called from somewhere behind me.

"I am fine," I said, forcing my voice to be strong. "I am simply . . ." For a moment, I could not think of a suitable excuse why I might have thumped down hard on the deck; but then I caught sight of the rainbow-colored hemlock tree painted on the wall not far from me. "I am simply contemplating the art," I said—because I did not want the others to treat me as a tottery invalid who could not participate in important activities.

"All right," Festina called. "You enjoy the art."

That is easy for her to say, I thought. The tree on the wall was not enjoyable in any way. For True Artistic Merit, a painting should have dried globs of pigment protruding from the surface so that viewers can pick off little bits and sniff what the paint smells like; at least that is what my sister and I concluded as we developed Our Own Personal Aesthetic with the ancient paintings on display in our home village. But the hemlock image in front of me was tediously two-dimensional, with no protruding bits at all. I was about to make an astute critical remark on this lack of texture, when I noticed the tree possessed a feature I had previously over-looked.

Two glowing red eyes burned dimly amidst the multicol-ored foliage . . . as if a certain headless creature was con-cealed behind the leaves.

Talking To The Painting

"Pollisand?" I whispered softly.

"Who else?" he replied. "The fucking Cheshire Cat?"

He was speaking in his normal raspy-sharp voice. I looked back quickly at the others, but they showed no sign of hearing him. Considering how loud he sounded in my ears, it seemed most strange they had not noticed.

"Nah," the Pollisand said, "your buddies aren't in on this conversation. It's just between you and me, sweetums."

"In other words, you are not really here. You are project-ing sights and sounds into my mind again . . ." I stopped. "But I am not connected to Starbiter! How can you contact my brain when I am not linked to anything?"

"Hey," the Pollisand said, "didn't I tell you I'm seventy-five trillion rungs above you on the evolutionary ladder? Why should I need a Zarett to do my projecting for me?"

"Hmm," I hmmed, thinking very hard. This Pollisand had a most irksome habit of not answering questions—he simply made it *seem* like he was responding, when he was really evading the subject. In this particular situation, it occurred to me he might be attempting to hide something most impor-tant indeed.

"Did you do something to me?" I asked in whispered out-rage. "When you took me away and mended my bones, did you do more? Did you perhaps place a Scientific Device in my brain that allows you to link with me at any time?"

"Ooo," said the Pollisand, "aren't we clever! At least one of us is. *Much* cleverer than Dr. Havel. He didn't find a thing. Then again, maybe there's nothing to find."

The red eyes grew brighter and pushed out from the hemlock's painted leaves. Attached to those eyes was the rest of the Pollisand's body, moving outward too—then thickening from flat to fat and coming straight off the wall. If you have ever seen a large headless alien step out of a two-dimensional painting, this was exactly like that . . . only better, because it was happening to *me*.

Since I was still seated on the floor, his huge white body towered above my head. He looked very real as he yanked his rump free from the wall and flicked his short tail to brush flecks of paint off his hindquarters; but no one else in the room even glanced in our direction. This was indeed just a projected image, and my brain was the only one receiving the signal.

"What are you doing here?" I asked, still whispering. "Have you come to observe another dreadful mistake?"

"Hope not," he said. "But let's see how you handle the Cashlings."

"So you will watch whether we anger them?"

"Of course I'll watch. I'm always watching."

He gave a full-body shake, and stray bits of paint showered off him onto the floor. They also showered onto my legs, which I had tucked in front of me. Glaring at him, I wiped the tiny flakes of green and red and black off my previously clean thighs. Meanwhile, the Pollisand eased his bulk past me until he stood between me and the other people in the room; only I was in a position to see his eyes, glowing deep in his chest cavity.

Suddenly, the eyes burst into white-hot flame, such as when a forest fire strikes some bone-dry deposit of leaves and pine pitch. The flash of that light flared down upon me, so blinding I shut my eyes . . . but I could feel the radiance pouring through my body with great invigorating intensity. In less than a second, I was sizzling—the same sort of sizzle one experiences after a full week of basking in the brilliance of an Ancestral Tower.

The heat faded quickly. When I opened my eyes, the Pollisand was back to normal, only a dim crimson glow shining from his neckhole. He reached out a foot and patted me lightly on the cheek. "You're such a skinny girl," he said with a strange feigned accent, "don't you know you gotta eat? And not just cotton candy," he added, waving his foot at the glow-wands I still carried with me. "Those things got no nutrition—they're ninety percent visible light, capiche? They go right through you, and where's the good of that? A pretty girl oughta put meat on her bones. X rays, gamma rays, microwaves: the high-energy stuff. Or maybe (such a radical thought!), you might try solid food once in a while. Okay, so a stranger's cooking can't match your mamma's lasagna; you still gotta get some nourishment or you'll shrivel down to a stick. How you gonna bump off the Shaddill if you keep starving yourself? I'm not always gonna be free to bring you take-out."

He finally paused for breath. Then he asked, "Feeling better now, bright-eyes?"

"Yes," I told him. "However, if this is all just a fiction projected into my brain, how can it affect me as if I was bathed in real light?"

"Oops," said the Pollisand, "look at the time. Gotta go, bambina. Ciao!"

With that, he simply vanished—not in a fancy way, but disappearing as abruptly as a light being turned off. His exit did not make the slightest sound.

I stared at the place where he had been. All those flecks of paint he shook onto the floor were gone, vanished like snow in a bonfire. When I looked at the tree on the wall, no red eyes stared back; there was just flat uninteresting paint.

"Hmph," I said to myself. As always, the Pollisand had proved himself an infuriating visitor . . . but I felt much better, no longer woozy.

Perhaps he was not quite the utter asshole he pretended to be.

Or perhaps he was simply preserving me for something worse later on.

The Advantages Of Immersing Oneself In Mindless Entertainment

Dumping my now-unnecessary glow-wands onto the floor, I rose to my feet and was halfway across the room when Nimbus said, "Listen!" Everyone went instantly silent; in the stillness, I could hear thumping noises to my right.

When I turned in that direction, I saw a heavy metal door embedded in the wall—the entry to the manual airlock. I had not noticed it before in the dim glow-wand light because it was painted the same flat white as the rest of the transport bay . . . as if someone wished to pretend the door was not even there. Perhaps the navy preferred to downplay the necessity for their ships to contain an emergency entrance.

"Okay," Festina murmured. "It's showtime. Everybody on your best behavior."

Quickly I retrieved my Explorer jacket from Lajoolie and slipped it on—one must endeavor to look official when alien guests arrive. As I was fastening the front flaps, Uclod said, "Hey, here's a wild thought: do any of us speak Cashling?"

"No need," Festina replied. "Cashlings spend every waking hour amusing themselves with entertainment bought from other species: Mandasar out-of-shell fantasies, Unity mask dances, human VR chips, the works. Makes Cashlings very cosmopolitan and knowledgeable about alien races. I guarantee whoever comes out of that airlock will speak colloquial English and understand mainstream human body language . . . as well as knowing the proper form of address for a Fasskister hetman, how to initiate a Greenstrider sex act, and which knife to use in a Myriapod auto-da-fé."

"Second knife from the left," Aarhus said. "The one with three black barbs and the engraving of the Horsehead Nebula."

We all stared at him.

"Hey," said Aarhus, "I have hidden depths."

Two Cashlings And Their Spacesuits

With another thump, the door opened. Two gawky figures stood on the other side, both wearing spacesuits of eye-watering flamboyance. One suit was a swirl of red and white stripes, the stripes spiraling down from top to toe and daubed with bright blue curlicues that might be letters in some alien alphabet. The decorations were just as thick around the helmet as anywhere else: if the helmet had a see-out visor, I could not discern where it was. The entire outfit seemed opaque.

The other suit was equally opaque and visorless, but sported an aggressive frost green background, with all manner of clashing violet images painted on top—animals and houses and fruit and farm implements . . . all of which might have been completely different objects than I believed, because with aliens, an item that appears to be a nice juicy peach may turn out to be your host's nephew in temporary chrysalis form, so it is best not to be too hasty at the supper table.[11]

The figures wearing these suits were of course Cashlings; and they had assumed their walking configuration, with long long legs and almost no torso at all. You might think they would look ridiculous, as if their pants were hiked up to their armpits . . . but in fact, they had a sinister air that made me most queasy. They were all limbs and dangly, like giant spiders who had reared up to human height. Even their garish colors and ornamentation were not as clownish as one might expect—not when most of the light in the room came from the glow-wands I had left in the far corner. The lanky faceless Cashlings stood poised half in shadow, reminding one of flashy-hued snakes about to strike.

When they quitted the airlock chamber, the motion was

---

[11]Or so I have been told by human Explorers. Explorers are *extremely* prone to lecturing on the Diverse Facets Of Alien Life . . . and then telling most entertaining stories ("This did not happen to me but to a friend") of instances when an Explorer *did* dare to eat a peach.

fluid and fast: two steps and they both had reached us, more speedy than a human could run, though it appeared they were not exerting themselves. The swiftness of their approach was enough to make Lajoolie gasp and back away, tugging Uclod with her. Nimbus retreated too, curling more tightly around his child. Festina and Aarhus did not flinch, but I could see it cost them an effort—they clenched their jaws and silently held their ground as the Cashlings loomed in toward them, shoving their eyeless heads close to my friends' faces.

Angry at these bullying tactics, I thrust myself forward and declaimed in a loud voice, "Greetings!"

The two Cashlings turned their blank rainbow helmets in my direction.

"I am a sentient citizen of the League of Peoples," I told them. "I beg your Hospitality."

For a moment, there was nothing but silence. Festina's face looked aghast, as if I had made a hideous mistake speaking the League of Peoples' words. It struck me belatedly there must have been a reason why she did not proclaim the speech herself; perhaps these Cashling ones took offense at rote recitations. But there was nothing to do except maintain my poise—stand straight with dignity, attempting to project cool confidence. The Cashlings remained motionless for another long moment . . . then broke into peals of laughter.

First Impressions

It was not true laughter as came naturally to my own race and humans—it was more an imitation, a mimicry from beings who knew the *sound* of laughter but not the sense. Festina had said these creatures were familiar with human ways from watching entertainment shows . . . but one had to ask how much entertainment they actually derived if they could put no genuine feeling into their ha-ha's.

One also had to ask why they chose to respond to the League of Peoples' greeting with guffaws . . . and insincere-sounding guffaws at that. But it would be imprudent to punch them in the nose for being discourteous; I did not even chide them as crazed and foolish ones under the influence of inappropriate chemicals in their brains. No, no—I was exercising *diplomacy*. Therefore, I simply glared at them with distaste, waiting for them to cease their nonsensical noise.

When they did stop laughing, they did not taper off; the laughs died abruptly, as if someone had grabbed the two Cashlings by their throats and squeezed very hard, then knocked their eyeless heads together with a resounding bang. (But that did not happen, because I was being Diplomatic.)

"Greetings yourself," said the red-and-white striped one. Though it spoke Earthling words, its voice was nonhuman: not just one tone but many, as if a dozen people were softly murmuring the phrase in unison. I recalled the pictures I had seen of Cashlings, with a multitude of mouths spread over their bodies. Clearly, this Cashling could speak out of several mouths at once . . . and perhaps it *had* to do that in order to be heard, for its multiple lungs were all much smaller than a real person's. No single mouth had enough air power to achieve acceptable audibility; the only way to produce sufficient volume was to make one's mouths speak together.

The red-and-white Cashling had not finished talking. With a single step, it crossed the space between us and thrust its head close to mine. "You are so . . . so . . ." It made a whooshing sound that might have been a sigh or a word in its own language. One hand lifted toward my face; I thought it was going to touch my cheek, but suddenly it seized the front of my jacket and ripped the coat open wide. "What *are* you?" it cried, bending down to press its helmet between my wallabies, as if it were staring straight into my chest. "Apart from being the ugliest alien I've ever seen."

Before I could respond in a fitting manner, Festina threw her arm around me in a gesture that no doubt appeared companionable . . . while serving the purpose of restraining me from committing a Spontaneous Act Of Diplomacy on someone's intrusive face. "Oar's ancestors were human,"

Festina told the Cashling. "But her race was redesigned several thousand years ago."

"As some sort of punishment?" the frost green one asked.

"No," I said. "As a *gift*."

The other one was still peering into me, as if it could actually discern something within my glass anatomy. Perhaps it could; Festina had said these Cashling ones could see far into the infrared and ultraviolet, and I have been told I am not transparent on those wavelengths. The red-and-white creature with its face against my chest might be watching my lungs breathe and my heart beat . . . which was outrageously impudent, since I could not see those things myself. "What are you looking at?" I snapped, stepping back and haughtily fastening my coat again.

"I was looking at you," the red-and-white Cashling said. Once more it stepped in close, but this time it leaned to one side and thrust its helmet within a hair's breadth of my ear. I had the uncomfortable feeling it was staring straight into my brain; and that made me feel most *soiled*, for all my parts are supposed to be invisible, and I did not want some hideous alien implying I was actually opaque.

"Most fascinating," the Cashling said, one whispery voice at my ear, while more voices murmured the same words up and down its body. "I always thought humans were the ugliest creatures in the galaxy, but at least they have *some* charms." It lifted its head and turned toward Festina, who was still quietly holding me back from delivering a lesson in manners. "You, for example," the Cashling said. "Lovely purple splotch on your face. Blazingly conspicuous. Are you splotchy all over?"

This time, it was *I* who had to prevent an outburst of Extreme Diplomatic Behavior.

The Giving Of Names

"Perhaps," said Nimbus, gliding forward with dispatch, "we should begin by introducing ourselves. I am—"

"A vassal species," the striped Cashling interrupted.

"Who doesn't know his place. If I ever need to know your name . . . well, I'll cut out all my hearts and immerse myself in acid before I sink that low, so the problem will never arise. As for the rest of you—my human name is Lord Ryan Ellisander Petrovaka LaSalle, and this is my wife, the Lady Belinda Astragoth Umbatti Carew."

"Those sound like Earth names," I whispered to Festina.

"They are," she replied, with a wary glance at the aliens. "Cashlings have a fondness for acquiring names and titles from other cultures. Sometimes through legitimate purchase, sometimes through . . . different means."

Festina gave me a pointed look, as if I could guess what these "different means" were. I suppose she wished to imply theft or some other manner of crime . . . but I could not imagine how one went about stealing a name. Names are not the type of thing one can stealthily remove from another person's room. Then again, these aliens enslaved hapless victims of space accidents; perhaps they had devised a Science technique for expunging a slave's name from his or her brain so the Cashling could acquire the name instead. If so, it was a fearsome violation of personal identity . . . and something this pair of aliens must have done frequently if they had acquired such lengthy appellations as Lord Ryan Ellisander Petrovaka LaSalle and Lady Belinda Astragoth Umbatti Carew.

"And of course," the frost-green Lady Belinda added, "we have different names for interacting with different races. Human names for handling humans, Divian names for dealing with Divians . . ."

"By the way," the striped Lord Ryan said to Uclod and Lajoolie, "my name is Proctor-General Rysanimar C. V. Erinoun and my wife is Detective-Sergeant Bellurif Y. J. Klashownie."

Uclod opened his eyes wide and mouthed the phrase *Detective-Sergeant*. Perhaps he was scoffingly dubious . . . or perhaps, as a criminal, he was disconcerted to encounter someone who claimed a connection with the constabulary. Then again, he might simply have been impressed by anyone who could pilfer the very name from a detective-sergeant.

"Which brings us to you," the lady Cashling said, turning in my direction. "What sort of names do your people use?"

I stared back at her. "If you are Belinda to humans and Bellurif to Divians, on my planet you might be called Bell. A bell is a metal object that makes a melodious sound."

"I *know* what a bell is, you idiot." Only half her usual voices spoke the words—the rest of her mouths hissed angrily, as if I had demeaned her intelligence. "And what sort of honorifics do you use? Princess Bell? Queen Bell? *Saint* Bell?"

"None of those," I said. "You would just be Bell. A bell is a metal object that makes a melodious sound . . . when *struck*."

Festina placed her foot heavily on my toe in a Gesture Of Admonishment.

"So," said the stripy male Cashling, "I suppose my name would have to be Rye."

"Yes. Rye is a type of grain that can be made into a beverage."

"A *good* beverage?"

"Opinions differ," Festina said. "Now, if you'd like us to introduce ourselves—"

"No," Lady Bell interrupted. "You're slaves. You *have* no names. You may think you do, but we'll soon wipe that out of you."

"Before you do anything irreversible," said Festina, "we'd like to talk to your prophet about ransom."

"Would you really?" Lord Rye asked. "Then go ahead. I'm the prophet."

Vexatious Bickering

Lady Bell whirled on him. "No," she snapped. Many of her mouths made sharp under-hisses. "Today *I'm* the prophet."

"You're mistaken, darling." The word "darling" was stressed most oddly; as with the Cashlings' attempt at laughter, I got the impression Lord Rye was endeavoring to imitate something he did not understand. "You were the prophet yesterday. At that rally on Jalmut."

"That was *two* days ago, darling. Therefore you were prophet yesterday, and it's my turn again."

"But I didn't *do* anything prophetic yesterday—we spent the whole day just getting free of Jalmut airspace. Darling."

"That's not my fault, darling *darling*. You had plenty of time to do holy work. You could have whipped up a sacred revelation."

"One doesn't *whip up* revelations," Lord Rye said with many supplementary hisses. "They're supposed to come naturally. And they haven't of late." He made a whining noise. "I think I have prophet's block."

"Then I *definitely* should be prophet today." The lady turned to us all, sweeping her hands outward in a gracious gesture. "My friends—by which I mean, my worthless alien chattel—I am the Exalted Prophet Bell. Just a moment."

She reached to the neck of her spacesuit, slipped some sort of latch, and removed her helmet. Underneath she looked exactly like her suit . . . which is to say, frost green dappled with violet bits. The bits were not clean-edged pictures like the ones on her clothes, but they were similar in size and color. Either the woman had tattooed herself to match her suit, or the suit had been decorated with little images that were chosen to be close matches for the natural spottles on the lady's skin.

She had no discernible eyes, nose, or mouth . . . or rather, she had numerous pocks and indentations all over her head which probably served as the usual facial organs, but when a creature has dozens of small eyes instead of two normal-sized ones, it is just not the same *at all*. How, for example, can one tell where the person is looking? And how can one read emotional expressions when the alien's face cannot smile, pout or frown? Perhaps that is why the Cashlings always moved with extravagant gestures, waving their hands and bobbing their bodies—with no facial features to convey emotion, they were forced to act everything out.

"That's better," Bell said as mouths all over her face sucked at the *Hemlock*'s air. "Now you wished to discuss ransom? I'm amenable. Your Outward Fleet has notoriously deep pockets."

"We don't need to bring the Admiralty into this," Festina replied. "I can pay all our ransoms with property I have ready to hand."

"Property?" Bell repeated. "You have no property, slave. The ship is ours. Its equipment is ours. Even your *clothes* are ours . . . although Miss See-Through Savage can keep her flea-bitten jacket. Dis*gust*ing."

"I was thinking of a different sort of property," Festina told her. "*Intellectual* property."

"Oh *merde*," said Lord Rye, with many mouths sighing. "You aren't going to offer us military secrets, are you?" By now, he too had removed his helmet; unsurprisingly, his head was striped red-and-white like his suit. "Some crusade thirty years ago accepted military secrets as a ransom, then couldn't sell them to *anyone*. Nobody *cared*."

"Don't be ridiculous, darling," Lady Bell told him, "that's a complete myth. A *legend*. Probably started by the Outward Fleet itself to discourage espionage." She turned back to Festina. "What kind of military secrets are we talking about? Access codes? Crypto algorithms? Names of spies in Cashling space?"

"I didn't say I was offering military secrets," Festina replied.

"Then what *are* you offering?"

"Military secrets. But not the kind you think. These secrets are fat, wet, and juicy. The kind a news agency would pay millions for. And it's all yours if you'll let us go."

Festina began the story of Alexander York and his exposé. Since I had heard this tale before, I did not pay attention; instead, I looked for something in the transport bay I might find amusing. There was very little there—I could not spot the Pollisand hiding in tree paintings, and the rest of the room was bare . . . except for the people, of course: Festina, the Cashlings, Aarhus, Uclod, Lajoolie . . . and Nimbus.

The cloud man was floating some distance away from the rest of our party. He had clearly been offended by Rye dismissing Zaretts as a vassal race; therefore, Nimbus had withdrawn, hovering like a storm cloud against the rear wall of the chamber. As his sibling-in-Shaddillhood, I did not like to see him upset . . . and anyway, it was tedious listening to Festina speak of things I already knew, so I sidled away from the group and went to offer Nimbus some sisterly consolation.

Umushu

"Hello," I said softly. "How are you feeling?"

Since he did not have eyes, Nimbus could not glare in bitter remonstrance; but the shudder that went through his mist conveyed a similar response. "Why should you care about the feelings of a vassal race?"

"Do not blame me for an alien's words." Lowering my voice, I added, "In my opinion, these prophets are arrogant and hurtful. Are all Cashlings like that?"

"They're all fools," Nimbus answered in a fierce whisper. "Dangerous ones."

I looked back at the Cashlings' spindly bodies; they had shown they could move most quickly, but they did not look strong enough to punch with any great effect. "How are they dangerous?" I asked.

A tendril of his mist swirled toward me, brushing my cheek like tingly dust. "They're *umushu*," the tendril whispered softly into my ear.

"What is that?" I whispered back.

"A fictional monster from Divian folklore. A corpse whose spirit has departed but who doesn't fall down. Going through the motions of life, but no longer truly conscious."

"Lord Rye and Lady Bell are zombies?" I asked with delectable horror.

"Not real ones . . . but they might as well be." The dusty tendril of his being still hovered close to my ear, brushing lightly against my skin. "There's something missing in Cashlings: some important spark has burnt out. Admiral Ramos told you they waste most of their lives in idle entertainment, bought from other species; and they spend the rest of their time on crusades, which are just another form of hollow amusement. Crusades don't really *mean* anything to them—it's just that their ancestors organized crusades, so the current generation does too. Do you think those prophets genuinely have anything to say about life?"

"No . . . but how does that make them dangerous?"

Nimbus did not answer right away. Finally he said, "Think about people on your planet, Oar—the ones with Tired Brains. Suppose that instead of lying dormant in towers, they actually moved around. Suppose they had parties, they traveled to other cities, they pretended to practice spiritual devotions . . . but their brains were still Tired. It was all just sleepwalking. They never built or manufactured anything, they never did anything new, they never dreamed of change; they simply lived in automated habitats filled with machines that did the bothersome work of keeping everyone alive. Wouldn't that be a form of hell?"

I did not answer immediately. The conditions Nimbus described were perilously close to the reality of my world— not just the state of my ancestors, but my *own* state through much of my life: creating nothing, and living by the grace of machines. "It would be most suffocating to the soul," I said at last. "But I do not see how it could be dangerous to other persons."

"It's dangerous," Nimbus whispered, "it's *terrifyingly* dangerous. Because after seeing the Cashlings, everyone else wants to be that way too."

The Resentment Of Vassals

"Everyone would wish to be Cashlings?" I whispered. "How can that be? They are *awful*."

"Other species agree with you," Nimbus replied, his whisper most gloomy. "They despise the Cashlings . . . then try to live exactly like them."

"That is nonsense!"

"Yes, it is. But nevertheless, it's happening. Believe me, I know—belonging to a vassal race teaches you a lot about your masters."

"But you work for Uclod, not Cashlings."

His mist fluttered. "Do you know how old I am?"

"No."

"Over two hundred Terran years. I've worked for *all* the local races."

I stared at him. "You are two hundred years old? That is quite most astonishing."

"Why?" the cloud man asked. "You and I are Shaddill technology; you're virtually immortal, so why shouldn't I be? In fact, I should be *more* immortal than you—the Shaddill created your race 4,500 years ago, while my race is less than a thousand. If the Shaddill continued to make scientific advances all that time, my design is 3,500 years more sophisticated than yours."

"Oh foo!" I exclaimed in outrage. Then I remembered we were supposed to be whispering and glanced around guiltily to see if anyone else had heard me. The other people in the transport bay showed no signs of noticing—the room was large, and we were quite some distance removed. Besides, everyone was still listening intently to Festina speak of Alexander York . . . though mostly they were listening to the Cashlings ask irrelevant questions about the whole business. Festina could only utter a few words at a time before Bell and Rye interrupted with more pointless quibbles.

I turned back to Nimbus and whispered sharply, "You are not more advanced than I!"

"Maybe not," he agreed. "I'm only a vassal race."

"Do not pretend to be pitiable. I do not see anyone persecuting you."

"Apart from the fact that I'm owned? That I'm a slave? That I'm sent to impregnate females I've never met before, I stay long enough to deliver the baby and get a bit attached to it, then off I go to some new master fifty light-years away, never to see my mates or children again? You don't call that persecution?"

I stared at him . . . or perhaps I was staring at the infant

Starbiter clutched tight in his belly. Perhaps it was not coincidence that he carried the child as a pregnant woman does—not in his hands but in the center of his being, at his body's core. "Very well," I whispered, "it *is* persecution. Your species is callously mistreated . . . though I shall not call you a vassal race, for *I* do not think of you that way."

"Everyone else does," he said, "and that's how I know about Cashlings. Not to mention it's how I know that all other sentient races are hell-bent on becoming Cashlings."

"Explain," I said.

And he did.

Coveting Folly

Though the majority of Zarett ships were owned by Divians, a number had been sold to alien races as well. More precisely, Divian breeders sold *female* Zaretts to non-Divians; they then leased male Zaretts (at high cost) to the aliens whenever paternalish services were required.

Therefore, as Nimbus said, he had spent his life drifting from one stud position to another, only staying long enough to mate with a Zarett female, help with the birth, and attend the first months of motherhood. Such a forced impermanence saddened him deeply; but it had also given him a unique chance to observe alien species at their most unguarded. Most of the time, the aliens did not know they were being watched—male Zaretts were microscopic eyes and ears hiding in a starship's walls, watching their "masters" at work and play.

Very much play. Very little work. Especially in alien species who had been Scientific for a long long time.

Nimbus spoke of diverse alien races—Earthlings and Divians and Cashlings and several other species whose names did not stick in my mind—but they all had two qualities in common. First, they had been "uplifted" by the Shaddill: approached in their native star systems, given new homes elsewhere in the galaxy, and presented with sophisticated Science Gifts as a welcome to the League of Peoples. Second, ever since their uplift, these species had all grown more decadent, temperamental, and culturally sterile . . . particularly those uplifted for the longest period.

As a simple example, one could compare Cashlings with humans. Cashlings had been uplifted four thousand years ago; with humans, it was only four hundred. You therefore might expect the Cashlings to be more sophisticated in the ways of technology, having had so much longer to develop . . . but in fact, the Cashlings were not superior at all. Partly, this was because Cashling civilization had lost all interest in Scientific Research. In addition, whatever advanced knowledge they *did* once possess they had speedily bartered to *Homo sapiens* in exchange for VR adventures, situation comedy broadcasts, and glossy picture books.

The Cashlings had sold their technology to other alien races as well—which meant *every* species now possessed the know-how to build self-repairing cities that could satisfy the physical requirements of inhabitants without those inhabitants needing to work. (*Much like our cities on Melaquin*, I thought.) And gradually, such places *were* being constructed by other species, humans and Divians and all.

Most of these other species declaimed loudly they were not imitating the despised Cashlings but simply exploiting Cashling technology . . . yet little by little, these races declined into lifestyles indistinguishable from the Cashling mode. Idle entertainment. The pursuit of faddish excuses for profundity. A deadened inner emptiness, reinforced by a self-righteous conviction there was no more worthwhile way to live—not that they felt satisfied with their own way of life, but they held an unquestioned certainty that no one possessed anything better.

So the diverse races of the galaxy were drifting toward the feckless ways of the Cashlings. Was this not the case with the human navy? Filled with venal admirals like Alexander York and puffed-up captains like Prope, not to mention foolish but inept saboteurs like Zuni. As for Divians, what could one say about the villainous marriage brokers who threatened to kill Lajoolie's family if she did not perfectly satisfy Uclod? Wicked, arrogant, and self-centered.

Of course, Lajoolie herself was not so bad. Neither was Uclod . . . nor Festina . . . nor perhaps Sergeant Aarhus and various other persons I had met . . .

When I voiced this objection, Nimbus said it merely demonstrated that Earthlings and Divians had not progressed so far into decadence as other species. Their races had only been uplifted for a few centuries; though decline was definitely creeping in, it had not yet infected everyone. Given a few more generations, however, Earthlings and Divians were headed for the same ghastly foolishness as Cashlings.

And apparently, Cashlings were very foolish indeed. Nimbus told me of numerous Cashling misdeeds he had observed over the years while riding in female Zaretts: Cashlings neglecting to pack sufficient hydrocarbons for long voyages . . . never bothering to calculate an optimal flight path, but simply aiming toward the apparent position of one's destination . . . forgetting the difference between internal and external gravity, and consequently landing their spaceships upside-down . . .

I giggled at that, but Nimbus said it was Not Funny, Oar, It Was Tragic. At one time, the Cashlings had been a great people—intelligent, sensitive, and thoughtful. They had created some of the greatest visual art in the galaxy; they had cared passionately about color and form and meaning. But that was long ago and those artworks were gone: sold off to pay for foolish games and amusements from other species. Soon there would be nothing left . . . and no one could tell what the Cashlings would do with themselves when they could no longer squander their ancient heritage to pay for short-term diversions.

"Perhaps," I suggested, "they will rouse themselves from fruitless indulgence and embark upon lives of industry."

Nimbus's mist swirled a moment. "No, Oar. They're no longer capable." He paused. "A lot of non-Cashling planets have Cashling communities: outreach crusades travel all over the galaxy, leaving bored drop-outs on every planet they pass. If someone doesn't take care of those Cashlings, they simply languish and die; they're too accustomed to having everything done by machines. That includes machines to rear their children—if a baby comes along, a Cashling mother has no idea how to raise an infant and no desire to learn. As a result, there've been lots of Cashling children raised by foster parents from different races . . . and those kids are just as useless as other Cashlings, no matter what their adoptive families do. Petulant. Disdainful. Negligible attention span. Unable to function, unwilling to be taught." Nimbus made a sighing sound. "Even children brought up with no knowledge of Cashling ways still grow up to be Cashlings. Every last one of them. Nature completely defeating nurture."

"But why is that odd?" I asked. "Rabbit babies grow up to be rabbits. Wolf babies grow up to be wolves. All creatures have instincts, and instincts cannot be erased."

"But Cashling instincts *have* been erased," Nimbus whispered intensely. "That's the point, Oar, that's the whole point. Cashlings haven't always been useless. Before they were uplifted, they had a thriving ambitious culture. If nothing else, they certainly possessed the instinct to raise their own children. Now they don't. *None* of them. Too flighty and easily bored. The only ones with the tiniest bit of initiative are the prophets, and you can see what *they're* like."

His misty hand wafted dismissively in the direction of Lord Rye and Lady Bell. "It's not surprising that affluence leads *some* people to indolence, but there should be others who buck the trend. Cunning schemers who want everybody else under their thumb, or strong-willed crusaders who fight to change the world. Cashling history has had plenty of striking individuals, both good and bad . . . but not in the past few millennia. No conquerors, no heroes, no devils, no saints." He paused. "The only way to explain such a universal absence is some crucial degeneration in the Cashling genome: a dominant mutation that's made them all peevish and ineffectual."

"In other words," I said, "some dire calamity has afflicted them with Tired Brains."

"Exactly. And the same thing is happening to other species. Fasskisters, for example—the greatest masters of nanotech in our sector, but these days they hardly work at all. Oh, they still take jobs if they find the assignment amusing (and if the price is right); but they haven't initiated anything themselves for quite some time. They don't dream up projects on their own. It's as if they're incapable of imagining what they might do: they need an outside commission to kick them into activity."

When the cloud man used the word "kick," I could not help picturing the way I needed to kick elderly persons on Melaquin in order to elicit any response. Hesitantly I asked, "What do young people think of this, Nimbus? The young Fasskisters and Cashlings. Do they ever look around and say, *Why are things not better? What is wrong with us that we cannot accomplish great deeds? Why do we waste hours and days and years on activities we know achieve nothing? How can we stop being broken?*"

The cloud man's mist floated close to me, becoming fog all around my eyes. I had the feeling he had actually surrounded me, wrapped himself about my body, enfolding me until I too looked like a creature of mist. "Of course they ask such questions," he whispered. "Once in a while. When they can force themselves to concentrate. Out in the depths of space, light-years away from anything, I've watched Cashlings weep over who they are . . . who they aren't . . . what their race has become. That's how prophets are born: a moment of clarity, the desire to transform themselves and the universe.

"But," he continued, "it never lasts. They can't *make* it last. They're *damaged*, Oar—even if they experience a flash of profundity, they can't sustain it, they can't use it, they can't preserve the desire to change. I've watched them; they can't become anything else, not even with other species to learn from. They simply lack the capacity. The Cashlings are lost, and other races are following them into the darkness. On their best days, they long to be truly alive . . . but they're physically incapable of pushing themselves past the emptiness." He paused. "You can't imagine their heartbreak when they realize they can't make it work."

"I believe I *can* imagine it," I said. My eyes had gone misty . . . and the mist was not cloud.

20

WHEREIN I FEEL SORRY FOR FISH

Exclusive Rights

I still had my eyes shut, squeezing them tight to choke off tears, when the twittering Lady Bell clapped her hands with jubilation. "Then it's settled!" she said in a gleeful voice. "Your lives for your story!"

My eyes snapped open. While I was conversing with Nimbus, Festina had apparently negotiated our freedom . . . which irked me no end since *I* had wished to be the one who persuaded the Cashlings to set us free. How else could I show the world I was not a worthless idle-head? I swiped the tears from my cheeks and stormed across the transport bay. "So," I demanded, "what is this sinister deal you have worked out behind my back?"

Festina blinked in surprise. "Nothing sinister, Oar. Lady Bell has agreed to transport everyone on *Hemlock* to Jalmut and let us go free once we get there in exchange for which, she gets exclusive rights to our story."

"Exclusive rights!" Bell crooned. "The most wonderful phrase in your language!"

"Of course," Lord Rye said, "tomorrow, the rights will be mine. Because then it's *my* turn to be prophet."

"Uh, yes, certainly," Bell replied. "It will be your turn." She whirled back to Festina. "No time to waste. We have to record your statement and broadcast it *immediately*. We have to record *everybody's* statement." She moved to my side with a single step of her long-legged gait and took me by the arm in a manner oozing with unearned familiarity. "Your statement particularly, dear. You were the one who suffered most; and you'll come across *fabulously* on camera. The moth-eaten jacket . . . the woebegone expression . . . the childish speech patterns . . . you'll tug like mad on everyone's heartstrings. Especially the prime demographic of men who like watching grown women behave like eight-year-olds. Boy, do those guys have disposable income!"

Festina seized my other arm before I showed Lady Bell what "disposable" really means.

No Such Thing As An Immediate Departure

"So," Uclod said to Bell, "you can do the broadcast right away?"

The lady whooshed gusts of air from several apertures in her skin. I believe this was a Disdainful Scoff. "We're running a crusade," she told the little orange man. "We have an instant-play contract with four major news-wires and enough broadcasting wattage to saturate every star system from here to the globular clusters. When we preach a sermon, we *preach* a *sermon*."

"Then what are we waiting for?" Uclod asked. "Let's go!"

Alas, it was not so easy as that—Arrangements had to be made. While the prophets' ship (called *Unfettered Destiny*) could hold those of us scheduled to give testimony, the rest of *Hemlock*'s crew had to be offloaded in ones and twos to other vessels in the flotilla. This would require significant coordination of effort, and neither Lady Bell nor Lord Rye wished to supervise the work: such "petty details" were beneath the dignity of important prophets. Moreover, Lady Bell insisted her broadcast witnesses could not possibly spare the time to help clear the navy ship. We had to start recording without delay; otherwise, she might decide to make us slaves after all.

This was merely an empty threat—anyone could see she did not care about slaves half so much as she cared about the broadcast. Bell literally jiggled with joy at the prospect of disseminating our testimony; she clearly expected to reap substantial benefits. No doubt she would become famous as the person who brought my poignant tale to the universe. Moreover, I suspected the broadcast was not going to be delivered free of charge—the audience would have to pay a fee in order to see my beauty. This meant Lady Bell would surely become rich, for everyone enjoys watching a person as lovely as I, especially when the person has a Sobering Tale To Tell.

The promise of forthcoming largesse explained why Bell grew upset with Festina. My Faithful Sidekick wished to remain on *Royal Hemlock* long enough to ensure there were no slip-ups in the evacuation . . . whereas Lady Bell desired to leave right away, and stamped her foot impatiently at waiting even a little bit. "If you *must* hang around here," she told Festina, "I'll take the others and get started without you."

But that did not please Festina: she had the air of a person who believes everyone else will make an Awful Cock-Up of giving testimony, emphasizing the wrong details, skipping important evidence, and generally creating a flawed impression with the viewing public. She did not trust us to do things correctly unless she was there to supervise.

In the end, Lady Bell agreed to wait just long enough for Festina to find Captain Kapoor and put him in charge of the evacuation. This, as it turned out, was merely a ruse on the lady's part—as soon as Festina left the transport bay, Bell attempted to persuade us to depart immediately.

"Can't do it," Sergeant Aarhus said, "even if we wanted to. No spacesuits."

"Why do you need spacesuits?" Bell snapped.

"Don't like breathing vacuum," Aarhus answered. "I hate the part where my eyes get freeze-dried. So while the admiral is gone, let's just mosey on down to where the Explorers keep their suits—"

"No, no, no," Bell interrupted, "you won't need suits. *Un-*

fettered Destiny is docked directly outside. An airtight link."
She waved her hand toward the exit hatch. "You can go over
right now."

"So why are you and Rye wearing suits?" Uclod asked.

Lady Bell made another whooshing sound with multiple
orifices. "We didn't know how much air you'd have," she
said. "You were floating derelict, no FTL field, no electrical
readings . . . for all we knew, you might not have oxygen either."

"Exactly," Lord Rye agreed. "We didn't know you'd fried
your own ship; we thought maybe all your power systems
had been disabled by that thing on your hull."

For a second, nobody spoke. Then we all howled in unison, "*What* thing on our hull?"

"I don't know," Lord Rye said. "It looked like a big stick."

Questions Of Security

Lajoolie fairly threw herself against Uclod, as if the little
man was the only creature in the universe who could protect
her; she nearly bowled him over, but somehow he stayed on
his feet. He put one arm around her hips and gave a comforting squeeze . . . but his eyes turned toward the exit airlock as
if he desperately wished to run for it.

The rest of us were unencumbered by large timid women.
We *did* run for the airlock—not because we were fleeing
cowards, but because the foolish human ship had no means
of looking at its own exterior. I wanted to see with my own
eyes what this big stick looked like. Nimbus and Aarhus
clearly felt the same.

"Where are you going?" Lady Bell asked as we passed
her.

None of us answered. I reached the airlock first, with
Nimbus gusting straight behind me, and Aarhus pounding
through the hatchway a moment later. The sergeant grabbed
the door as he passed; with a strong yank, he slammed it
shut while the Cashlings still gaped at us from outside.

"Spin that wheel," Aarhus yelled, pointing at a spoked

metal ring that stuck out of the wall. I grabbed the wheel and heaved; it moved so grudgingly, I was not certain I was turning it in the correct direction, but one does not like to embarrass oneself by sheepishly switching to go the other way, so I just pulled the wheel harder. *Much* harder.

The floor lurched beneath our feet.

"Hey," Aarhus said, "take it easy!"

"I did not do anything," I told him, "I just turned the wheel."

"The wheel's attached to gimbals," he said. "They change our orientation to match the direction of gravity on the other ship the last thing we want is to step out of the airlock and plummet straight up toward the floor."

"Why are spaceships so complicated?" I grumbled. "If I were in charge of the galaxy, I would pass a law that all ships must fly flat and level instead of at odd angles."

But I spun the wheel more slowly after that. I could feel the airlock chamber rotating and rolling in accordance with the wheel's revolution . . . but the direction of down continued to be more or less beneath our feet, as if gravity was continually rearranging itself to match our gyrations. Quite possibly, if I had been patient enough to move the wheel at a snail's pace, we could have turned completely upside-down while barely noticing the change.

"You know," Aarhus said as he watched me work, "technically speaking, what we're doing could be considered hijacking. Boarding someone's ship without permission."

"Do not be foolish," I told him. "The Cashlings can follow us as soon as we have gone through."

"I know that. But what will the Cashling security systems think? When strangers show up unaccompanied, the ship might consider us illegal intruders."

Nimbus made a dubious noise. "In my experience with Cashlings, half the time they forget to activate security systems when they leave the ship."

"That leaves the other half of the time," Aarhus said. "The half of the time when the ship-soul incinerates your ass and stomps on the cinders. Anyone know what anti-personnel weapons are popular in the Cashling Reach?"

"Gas," Nimbus answered immediately. "Doesn't hurt Cashlings because they adapt so quickly to airborne contaminants . . . but with humans, it makes you retch till you pass out from the dry heaves."

"Lovely," Aarhus muttered.

"Do you wish to go back?" I demanded. "Do you relish groveling before Lady Bell and apologizing for your rashness?"

"Nope," Aarhus said. "I just want to know what might happen when that door opens."

The wheel in my hands clicked and stopped turning. Aarhus smiled at me, then at young Starbiter inside the cloud man's stomach. "I'm tempted to say women and children first," Aarhus murmured, "but Admiral Ramos would never let me hear the last of it."

He grabbed a lever on the airlock hatch and threw the door open.

Why It Is Good To Have Airlocks

For a moment, I feared we *were* under attack by some noxious gas—a foul stench assailed my nostrils, like midsummer swamp rot combined with the scent of skunks and boar feces. Of course I held my breath; but even without inhaling, I could feel the horrid reek pressing in upon my nose, like the sharp tip of a knife just waiting to plunge to the hilt.

"God damn!" Aarhus cried, throwing up his hand to cover his mouth and pinch his nostrils shut. "Holy fucking shit!"

He reached out to close the door again, but Nimbus said, "Wait." The cloud man's top half separated into a dozen foggy ribbons, while the lower half of his body—the part containing baby Starbiter—retained a vague eggly shape. "Wait. Wait. Wait."

Nimbus swirled out of the airlock, his upper half combing the air in long strips, turning a full circle horizontally, then rotating back in the reverse direction. At first, I did not understand what he was doing . . . but then I remembered how he had originally sensed me as a "chemical imbalance" (hmph!) back on Starbiter Senior. His little misty bits must possess the ability to analyze the air for toxicity; now he was testing to determine if the smell was harmful or just foul.

After another two circles, the streamers of his upper body coalesced into his former egglike shape. "The air's not dangerous," he told us. "Not in the short term anyway. It's just putrid as hell."

"But why?" Aarhus demanded . . . though it is difficult to sound truly demanding when one is muffling one's mouth with one's hand. "Have they sprung a leak in their sewage recyclers?"

"No. Cashlings simply have an impressive capacity to counteract atmospheric pollutants. Their *stibbek* automatically compensate for extreme degrees of . . . uhh . . . odorous infelicity. Therefore, I've noticed—in the times I've served on Cashling ships—they don't maintain high standards of sanitation."

The sergeant's expression turned aghast. "You mean they leave garbage lying around?"

"Anything and everything. They simply can't be bothered to clean up after themselves. If they're eating something as they walk down a corridor, they'll drop whatever they don't want and leave it to rot. Then they'll step over the mess for weeks afterward, rather than bend down and pick it up. As for personal hygiene . . ." A shudder went through Nimbus's body. "You don't want to know. Every few years, they have to dock their ships at an orbital station and get robots to scour all exposed surfaces. You and Oar should watch your step; personally, I intend to hover at least half a meter off the floor."

"Christ Almighty," Aarhus muttered. "Now I understand why the navy sends Explorers to enter alien vessels. We ordinary swabbies aren't cut out for stomaching hostile environments."

"You are not the one with bare feet," I told him. Then I

headed out the hatchway, my eyes most diligently watching the ground.

A Glimpse Of Unfettered Destiny

The Cashling ship *Unfettered Destiny* was indeed a most God-Awful Mess. Not only was the receiving bay be-smirched with organic substances of disgusting provenance (discarded fruit turned spongy brown, hunks of desiccated meat, stains of spilled liquids in a variety of colors and de-grees of stickiness) but the bay was full of bric-a-brac: pos-sibly gifts or tribute from the prophets' disciples, but maybe just foolish knickknacks procured on impulse and tossed aside two seconds after arriving on ship.

How else to explain at least thirty bolts of cloth piled hap-hazardly against the wall—with every bolt displaying the same pattern. (Jagged green and red zigzags moving jerkily across an electric blue background . . . and I do mean elec-tric, since the cloth occasionally gave off sparks.) There were also statues lying about, some recognizable (trees, horses, arches) and some depicting objects that did not exist in nature . . . unless somewhere there is a spherical creature who has a habit of shoving both hands all the way down its throat until they come out the other end.

I will not bother to describe the other items heaped around the room—and there were many heaps indeed, in-cluding mounds of gold coins, stacks of data-bubbles, and buckets of glittery crystals that might have been genuine jewels—but I must note the cages, crates, and pens that once contained living animals.

Now those same containers held corpses, many in ad-vanced states of decomposition.

I could not identify any of the species. Some were clearly alien—things with eight legs, or with shells shaped like flat orange octagons. Others might have been creatures I knew, but were too dried and withered to recognize anymore. Skeletons covered with shriveled skin. Mounds of decaying fur still pressed desperately against the wire of the cages where they had died.

All these animals perished from neglect: unfed, unwatered, uncleaned. I suppose they had been brought to the prophets as pious offerings, then simply ignored. They might have been nice *pretty* creatures—fluffy and gentle, or scaly and playful—but the Cashlings apparently could not be bothered to fill up food and water dishes. These "holy sacrifices" had suffered most horrible deaths from sheer lack of attention . . . and the sight made me sad and angry, both at the same time.

Had Lady Bell and Lord Rye been the ones responsible for such starvation and thirst? Or were these creatures left over from previous prophets—prophets who accepted live offerings from their followers, then left the animals to rot? I did not know. I strongly hoped the two current prophets were not the guilty parties; but even if Rye and Bell were innocent of these animals' deaths, they were obviously not much different from their predecessors. Whatever awfulness they had inherited, they had simply allowed it to continue: a dirty, messy, stinky ship that made one want to cry.

The most tragic part was that *Unfettered Destiny* was made of glass—beautiful, beautiful glass, so grimy and grubby it broke one's heart.

The floor tiles were see-through: if you looked past the crusty smudges and mounds of rubbish, you could stare at the next level below (chockfull of machinery that might have been the ship's engines, its computers, or its entertainment systems). Through the walls, one could see more machines—some with screens that flashed pictures, some with screwlike attachments that spun at high speeds, some that just brooded silently over their dour lack of ornamentation. As for the view through the glass ceiling . . . the entire length of *Royal Hemlock* rose straight above us, like a great white tower jutting into black space.

It made me dizzy to look at—as if the giant white ship might topple onto my head at any second. I could barely stare up at it without going woozy. Perhaps it might have been easier if I had lain down flat on my back, but I was not about to lie on *this* floor.

Therefore, I closed my eyes, steeled myself, and looked again. This time, I scanned up the *Hemlock*'s length, beginning at the bottom, moving carefully toward the top . . . until far far away, near the ship's nose, my gaze fell on a dark object attached to the *Hemlock* like a leech on a trout.

It was a stick; or perhaps I should call it a twig compared to the much bigger sticks of the Shaddill ship. Even so, I could see it was the same type of thing: a flexible tube that had embedded itself in the *Hemlock*'s forward hull. As I watched, it waved back and forth in lazy patterns, like seaweed in a gentle current.

How long had the twig been attached there . . . and what was it meant to accomplish? Had it perhaps injected Dangerous Substances through the *Hemlock*'s outer skin, horrible gases or diseases that would soon incapacitate those aboard? Or could it have contained horrid alien warriors who were even now creeping through the ship's pitch-black corridors, ambushing crew members in the darkness? Perhaps the alien invaders could transform their persons into a semblance of those they ambushed, and the entity who appeared to be Sergeant Aarhus was actually a loathsome jelly-thing waiting for a chance to implant me with its gibbering spawn.

. But I did not think so. All the aliens I had met since leaving Melaquin were stodgy disappointments who did not shapeshift or *anything* . . . and what is the point of *being* an alien if you do not have Uncanny Abilities with which to incite terror in other species? If you cannot disrupt the lives and sanity of other races, you might as well stay at home.

But of course, aliens never listen to *me*—the big poopheads.

The Purpose Of The Twig

"Holy shit," Aarhus whispered, staring up at the twig. "We got tagged, didn't we?"

"Apparently so," Nimbus agreed. "The Shaddill must have shot that at *Hemlock* like a torpedo."

"What do you think it is?" Aarhus asked. "Maybe a homing beacon?"

"Probably. When Starbiter hit the Shaddill ship, she obviously disabled them somehow—maybe took out their engines. The Shaddill saw us get picked up by *Hemlock* and knew they couldn't follow until they'd made repairs . . . so they harpooned your ship with a signal device that would let them track us."

"Are you sure it is just a signal?" I asked. "Could it not be a tube full of shapeshifting warrior-droids programmed to replace us one by one?"

"Let's stay with the signal theory," Aarhus said. "But if we're lucky, the Shaddill won't get their ship repaired till everyone's evacuated and halfway to Jalmut. I like picturing the bastards coming to capture *Hemlock*, only to find it's nothing but a big empty paperweight."

Behind us, the airlock made thudding sounds. Aarhus had closed the door once we entered the receiving bay; now the hatch opened again, revealing Uclod, Lajoolie, Lady Bell and Lord Rye, plus my friend Festina, who must have finished making arrangements with Captain Kapoor.

Festina's nose wrinkled as the stench of *Unfettered Destiny* struck her, but she quickly assumed a straight face. Uclod, on the other hand, doubled over and began making hiss-whistle sounds, clutching at his stomach. A moment later, he disgorged his last dinner with a great resounding splash. Lajoolie placed her hand on his back and bent as if to say, "There, there" . . . but then, she too began to hiss-whistle, her whole body shaking.

When a woman that large gets the shakes, it is a titanic vibration indeed. I believe I could feel the ship trembling in response. This impressed me so much, I barely had the presence of mind to leap backward; I am fortunate to be an excellent leaper, because Lajoolie's subsequent spew splattered widely in all directions.

"Divians," Aarhus muttered, looking down at his dampened boots. "Meticulously bioengineered into thirty-five different sub-breeds, and they *all* have weak stomachs."

"You pigs!" cried Lady Bell to our friends. "You're making a mess of my floor!"

We all stared at her for a moment; then even Uclod and Lajoolie started to laugh.

Supreme Impatience

Lady Bell was not such a one as to tolerate laughter. Muttering angry whoosh-whoosh sounds, she tapped a button on her spacesuit's stomach, making the suit slump off like wilting blades of grass. Underneath, her entire body was identical to the suit, frost green with violet spottles. She paused for a moment with the clothes in a heap around her ankles . . . and I had the impression she was striking a pose, hoping someone would say admiring things about her unclad person or at least gawk with envy. When none of us did, the lady petulantly kicked the suit loose from her feet and stomped toward an electronic console set into the wall. Using many orifices at once, she began making gushy noises; these must have been instructions in the Cashling tongue because seconds later, the airlock closed and the ship gave a tremendous shudder.

"Finally!" she exclaimed in English. "If everyone's wasted enough time, may we *please* start recording the broadcast?"

Nobody answered. The Divians were still doubled over, and Festina was staring through the roof at *Royal Hemlock*. I could tell the moment she caught sight of the twig-thing clinging to the hull; her jaw grew tight under the purplish skin of her cheek. She turned to Lady Bell and asked, "Does your ship have long-range scanners?"

"Of course."

"Can you call up a readout?"

"When we get to the broadcast studio," Lady Bell snapped. "Let's *go!*"

Without waiting for a reply, she strode toward a door at

the far end of the room. Her elongated limbs let her cover the ground most rapidly indeed—we could not have kept up with her, even if we ran. As it turned out, none of us showed any desire to match her speed; therefore she was forced to stop at the exit, gesturing peevishly for us to hurry along.

Festina was not to be rushed. She crouched beside Uclod and Lajoolie, asking in a low voice, "Are you okay?"

"Yeah, sure," Uclod mumbled. "Just . . . getting used to the smell . . ."

"I'll stay with them," Nimbus told Festina. "To make sure they're all right."

"No need," Uclod said, wiping his mouth. "We'll come with you." He turned toward Lajoolie. "Right, honey?"

Lajoolie said nothing, but nodded. She looked most miserable indeed; I wondered if she was simply feeling ill or if she was ashamed to have vomited in public. The precepts of "femininity" demanded by her strange upbringing were still a great mystery to me. Nevertheless, I suspected that spewing half-digested *choilappa* was not considered the height of womanly allure.

Thoughts On A Spiritual Vocation

The corridors of *Unfettered Destiny* were no cleaner than its receiving bay—specked with patchy nubbins of substances best unexamined, and cluttered with boxes containing wrinkly clothes, water-stained paper, or cracked ceramic candleholders. Most of these boxes had been shoved against the wall in an attempt to leave a clear path down the middle . . . but the ship's passageways were so narrow, one was often forced to step over chunky obstructions. With their long legs, the Cashlings experienced no trouble; those of us with shorter gait did not have such an easy time.

Festina in particular was constantly compelled to hop over ungainly hurdles. She succeeded with admirable grace, for I never noticed the slightest stumble or hesitation. However, the look on her face was not gracious *at all,* and from time to time I heard her muttering imprecations in the colorful tongue of her ancestors.[12]

On the positive side, *Unfettered Destiny* appeared to be constructed of glass all the way through, not just in the receiving bay. As we walked, I could glance behind my shoulder and see our ship drawing away from the *Hemlock*. We drifted silently into the blackness as another small ship from the crusade took our former position at *Hemlock*'s airlock. Lady Bell must have sent instructions to her followers while she was at that control console back in the receiving bay; now the disciples were hurrying to obey their prophet's commands.

I could not help thinking, *It must be excellent to be a prophet, if people do whatever you say.* So I spent a brief time wondering how one became a prophet in the Cashling culture, and if there were any negative aspects to a prophet's calling. Having a flotilla of docile adherents was all very well, but prophethood would not be so fine if one was required to practice overzealous chastity or to cut out one's heart in a ritual manner at the coming of winter. On the other hand, if one simply declared, "I am prophet," and people bent themselves obsequiously to fulfill your slightest whim . . .

That would not be a bad profession for a woman trying to make her way in an unfamiliar world. It would not be a bad job at all.

---

[12]Festina curses most casually in English. When she curses in Spanish, it is *serious*.

21

WHEREIN I MAKE A VAIN ATTEMPT TO BECOME A RECORDING STAR

Reaching The Studio

"Oar? Oar? Oar!"

Someone was tugging on my arm—Festina, gripping me tightly in *Unfettered Destiny*'s corridor.

"What is wrong?" I asked.

"We're here. At the studio. You walked straight past it." She stared at me keenly. "Are you all right?"

"I am fine, Festina. I was simply lost in thought."

"Really." She did not let go of my arm. "You're sure you're okay? Sergeant Aarhus told me you passed out in Nimbus's room . . . and I noticed you acting strangely in *Hemlock*'s transport bay."

"There is nothing wrong with me," I said, detaching myself from her grasp. "If you think my brain has become faulty, you are quite mistaken." The look of concern on her face did not lessen. "Truly," I told her, "I am perfectly well . . . though I have not eaten in four years, and therefore would benefit from the intake of appropriate nourishment."

"We'll get you some food, don't worry," Festina said. "Come into the studio and sit down; I'll ask Lady Bell . . . no, I'll ask Lord Rye to bring you something from the galley."

She attempted to take me by the arm and guide me through a nearby door. I did not wish to be guided—I was not some frail muddle-head whose brain might go blank at any moment, I had simply been distracted by the notion of becoming a prophet. There is nothing sinister about a momentary preoccupation; it was most annoying for Festina to Show Undue Concern. Therefore, I shrugged off her efforts to baby me, and surged boldly through the door myself.

I had never visited a broadcast studio before, but I expected such a place to contain ostentatious banks of Technology. Instead, the room was just a large empty space with jet-black carpet on the floor. The walls were glass, but with a fuzzy feathered texture; this had the effect of suppressing echoes, for the room was extremely quiet, as if some Uncanny Force were muting every sound we made. The very air seemed to press against my eardrums, stifling noises before they reached me: a most eerie and disturbing effect. Compared to the clutter in the rest of the ship, an area with no knickknacks or dead animals should have cheered my heart . . . but the atmosphere made me most edgy, as if I were cut off from important auditory input that might warn me of danger.

Lady Bell, on the other hand, was clearly glad to reach the place after fretting through so much delay. No sooner had she entered than she threw herself down on the carpet . . . and the woolly black surface reshaped itself beneath her, the floor acquiring bumps and hollows molded perfectly to the lady's body. I had to admit she looked striking, the frost green of her skin almost fluorescent against the heavy black background. This might have been why the floor was so dark; she would not have stood out as well against the ship's clear glass.

"Sit down, sit down," she said with expansive cheer, gesturing to the floor beside her. "Make yourself comfortable. Can my darling husband get you anything? Accelerants? Placations? Our synthesizers have complete pharmaceutical indices for Earthlings and Divians; it'll only take a second to whip up your favorite stimulant."

"How about food?" Festina said, making no effort to seat

herself. "Something humans can digest." She glanced in my direction. "Preferably transparent."

I lowered my head, trying not to show shame. It is mortifying when your Faithful Sidekick believes you are crazed with hunger and she makes a scene to ensure you are properly fed. I knew I could not die from starvation, but I was not so certain about embarrassment.

Fortunately, Lady Bell was not such a one as could feel urgency about someone else's problem. She therefore did not make a fuss: *Oh yes, we must quickly bring sustenance for the poor dear and make her lie down in the meantime.* She merely told Rye, "See to that, darling!" and puckered several of her cranial orifices at him. He muttered something in the universal language of unappreciated persons and slunk out of the studio.

"Now everyone just sit down!" Lady Bell said brightly. "I don't want you pacing during the show. Pacing will upset the audience—not to mention that the lights and cameras will have a hard time following you. Shadows on one's face can completely ruin credibility. Sit down, sit down!"

"Where are the cameras?" I asked, looking around the blank room.

"Built into the walls, dear."

"But the walls are clear glass. They do not contain cameras."

"*You're* clear glass, and you contain all kinds of things: lungs, kidneys, a heart . . . pity you only have one of those, but let's pray it holds out till the recording is over. And your heart will last ten times longer if you just *sit down!*"

Grudgingly, I lowered myself to the floor. I do not enjoy *anyone* offering advice about my health; and I knew I would not enjoy the floor either. Sure enough, the moment my bottom touched the carpet, it began to squirm beneath me. (The carpet, I mean, not my bottom.) A sizable gully sank down to accommodate my feet, while a woolly black hump rose to support my back. I grant that the seat was comfortable—like reclining on a mound of dead sheep whose bones have been softened with hammers. The problem was I did not *wish* to be comfortable. I did not wish to be soothed because . . .

. . . I worried I would not retain consciousness.

There. I have said it. Though I told Festina I was fine and resented her suggesting otherwise, I feared my mind would go blank if I allowed myself to relax. Perhaps it would happen even if I did *not* relax. No matter how hard I fought the Tiredness, I still was most terrified I would sink into the cozy carpet and my brain would cease to function. Mental emptiness had swallowed me too often in the past few hours; it seemed as if I could not spend an idle minute without slipping away from the world. Being forced to sit in a comfy place was almost a sentence of execution . . . but of course I could not say that for fear of being called a coward.

So I sat and cringed and shivered.

"Excellent," Lady Bell said as the others also claimed sections of carpet. Festina sat right beside me, probably wishing to be within reach in case my brain dribbled out my ears: a gesture which infuriated me greatly.

"Now," said Bell, "we'll record everything before we broadcast, so we can edit out slips of the tongue, and perhaps passages of testimony that don't work . . . though I don't want anyone to be self-conscious, just say whatever you want and let *me* decide whether you're being tedious and pedantic. By the way, I hope you can all take direction. And perhaps it would be best to do vocal warm-ups right now: run through some tongue-twisters, practice speaking from the diaphragm. You all have diaphragms, correct? Except for you, cloud man, I don't know what you have. Why don't *you* practice holding a nice solid shape rather than wavering about. Try to look like a *person* instead of a *pukka*-ball. And make your arms bulgy to suggest muscles. Viewers like muscles. Taut lean muscles gleaming with sweat. Perforated with tight puckered orifices and preferably highlighted in at least two of the primary colors. Umm, well . . . work on that, do your best. Meanwhile, I'll call a newsbroker I know on Jalmut—have him put out the word that we'll soon have some hydrogen-hot footage for sale."

She raised her voice slightly and said something in Cashlingese. I did not know whom she was addressing; but a moment later, a gusty voice whooshed and fribbled an answer from the ceiling. Either the words came from another person elsewhere in the ship, or it was the voice of *Unfettered Destiny* itself: what humans call the "ship-soul." I have been told that in the Technocracy navy, the ship-soul is intentionally given a mechanical-sounding voice so it can be distinguished from humans. On *Unfettered Destiny*, the voice sounded more *windy* than Bell or Rye, as if it were powered by huge ship-sized lungs instead of the many little lung-ettes of real Cashlings.

The ship-soul spoke briefly, then fell silent. Lady Bell seemed waiting for more; I suppose she had instructed the ship to contact her newsbroker and was now expecting a reply.

In the meantime, I squirmed in my too-comfy seat. Uclod and Lajoolie still appeared bleary after their nausea in the receiving bay; Nimbus hovered near them while Festina whispered to Aarhus in confidential tones. I disliked my friend speaking in a manner I could not overhear . . . but it seemed a great deal of trouble to move into a position where I could eavesdrop, especially when she and the sergeant were probably just discussing tiresome navy topics.

It was all too much bother to pay attention. In fact, everything in the world seemed excessively complicated. I remember thinking, *Why can't I just sleep for a while?* Then I snuggled into the soft woolly floor.

Enough To Wake Me Up

Lady Bell said something sharp in Cashlingese. I sat up abruptly, unsure how much time had passed since my last conscious thought. As far as I could tell, no one had changed position at all. Perhaps it had only been a few seconds.

But I did not know how long I had blanked out, and that terrified me.

"Is something wrong?" Festina asked. I opened my mouth to say, *I am very very scared* . . . but she was looking at Bell, not me.

I pushed myself up to look at Bell too. Even though the

Cashling woman had no face, it was clear she was most upset. In fact, Ms. Prophet was wheezing indignantly from a
dozen orifices at once.

"This stupid ship!" Lady Bell said. "The most important
day of my life, and wouldn't you know, the communication
system breaks down. We can't raise a peep from Jalmut; no
trans-light communications at all."

As the human phrase goes, a chill went down my spine. In
fact, it felt more as if the chill moved upward from my stomach to my shoulders and thence to my face, but perhaps
chills behave non-traditionally in artificial gravity.

"Uh-oh," muttered Uclod. "I hate to say it, missy," he told
Bell, "but it sounds like you're getting jammed."

"Jammed?" Aarhus repeated. "Oh crap."

"Quick!" Festina said. "We need a long-range scan right
now!"

"No, we don't," Nimbus answered quietly.

He waved a foggy arm, pointing behind our backs. We all
whirled to look through the glass bulkhead.

There, looming across half the sky, was the stick-ship.

Big Bully

"Damn, that's a big sucker," Festina whispered.

The Shaddill had appeared alongside *Royal Hemlock*, a
vast brown forest beside a single white tree. Every stick in
the Shaddill ship seemed larger than the entire *Hemlock*:
longer and wider, like oaks crowding in on a paper birch.
There were hundreds, maybe thousands, of the brown
sticks, one of which telescoped lazily toward the dwarfed
navy vessel.

"What are the odds," Uclod asked, "those bastards will
just grab *Hemlock* and fly away?"

"They don't want to fly away," Festina said. "They want
to capture everyone who knows too much. You. Oar. Anybody you might have talked to."

"Which means the whole damned crusade."

"Right. They want to nab every last ship."

"How the hell will they do that?" Uclod asked. "We've got dozens of little ships. If we scatter in different directions—"

"They won't let us," Festina said. With sudden urgency, she rolled to her feet. "Lady Bell, is there any way to opaque this ship's hull?"

"Why would I want to do that?" the lady asked.

A flash of blue brilliance burst upon us like lightning. For a moment, Festina's face was reduced to pure black and white: white eyes, black pupils, white skin, black birthmark, white anger, black "I knew this would happen" expression. Then her body crumpled limply to the floor.

Everyone else was already lying down.

Another Ship Bites The Dust

I am such a one as thrives on bright light. I did not feel invigorated by this particular light, but I did not slump over unconscious either. Perhaps, as the Pollisand had joked, many types of light just pass right through my body. At any rate, I am not so weak as opaque persons, so it takes more than a garish flash to subdue *me*.

The others, alas, were unconscious . . . everyone but Nimbus, who still hovered mistlike above the unmoving bodies. It annoyed me that he too had remained awake; one enjoys being special, or at least more special than an entity made of fog. Nevertheless, I could guess why he had not succumbed: a creature consisting of tiny floaty bits might not be affected by Sinister Weapon Beams in the same manner as creatures made from meat . . . and of course he was nearly as transparent as I, not to mention he too had been designed by the Shaddill.

Perhaps we had both been constructed immune to Shaddill weaponry. If so, the stick-people were greatly foolish—if *I* were designing artificial beings, I would make them *especially* susceptible to my favorite weapons, so I could quell rebellions with dispatch. But then, the Shaddill were villains; and if I had learned anything from the fictional writings of my people, it was that Villains Always Make Mistakes.

"What shall we do now?" I whispered to Nimbus. "If the Shaddill think we are unconscious, this is an excellent time to take them by surprise."

"Don't be too hasty," the cloud man replied. "They know you're here, right? Catching you seems to be a priority for them. And they must suspect their stun-beam doesn't work on you—it didn't work when you were in Starbiter, so why should it work now?" He drifted across the floor a short distance, then drifted back again: the cloudish equivalent of pacing. "Maybe they're *hoping* you'll do something noticeable so they can tell where you are."

"Ahh," I said. "That is astute reasoning." I looked up at the glass roof. "Of course, they will see me as soon as they look in this direction. I am harder to notice than opaque persons, but I am not invisible."

"Don't worry about that," Nimbus told me. "In a Cashling ship like this, the hull is only transparent one way; you can see out, but no one can see in. The Shaddill won't spot you that easily."

Which meant that with so many ships in the crusade, the Shaddill faced great difficulty determining where I was. Our trying to flee or attack would be a mistake, since it would catch the Shaddill's attention . . . but then, I doubted that we *could* flee or attack. *Unfettered Destiny* would almost certainly refuse to take commands except from the Cashlings themselves. Indeed, I did not know if I could even leave the studio—without Lady Bell's or Lord Rye's permission, the ship's security systems might not open the door for me.

That is often the way with mechanical devices—they are most exceedingly mulish. Back in my village on Melaquin, many buildings contained shiny equipment with display screens showing excellent three-dimensional curve-graphs in bold fluorescent colors. The village's maintenance robots kept these devices free of rust, and presumably in perfect running order; however, no one knew what the machinery did. According to tales from my mother (who received the tales from *her* mother and so on back through the centuries), the equipment would only respond to commands spoken in the ancient language my ancestors used more than four thousand years ago. That language was not the tongue we had learned from the village's teaching machines; therefore, my sister and I could only stare at the waves of color constantly painting themselves on the monitors, and dream of what excellent deeds we might do if only we learned the correct words to say.

Was I not in the same position now?

Reflecting gloomily on my inability to control the Cashling ship, it struck me that once again I had boarded a vessel, only to find it rendered inoperable shortly after my arrival. This was not an amusing pattern of starship behavior. Moreover, the trend was accelerating. I had lasted seven hours on Starbiter, before she ripped herself apart; then an hour on *Royal Hemlock* before the dreadful act of sabotage; and finally, only ten minutes on *Unfettered Destiny* before the attack on the Cashlings made it impossible to command the ship to do anything.

Perhaps I should endeavor to board the Shaddill craft. If I managed to do that, the stick-ship might explode instantly into a cloud of radioactive dust.

Hah!

The Fate Of The Hemlock

Thinking about the stick-ship, I raised my head to the glass ceiling and stared at the alien vessel. A hollow tubelike stick now extended from the Shaddill ship's belly: reaching out slowly like a snake slithering up to its prey, the stick thwacked against the *Hemlock*'s hull. Of course I heard no sound through the vacuum of space; but the navy craft shuddered and shook silently with the impact. The collision must have been forceful enough to knock people in *Hemlock* off their feet—if any of them were still standing after the beam weapon's attack.

For a moment, the pair of ships just floated there, as if the white navy cruiser were impaled on the big brown stick. Then a thousand tiny vines sprung from the end of the stick, some circling the *Hemlock* widthwise while others streamed out along the ship's length, and still more wrapped around the hull in long weaving spirals. In places, the vines criss-crossed each other; in others, they sprouted side tendrils that intertwined and appeared to fuse together. Considering how far we were from the two vessels, the vines must have been quite thick—perhaps as wide around as my entire body; otherwise, I would not have been able to see them at such a distance. But they moved with the speed and flexibility of much smaller strands, until they had completely bound the *Hemlock* in their great sinister web.

The telescoping stick began to retract: back into the body of the Shaddill ship, dragging with it the trussed-up *Hemlock*. Two nearby sticks snaked out of the woodpile as if they were interested in having a closer look at the captured prize. They drifted lazily outward, skimming their heads along the length of the navy ship in opposite directions; then they struck simultaneously, jamming their open mouths onto either end of the cruiser. Once the *Hemlock* had been capped fore and aft in this fashion, it was quickly pulled down into the weaving brown forest. I lost sight of it as dozens more sticks slithered up and over the ship, like a mass of brown snakes squirming onto a single white one.

So that is the end of the Hemlock, I thought. *And how long before the Shaddill gather up the crusade ships as well?* Even as the words crossed my mind, a new stick telescoped from the Shaddill vessel, reaching for one of the crusade's smaller craft.

Our own ship had pulled a goodly distance away from *Hemlock*; therefore, if the Shaddill began scooping up the nearest crusade ships, they would not get to us for a few minutes. However, it was only a matter of time before they swallowed us all.

A Gargantuan Sneeze

I turned to say something to Nimbus—I do not know what it was going to be, I simply wanted to speak and hear his voice in return—but the cloud man had vanished. I blinked and peered around the room. There was no sign of him, not even a little bit. I was about to cry out in anger and fear when I noticed baby Starbiter resting in the pit of Festina's stomach.

That was a strange place indeed for an infant Zarett.

I moved nearer for a better look. Festina had fallen into a twisted three-quarters position, her bottom half lying sideways on her right hip, but her top half slumped over so her chest and arms lay almost flat on the floor. This left a covered nestlike area under the shelter of her belly, a dark little cave where a small Zarett person could rest safely. Nimbus must have placed Starbiter there in the shadow of my friend's body, where the little girl would be protected while her father was busy with other activities.

But what was the foolish man doing? Where had he gone?

I looked around frantically. The recording studio possessed numerous air vents in its floor and ceiling; a creature made of bits could have left through any one of them. Perhaps he planned to seek *Unfettered Destiny*'s bridge, hoping to take control of the ship. Nimbus might well speak the Cashling tongue—he had, after all, served on ships owned by Cashlings, and had demonstrated an ability to learn languages quickly. If he could give orders to this ship in Cashlingese, he might . . . he might . . . I did not know what he might do, since we had already agreed not to draw unwanted attention. But the bridge was the only place I could imagine the cloud man might go . . .

. . . until I saw wisps of mist dribbling out of Festina's nose.

"Nimbus!" I cried. "Are you inside my Faithful Sidekick? It is very very wrong to enter a woman when she is unconscious and helpless!"

The cloud man did not reply; but Festina made a choked "Uhh" noise that sounded as if her entire head was congested with mucous. One arm moved and her body shifted. Seeing the potential for a horrible occurrence, I snatched up little Starbiter and clutched her to my breast mere moments

before Festina groaned and rolled over. (Festina rolled onto
her back, so she would not have crushed the baby after all.
Still, I felt heroic for my lightning-quick reaction. With
heroism, it is the thought that counts.)

As for my friend, she ended spreadeagled face up on the
jet black carpet. The carpet sank beneath her, molding itself
into a Festina-shaped hollow . . . as if she had struck the
floor after falling from a great height. Festina lay in this per-
sonalized gully for nearly a minute, all the time making loud
congested grunts and wheezes that were most undignified. I
knelt beside her, cradling her head and offering words of en-
couraging comfort: "Stop those ugly sounds at once, you
foolish one! You must not be ill or dying, because that is not
how a proper sidekick behaves."

As I held her, more mist trickled out of her nose. The bits
did not *stay* outside; whenever she inhaled, all the mist went
back in again. After one exhalation, I waved my hand
through the fog around her face in an effort to disperse it . . .
but the tiny particles simply swirled past my fingers and returned inside with the next breath. Of course, I could have
prevented this by squeezing Festina's nostrils shut. However,
I did not wish to asphyxiate my friend, so I stayed my hand.

Suddenly, Festina let loose a colossal sneeze. The sneeze
was remarkable in several regards: volume of sound, volume
of air, and volume of sputum discharged into my face. I
wiped off the moisture with great dispatch (or more precisely, with the sleeve of my jacket); and as I was doing so, a
burst of fog exploded from my friend, streaming out her
nose and mouth, and even little wisps from her ears. In seconds, Nimbus floated before me . . . while in my arms, Festina opened her eyes and said, "Christ, I feel like shit."

"That is because you had a cloud man in your head," I told
her. "It seems he saw you unconscious and succumbed to
penetrative urges."

Festina stared at me a moment, then closed her eyes, murmuring, "This is all a dream, this is all a dream, this is all a
dream." She opened her eyes, looked at me, and said,
"Damn. So much for that theory."

The Cloud Man Gets Huffy

I helped my friend sit up—which was not as easy as it sounds. First, I still held the gooey infant Starbiter in one hand and was attempting not to hurt her (or get too much of her ickyness on me). Second, the floor kept shifting, trying to reshape itself to Festina's body the moment she moved in any direction. It made me wonder how many people died because of these foolish floors; one could easily sink into a customized crater and starve to death because one could not get out.

Starvation was a subject much on my mind.

When Festina finally reached the vertical, she shook her head as if trying to clear her wits. Then with a groan she said, "Shit . . . what's happened since I went down?"

"Very little. The Shaddill have seized the *Hemlock* and have begun to capture smaller ships."

"That's all they've done in six hours?"

"It has not been six hours," I told her. "It has been less than five minutes."

"But I thought . . . the first time the Shaddill flashed you, Uclod and Lajoolie were unconscious for . . . I shouldn't be awake yet."

Nimbus drifted closer—which is to say, closer to Festina. His tiny bits avoided me, as if his whole body were leaning back from my presence. "I thought it advisable to wake you," he told my friend. "Stimulate your glands and nervous system; get some adrenaline pumping; counteract the effects of the beam."

"You can *do* that?" Festina asked.

"Apparently," he said. "I haven't had much practical experience with *Homo sapiens*, but my medical training covered first aid on familiar alien species. Apologies if my methods lacked finesse; how are you feeling?"

"Like crap, but I'll live. Thanks."

Nimbus fluttered, temporarily losing his human shape. "Then I'll move on to someone else. The more of us who are conscious, the better we can deal with the Shaddill when they arrive." He swirled above the other bodies as if looking them over one by one; then he coalesced next to Lajoolie. "This one next," he said. "We may need muscle."

"I have muscle," I told him. "I am excellent at feats of strength."

He did not answer. In fact, his body tightened at the sound of my voice. Perhaps he was simply compressing his components in preparation for flying up Lajoolie's nose; but it occurred to me, he might be upset at certain insinuations I had made about his behavior: specifically, my remarks about penetrative urges. He was, after all, a creature who burned with shame over something as simple as tickling his daughter or seeing through her eyes. Perhaps he felt equally guilty about entering Festina's body and forcibly rousing her to consciousness. It was much the same, was it not? Invading a woman's anatomy without permission, even though the act was justified. And a man in such a state of guilt might be *sensitive* to allegations that he was acting from base motives.

He might be very hurt indeed.

As Nimbus flowed up Lajoolie's nostrils, I called to him, "I am sorry I suggested you behaved improperly when you entered Festina. I was foolish to jump to such a mistaken conclusion. But it is amusing, is it not, how misjudgments occur? And it is also most traditional. You and I, we are son and daughter of the Shaddill; and as siblings, it is common to fall into ill-founded petty disagreements . . ."

I stopped speaking because he had disappeared—completely ignoring my words. Pretending I did not exist, because he was fiercely angry at me.

Sometimes it is hard to have a brother. Especially when you both make each other feel bad.

More Arousals

I do not know if Divians are easier to wake than humans, or if Nimbus had simply gained experience in rousing persons from this type of unconsciousness. Whatever the explanation, the cloud man did not take nearly so long to bring

Lajoolie around as he had with Festina. As soon as her eyes flickered open, he proceeded immediately into Uclod's sinuses, not giving me the tiniest opportunity to apologize again.

Watching Nimbus work on the two Divians, I wondered why he had not woken them the previous time they had been shot with the Shaddill's beam. The probable answer was that invading other people's bodies truly filled him with abhorrence. On the previous occasion, I had been doing an excellent job of piloting Starbiter so there was no need to rouse the two Divians; now, however, our predicament was so dire that it called for Extreme Resuscitation.

Of course, extreme resuscitation is not pleasant, and neither Festina nor Lajoolie looked to be enjoying their newly regained consciousness. Lajoolie showed a marked preference for lying in a fetal position, occasionally whimpering with pain. Festina remained sitting up, but drooped her head between her knees and muttered unintelligible phrases conspicuously featuring the word "hangover."

In an attempt to divert them from brooding on their pain, I said, "Come, we will soon face the villainous Shaddill, so we must make plans for a fight." But this did not rally their spirits. Lajoolie just groaned and Festina mumbled, "If there *is* a battle, pray God I get shot."

When Uclod regained consciousness, he was no more eager to spring into action than the other two. Nimbus still would not talk—he went directly into Sergeant Aarhus without an instant's pause. From Aarhus he moved on to Lady Bell, splitting himself into a dozen small fog patches and seeping into her body through a variety of orifices.

I do not know how he could tell which openings led into lungs, which into stomachs, and so on. However, the cloud man had the lady awake in under a minute . . . after which she howled most piteously. I opened my mouth to ask why she made such an appalling racket; but I closed it again when her head sank into her body as if being sucked down the neckhole. The skull fit exactly into her tiny torso.

This was something one did not see every day.

The now-headless Bell shifted her position on the floor to

lie flat on her spine. Immediately her legs lifted up from the hips, slanting back and arching above her body until her toes touched the carpet near her shoulders—her legs completely covering her torso like two logs laid lengthwise down her chest. Reaching up, she wrapped her arms tight around her thighs, then bent her knees so that her calves were on top of her arms, on top of her upper legs, on top of her headless body. She held that tucked-up position for a brief moment; then the whole stack of Bell crushed in on itself with a sound like knuckles cracking. In a moment, she had reduced herself to a tight little basket of a person, a bundled-up woman who lay on the ground in a heap that reminded me of a discarded turtle shell.

This was the Cashling defense configuration I had seen in pictures. It may have been quite excellent for protecting vital organs under a thick arrangement of bones . . . but I did not think it clever to reduce oneself to a form that practically *demanded* other persons use you as a kickball.

Our Turn Next

All this time, the Shaddill ship had been snatching crusade vessels out of the sky. It did this with an extendible tube-stick, a big hose that reached toward one little craft after another and slowly sucked them in. None of the ships tried to flee or dodge the hose—the Cashlings on board must have been unconscious, everyone brought low by the blue-white flash.

Though I despised the Shaddill, I had to admit they built excellent weapons.

Each time a ship was captured, the mouth of the hose-stick squeezed shut for a few minutes. I suppose it took that long to swallow what had been eaten, to clear the stick's mouth so it could gobble up more. In my imagination, I pictured a huge stomach inside the stick-ship, where little crusade craft bobbed listlessly amidst foul digestive juices. *Well,* I thought, *I shall give those great poop-heads a tummy-ache to remember.*

No sooner had those words passed through my mind than the great sucking hose turned its mouth toward us.

"Uh-oh," I said. "Uh-oh."

Blacking Out Destiny

"We must now be very brave," I announced to my comrades.

Festina lifted her head, saw the oncoming hose-stick, and staggered to her feet. She required a moment to steady herself once she became wholly upright; then she tottered her way to Lady Bell, who was still closed up tight in her basket configuration. "Hey," my friend said, nudging the Cashling woman with her toe. "Open up."

"Go away," muttered a mouth in the lady's back.

"No," Festina said. "Not till you talk to your ship-soul."

I told Festina, "It would be unwise for *Unfettered Destiny* to take evasive maneuvers. We would only give away that we were conscious."

"I know; but we still have things to do." Festina gave Bell another nudge with her toe . . . though perhaps it was less a nudge and more of a kick.

"Leave me alone!" the lady hissed . . . which is to say, a small number of her mouths spoke the words while the rest did the hissing.

Festina took no notice. "I won't leave you alone till you do what I want. It's in your best interests too. If they take you prisoner, you'll never be seen again. Do you want to go down in history as the prophet who lost an entire crusade?"

Lady Bell made a barking wheeze. I suspect this was a rude word in the Cashling tongue. However, as Festina prepared to deliver a kick that showed every promise of being full strength, Bell said, "All right, all right." An eye opened in the middle of her back. "What do you want?"

"Tell the ship-soul to opaque the hull. As thick as possible so we can't see out."

"Why?" Lady Bell asked sullenly.

"In case the Shaddill flash us again."

"They've already flashed us once. What's the point of a second shot?"

"Insurance," Festina said. "If I were the Shaddill, I'd keep shooting the whole damned crusade every five minutes, just to avoid surprises. They haven't done that, so maybe the weapon draws too much power to let them bang away indiscriminately. Even so, they might have a smaller version of the weapon inside, and they'll zap us just before they board our ship."

"You think blacking out the hull will protect us?" The lady's voice sounded most sneerful. "I bet that beam isn't real light at all—it'll affect us even if we can't see it."

"You're probably right," Festina said. "But I'd feel stupid if we could save ourselves with simple measures and never bothered to try. Do it."

Lady Bell muttered something in Cashlingese. I thought it might be an insolent retort, but it must have been a command to the ship; a moment later, the glass roof went completely black. "There," Bell said. "Happy?"

"Ecstatic," Festina replied.

I myself was not so cheered by the change—without the see-through ceiling, the recording studio felt confined and glowery. It did not help that the floor was black . . . and the muted silence of the room added to the air of oppression that encompassed me.

"Let us go a different place," I said to Festina. "It is not pleasant here."

"I don't like it much myself," she replied, "but the place is soundproof. That might be important."

"You think the Shaddill are listening for us?" I asked. "How can that be? We are surrounded by the silence of space."

"Yes . . . but if we weren't soundproofed, any noise we made would be conducted throughout the ship, eventually making tiny vibrations in the hull. If the Shaddill bounce a laser off the ship's outer skin, they'll be able to detect those vibrations. They'll know we're in here talking."

Lady Bell made a disgusted whoosh. "Are you always this paranoid?"

Festina glared at her. "Usually I'm *more* paranoid, but right now I'm still hungover."

The ship gave a sudden lurch. "What was that?" Lajoolie cried out.

"I think we've just been swallowed," Festina answered.

"Do not worry," I said, patting her shoulder. "This happens to me all the time."

My Plan

"All right," Festina said, "we need a plan."

"To do what?" Lady Bell asked.

"To escape. Or at least, to survive."

I said, "The villains will come through the receiving bay, will they not? So we should lie in wait behind the boxes cluttered in that area. When the Shaddill arrive, we shall leap from concealment and punch them in the nose." I paused. "Provided they are such creatures as possess noses. If we leap from concealment and do not see noselike facial features, we shall have to improvise."

"Sounds good to me, missy," Uclod said. "Of course, if the Shaddill *do* have noses, they'll probably pass out the second they get a whiff of this place."

"Watch your tongue!" Bell snapped.

Sergeant Aarhus cleared his throat. All this time, he had been sitting on the carpet, no doubt gathering strength after being unconscious. Now he rose and told Festina, "I hate to admit it, Admiral, but Oar's plan sounds as good as we'll get. We sure can't stay in the studio here—it's got see-through walls and nowhere to hide. We'll be sitting ducks."

"I know." Festina made a face. "All right—an ambush in the receiving bay. Everyone ready to fight?"

Uclod, Lajoolie, Aarhus, and I all chorused yes. Nimbus floated delicately forward. "I won't be much use in a scuffle . . . and I have to protect my daughter."

"Understandable," Festina said. She glanced at me; I still held the little Zarett girl in one hand, and gooey though the infant was, I did not mind the feel of her so much. She was very most delicately soft, a small light person who seemed so fragile and breakable that Deep Adult Instincts made me want to take care of her. To be honest, I wanted to snuggle her a little while longer . . . but time was short, and I could not throw punches with a child in my fist.

"Here she is," I said, cupping her in both hands and holding her out to her father. Nimbus swirled forward, and for a moment, I felt his cool dryness playing around my fingers. It might have been a nudge of forgiveness; one cannot tell with fog, but I do believe it was more than just the bare minimum of contact required to take the girl. Then he was gone, and baby Starbiter was gone too, wrapped in a thick ball of mist.

"All right," Festina said, "now what about you, Lady Bell? Are you up for some fisticuffs?"

"I've heard," Aarhus put in, "that Cashlings are excellent fighters. Stunningly powerful kicks."

He said this so unctuously, even naïve baby Starbiter must have recognized his words as purposeful flattery. Lady Bell, however, was not so perceptive; she loosened slightly from her wrapped-up form, with orifices fluttering all over her green skin. It looked like the Cashling form of simpering. "I can handle myself quite well," she answered in a creamily smug tone of voice. "If it's absolutely necessary . . ."

"It is," Festina said. "Now let's get down to the airlock. And once we're outside the studio, no talking. The engines make enough background noise to cover our footsteps, but let's not get sloppy."

"Sloppy!" Lady Bell said, continuing to unfold back to her more personlike configuration. "I am *never* sloppy."

Sergeant Aarhus opened the door and the odor outside assailed my nostrils. I believe we all wished to take exception to Lady Bell's last statement; but it was too late for cutting remarks.

Silently, we headed for the receiving bay.

22

WHEREIN I BATTLE THE ENEMY WITH PRECIOUS METALS

Waiting

When I say we headed out silently, I mean as silently as possible. Though I am excellent at stealth in natural settings, it is most unreasonable to expect hard glass feet not to clack on solid tiles. The noise was enough to make me self-conscious; I also believe Lady Bell was glaring at me, though her lack of a face made it difficult to be certain. I mouthed the words, *I am doing my best*, then spent the rest of the journey staring down at my feet . . . which was just as well, considering the quantity of vile substances I had to circumnavigate on the floor.

Once we reached the receiving bay, we chose separate hiding places close to the airlock door. I took a strategic position between a chest-high crate stacked with platinum ingots, and a container made of blue sheet-metal whose interior was littered with fish skeletons. At one time, the container must have been filled with sea water—the metal was crusted with salt deposits and the dried remains of lacy seaweed—but the water had evaporated and the fish had died of dehydration . . . or suffocation . . . or starvation . . . or sheer lack of hope. I found myself staring at their with-

273

ered carcasses and feeling most teary-eyed over their unde-
served fate; so I forced myself to turn away and grabbed a
chunk of platinum from the other box, promising the ghosts
of those fish I would hurl the heavy ingot with great strength
at someone who truly deserved it.

I settled down in my place, squeezing the cool platinum
while I waited for Shaddill to arrive. It was too bad the hull
was no longer transparent—I would have liked to observe
the process of being sucked into the bowels of the stick-
ship. But such was not to be. I could only crouch in Nervous Anticipation, trying to guess what was going on
outside and doing a poor job of it. In my head I would say,
Ten seconds from now, I shall hear something; but then I did
not hear something, so I thought, *Another five seconds and
someone will come*; but the five seconds passed without incident, whereupon I started counting to see how long it *did*
take for something to occur, but I lost patience when I
reached fifteen, so I crossed all my fingers and even my
thumbs to *force* the Shaddill to do something, and I
squeezed my eyes shut and *everything* . . . then I counted
some more, then stared at my reflection in the platinum ingot
to see how I looked when I was Fraught With Expectation,
but there were too many smudges from my fingers on the
metal, and I was just cleaning the ingot on my jacket sleeve
when *Unfettered Destiny* struck something with a thud.

Hah! I thought to myself, *this is it! And despite the terrible wait, I did not let my brain become Tired And Distracted
at all.*

The Enemy Arrives

Events did not transpire immediately. After the bump
(which I assumed was our ship settling onto a landing pad),
there was a tedious delay of at least ten seconds before I
heard noises in the airlock. Then the airlock took an uncon-
scionably long time to perform its function, so that I just
knew the awful Shaddill were playing foolish games punching the control buttons for mere entertainment rather than

Getting Down To Business. At last, when I was so keyed with frustration I was ready to dash over and rip open the airlock with my bare hands, the door gave a resounding click and swung ponderously inward.

An object was tossed into the room: a dull silver orb the size of my fist, sailing in a lazy arc upward, then down toward the floor. The object had WEAPON written all over it . . . not literally (as far as I could see) but I knew something unpleasant would happen when it struck the ground. I squinched quickly behind the crate of ingots, putting all that heavy platinum between me and the silver ball. However, because I was still trying to keep silent, I did not move quite speedily enough—my right arm and shoulder were still exposed when the ball hit the floor with a clink.

I did not see or hear any spectacular result—no flash, no explosive boom. My unprotected arm simply went numb from shoulder to fingertips. I could see the arm was still there, but it had no sensation at all. Even worse, it had no strength; and that was the hand which had been holding the platinum ingot. Before I realized the danger, the ingot slipped from my limp fingers and dropped to the ground.

Clunk!

So much for lurking in secret. Without hesitation, I let forth a gasp of Poignant Distress and slumped into an aesthetically pleasing sprawl on the floor. Since I had accidentally revealed my presence to the Shaddill, I would let them believe they had bested me with their numbness device; that way they might not embark upon more drastic action to overpower me or my comrades. When they came to collect my unconscious body, I could still take them by surprise and rain punches on their villainous noses.

I lay where I was, cleverly opening my eyes in tiny slits to observe what was going on. At first, I saw nothing; but I heard heavy footsteps walk cautiously out of the airlock and advance in my direction.

None of my hidden comrades attacked. I did not know if they had fallen victim to numbness themselves or if they had been sufficiently shielded behind crates and were simply biding their time, waiting for the Shaddill to advance farther

into the room. It was also possible there were multiple Shaddills to consider—if a single one ventured into the receiving
bay while others remained in the airlock to provide covering
fire, the situation required delicate handling. As for me, all I
could do was lie still and wait . . . until I saw a pair of feet
step around a box some four paces away.

They appeared to be human feet. More precisely, they
were feet wearing human-style boots—very much like the
boots both Festina and Aarhus wore.

Sturdy *navy-issue* boots.

A Ghastly Realization

The boots took a step toward me. My head lay at an angle
that prevented me from seeing more than the person's
legs . . . but they looked very much like human legs enclosed in human trousers. *Gray* trousers. Gray trousers exactly like Festina's—the color that denotes an admiral in the
human fleet.

I suspected this was not just an Eerie Coincidence.

The person in gray made rustling noises: I could not see
what this person was doing, but it sounded as if he or she
was rooting inside a jacket pocket. Then a man's voice said
in conversational tones, "It's Oar. We've got her."

No doubt he was speaking to someone else via a communication device. This in itself was enough to give me
chills—confirmation that these people were looking for me
in particular. But even more terrifying was *how* he spoke:
not in English, but *in my own language*. The tongue I had
learned from infancy, the language of my mother and my
sister and all the teaching machines on Melaquin.

Suddenly, I had a terrible thought. Those teaching machines had been built by the Shaddill . . . and I knew our current language was not what my ancestors spoke when they
first arrived from Earth.

What if all this time—from my very birth and from the
births of untold generations of my glass predecessors—we
had been speaking the Shaddill's own tongue? What if they

had created the teaching machines to make us over in their own image? Our flesh-and-blood ancestors could not have prevented it; they were mortals who died in their natural time, and after that, our only instructors were the machines. Perhaps somewhere on Melaquin, in some well-lit Ancestral Tower, members of the first glass generation still remembered words from ancient human tongues . . . but those ancestors had not made sufficient effort to pass on the words to subsequent generations, and now we were thoroughly immersed in the language of our enemy.

In a horrid way, *I* was a Shaddill.

I hoped that beneath the gray pants, the man in front of me did not have glass legs.

I Make First Contact With The Shaddill

The man stepped closer. Indeed, he came near enough to nudge me with his foot. I let him do so; he gave a satisfied grunt, then turned away. That was the moment I swept my right leg in front of his ankles, while kicking at the back of his knees with my other foot. His knees buckled most satisfactorily—he fell backward on top of me, his head striking my stomach with a satisfying thump.

It was an Earthling head with genuine hair. Not my lovely glass species at all.

My right arm was still entirely numb. However, I threw my left around the man's throat in an arm-bar and squeezed tight. He tried to yell, but could draw no air. Desperately, he grabbed my arm with both hands and tried to pull it away. If I had possessed a functional right hand to reinforce the arm-bar, he never would have pried me loose. As it was, he still had to work hard for it—after five seconds, he was just able to inhale, readying himself for a shout, when a large orange hand clamped down hard on his mouth.

Lajoolie. I had not heard the tiniest whisper of her approach.

She was not quite so silent in finishing the man off—one cannot throw eight successive palm-heels into a man's solar plexus without making noticeable thumps, not to mention the "Whuf!" sounds that emerge from a man's mouth no matter how thoroughly you have him muffled—but the noises were scuffly and vague, rather than clear-cut evidence of a fight. If other persons were listening, I hoped they would think the man was merely struggling to drag my unconscious body out into the open . . . and indeed, a moment later, a woman's voice called, "Do you need a hand with her?"

Lajoolie looked at me helplessly. The words had been spoken in my own language; Lajoolie did not know what had been said, and no doubt feared it was something like, "I know you have pummeled my partner, and now I will shoot you like dogs."

I gave Lajoolie a reassuring smile and called back in a throaty whisper, "Yes, come help." One would never pretend it sounded *exactly* like the man, but my performance was good enough to fool the unseen woman—her footsteps came slowly out of the airlock, moving in our direction.

As she approached, there was time to inspect the man Lajoolie and I had just bludgeoned. His hair was jet black, cut close to the skull, and he sported a fussily trimmed goatee; his skin was golden, about halfway between Aarhus's light pinkness and Festina's deep tan. As for his clothes, they were indeed a Technocracy admiral's uniform—something that raised important questions, but I had no time to ponder such issues. The man's female colleague would soon be upon us and . . .

And . . .

The man was not breathing. In fact, he had gone quite limp; I could not remember him moving so much as an eyelid since Lajoolie finished hitting him.

Oh dear, I thought, *the League of Peoples is not going to like this.*

I Make Second Contact With The Shaddill

The man's female partner was almost upon us. Silently, Lajoolie slipped out of sight behind the crate of platinum. As for me, I was left as I had been while trying to choke the foe: lying on my back with the man slumped on top of me.

Knowing that any second, the Shaddill woman would come around the corner and see what had happened, I used my good hand to snatch up the ingot I had dropped earlier. When the woman appeared—a beefy red-faced human with hair of stringy white, her body clad in admiral's gray—I hurled the chunk of metal with all my strength straight into her stomach.

The impact made a satisfying thump. Her shoulders jerked in a sharp spasm, but she did not buckle over. Instead, she reached toward her belt where a pistol hung in a holster; I recognized the gun as a hypersonic stunner, the type carried by human Explorers. Such a weapon had murdered my sister and nearly killed me as well. Therefore, I was desperately trying to roll away from the line of fire, when a slim brown hand slammed the pistol out of the woman's fingers.

The slim brown hand was attached to Festina's arm.

A moment later, a slim brown fist attached to Festina's other arm caught the woman with a cracking blow to the jaw. The woman's head snapped sideways, but she showed no sign of being hurt. In fact, it was Festina who yelled, "Fuck!" and jerked her fist away as if in great pain. Even so, my Faithful Sidekick went back on the offensive within a split-second: she slammed her forearm across the woman's chest while simultaneously sweeping a leg behind the woman's knees. The alien admiral woman toppled backward, striking the floor with a bang. Then Aarhus and Uclod were there, pounding and stomping and generally committing mayhem until the woman lay still.

"Damn!" Uclod panted. "That was one tough honey."

"Her partner was not tough at all," I said. "He is no longer breathing."

"Christ!" Festina cried. She raced toward me and dropped to her knees, touching her fingers to the fallen man's throat. Her face turned even more anxious; after probing the man's neck at several points, she said, "I can't find a pulse. Shit!"

With desperate urgency, she dragged the man off me, flat

onto the floor. Kneeling beside him, she tipped back his head, blew two breaths into his mouth, then began pushing down on his chest. Under her breath she whispered, "One and two and three and four and five and . . ."

"Oh, missy," Uclod said, hovering behind Festina's shoulder, "this is not good. They only had zappers and stun-grenades. We had no justification for using deadly force . . ."

Lajoolie, still crouching beside the crate of platinum, let forth an anguished sob. "I just . . ." She buried her face in her hands.

Uclod rushed to her side, calling out to the whole room, "It's not her fault. She didn't know her own strength."

"I *do*," she moaned, "I *do* know my own strength. Over and over again, they told me never to hit people or else . . . or else my brother . . ." She sobbed and crumpled.

"I've got bad news," Sergeant Aarhus called from a few paces away. "This woman isn't breathing either."

He was squatting beside the red-faced admiral; he had placed his hand on her throat in the same manner as Festina had touched the man. "No pulse," he said.

"Both of them?" Festina broke off pumping the man's chest and sat back on her heels. "Shit—the League is going to love this."

"Yes," agreed Aarhus. "To lose one opponent may be regarded as a misfortune; to lose both looks like carelessness."

Festina stared at the man she had just been attempting to revive. "How the hell could we kill them both?"

"Perhaps these Shaddill are shamefully weak and fragile," I suggested.

"These people aren't Shaddill," she told me. "This man is Jhimal Rhee, Admiral of the Brown. The woman is Gunsa Macleod, Admiral of the Orange. They're members of the navy's High Council; I've met them a few times."

"Oh goody," Aarhus said, "I just helped snuff a high admiral. Correct me if I'm wrong, but I'll bet that's a court-martial offense."

"Rhee and Macleod?" Uclod asked. "Killing them isn't an offense, it's a humanitarian service. We should all get a bounty."

The little man was holding Lajoolie, stroking her shoulders . . . and for once, she was no taller than he, for she had sunk to her knees and was hunched over almost to the floor. She wept piteously—the sort of weeping when the weeper seems terrified to make the tiniest sound, so it is all choked whimpers and sniffles. Uclod squeezed her and spoke gently. "It's all righ* sweetheart, you don't have to worry. You've read the ~~s on these bastards. Rhee and Macleod were two of the worst on the council. Rhee arranged for that colony to starve to death, remember? He tampered with the food shipment schedules. When the colonists were dead, he sent in settlers of his own and claimed the whole planet for himself. As for Macleod, she killed her first three husbands for their money. The files absolutely proved it. Remember that, honey? Rhee and Macleod were both dangerous non-sentients, and the League doesn't give a self-righteous crap what you do to them."

"I do not understand," I whispered to Festina. "If these humans were dangerous non-sentients, how could they journey through space? Would the League not prevent them from doing so?"

"Damn right it would."

She stared at the man, Admiral Rhee, lying motionless before her. Suddenly, she reached for his jacket, ripped up the slap-tab, and tore open his shirt. In the pit of his stomach, where Lajoolie had struck him so many times, his skin had burst under the force of the blows. Beneath lay a crushed mass of wires and electronic circuitry.

"Okay," she said to everyone in the room, "I have good news and bad news . . ."

The Shaddill And The Admiralty

It did not take long to ascertain that the red-faced woman was also a person of mechanical construction—Aarhus rubbed her arm hard against the sharp edge of a sheet metal container and the woman's skin split open, revealing a collection of shiny steel armatures.

"You see, honey?" Uclod murmured to Lajoolie. "They were just robots. You didn't do anything wrong. Doesn't that make you feel better?"

Lajoolie made an indeterminate noise.

"Makes *me* feel better," Festina said. "I thought I was losing my edge when I socked that bitch in the jaw and damned near broke my fist."

"Of course," Aarhus said, "you have to wonder why the Shaddill have perfect copies of two Technocracy admirals." He touched his fingertips to the robot woman's cheek. "The skin feels amazingly authentic—best meat-puppet I've ever seen. Bet she even had a neck-pulse before we bashed the crap out of her."

"What I'd like to know," Festina said, "is whether the real Rhee and Macleod are still back on New Earth . . . or if they've actually been missing for years."

Uclod blinked. "You think these robots had replaced the real admirals? Like . . . the originals had been bumped off and these robots were the ones sitting on the High Council?"

"It's possible," Festina said. "Your files claim the original Rhee and Macleod were both murderers. Okay: that means they weren't sentient. The Shaddill could cold-bloodedly kill the two of them without upsetting the League. Once the real Rhee and Macleod were gone, android duplicates could quietly step in."

"After which," Aarhus said, "the meat-puppets took their places on the council, all the while working for the Shaddill. Sending their masters Admiralty secrets, and doing their best to influence council decisions."

"Yeah," Uclod agreed. "But then the council caught wind of York's exposé. If it ever became public, every high admiral scumwad would get thrown in jail . . . at which point, they'd be strip-searched and put through medical exams. An X ray was bound to show that the fake Rhee and Macleod had gears between their ears. So the Shaddill swooped the robots off New Earth, whisking away the evidence before anyone learned the Admiralty had been infiltrated."

Festina nodded. "It explains what brought the Shaddill into this whole mess—when the High Council found out about the exposé, the robots did too. They immediately reported to Shaddill Central."

"Hey," Uclod said, glaring at the two machine people, "do you think these ratchet-brains killed Grandma Yulai?"

My friend shook her head. "If your Grandma Yulai was sentient, the Shaddill couldn't kill her. More likely, the murderer was sent by *real* human admirals."

"Bastards," Uclod said.

"Utter ones," I agreed. I had spent much of the past few minutes massaging my numbed arm, trying to wake it up. An unpleasant pins-and-needles sensation had begun to twang through the muscles—most uncomfortable, but any feeling was better than none. Meanwhile, I told Uclod, "We shall bring your grandmama's killer to justice, all in the fullness of time. For now, however, we must deal with the Shaddill . . . who are also utter bastards, and much closer to hand."

"Good point," said Festina. She got to her feet and called, "Bell! Where the fuck are you?"

Some distance away, I heard the crackly sound of gristle popping. Lady Bell had obviously folded up again, to protect herself during the fight . . . and she had remained in that position long after the fisticuffs ended. So much for Aarhus's claim that Cashlings were excellent kick-fighters. It seemed they were simply cowards.

"What do you want?" Bell's voice asked weakly.

A moment later, she came into view—hobbling most ostentatiously, as if she were desperately injured. I had no intention of inquiring what was wrong, but my Faithful Sidekick asked, "What happened to you?"

"The stun-grenade," Lady Bell answered, a theatrical quiver in her voice. "It caught my right foot; I'm sure it shut down at least one of my hearts and three whole lungs."

"Stunners don't interfere with hearts and lungs," Festina said. "Otherwise, they'd be lethal weapons, wouldn't they?"

"Are you implying—" Lady Bell began, but Festina cut her off.

"Don't start. Just ask the ship what the conditions are like outside the airlock."

I expected the lady to whine in protest . . . but for once

she did not argue. Instead, Bell muttered a few words in Cashlingese; a moment later, the gusty ship-soul voice answered with a rapid-fire report that would have interested me greatly if I had understood a word of it.

At last, the ship-soul stopped speaking. "Well?" Uclod asked.

"We're inside the Shaddill vessel," Lady Bell said. "In a big hangar with lots of other captured ships. Nitrogen-oxygen atmosphere—almost the same as we're breathing now."

"And the temperature?"

Lady Bell called to the ship-soul, got an answer, and said, "In human measurements, thirty-four degrees Celsius."

"Toasty," Aarhus grumbled. "We'll all end up sweating like pigs."

"Speak for yourself, Viking boy," Festina said. "Where I come from, thirty-four is a nice spring day." She looked around at the rest of us. "Care for a walk outside?"

"I wish to locate the Shaddill," I said, "for I have not yet punched *anyone* in the nose." My right arm was clumsily able to move on its own now—the fingers felt as weak as worms, but I trusted the debility would pass. I am excellent at speedy recuperation.

Uclod said, "I wouldn't mind kicking some butt myself." He turned to Lajoolie. "How about you, honey?"

The big woman did not answer. Her eyes and nose were still runny, and her face had a look of haunted guilt. I do not think she found any consolation in knowing the creature she destroyed was only a robot; she had thought he was a living man when she struck him, and her act of violence weighed torturously upon her mind. Perhaps she even realized one other thing—with a few blows of her hand, she had crushed a gut made of metal. How much more damage would she have done to mere flesh and blood?

"Lajoolie does not wish to kick butts," I told Uclod, "and she does not have to. The rest of us are fully capable of handling dangerous situations."

"Sure," said Festina, laying her hand on Lajoolie's arm, "if you want to take it easy for a while—"

"What?" Lady Bell interrupted. "You're just going to let

her play coward? If you get in another fight, you'll say, 'Oh, it doesn't matter if the strongest person on our side hides in a corner, we don't care if we win or lose so long as we don't hurt someone's feelings!' "

The Cashling was only saved because Uclod and I jumped toward her at the same time. The little orange man bounced against my shoulder, knocking me aside and knocking himself the other way; before we could converge again, Festina and Aarhus had stepped in to stop us from ramming Lady Bell's head through any orifice it would fit.

"We don't have time for this!" Festina snapped. "You two," she said, pointing at Uclod and me, "back off. You," she said, pointing at Lady Bell, "shut the fuck up. You," she said, pointing at Lajoolie, "you I trust to do the right thing if it becomes necessary. Even if it means using your fists again. Got me?"

Lajoolie hesitated a long moment, then nodded silently. Her eyes were rimmed with red.

"Fine," Festina said, "we have an understanding. Now let's get moving."

She headed for the airlock door, with Aarhus striding at her heels. As Festina passed the robot of Admiral Macleod, she stopped and picked up the stun-pistol that had fallen from the android's hand. The sergeant nodded approvingly.

Lady Bell lingered sullenly behind for a count of three; then she must have realized she was standing within arm's reach of Uclod and me without anyone near enough to intervene if hostilities broke out. She hastened most speedily after Festina and Aarhus.

Uclod took one of Lajoolie's arms and I took the other. Together we guided her forward. When we reached the airlock, Nimbus was already there, hovering in a foggy ball above everyone's head.

"All right," Festina said, "time to attack an entire shipload of hyper-advanced aliens on their home turf." She sighed. "Why I love being a goddamned Explorer."

"I too love being a goddamned Explorer," I said, proudly fingering my black jacket.

"Oar," Festina said, "you're a total fucking lunatic. Fortunately, that's exactly what we need." She waved a hand at Aarhus, who was standing by the airlock controls. "Push the button, Sergeant. Immortality awaits."

23

WHEREIN I CONFRONT UNPLEASANT TRUTHS

Lady Bell's Personal Limitations

The door of the airlock opened—and the first thing I noticed was dirt. The smell of dirt, loamy and cloying; the sight of dirt on the ground, dark and glinting with flecks of minerals; the feel of dirt in the air, gritty and humid and hot. Festina, standing in the airlock doorway, took a moment to inhale the deep soil scent . . . then she threw herself outside and assumed an aggressive posture with pistol in hand, quickly scanning the area for hostile forces.

After five seconds, she gestured for the rest of us to join her. We clambered out into dank sluggish air that pressed most tepidly against one's skin—all except Lady Bell, who remained shuddering in the airlock.

"What's wrong?" Festina asked her.

The lady replied, "It's horrid!"

She stared at the area surrounding us. It had the appearance of a vast tropical mud flat, simmering in twilight just after the sizzling sun has gone down. It even had some kind of foliage—not close to the ship, but off in the distance, clusters of trees and undergrowth rose high from the soil. Farther away still, dirt-covered walls towered up, up, up; in the dusky light, the top of the walls disappeared into shadow, but I assumed that far overhead there must be a roof closing us off from the vacuum outside. We were, after all, inside the stick-ship, even if this great chamber was so huge it seemed like out-of-doors.

"What is so horrid?" I asked Lady Bell. "The temperature is hotter than one enjoys, but there are no robots trying to shoot us. Also, in a spacious enclosure such as this, one can see potential enemies from quite far off, yet there is no sign of anybody. I believe for the moment we are safe."

"Knock on wood," Aarhus muttered under his breath.

"But . . . but . . ." Lady Bell said, "it's so . . . raw. And open. And *exposed.*"

"Bloody hell," Uclod said to Festina, "are Cashlings agoraphobic?"

"Now that I think of it," Festina replied, "they put all their cities under opaque force domes—which is completely unnecessary on most of their planets. And my old partner Yarrun once told me he visited a Cashling city and wanted to leave the dome to see the countryside . . . but nobody knew if there was a doorway out. He thought it was crazy: they had a constant flow of people shuttling up and down to orbital space stations, but the Cashlings never went sideways, out into the trees and fresh air."

"We don't *need* trees and fresh air," Lady Bell said, clutching one edge of the airlock doorway as if she were afraid we might drag her outside. "We're *civilized.* Cities have all the necessities of life . . . and they don't have insects. Or poisonous weeds. Or trees that might fall on you."

"If a tree attempts to fall on you," I told her, "jump out of the way. Trees are famed for their slow reaction times."

Lady Bell ignored me. "I think . . ." she said. "I think I should check on my husband. Yes. That's what I should do. He must be lying unconscious, somewhere inside. The poor *darling.* I'd better find him and make sure he's all right."

Without waiting for an answer, she pushed a button on the airlock control panel and the door swished shut in front of her. Uclod stared after her a moment, then made the odd hiss-whistle noise he and Lajoolie had produced just before vomiting. Obviously, this was his race's expression of supreme disgust. "I was wondering when she'd remember her missing husband. That Rye guy goes off to fetch food, he gets zapped by the Shaddill, and our godly prophet-lady doesn't give him the least little thought till she decides to turn chicken."

"Some men don't like their wives to fuss," Lajoolie murmured. "And some women learn to hide their concern."

We all stared at her a moment; then we quickly turned away and gazed at our feet. "Let's take a look around," Festina said in a muttery voice. We were glad to follow her forward.

Footprints

The great mud flats stretched in all directions. There was plenty of space to hold all the Cashling ships that had been captured thus far; and even as we watched, another small crusade vessel descended from the sky on a red beam of light, to be deposited a short distance from *Unfettered Destiny*. The other Cashling craft sat close by—no doubt to make it easier for the admiral robots to move from one ship to the next, looking for . . . well, looking for me.

I had clearly been their quarry. Apart from wondering why that was—and I wondered about it a great deal—one had to ask what the robots were supposed to do after I was secured. If, for example, they were under orders to carry my unconscious body to a place of imprisonment, how long before the Shaddill realized the robots had been waylaid? Perhaps only a few minutes. We must needs act quickly, before an alarm was raised; we had to bring the Shaddill to their knees (if they were such creatures as possessed knees) before they even knew we were coming.

But where to go? We were in the middle of the flats, with no exit in sight. Almost certainly, there had to be a door in the distant wall of the chamber—perhaps many doors. But the wall was curtained off by those thick stands of trees, and in the grayish twilight, it was impossible to see where doors might be hidden. Considering how large this hangar area was (almost the size of the cavern that held Oarville), it would take hours to walk the circumference . . . perhaps longer if the jungle-ish forests at the edge hindered our progress.

The same thoughts must have passed through Festina's mind. She had stopped on a clear patch of ground and was turning in a slow circle, peering at the horizon with narrowed eyes. "Wish I had a Bumbler," she muttered. That was a device human Explorers carried for scanning their surroundings; it had many Scientific Abilities, such as amplifying dim light and magnifying faraway objects. However, we did not possess such a device, so we would be forced to rely on our own ingenuity.

I am excellent at ingenuity.

"Here is what we must do," I said. "We must spread out to look for tracks. The robots were heavy creatures of metal, and the ground is only dirt. They must surely have left discernible footprints. We shall find those footprints and follow them back to the point where the robots entered this chamber."

Uclod's mouth dropped open. "Missy!" he said, in tones of admiration. "Good thinking!"

"Oar's right," Festina agreed. "Let's be quick about this."

The footprints close to the Cashling ships were too jumbled to read; but when we fanned out a short distance, Sergeant Aarhus found a clear pair of booted tracks leading back in a straight line toward the distant walls. They were like a great big sign saying THIS WAY OUT.

Since time was short, we followed the tracks at a run . . . and since Uclod was short, Lajoolie carried him. (Nimbus showed no apparent difficulty keeping up with our pace—he simply compacted his body into a horizontal raindrop shape and flew right along beside us.)

It took five minutes to reach the trees: five minutes during which we saw nothing but mud, mud, mud. The mud was not the deep mucky kind, and our feet were not completely swallowed with every footfall; nevertheless, the run was strenuous business, especially for one with low reserves of energy. If at the end I was wheezing, it is not evidence I was piteously out of shape—I was in *excellent* shape. How many of *you* could pass four years without food, then run for five minutes on muddy terrain? You would most likely die from exertion . . . and when you arrived in the afterlife, you would say to the Hallowed Ones, "We are sorry we mocked poor Oar for gasping a little bit. She is clearly a splendid physical specimen, and doubting her was very very wrong."

Apology accepted.

Mini-Chilis

As we came in under the trees, we were forced to slow down—not because I was panting for air and feeling most fluttery in the stomach, but because the undergrowth was prohibitively profuse. The only way forward lay along a narrow path that had apparently been slashed by the robots; this was not a long-established trail, but a route that had recently been forced through the snarl by dint of brute strength. If there was indeed an exit door somewhere ahead, it must not be used very often.

We had only gone a short distance forward when Festina stopped and craned her head back to look up into one of the trees. Here in the forest shadows, everything was harder to see than in the open . . . but I could make out yellowish objects hanging amongst the tree's dark leaves. Festina jumped high and grabbed one, pulling it off its stem with a soft pop. When she held it out for the rest of us to examine, I saw it was a waxy fruit the color of dandelions, two fingers wide at the stem and narrowing down to a point.

"Looks like a half-sized yellow chili pepper," Aarhus said.

Festina nodded. "Back home, we called them mini-chilis. The trees grew wild all over Agua."

"This is a tree from your home planet?"

She shook her head. "It wasn't native to Agua, it was a transplant. Don't know where it came from originally, but it was brought by Las Fuentes . . . those aliens who abandoned their colonies five thousand years ago." She looked down at the fruit. "Everywhere Las Fuentes went, they planted mini-chilis. Must have been one of their favorite foods."

My mouth watered. "Are mini-chilis tasty?"

"Don't know," Festina told me. "Humans who try to eat them always keel over and die before describing the flavor. Totally poisonous to terrestrial life. Our farm lost dozens of cattle because of the damned things—whenever a cow escaped from pasture, she headed straight for the nearest mini-chili tree and gobbled whatever fruit she found on the ground. I guess animals liked the smell; either that, or our herds were suicidal."

Festina looked at the chili a moment longer, then folded her fingers over it in a tight squeeze. "Nasty stuff," she murmured. I thought she intended to hurl it away, but instead she tucked it carefully into a jacket pocket.

Explorers are like that—even in moments of tension, they feel compelled to take plant samples.

Overmany Coincidences

"So," Aarhus said in pensive tones, "this tree was a favorite of Las Fuentes . . . and it's here on a Shaddill ship."

"Makes you think, doesn't it?" Festina took a few more steps down the trail, her gaze moving carefully over the jungle. "A lot of these other plants look familiar too—things from the Agua rainforest. That vine . . . we called it monkey rope. And this thorn bush is *madre sangrienta*. Both came to Agua courtesy of Las Fuentes." She stared at the *madre* bush a moment longer, then turned back to us. "It would take a laboratory to prove these were the same species as the ones on my world; but at first glance, they seem identical."

"Which means what?" Uclod asked.

Festina shrugged. "Las Fuentes abandoned their holdings five thousand years ago. A few centuries later, the Shaddill made their first appearance when they removed Oar's ancestors from Earth. Could be that in those missing years, Las Fuentes became the Shaddill."

"But," said I, "Las Fuentes became horrible purple jelly."

"That's what the horrible purple jelly claimed," Festina told me. "It wouldn't be the first time an alien told a lie."

She started down the trail again. We followed glumly . . . and I for one made sure I did not step on the poison fruit.

How To Talk To Doors

It turns out that jackets catch on thorns and nettles. Jackets catch on such things *all the time*. Back on Melaquin, I had never bothered to give wide berth to these hazards, for my skin is impervious to prickly annoyances; now, however, I was constantly getting snagged on passing vegetation, to the point where I strongly considered taking off my jacket and flinging it into the bush. I suppressed this impulse only because Festina had inducted me into the Explorer Corps . . . and perhaps, if she saw me treating the uniform in cavalier fashion, she would think she had made a mistake. It would be very most sad if Festina said, "Oar, you do not behave like a proper Explorer, so you cannot be one any longer." Therefore, I continued to wear my jacket and simply yanked it loose whenever it got hooked on grabby undergrowth. Sometimes bits of cloth remained behind on the thorns, but it is not my fault if navy apparel suffers from shoddy manufacture.

Because of the snagging and yanking, moving through the jungle was almost as strenuous as running. It was not out-of-breath strenuous; but the constant exertion made my insides feel watery. Then my head went watery too—not a sudden dizziness but a growing sense of disconnection, as my feet kept walking but my mind drifted off. I found myself dreaming of the lovely brightness in my Tower of Ancestors: how peaceful it had been to lie empty for the past four years, without worrying about thorns, or awful Shaddills, or the many ways my life had never gone *anywhere* . . .

Muddled blankness crept up on me so stealthily I did not feel it: blankness from fatigue and insufficient food. Time passed in a blur, which is to say, in a discontinuous jump . . . because the next thing I knew, I was leaning in great exhaustion against a dirt-encrusted wall, with my cheek and nose pressed into the grimy surface.

I turned my head blearily and saw Lajoolie staring at me with fearful concern; the others, however, had focused their attention on a door in the wall a few paces away from me. This door was the metal kind that slides open and shut. At the moment, it was closed . . . and there was no obvious mechanism for opening it. No doorknob, no latch, no button, no dial.

"We could bash it down," Uclod suggested. He turned to Lajoolie. "You wouldn't mind doing that, would you, sweetheart?"

Lajoolie gave me a plaintive look, suggesting she would mind very much: I do not think she wanted to use her great strength ever again. Her face overflowed with relief when Festina said, "No bashing if we can help it. For one thing, it'll make noise. For another, the door might have defense mechanisms—alarms or maybe stunners."

"So what do we do instead?" Uclod asked.

Festina ran her hands over the door's surface, obviously groping for unusual features. As she did, she told the rest of us, "Look around nearby. Maybe there's a hidden switch."

"Or maybe it can only be opened from the other side," Uclod said. "Maybe it's voice-activated and you have to know the password."

"I *realize* that," Festina answered testily. "But let's check for other alternatives."

So they checked, looking under bushes, digging in the dirt and fingering the blank wall as if it might conceal some secret access mechanism. Their earnest activity soon maddened me; still propped against the wall, I cried out in my own language, "Open up, you foolish door!"

The door slid silently open.

How To Talk To Me

Festina's mouth gaped wide and she stared at me. "What did you say?"

"I told it to open."

"In what language?"

"My own . . . which I now suspect is actually the Shaddill tongue. And do not shout at me for not telling you sooner; I am very upset the Shaddill indoctrinated my people to speak their villainous language, and perhaps I am also in a weakened state physically and emotionally, so if you scold me, Festina, I shall cry."

She came forward and wrapped her arms around me. I leaned into the embrace . . . and unlike the time when she hugged me in the *Hemlock*'s transport bay, I did not feel self-conscious at all. To tell the truth, I was too tired to feel much of anything; but it was comforting and agreeable to be held, not to mention that it helped me stay on my feet.

Festina whispered, "Do you really speak Shaddill?"

"I believe I do."

"Under the circumstances, that's a wonderful thing. It gives us a valuable edge."

"It doesn't feel . . ." I caught my breath. "It does not feel wonderful or valuable—to know that all your life, you have been someone else's creature. One could easily become downhearted, Festina."

She gave me a squeeze . . . which became more of a shake as she said, "Stay with us, Oar, come on, stay with us. If you stay awake, you might get to punch a Shaddill in the nose."

"Oh. That might be pleasant."

I forced myself to stand straighter. Festina did not release me; she propped herself under my arm and gripped my back to make sure I did not fall. "This is only a temporary weakness," she told the others. "Oar just needs food."

"Temporary my ass," Uclod replied. "She keeps going blank on us. Lajoolie told me she conked out for a full hour on *Hemlock* . . . and I've caught her drifting off a couple other times too. Not to mention she was a zombie for four whole years before I showed up on Melaquin." He turned to me. "I hate to say it, missy, but your brain is turning to toffee."

"It isn't!" I cried. "It isn't!" Lajoolie flinched; otherwise, I would not even have noticed my slip of the tongue. Two contractions in a row. Suddenly blazing with anger, I pushed myself away from Festina and said, "I am perfectly fine. I

am, in fact, quite splendid. Now cease your foolish insinuations, for it is high time we found the enemy."

I strode majestically toward the open door . . . but not before I caught a look passing between Festina and Uclod. One
might think she would be reproving him for making me so
furious; but in fact, her lips mouthed the words, "Thank
you"—as if he had done something praiseworthy instead of
driving me into a rage. And the little man actually winked
back at her.

There is no understanding aliens *at all*.

Burrows

The door led into a corridor that was nothing like a
proper ship corridor—just a dirt-lined tunnel, as must be
dug by rabbits or gophers if the animals were almost the
size of a real person. I say *"almost* the size" because the tunnel roof was not quite my height; I had to duck slightly,
which did not improve my mood. Aarhus too was forced to
stoop, and poor Lajoolie needed to bend most uncomfort-
ably. I expected the short people to boast that *they* had no
trouble at all . . . but Festina was too polite, and Uclod too
busy fussing with his wife, trying to think of ways to make
movement easier for the big woman. ("Would it help if . . .
suppose I . . . maybe you could . . ." None of this improved
things in the least, but perhaps Lajoolie found his efforts endearing.)

Nimbus, of course, floated down the middle without difficulty. As we started forward, the cloud man told Festina,
"You realize this tunnel is just a mock-up? I sent a few of my
cells to check the wall; it's a type of artificial dirt sprayed
over a base of solid steel-plast."

"Doesn't surprise me," Festina replied. "It looks like the
Shaddill evolved from burrowing creatures. All this soil
must make them feel comfortable."

"Then they are giant space gophers?" I asked.

"Gophers aren't the only animals who burrow," Festina said. "Rabbits . . . worms . . . beetles . . . snakes . . . and those are just terrestrial species. I could list thousands of even stranger burrowers from other planets."

"Do you know what Las Fuentes looked like?" Uclod asked. "Before they changed into purple blobs."

Festina shook her head. "They cleaned their worlds meticulously before they abandoned their settlements— made a determined effort to eliminate any direct clues about themselves. Oh sure, they overlooked a few odds and ends: a small number of tools that were probably designed for four-fingered hands . . . broken furniture that suggests they always lay down rather than sitting, so they were probably jointed differently than we are. No bodies, though; not a single bone. Shows how advanced their technology was if they could make such a clean sweep. Also shows Las Fuentes didn't want us to know what they looked like."

"Just what you'd expect of burrowing creatures," Aarhus said. "Obsessively secretive."

"It is not obsessive," I told him, "it is simply good sense. One must always take pains to go unnoticed, or one might be observed by persons of unknown provenance . . ."

I stopped. Festina was looking at me keenly. "Your race *is* secretive, isn't it? And you all live in hidden enclaves like that underground city."

"Are you suggesting *I* am a Shaddill? That is very most rude of you, Festina. I may speak their language, but I am not such a creature as burrows . . . or has small four-fingered hands . . . and I bend in the middle with perfect ease, thereby allowing me to sit wherever I choose."

"I'm not saying you're a Shaddill lookalike," Festina replied, "but your planet Melaquin was the earliest known settlement established by the Shaddill after Las Fuentes disappeared. The Shaddill may have created you as an artificial race who looked human enough to please people taken from Earth, but who had Shaddill-ish characteristics too. The secretiveness, the instinct to hide. They built you concealed towns and villages all over the planet; and they made you transparent, so you'd be damned hard to see, even when you ventured out into the open. If the Shaddill are, uhh, reclusive space gophers, they constructed you to follow in their footsteps."

"And they taught you their language," Aarhus put in. "They didn't do that with any other race they uplifted."

"The other uplifted races were scientifically advanced," Festina said. "At least advanced enough to have launched a few rockets and satellites. But Oar's people got picked up when they were still trying to get the hang of smelting bronze." She puckered her brow. "Makes you wonder why the difference. What did the Shaddill want with . . ."

"Children!" Lajoolie blurted out. "The Shaddill wanted children."

We all turned to look at her. I noticed Uclod turned faster than the rest of us—the little man's head fairly snapped like a whip. Perhaps a man has especially rapid reflexes for responding when his wife broaches the subject of offspring.

Childlike, Most Childlike

"Uhh," said Lajoolie, wilting under our collective gaze. "It's just . . . well . . . maybe the Shaddill wanted children. To watch growing up . . . and . . . playing . . . and . . . things. Because maybe they'd done something to change themselves from burrowing creatures into blobs of jelly, and maybe the blobs of jelly couldn't have babies, or anyway not normal ones, so the Shaddill . . . Las Fuentes . . . were nostalgic for children. They created an artificial race that was sort of like what they used to be—secretive, you know, and hard to notice—but the kids would always be, uhh, *childlike* throughout their entire lives."

She looked at me with her big brown eyes. "Yes, childlike. And maybe the Shaddill couldn't take care of the children one hundred percent of the time, so they brought in bronze-age humans to be, uhh, nannies. At least for the first generation. The Shaddill made the children look and act like humans, so the Earthlings would feel more comfortable tending them, but inside, the kids had attitudes that would make the Shaddill find them . . . lovable."

There was a silence; for some reason, everyone was now looking at me instead of Lajoolie. "But that is not how it was," I told them. "My people have stories and records. Flesh-and-blood Earthlings were brought to Melaquin, and the Shaddill asked, 'Do you want your children to live forever?' The Earthlings said yes, that is what they wanted . . . and the Shaddill changed the humans inside, so their offspring would be made of glass. My ancestors were not baby-sitters; they were loving parents who cared so much for their children, they desired us to be perfect."

Festina put her hand on my shoulder. "Oar—you shouldn't put faith in your written records. The humans on Melaquin came from 2000 B.C. Almost no one on Earth could write back then . . . and if any of the settlers *were* literate, they'd write in their own language, not yours." She took a breath. "It must have been the Shaddill who wrote your history books."

I stared at her, feeling a tear trickle down my cheek.

"It might not have been a total lie," she said. "The Shaddill *may* have altered the humans physically to become . . . surrogates. The women could have served as hosts for implanted embryos: they'd be more likely to take care of you if they thought you *were* their own children."

"But if the Shaddill made us to be their children," I said, "why did they make our brains Tired?"

Silence. I was about to say, *You see, I have defeated your arguments*, when Nimbus spoke softly. "Perhaps they didn't want you to grow up."

I whirled upon him. "What do you mean?"

"Perhaps," he said, still very quiet, "there comes a time—even for beings designed to remain childlike as long as possible—perhaps there comes a time when childhood has to end. When the brain reaches a point where it must either become adult . . . or become nothing. And the Shaddill preferred you to be nothing."

His fog wisped in close to me, brushed my cheek, then

swirled toward the others. "A while ago," he said, "Oar and I had a conversation about the Cashlings—how much they've degenerated since they were uplifted. Other races have too; even humans and Divians are getting worse."

He paused, as if waiting to see if anyone would challenge him. The others said nothing; indeed, Festina and Uclod both nodded in solemn agreement. "Suppose," Nimbus said, "the Shaddill are behind that degeneration. Suppose it's not just the result of affluence and indolence, but something else: a poison, a virus, radiation, who knows? The Shaddill are advanced enough to sneak some subtle contamination into our environment without us noticing."

"I find that hard to believe," Aarhus said. "With all the monitoring we do for pollution, medical threats, any sort of harmful influence—"

"Sergeant," Festina interrupted, "how long have we had FTL fields? Yet we never discovered how they could be strengthened by the sun. If the Shaddill could hoodwink us on that, why not something else? YouthBoost treatments, for instance—supposedly a gift from the Shaddill to help us all live longer. Every Technocracy citizen over twenty-five gets regular doses. If there was something in YouthBoost that very very slowly, over the course of centuries, damaged the human genome . . . caused cumulative mental regression . . ." She shook her head angrily. "And YouthBoost is just the most obvious possibility. Degenerative agents could be hidden in any of the other so-called 'gifts' they gave us. Or disseminated in some other way entirely."

"But the Shaddill wouldn't do that!" Lajoolie protested. "They're good . . . and benevolent . . ."

Her voice trailed off. After everything that had happened, not even the warm-hearted Lajoolie could force herself to believe the Shaddill were generous benefactors.

"I think," Nimbus said, "the Shaddill have been waging a war against other sentient races for thousands of years. Not to conquer territory, but to suppress competition. When a species reaches the point where it's beginning to venture into space, the Shaddill show up with armloads of gifts; and somewhere amidst those presents is a booby-trap that gradually turns the uplifted race into mental defectives who will never cause the Shaddill trouble."

"But that is horrible!" I cried. "Surely the League of Peoples would object."

"No," said Festina, "not if the poison doesn't actually kill. And not if the uplifted race accepts the gift freely. The League prevents outright murder . . . but it doesn't stop anyone from making choices that are suicidally stupid."

"But why would the Shaddill *do* such a thing?" Lajoolie asked in a trembly voice.

"Maybe from fear," Uclod answered, taking her hand in his. "Think about it from the Shaddill's viewpoint—there were all these other intelligent races in the same region of the galaxy, and bit by bit, those races were developing their own technologies. Sure, the Shaddill had a headstart . . . but maybe they were afraid someone else would catch up. If another species was a tiny bit smarter or luckier or harderworking, the Shaddill might eventually get left in the dust. And what could they do to stop it? The League doesn't tolerate violence, so the Shaddill couldn't directly destroy potential threats. Instead, they got sneaky."

"Trojan horses," Aarhus murmured. "Gifts that slowly but surely neutralized any race who was close on the Shaddill's heels. Turning us all into vapid idiots like the Cashlings." He turned toward me. "Or even worse, what they did to your people on Melaquin. You might have been the Shaddill's substitute children, but your creators didn't want you growing up and becoming serious competition. So they damaged you mentally—made certain you'd never mature."

"Yes," Nimbus told me, "by keeping your people childlike, the Shaddill eliminated you as a threat and made you all the more endearing: a society filled with happy healthy kids, rather than the usual messiness of a civilization run by adults. When your brains get to the critical point of *Grow up or shut down* . . . you're designed just to go to sleep."

"Not much better than dying," Uclod growled.

"But," Nimbus replied, "less distressing as the Shaddill

look down from the sky. That cute little boy they watched three hundred years ago . . . he's not dead, he's just at a slumber party with his friends. Perhaps the Shaddill could give him a stimulant so he'd get up for a while, walk around, show off the sweet little mannerisms that made his creators feel so fond. Then away they'd go again until the next time they felt like visiting the kids for a few hours."

"Bloody hell," Festina whispered. "Very neat . . . and despicable." She gave my shoulder a squeeze. "If all this is true . . ."

I waited to hear how she would finish the sentence. But what could she say? *If all this is true, poor Oar, poor you! It is too bad you face a malfunctioning brain because your creators wanted you lovable but helpless. We too find you lovable, and are charmed by your naïve innocence; we will be very most sad when you finally fall to the ground and do not get up.*

In the end, all Festina could do was give my shoulder another squeeze.

My Vow

I looked around at my companions—their somber faces, their eyes shifting away from me as if I were already some walking dead *umushu* whose gaze they could not meet—and for one brief moment, I nearly lost heart. These were my only friends in the universe, and they believed I was doomed: a wind-up toy to amuse foul aliens, and now I was running down. They thought of me as a frivolous child who did not understand the world, a person who had not grown up and *could* not grow up. For one brief moment, a great sorrow washed over my soul, as I feared they were correct.

Perhaps I was not a glorious heroine, destined for grandeur.

Perhaps I was just a silly girl-child who had filled her own head with nonsense—deluded herself into thinking she was special.

For I had to admit, my brain *was* getting Tired. It had been that way for the past four years. Recent events had temporarily stirred me from my stupor . . . but over and over again, I had almost slipped back to nothingness. How long before I reached the point of no return?

If the Pollisand was telling the truth, I could still be cured—provided I embraced his cause to "wipe the Shaddill off the face of the galaxy." When he first made his proposition, I had glibly answered, *Yes, I shall help*; but I had understood so little of who and what the Shaddill were. Even now . . . even now, there were only conjectures. I did not *know*. But if all those conjectures were correct . . .

. . . I wished to do more than just punch the Shaddill in the nose. I wished to keep punching and punching until they said they were sorry, and even then, I did not think I would stop. I truly wished to hurt them, not because I wanted to win favor with the Pollisand, but because it was what such villains deserved.

After all, working with the Pollisand might not save me—why should I trust an alien to keep his word? The universe was full of betrayal. And what would it mean to be cured? Who would I become? A tedious plodding grown-up? A stodgy sighing person who did not fall down from Tiredness but who went around three-quarters Tired all day, pretending that because her feet were moving, her brain must still be alive?

Nimbus suggested I must become adult or become nothing; I did not know which option I feared more. But whatever happened to me, I swore I would not succumb to oblivion until I had made the Shaddill regret what they had done.

That was my vow. That was what I solemnly promised to the universe: to every glass elder lying comatose in a tower, to my original flesh-and-blood ancestors, and even to alien races like the foolish Cashlings whose brains were crumbling wrecks. *Somehow,* I thought, *this must all be avenged.*

Therefore, in my most secret inner soul, I swore a terrible oath to do so.

"Come now," I said to my friends, "we are wasting time, and perhaps I have little time left. Let us perform at least one great deed in our lives before we vanish forever."

I did not wait for them to answer—I strode down the dirt-caked tunnel, trusting that somehow I would find the Shaddill. My friends hesitated a moment, then followed close behind me.

24

WHEREIN I EXPLORE
THE ENEMY'S LAIR

In The Tunnels

The entire stick-ship seemed filled with tunnels: some narrow with little head-room, some wide and reaching up into darkness. Darkness was indeed the most salient feature of these tunnels; there *were* occasional lights—dim orangey plates the size of my palm, set into the wall at waist level—but I counted a full twenty-two paces from one plate to the next, and considering the lights were scarcely as bright as a single candle, they did not provide substantive illumination. Their sole function must have been to prevent one from getting lost in total blackness.

Festina still had her glow-wand, but she used it sparingly: she only activated it when we came to an intersection. Since the floor was dirt, one could see which tunnels were more frequently used than others—the ones where the soil was tamped down more solidly, with the occasional discernible footprint. (The footprints were always from human boots, their tread identical to those worn by the robot admirals.) We always chose to follow the direction of greatest traffic, on the theory that this was most likely to lead us to Shaddill.[13]

---

[13]At every intersection, we made clear deep gouges in the soil, pointing back the way we had come. Festina called this "our trail of bread crumbs" . . . which does not make me eager to eat Earthling bread.

Of course, the stick-ship did not merely consist of earth-lined tunnels—there were also multitudinous rooms opening off the tunnels. Many of these rooms did not have doors, just open entranceways . . . but the rooms were even darker than the tunnels, so peeking inside only showed bulks of anonymous machinery enclosed in metal shells. From time to time, we saw robots scurrying in the darkness, things that were no more than wheeled boxes with arms sprouting out of their tops. The robots took no notice of us; they were too busy with their programmed tasks to worry their mechanical brains about strangers.

As for the rooms with closed doors, we did not attempt to open them. I had no time to waste on side trips, since I did not know how much longer my brain would stay active. Besides, as Festina pointed out, doors are often closed to protect passers-by from dangerous things on the other side, whether those things were wild beasts, aggressive nano, or machines that produced incinerative quantities of heat. (Nimbus assured us he was keeping watch for high concentrations of nano; according to him, there were light sprinklings everywhere we went, but the nanites showed no more interest in us than the boxy robots.)

Minutes slipped by and still we did not see anything that might have been a living Shaddill. Of course, the stick-ship was huge; there might be millions of Shaddill in some other part of the craft, a residential section that was kept separate from the place where they imprisoned captives. But as time went on with no sightings, I wondered where the great poop-heads were. Was the entire stick-ship run by robots and nanites? Did the machines need no supervision at all? And if the ship could run itself, what about other Shaddill projects?

I knew the Shaddill had changed Melaquin from whatever it once was into a near-duplicate of Earth, with terrestrial weather and plants and animals . . . not to mention all the cities built underground and at the bottom of lakes. Was it possible such construction had been accomplished entirely by unsupervised machines? Perhaps so—aliens of advanced technical abilities might do *everything* with machines instead of physical labor. For all I knew, there might only be a handful of Shaddill left in the universe; they languidly gave a command, then years of work (including planning, design, and terraforming) were carried out by mechanical servants.

And if *that* were possible . . . why did there have to be living Shaddill at all? Suppose the old race, Las Fuentes, had created this stick-ship and programmed it to operate on its own. The living Fuentes then turned themselves to jelly, leaving the ship to work unattended.

It would be very most irksome if we reached the stick-ship's control center, only to find it filled with more bulks of anonymous machinery: artificial intelligences running the whole show. One cannot punch a computer in the nose.

On the other hand, one can kick loose a computer's metal housing and rip out its wires, dancing upon its circuit boards and smashing anything that says FRAGILE, DO NOT STOMP. Even better, the League of Peoples would not consider me a bad person for doing so—if the League dealt with computers on a regular basis, they probably felt the urge to dance on circuit boards themselves. Perhaps they would appear before me in a pillar of fire and say, "Oar, most good and faithful servant, you have done exactly what we would have done ourselves, if only we had feet." It would turn out the League people were giant space butterflies; they would give me a medal for heroic achievement, then seat me upon their backs and we would ride off for Glorious Adventures on the far side of the galaxy.

That is what was going through my head when I saw the Pollisand.

In Good Paintings, The Eyes Follow You; In Stick-Ships, You Follow The Eyes

We had come to a T junction and Festina was examining the dirt on the floor, trying to determine which way was used more often. Both left and right were quite trampled, indicating we had finally reached a major thoroughfare. While the others busied themselves debating which direction looked better, I kept watch for hostile elements . . . which is how I caught sight of familiar red eyes glowing in the darkness to my right.

The Pollisand was so far off in the shadows, I could not make out his body; but his eyes were unmistakable. They glowed for the briefest of moments, just long enough for me to recognize them. Then they winked out as if they had never been there.

"This way," I said, pointing in the direction of the eyes. "That is the proper route."

Festina looked up as if waiting for an explanation. I did not think she would be happy to learn I had seen the Pollisand again—Festina believed he was a Creature Of Ill Omen, and perhaps she would insist on going exactly the opposite way. Therefore, I said nothing. Eventually, she shrugged and muttered, "Why not? Right looks as good as left."

So we moved in the direction I had seen the glowing eyes. I kept close watch on the ground as we walked, hoping to observe deep footprints from a rhinolike beast . . . but I saw nothing except packed-down soil. Perhaps all I had seen was an illusion inserted into my brain. Still, we pressed along the tunnel until we came to another intersection; and once again, I caught a fleeting glimpse of eyes down one of the passages.

"This way now," I said pointing.

Of course, it was not so easy as that—Festina wished to examine the ground, and we had to pause as Aarhus made grooves to mark our way back. In the end, however, Festina agreed the direction I indicated was as good a choice as any, and we proceeded accordingly.

Several minutes passed in that manner. None of the others noticed the glowing eyes: they were only visible to me. Nevertheless, at each junction, the Pollisand marked a reasonable way forward, so the others were willing to follow my lead.

Once or twice, Festina peered at me with suspicion—she obviously wondered why I had started to make snap judgments at each cross-tunnel. By now, however, she must have become accustomed to me behaving in a manner too deep for humans to understand; and as my Faithful Sidekick, she chose not to question my will. She simply made sure the sergeant continued to mark our way back, and little by little she took less time to examine the ground before declaring, "Let us do as Oar says."

Therefore, we made swifter progress, though we were now in a part of the ship where the ground was exceedingly well trodden. In spots, the dirt had worn away entirely, revealing solid flooring beneath. Festina said all these floors were made from steel-plast, a material found in human starships as well—which made sense, considering the Shaddill had taught humans how to make starships in the first place. One wondered what other features the stick-ship possessed in common with a vessel like *Royal Hemlock* . . . and we soon discovered such a feature, as a door we were approaching swished open automatically at our approach.

Doors had opened for us in this fashion several times on the *Hemlock*; however, this was the first such occurrence on the stick-ship, and Festina halted our march immediately. More precisely, since I was walking in front, she grabbed me by the collar of my jacket and yanked me back sharply.

I turned with a reproachful look and was about to tell her she should not handle me with such brusqueness . . . but she threw her hand over my mouth before I could speak a word. Apparently, she did not want any lurking Shaddill to hear us talking. When she was certain our companions would also keep quiet, she motioned us to stay where we were, then crept forward stealthily toward the open door.

She stood just outside the door for a tediously long time, holding her breath and listening for any sort of noise from the inner room. The rest of us listened too—Uclod and Lajoolie rolled back the coverings of their spherelike ears, exposing raw eardrums to the world. Perhaps this made their hearing even keener than mine; at any rate, Festina must have believed they had the best ears among us, for she turned to them and mouthed the word, "Anything?" Both Divians shook their heads. Festina shrugged, clenched her stun-pistol in both hands, and hurled herself forward into the room.

Nothing happened. No shots, no shouts, no scuffles. After some tense moments, Festina reappeared in the doorway and waved us forward.

The Milk Of A Million Mothers

By normal standards, the light in the room was dim: just-after-sundown twilight like the hangar where we first landed. After the darkness of the tunnels, however, the soft dusky glow seemed pleasantly welcoming.

It was bright enough to show that the room was empty . . . which is to say, there were no robots or Shaddill or bulky machines. Instead, three mini-chili trees grew in a widely spaced triangle, their trunks arrow-straight and their branches heavy with yellow fruit. Nothing else sprouted from the surrounding soil—no bushes or undergrowth, not a single blade of grass—but in the center of the triangle formed by the trees stood a fountain carved from gray stone.

We had all seen such a fountain before—in the pictures Festina showed of her world, Agua. This was unmistakably a creation of Las Fuentes.

The fountain was simple: a low bowl-shaped basin ten paces across with a knee-high wall surrounding it, and a single unadorned pillar rising from the center. The pillar stood a little higher than my head; it had three spouts just down from its top, each oriented toward one of the mini-chili trees. At the moment, however, the spouts were not spouting. Indeed, the entire fountain was bone-dry, as if it had not operated in ages. It sat in stony silence—a silence that was somehow more intense because it ought to have been broken by the cheerful gushing of water.

"Okay," Uclod said softly, "this clinches it. The Shaddill *are* Las Fuentes."

It seemed appropriate to talk in near-whispers. We had stopped just inside the door, none of us ready to venture farther. "Admiral," Aarhus murmured, "those fountains on Las Fuentes planets—did any of them work?"

Festina shook her head. "By the time humans arrived,

they'd been sitting idle for thousands of years—gummed up with dirt and mold. A lot were completely buried under normal soil accumulation; they were only found because they sat in the middle of those huge craters and archaeologists knew where to dig."

"But did the fountains have pipes? And water sources?"

"They had pipes, but they didn't actually draw from the surrounding water table; the water came from big sealed reservoir drums buried under the ground." Festina shrugged. "Using a self-contained water source might have been a religious thing—maybe the water in the fountain had to be specially blessed by priests, and Las Fuentes didn't want their holy water mixing with unsanctified stuff from local rivers. For that matter, the reservoir drums and the fountains may not have contained normal H_2O. The fountains could have held a sacred drug used in worship ceremonies . . . or blood from animal sacrifices . . . or milk ritually obtained from a million mothers . . . and before you ask, no, we don't know if Las Fuentes actually produced milk, I just made that up as an example."

Example or not, it was something that caught my attention. I should very much like to see a fountain that sprayed milk or blood. Perhaps the fountain before us had an ON switch. At the very least, it might contain crusty stains one could pick off with one's fingernail and stare at with haughty disapproval. I moved toward the triangle of trees . . . then found myself jerked back again as Festina once more grabbed my jacket.

"No," she said with quiet urgency, "it might be a trap. The door to this room opened as we approached, unlike every other door we've passed. That's way too convenient."

"Don't be so grim, missy," Uclod told her. "There's nobody here, right? And if this fountain is a Shaddill shrine, maybe the door always opens automatically as a sign of welcome. 'Come in, whoever you are, sit down and pray.' "

Festina did not look convinced . . . and it dawned on me she might be correct in saying the door did not open by accident. The Pollisand's eyes had led us here; perhaps the Pollisand himself had arranged for the door to open because there was something we ought to discover. "I do not think there is danger," I told Festina. "If this is a holy place, surely it is the last location the Shaddill would set a trap. An attack on us might damage the fountain."

"Unless," said Aarhus, "they're the sort who think shrines look holier when splashed with the blood of enemies."

"Oh, you're a barrel of laughs," Uclod muttered.

Yet Another Thing That Might Be Wrong With My Brain

"If I can make a suggestion . . ." Nimbus said.

We all turned toward the cloud man. In the dim light, he had been so nearly invisible it was easy to forget he was there. "If you think it's important, I could send some of my components over to the fountain. It's unlikely the ship would notice a few stray cells drifting through the air . . . and I could do a quick chemical analysis on any residue in the basin."

"That is excellent," I said. "It could provide us with important information."

"Why?" Festina asked. "Why do we care what the Shaddill put in their fountains? Why should it matter if the stuff is water, blood, or fucking sangria?" She stared at me most piercingly. "You've got some idea in your head, Oar; I can tell. That's scary enough on its own, considering what your ideas can be like. But with you being a Shaddill creation, I also worry the bastards might be influencing you somehow. Beaming notions straight into your cerebral cortex. They could have built your brain with receptors that would let them control you when it became necessary."

"That is very foolish!" I answered hotly. "I am not being controlled by anyone!" But . . . was I sure the Pollisand eyes I had seen were actually attached to the Pollisand? He had left no footprints; no one else had seen the dim crimson glows. If the Shaddill had constructed my brain in such a fashion as to delude me with False Sensory Input . . .

Oh, it was very most irksome being a creature designed by evil aliens!

"All of you, step back," I told the others with great anger. "Go far away, out of the room . . . because if I have been deceitfully led here by villainous poop-heads, I intend to find out once and for all. I am going to walk straight up to that fountain, and then I shall do something drastic. If I see a large button labeled DO NOT PRESS, I shall press it. If I see a big X scratched into the floor, I shall step on it with all my weight. If the trees come alive and attempt to stuff poisonous mini-chilis down my throat, I shall beat them to death with their own branches. The one thing I shall *not* do is dally in forlorn uncertainty, wondering if I am another creature's dupe. If something is going to happen, I shall make it happen *now*."

The others all turned to Festina to see her response to my words. "Well," she said slowly, "there *is* some benefit in knowing where we stand . . . and maybe provoking a confrontation is better than wandering forever with no idea where the Shaddill are hiding."

"Sounds good," Uclod agreed. "No offense, missy," he said to me, "but if the bad guys have some hold over you, it's better you *do* walk into a trap. I mean, the trap couldn't be lethal, right? The League won't let the Shaddill kill any of us. And if they're playing games inside your head, they'll bloody soon use you against us if you're not taken out of the equation."

"That is the sort of logic one expects from a heartless criminal," I told him, "but it is logic all the same. Now depart to a safe distance . . . and we shall see if I can cause dramatic events."

Festina scowled a moment; then, slowly, she nodded. "All right. I don't like it, but the Shaddill really *can't* kill you, not out here in space. And maybe if you cause enough ruckus, one of the bastards will show up personally. That's what we really want: someone we can talk to. The only way we'll get out of this mess is peaceful negotiation . . . preferably while we hold a pistol to somebody's head."

She turned and left the room. The others followed—with

Lajoolie giving me a plaintive look before she disappeared. "I will be all right," I called to her. "I am practically unbreakable. And quick. And clever. And . . ."

But by then I was alone; and suddenly I felt less confident about my plan. It is one thing to speak bravely in front of others. It is quite a different thing to stand in solitude, staring at a room filled with dirt and wondering if this is the last sight you will ever see.

Tentatively, I took a step forward. No awful disaster happened.

Taking a deep breath, I counted to five. Then I strode briskly forward, straight toward the fountain.

A Fruit In The Fountain

The moment I passed between two of the mini-chili trees, something gurgled beneath the floor. I leapt back quickly, but nothing attacked. Feeling my heart pound, I waited; and I kept my eyes moving, frequently looking back over my shoulder to make sure nothing was creeping up on me from behind.

There was no motion anywhere in the room . . . until another rattling gurgle came from the fountain and a stream of reddish fluid gushed out the top. It squirted a short distance up into the air, then fell back down, splashing crimson spatters into the basin. A moment later, the three lower spouts also began pouring liquid—the same reddish stuff that was shooting from the top.

It was not blood . . . at least not the sort of blood I had seen ooze from human injuries. The fountain's fluid was more viscous, like the thick liquid resin that maintenance machines on Melaquin employed to fill up ax gouges in the wall. Of course, the resin on Melaquin was pleasantly clear; the liquid in the fountain was transparent, but tinted the crimson of fall leaves. It also had a sweetish smell to it, not at all unpleasant: the scent reminded me of fresh-cut fruit, but which type of fruit, I could not say.

"What's going on?" Festina called from outside the room.

"The fountain has started on its own. I did nothing to provoke it. The fluid it emits is red."

A pool of the liquid began to accumulate in the basin. I approached, still watching for signs of trouble. Nothing moved anywhere in the room except for the fountain's central squirt and the streams pouring through the three lower spouts. All the flows were lazy, without much pressure; there was no chance of me being hit by the tiniest splash. I considered that a good thing—the fountain's dribbly babble was pleasant to listen to, but I was not yet ready to allow the red fluid to touch my skin. For all I knew, it might be a powerful Chemical that would burn my flesh or render me unconscious at the slightest contact.

Instead, I moved to the nearest mini-chili tree and plucked a low-lying fruit from its branches. Taking great care not to squeeze the little chili, I went back to the fountain and tossed the small fruit into the basin, very near the pool that was filling out from the center. The fruit landed neatly with its pointy end aiming inward toward the middle of the bowl. Bit by bit as liquid continued to flow, the level of the fluid rose and its edge inched up the stone toward the chili's tip.

"What's happening in there?" Festina called.

"I am performing an experiment. I am exposing an organic object to the influence of a sinister alien liquid."

"The organic object wouldn't be your hand, would it, missy?"

That, of course, was Uclod. "No," I told him, "I am not such a fool as to use myself for an experimental subject."

"Oh yeah? Then why are you in there, when we're all out here?"

One had to admit he had a point. But one did not have to admit it out loud, and anyway, the edge of the liquid was almost touching the chili's bottom tip. I held my breath in anticipation, hoping perhaps the small yellow fruit would burst into flame when the liquid made contact; but the result was more interesting than mere fire. As the fluid nudged the chili's surface, the fruit's yellow skin slowly changed color—not to red, as you might think, but to a dark purple. Even more intriguing, the chili's waxy texture grew puffy, bulging and bloating with purplish glee . . . until the sharp tip of the chili had turned to an ill-defined blob of purple jelly.

I stepped back several paces from the fountain. Several *long* paces. Taking care not to let my voice quaver, I called to the others, "Um. You will be pleased to learn my experiment has had a Result. Perhaps it would be useful if some independent observer were to witness this Result, so I may believe my own eyes."

Festina was inside the room even before I stopped speaking. She came quickly forward, close enough to the fountain that she could see the chili lying half-in, half-out of the clear crimson liquid. The top of the fruit was still recognizable as a chili; the bottom was equally recognizable as a dollop of purple gloop.

"Holy shit," Festina whispered.

"The holiest," I agreed.

Gray Foam, Purple Goo

I quickly explained what had happened. All the while, the liquid continued to rise in the basin, turning more and more of the chili into quivering gel. When I finished my tale, I asked Festina, "So . . . is the chili changing into a Fuentes? And if it is, is it now intelligent and lying there listening to us?"

Festina gave a little laugh. "I doubt that a fruit can become sentient just from getting dowsed with liquid. More likely, the fluid is breaking down the chili's cell structure— like the Modig powder back on *Hemlock*. With Modig, biologicals always decay into gray foam, whether you start with data circuits or human fingers. With whatever's in that fountain . . . I suppose it rips the shit out of something in living cells, and the result is purplish guck."

"If the Fuentes are also purplish guck, they must have used this fluid to rip up their own cells. Why would they do that?"

"Presumably it was the only way to reach the next level of

evolution. Maybe you can't transcend the limitations of physical form unless you break down your body structure. That could be the only way to free your consciousness." Festina shook her head. "Or I could be full of crap. It's not like I understand this any better than you do."

She turned her gaze to the mutating chili. The little fruit was almost entirely covered with fluid by now . . . which meant it was almost entirely converted to goo. Festina stared at it a moment, then shivered.

I was feeling the shivers myself. "Perhaps I am just an un-civilized one, but I would not wish to turn into jelly. Not even if I became a million times smarter."

"I'm with you on that," Festina replied. "But hey, I'm just a dumb old human. Maybe when you're truly ready to jump up the evolutionary ladder, turning into glup seems perfectly sensible. Easiest thing in the world: wake up in the morning, eat breakfast, say, 'Shucks, it's time I evolved,' and splash, you go for a dip in the nearest fountain."

"No," said a whispery voice. "It is not an easy thing. It is the hardest thing in the universe."

A blindingly brilliant light stabbed down from the room's ceiling, and suddenly two furry creatures stood shoulder-to-shoulder before us.

25

WHEREIN I FACE THE FOE

Tahpo

The two were no taller than Uclod. One's fur was brown and the other's was black; apart from that, they appeared exactly identical. Same height, same width, same pose.

Despite their fur, they seemed more like insects than mammals—each had two faceted eyes as big as my fist, and four mandible attachments arranged in a diamond shape around their mouths. The mandibles were constantly in motion: first, the two side ones would rub together furiously, the way a fly rubs its forelegs before eating; then those side parts would spread wide, giving room for the top and bottom attachments to sweep lightly across the lips, as if wiping off whatever dust might have landed in the past few seconds. After that the cycle repeated, with the same fierce rubbing once more.

As for the rest of their bodies, each alien had two short but muscular arms ending in small hands with three clawed fingers and a thumb. At first glance, the creatures appeared to stand on three legs; but when I looked more closely, I saw that only two of the lower limbs were legs (hinged like a rabbit's haunches). The third limb was a thick tail that ended in a chitinous scoop: the edges of the scoop looked sharp and sturdy, while the tail appeared muscular enough to move the scoop with great force. One supposed having a shovel on one's tail would be useful for creatures who burrowed underground . . . but it would also be a powerful weapon in a fight, especially if someone attacked from behind. Indeed, with shovel-tails at the rear, and claws and mandibles at the front, these creatures would be formidable opponents if encountered in a narrow tunnel.

The instant the beetle-things appeared, Festina dived to one side, rolling across the dirt and vaulting to her feet again with her pistol trained on the newcomers. She stood that way for several seconds, no doubt noticing that the aliens carried no obvious weapons and showed no sign of combative behavior. Without lowering her gun, Festina said, "Greetings. We are sentient citizens of the League of Peoples. We beg your Hospitality."

The two furry beetles turned in her direction. This required a sort of hopping move on their back legs; but despite the awkwardness of the maneuver, they remained pressed against each other, keeping in physical contact at all times. After they faced her, they said nothing for several seconds— long enough that I wondered if they had understood what she said. Perhaps they only spoke their own language . . . in which case, it was fortunate I could serve as interpreter. I was preparing to translate what Festina said when the black-furred beetle opened its mouth and a glowing gold ball emerged from its throat.

I had never seen a creature vomit a ball of glowing gold. The ball was not solid, but a tight clot of mist about the size of my head. Its consistency was highly reminiscent of Nimbus (who of course was a product of Shaddill engineering). The mist floated upward to hover above the black beetle's head . . . whereupon a voice sounded clearly from the gleaming fog.

"Greetings yourself," the voice said in English. The sound was identical to Festina's own voice; and it is most disconcerting to hear what seems like your Faithful Sidekick speaking from a ball of fog perched atop an alien bug. Clearly, the voice had to be a simulation . . . and when I thought about it, if I were creating a golden mist-ball to communicate with others, I might construct the ball to imitate the other person's voice as closely as possible. This would not only ensure the mist-ball's speech was pitched at a frequency the other person could hear, but it would also make one's words sound agreeably dulcet to the listener. If I were designing a speaking mist, I might also make it float above my head, so people would hear the mist's voice coming from my direction . . . but the whole idea was still most icky, and if I were an alien, I would not employ fog as an intermediary for communication. Especially not fog that resided in my stomach when it was not needed.

"I am Immu," the black beetle's fog-voice said. "This is my mate, Esticus."

The brown beetle (Esticus) clacked all four mandible attachments twice. This was probably a gesture of polite acknowledgment, though to my eyes it looked most fearsome. "So you are spouses?" I asked.

"Yes," said Immu.[14]

"Are you the husband or the wife?"

Immu did not answer; the two beetles just stared with their goggly eyes. Perhaps they were offended by my inability to recognize which was male and which female. Since neither of the creatures possessed obvious gender characteristics, I decided to regard Immu as the wife: she was the one who took a leadership role, and besides, she sounded like Festina.

"Are you Shaddill," I asked, "or Fuentes?"

"We've been called both names," Immu answered, "but it's not how we speak of ourselves."

The other one, Esticus, sighed. It was a soft sigh that breathed out another glowing ball of mist. Even before the mist could drift into position above Esticus's head, the fog murmured, "We are not Shaddill or Fuentes. We are Tahpo."

I blinked in surprise, and for two reasons. First, the voice that emanated from Esticus's fog-ball sounded suspiciously familiar: it was my own! It did not sound exactly like the tones I customarily hear in my head, but I have been told

---

[14]Of course, it was Immu's fog-ball speaking, but I assumed the beetle was transmitting its thoughts to the mist in some way, whereupon the mist provided an appropriate English translation.

one's voice never sounds the same in one's own ears as it does to other persons. Furthermore, it made sense that if Immu imitated Festina, Esticus would mimic me. Even so, I did not like the idea of an alien who spoke with my voice; it was most sinisterly creepy, like the first step in acquiring an evil twin.

The other reason I reacted in surprise was because in my language (and therefore in Shaddill-speak too), Tahpo means "the last" . . . or perhaps a better translation would be "the dregs." Whatever Esticus meant by the word, Immu disapproved—she nudged him warningly with her hip. Perhaps she did not intend for us to see her action, but she hit Esticus hard enough to make him flinch.

If Festina noticed, she did not comment. Instead, she told the aliens, "We're honored to make your acquaintance, but the circumstances are unfortunate. Why did you capture our ship? What do you want from us? If we've inadvertently offended you in some way . . ." She glanced in my direction, as if *I* might have been the one who provoked the Shaddill into reprehensible deeds . . . which was most unfair, because the Shaddill had started misbehaving first. "If there's any kind of problem," Festina said, "let's discuss it and resolve things amicably."

Immu made a raspy sound in her throat. I did not know if this was a growl of anger, the Shaddill form of laughter, or simply a clearing of phlegm. "Admiral Ramos," Immu's fog-ball said, "we know your reputation—our substitutes for Admirals Rhee and Macleod kept us apprised of all activities in the Outward Fleet. We know you are an intelligent creature; you must realize you have seen too much for us to consider releasing you. This room, for instance."

She gestured toward the fountain, pointing a claw toward the mini-chili. The small yellow fruit had completely disappeared; now, there was only a mush of jelly. "We don't know how you found your way here so unerringly," Immu said, "but it's a pity we didn't notice until you had already reached the fountain. Quite possibly, you've seen additional secrets on our ship: secrets we can't let you share with the outside world."

"Then keep us here, but let everyone else go—everyone in the crusade and *Royal Hemlock*. They haven't seen any of this."

"They still know too much," Immu replied. "For example, they know FTL fields can be hypercharged by entering a star." The mist above her head reshaped itself slightly—a tiny bit of fog broke off from the main gold ball and circled for a bit before plunging back inside. I realized this was intended to suggest Starbiter looping about the sun before she finally entered the fire . . . and I was most envious the Shaddill mist-clouds could not only perform English translations but provide delightful visual effects.

Even as the fog was pretending to be Starbiter and the sun, its voice continued to speak. "This information is something we sought to keep secret. We replaced high officials in every culture we uplifted—like your Admirals Rhee and Macleod—and had them pass laws to prevent disclosure. For example, all starship computers in the Technocracy must be programmed to stay well clear of suns . . . supposedly as a safety precaution."

"So," said Festina, "if someone ever wanted to get near a star, the ship's computer just wouldn't let it happen. Simple, but elegant."

"And yet," I said, "Starbiter flew into the sun. She was reluctant to do so, but she obeyed me."

The fog above Immu's head flared brightly and made a harsh fizzing sound. I do not think the noise was intended to be speech—it sounded as if Immu was transmitting such angry thoughts to the cloud, the translation nanites had caught fire. In a moment, however, the fizzing spittered into silence and the cloud muttered, "We never should have given the Divians living starships."

"It was part of their culture," Esticus said softly. "It was what they were used to. They would have been most suspicious of ships made from inorganic parts."

"I know," Immu snapped, her cloud threatening to fizz again. "We still shouldn't have taken the risk." She turned back to Festina and me. "The moment we gave the first Zaretts to the Divians, we surrendered control. You don't build Zaretts, you breed them; and in the breeding process, random factors inevitably creep in. The first Zaretts we made would never go close to a sun; we designed them to have an absolute phobia against it. But in every subsequent generation, a few individuals weren't quite as afraid as their parents. Inhibitions just don't breed true, especially when they're groundless. By now, half the Zaretts alive can be bullied into entering a star if you scream at them loud enough. Fortunately for us, no one ever tried it persistently."

"Until I came along," I said proudly.

Immu did not answer . . . but her translation mist gave another angry fizz.

"Why did you do it?" Festina asked the Shaddill. "Why create this elaborate lie about the limitations of FTL fields?"

"To slow you down," Esticus said. "To disrupt your species' development. And to make sure our own vessel was always much faster than the craft of lesser races."

"Surely you've realized by now," Immu said, "everything we do is aimed at weakening you. We approach cultures as they start into space; we offer them technology and flawed but plausible scientific models that completely bypass certain discoveries those races would otherwise make on their own." The cloud above Immu's head split into two hemispheres with a slight gap between left and right. "We create a discontinuity in a species' scientific progress," she said. "We give them devices they don't understand and *won't* understand, because they've been deflected from developing the necessary scientific background."

"And of course," Festina said, "you place robot agents in positions of authority to make sure the background science is never filled in."

"Exactly," Immu agreed, her cloud fusing together again. "Our robot replacements control the purse-strings for almost all research in your sector. If someone begins to investigate topics we dislike, that person is diverted to a different project." A part of her cloud spun off on its own. "When that doesn't work—and scientists often prove difficult to sidetrack—we take steps to remove the irritant." A strand of fog lashed out from the main ball of mist, struck the little separate piece, and pulled it back into the whole again . . . like a frog swallowing a fly. "The annoyingly keen scientist simply disappears, and ends up in a comfortable holding facility on this very ship: a facility you'll soon see for yourself."

Festina lifted the muzzle of her stun-pistol. "Think again."

Immu made the raspy throat-noise. This time it definitely sounded like laughter. "You obtained that gun from our robots. Do you believe we would arm them with weapons that would affect us?"

"You might," Festina replied. "For all your fancy technology, you don't seem very smart."

"We aren't," Esticus whispered. Immu gave him another hip-bump, this time making no effort to conceal it. She also made a hissing sound and clacked her mandibles in a gesture that was clearly a Shaddill short-hand for, "Shut up, you fool!"

"Here's what I think," Festina said. "I think five thousand years ago, your people were science whizzes who built this ship and a lot of other fancy stuff. Somewhere along the line, you developed a way to evolve to a higher state of being—to make yourselves smart as all hell, even if you ended up looking like blobs of purple jelly." She glanced at the liquid spurting out of the fountain. "What's this stuff called?"

There was a pause. The clouds over both Shaddill heads dimmed, as if they were trying to deal with some difficult concept and had to use all their power for the translation process. Finally, the mist above Esticus spoke softly: "Blood Honey," it said.

Immediately, both speaker clouds brightened to their usual golden luster . . . or perhaps a bit shinier than before, greatly pleased with themselves for devising an elegant translation of the actual Shaddill name.

"Blood Honey," Festina repeated. "Cute. Anyway, your people built Blood Honey fountains so you could all advance together. You carefully cleaned up the worlds where you lived, then you prepared to jelly out. The only problem was, some of you didn't *like* the idea of turning into purple goop. I think it scared you shitless. So when everybody else went to bathe in the fountains, a bunch of you just turned tail. You buggered off on this ship, and you've been running ever since."

"You mean," I said, "these Shaddill ones are cowards? All others of their kind pursued Celestial Transcendence, while these turned away in fear?" I glared at the two furry beetles with contempt. Suddenly, I understood why Esticus had called himself Tahpo: the dregs.

"So how many of you are left?" Festina asked the beetles. "Hundreds? Thousands? Millions? Or could it be you two are the only ones who didn't have the guts to change?"

Immu didn't answer—just turned her head away and lowered her gaze to the floor. Her mandibles fell still, as if she were paralyzed with shame. Finally, it was Esticus who spoke, his fog-cloud dim and drooping.

"There were others once," he said. "*Many* others. It isn't an easy thing to contemplate changing to the Soft Form— even when you've been assured it will . . . expand your horizons."

He closed his eyes: great brown eyelids rolled down from his forehead. "Once upon a time, this vessel was full of Tahpo. We spoke as if we were on a grand adventure—the last of our race, a single brave ship against a hostile galaxy. A grand, most *noble* adventure . . . and we formed a plan we all agreed was necessary for our survival. We would undermine lesser races before they could become our equals. There weren't enough of us to compete any other way; our only defense was sabotage. So we all agreed. We all . . ."

Esticus's mandibles suddenly clenched tight against each other. They squeezed for a long shuddering moment; then they fell limp and motionless. "We all agreed. But over the years—the long, long years—the others left, one by one. They found the courage to change . . . or perhaps it wasn't courage but despair. Despair at what our lives had become."

Esticus sighed. "In a way, we'd become as lifeless and tired as the alien species we subverted. We all knew it. As the centuries passed, our comrades listened to the voices of . . . of those who had changed in the fountains." He

paused. "The Soft Ones speak to us now and then. Or at least
they used to. I haven't heard them in years; perhaps they've
given up on Immu and me. But when there were more of us,
the Soft Ones whispered how profound their lives had become since the transformation . . . and slowly the other
Tahpo surrendered. We'd discover that one of our number
had vanished; we'd come to this room, and the fountain
would be bubbling smugly."

He opened his eyes and looked over at his mate. "Immu
always turned off the Blood Honey and let the fountain
drain . . . but eventually, the basin would be full again and
another of us would be gone. Until . . ."

Esticus's voice trailed off.

"You *are* the only two left," Festina said. "Aren't you?"

"Yes," Esticus whispered. "We are the greatest cowards of
our race."

He closed his eyes again. The two Shaddill stood there,
huddled against each other in silence.

The Effects Of Blood Honey

They did not hold the pose long. Immu suddenly lifted her
head and glared at us, her mandibles once more working furiously. "So!" she said. "Now you know how pathetic my
mate and I are. No doubt you'll have a good laugh about
it . . . once you're locked in our jail."

"I would not enjoy imprisonment," I told her. "That would
be unfair treatment . . . and I am fed up with cruelty at your
hands. You gave me a Tired Brain! You made all my people
that way! And since you first appeared above Melaquin, you
have hounded me unmercifully for no good reason."

"There was a reason," Esticus said. "I don't know whether
you'd consider it good . . ."

He turned toward Immu with what I suspect was a plead-
ing expression. Immu made an unpleasant grunting noise, as
if she really did not wish to explain; but gazing on Esticus's
face, she relented. "When we picked up the Rhee and
Macleod robots from New Earth," Immu said, "they told us

a woman had died on Melaquin four years ago." The fog cloud above Immu's head reshaped into an arrow pointing in my direction. "Few among your people ever die . . . and we thought we could use your corpse."

"What for?" I demanded.

"For an experiment. To see . . ." Immu glanced at the fountain, its basin now nearly full. "It's been centuries since that was last turned on. Not since our final companion changed to the Soft Form. We don't know if the Blood Honey is still potent."

"Of course it is potent," I chided. "You could discover that with a simple test." I waved toward the basin. "I placed a mini-chili in the bowl . . . and behold, it has turned to jelly."

"Jelly is only the first part of the transformation," Immu replied. "The *easy* part—breaking down a cell's exterior to expose the DNA inside. After that, there's a second process to convert the DNA into . . . something else. Something that can hold a vastly expanded consciousness."

"The process is complicated," Esticus put in. "It has to maintain existing neural connections in the brain to preserve the original psyche, while adjusting selected portions of the genome in a particular sequence . . ." His voice cloud began to reshape itself into some sort of twisty ladder, then collapsed back into a ball. Esticus must have decided this particular visual effect was too much bother. He said with weak sheepishness, "It's very complex."

"How does Oar fit into this?" Festina asked.

"We wanted to put her body into the fountain," Immu answered. "Using a living person would be too much of a risk; it's been so long since the Blood Honey was tested, the League of Peoples might condemn us for endangering another sentient being. But there'd be no problem with a corpse. We'd put Oar in the fountain, then examine her afterward to see if her cells had undergone the desired transformation." The alien glanced toward her husband. "Merely out of curiosity," she said. "To see if the Blood Honey still worked."

"Yes, just to see," Esticus agreed, gazing back at her. "A way to pass the time."

"But what good would Oar be?" Festina asked. "It sounds like the transformation is specific to your species. Any other species will just get broken down into purple goo, without being put back together the right way."

"Of course," Immu said, as if that should be obvious to anyone. "But Oar *is* our species. Haven't you figured that out by now?"

The Stupidest Creatures In The Universe

"I am not a villainous Shaddill!" I replied hotly. "Not even a little bit."

"You are," Esticus said, his voice cloud sliding a short distance toward me. "Your genome is 99.999 percent the same as ours."

"The differences between you and us," Immu said, "are no greater than the differences between your Freep and Tye-Tye companions out in the corridor. Or between female Zaretts, who are large and spherical, versus males, who are small and cloudy. External looks are insignificant compared to what's in your chromosomes and cytoplasm. We made your race to be just like us."

"But I am beautiful glass! Not fur at all. And I have five fingers, without claws . . . and no tail or mouth attachments . . ."

"All trivialities," Immu said. Her translation mist shaped itself briefly into an approximation of me, pleasantly tall and humanoid—then the image shifted into something more squat and beetle-ish. "Inside," she said, "you have the same organs that let you go without food for long periods of time, the same cellular structures that prevent you from aging, the same defensive systems that make you practically impossible to kill. We've lived more than five thousand of your years. Your people have the potential to live that long too."

"But it is five thousand years with Tired Brains!" I snapped. "That is another difference between you and me."

"It was necessary," Esticus said. "To make sure you didn't get too . . ." His golden cloud broke into a large number of thready wisps surrounding two little lumps—perhaps suggesting a horde of my people vastly outnumbering the two Shaddill.

"We wanted children," Esticus continued, "but the Soft Ones changed us somehow so we couldn't . . . it didn't happen naturally. They wanted to be sure we *were* Tahpo: the last of our kind. Lucky for us, this was originally a colony-building ship; it still had full terraforming capabilities and a supply of frozen fertilized ova. We altered the DNA in the ova just a bit to create a human-shaped race and . . . well. You really *are* like us, Oar, even if there isn't much external resemblance."

I still did not think it could possibly be true; but Festina was nodding to herself. In a quiet voice, she said, "If we get out of this, Oar, I'll show you pictures of a Chihuahua and an Irish Wolfhound—unquestionably the same species, but different as night and day. External appearance just isn't a reliable guide to cellular composition." She turned back to the Shaddill. "So you wanted Oar's corpse to test the Blood Honey. Just out of curiosity. You had absolutely no thought you might take the big step."

Esticus turned his eyes toward Immu; she looked back at him. For a moment, they did not speak . . . and although they were horrid fur-beetles, the image arose in my mind of lovers from some tale of romantic misapprehension: the kind of lovers who fervently want the same thing but believe the other does *not* want such a thing, so they say, "No, no, I do not want that either."

Fools! I thought. *They both wish to transform, but they fear to admit it.* I could see it in their eyes—as if some deep-down Shaddillish part of me knew instinctively how to read such googly insect expressions. Perhaps Immu and Esticus had once feared the honey fountain, but now they longed for it. Even if it meant death, they wanted release . . . but each was holding back for the sake of the other.

"You are both quite absurd," I told them. "Are you not secretly eager to jellify yourselves? I believe you have been so for years. Yet you each think the other person is afraid, so

you say nothing—never mentioning what you feel, for fear
of upsetting your mate. Is that not the case? You have been
shielding one another needlessly for five thousand years, because you are the stupidest creatures in the universe." I
pointed to the Blood Honey filling the fountain. "Please
jump in now, and get out of our lives."

The Tahpo/Shaddill/Fuentes stared at me pop-eyed for a
good five seconds; then they looked back toward each other,
their mandibles moving with great slowness. Esticus whispered something—a real whisper coming out of his mouth,
not the cloud above his head. Immu whispered back. In a
moment, they were nose to nose, whispering, whispering . . .
and holding each other's hands as their great shovel-tails slid
forward to entwine.

Festina leaned toward me. "If they've just been holding
off for the sake of each other . . . that's so fucking soppy, I
may puke."

"It is not soppy, it is merely ridiculous," I told her. "Many
creatures in the universe are ridiculous. Besides," I continued, "these two claim to be the same species as I . . . and I
am such a one as may soon succumb to a Tired Brain. Perhaps Shaddill brains get Tired as well, especially after five
thousand years. The Shaddill may not fall dormant, but perhaps there comes a point when they do very little actual
thinking."

"Perhaps," Festina agreed, watching Immu and Esticus
whisper. "I'll be ecstatic if they decide to go for a Blood
Honey skinny-dip. Once they're in 'Soft Form,' I don't think
they'll see us as threats—the jelly-guys aren't afraid of humans or any other species at our development level. With a
bit of luck, we'll be free to go; for that matter, they might
give us this ship. Once they jelly out, they won't need it anymore."

"You mean they will say, 'Now we see the light,' and all
will be well? We will not get to punch *anyone*?"

Festina tapped my jacket with one finger. "You're an Explorer now, Oar. The ideal outcome of any Explorer mission
is to walk away safely—not to kick butt, not to make your

opponents cry uncle. I don't know if there's ever been a mission where Explorers faced alien enemies and the enemies said, 'So sorry, we won't bother you anymore . . . and by the way, take the keys to our spaceship.' But by God, every Explorer *prays* for something that works out so tamely. Tameness is good. Tameness means you live another day."

"But they are horrendous villains!" I whispered. "They may seem like foolish beetles, but they and their kind have wreaked havoc throughout the galaxy. On my people. On your people. On the Divians and the Cashlings and all those other species the Shaddill uplifted. Long ago, Cashlings were a sensible species, but now they are vain and obnoxious: is that not a result of the Shaddill's deeds? And Immu said they did it deliberately! They intended to make the entire Cashling race silly and ineffectual; in a spirit of utter selfishness, these harmless-looking beetles have degraded billions of creatures into jokes."

"You think I don't know that?" Festina replied. "You think I don't know how humans and everybody else have been screwed around? Hell, Oar, *Homo sapiens* is a travesty of what it once was; the whole damned Technocracy is lazy, stupid, and corrupt, all thanks to a bunch of fur-balls who didn't give a fuck how much trouble they caused, so long as it let them avoid a scary decision. That infuriates me, Oar— the whole damned thing makes me livid. I want to snap the mandibles off these shitheads and stuff 'em down their rotten little throats. But I'm not in the business of vengeance; as always, I'm just trying to make the best of a crappy situation. So we grit our teeth, forget that the Tahpo have fucked over more sentient creatures than anyone else in history, and just cross our fingers the last two will remove themselves from the playing field. Once they're gone, once everybody on our side is safe, *then* we'll see if we can fix the damage these bastards have caused."

This plan did not please me at all: letting the villains quietly achieve transcendence after all the disruption they had wrought. But I did not have time to devise an alternate strategy because Immu and Esticus were turning our direction.

Their faces looked just as ugly as ever . . . but their mandibles moved less frantically, as if some inner tormenting tension had eased away.

"You were correct," Immu said. "We had both . . . we had both been foolish on each other's behalf. All this time . . ." She made a rasping noise in her throat. "We intend to transform as soon as possible."

"I'm fucking thrilled for you," Festina replied. "Now before you go all jiggly, please release our ships . . . or even better, tell your computers to obey our instructions and let us take care of—"

"Before any of that," Immu interrupted, "we have to make sure the Blood Honey is effective. It's been centuries since anyone used it, and some of the ship's systems are failing from sheer old age. Therefore, we must still try our experiment."

She turned to stare directly at me.

"Uh-oh," Festina said. She turned toward me too.

"What?" I asked. "What experiment?"

Then I remembered. "Oh."

The Nature Of Cowardice

"The fountain shouldn't hurt you," Esticus said, his shovel-tail twitching nervously. "We've analyzed the Blood Honey as well as we can. We think it's still all right; we just aren't sure."

"But it will turn me into jelly! *Purple* jelly!"

"If it works," said Immu, "you'll be a million times more than you are now. Transcendent. With power and intelligence far beyond your wildest dreams."

"But I will be purple jelly! I do not wish to be jelly, regardless of the quality of its dreams."

Immu stepped toward me. It was the first time she had ventured out of direct contact with Esticus. "Weren't you the one who called us cowards for refusing to change?"

"You *were* cowards!" I cried. "And you still *are*—if you cannot muster the courage to act unless I do it first."

"All right," Immu said, taking another step toward me. "So we're cowards. We've thought of ourselves that way for thousands of years—the most cowardly dregs of a race noted for how much it loved to hide. We're willing to do one last cowardly thing."

She took another step toward me. Festina moved in between us. "You don't want to do this," she told Immu, ignoring the mandibles that twitched right in front of her face. "If you dump Oar into the fountain and it kills her, the League of Peoples will consider you murderers. You yourself said it was too risky to try with a living person."

"At this point," Immu answered, "I'm willing to take the gamble."

"And it isn't really a gamble," Esticus said, scurrying up beside his wife. "We've done everything possible to check that the honey's okay. So long as we make our best efforts to ensure Oar's safety, we won't be held responsible if something goes wrong." He reached out tentatively to touch my arm. "It'll transform you into something amazing. Really."

I pulled sharply away from him. "I do not find jelly amazing. I should very much hate turning soft."

"But," said Immu, "it will cure your Tired Brain."

Suddenly, I felt as if everything in the world had gone silent. The fountain continued to burble, the Shaddill swished their mandibles together, Festina breathed softly . . . yet those sounds all seemed very distant. Very quietly I said, "It will cure my brain?"

"Yes," Immu replied, her translation cloud sliding closer to me. "The honey adjusts cellular activity and DNA . . . especially anything related to mental capacity. It vastly expands your intellectual power; and in the process, it will correct the genetic blockages that make your brain Tired."

"That's right," Esticus put in most eagerly. "We've, uhh . . . you're not the first of your people who's gone through this test. Back at the very beginning, when we were certain the Blood Honey was still good, we . . . we captured one of your men and we . . . he thanked us afterward, he really did. Before he left to join the Soft Collective. He thanked us, then teleported away by sheer force of will. So there's nothing to be afraid of, and everything to be gained."

I turned to look at the fountain, still gushing with thick-flowing honey. Out near the edge of the basin, the surface of the pool was calm—like a mirror of clear crimson, barely rippled by the splashing in the middle.

It did not surprise me to see two fiery red eyes glimmering up from the liquid's glossy surface.

The Pollisand had led me to this room. He had promised to cure me, and guided me straight to the remedy I needed. He had simply neglected to mention the medicine would turn me into purple gloop.

One should never trust alien promises. I ought to have known that by now.

"Perhaps someday," I said, "it will become necessary for me to take this step." I turned to Festina. "If I become such a one as does nothing for weeks on end and refuses to answer no matter how nicely you speak, you have my permission to take drastic action rendering me into a jellylike state. But *not yet!*" I glared at the two Shaddill. "Do you hear me? I do not wish to bathe in Blood Honey at this time."

"Perhaps not," Immu answered, "but you're going to anyway."

Her great shovel-tail swept up from the floor. She intended to smack me into the fountain; but Festina was ready for such a tactic. My friend shot her hands forward, striking nasty little Immu hard in the chest with the heels of both palms. Immu staggered back, her aim spoiled; instead of striking me, the tail's chitin edge swept harmlessly past, barely grazing my jacket sleeve.

Even that tiny graze was enough to slice a gash in the jacket fabric. The tail was strong and fast and sharp . . . and it was still whipping wildly through the air as Immu tried to regain her balance. Esticus squealed and ducked as the shovel-scoop slashed past him; I tried to catch the tail, but it plunged away from me, spearing into the soil beside my feet. In a split-second, the shovel was snapping up again, jerking clots of dirt loose as it freed itself from the hard-

packed earth. I stomped down hard, hoping I could pin the
tail under my heel . . . but it moved too fast, swishing out of
range before my foot touched the floor.

For all their foolish appearance, the Shaddill were fast
and elusive. Then again, what does one expect from cowards?

Immu may have evaded me, but she was not so lucky with
my Faithful Sidekick. Festina stepped right onto the alien's
rabbitlike foot and slammed another double palm-heel into
Immu's chest. With her one foot trapped, Immu could not
backpedal to keep her balance; she toppled back heavily,
twisting at the last moment so she hit the floor with her
shoulder rather than flat on her spine. Festina tried to press
her advantage, jumping forward with the obvious intention
of delivering a punch or kick . . . but Immu still had the use
of her tail. It swept up fast and hard, not well-aimed but as
dangerous as a swinging ax. Festina was forced to dodge out
of the sharp shovel's reach.

"Stop!" Esticus cried. "Stop, stop, stop!"

He was still crouched down, exactly where he had landed
after ducking Immu's tail. His own tail was tucked tight beneath him; he showed no sign of joining the fight. And
yet . . . he had spoken in Shaddill-ese, not English. That was
because his translation cloud was gone—it had vanished in
the past few seconds, while I was concentrating elsewhere.
Had the cloud's component bits been scattered by Immu's
tail as it swept through the air? Or had the cringing Esticus
sent his cloud on some terrible mission?

A look of horror passed over Festina's face. Suddenly, she
began to choke

26

WHEREIN I FACE THE GREATEST RISK OF ALL

Four Starbiter Lookalikes

Esticus was only a step away. I planted my foot on his tail, just below the scoop so he could not swing it. Then I grabbed him by the wrists and heaved him up as high as I could lift. Since I was so much taller, he ended up dangling by his arms, feet off the ground.

In this position, I did not have to worry about his claws or tail, and I held him out far enough that he could not reach me with his mandibles. That only left his feet . . . and with haunches like a rabbit, he was well built for kicking at things behind his back, but not so good for attacking persons in front of him. Anyway, he seemed too scared to put up a fight—his mandibles trembled, his eyelids fluttered, and he made anxious grunts in his throat.

I too may have uttered the occasional grunt. A creature of Esticus's size may not be as heavy as a human, but it took great strength to hold him hanging in that position. There was no chance of keeping him suspended for more than a minute . . . but with luck, that was all the time I needed.

"Let Festina go!" I shouted into his face. "Whatever you are doing, stop at once."

Esticus did not answer. Neither did Immu. As for Festina, she was clutching her throat and making horrible wheezing sounds. It had to be the work of the missing translation clouds . . . for Immu's cloud had disappeared too. I could imagine billions of translation nanites crowding inside my friend, sealing off her windpipe, clotting up her lungs. She was still on her feet, having staggered back to get away from Immu's tail; but her face was turning dark with blood, and her eyes were bulging. With the hand that was not at her throat, she raised her stun-pistol and fired at Immu.

Immu gave a raspy laugh. "I told you. Those guns don't work on us."

"Let Festina go!" I yelled at the two Shaddill. "Perhaps the gun cannot hurt you, but I surely can." I gave Esticus a shake and he gasped out a hiss.

"You're the one who should let go," Immu said, speaking in my own language. Without the translation cloud, her voice was nothing more than a whisper. "We have enough nanites to choke you too."

"Do not try," I said. "If I feel the smallest tickle in my throat, Esticus will regret it."

At that, Esticus wriggled and squirmed, trying to slip from my grip. He could not. The foolish Shaddill had made me stronger than they were themselves.

Immu got to her feet, her tail lashing angrily around her haunches. I turned quickly, placing Esticus between me and his wife as a protective shield.

"Lajoolie!" I shouted. "Sergeant Aarhus! Nimbus and Uclod! Could you please lend me assistance?"

"Save your breath," Immu said in her whispery voice. "Did you think we'd be stupid enough not to deal with them?"

She clapped her hands: a sharp smack with an after-clatter of claws clicking against each other. It was obviously a signal of some kind; I looked around quickly, wondering if I would be attacked by robots or nanites. But the attack was not aimed at me . . . and by all evidence, the attack had taken place some minutes earlier, so quietly I had not noticed it.

Four stringy blobs rolled in through the door. They looked like human-sized versions of baby Starbiter—gray threads sunk into damp goop that glistened wetly in the dim light. In this case, however, the goop was not white but murkily

clear . . . making it possible to see dark silhouettes embedded in the heart of the blobs. I had no trouble identifying the
silhouettes by their shape and size. Lajoolie. Sergeant
Aarhus. Uclod. The last blob had no figure visible inside, but
I did not doubt it contained Nimbus and his child.

Somehow my friends had been taken by surprise. They
had been encased in guck, caught like mosquitoes landing
on pine gum. If they were trying to struggle free, I could not
see any evidence of it—they seemed frozen in place, helplessly stuck as the blobs rolled across the floor and stopped
in a ragged line behind Immu's back.

"You see?" Immu said. "You're all alone." She glanced
toward Festina. My friend had toppled onto her knees and
was doubled over now, her head almost touching the floor.
Her whole face was approaching the port-wine color of the
birthmark on her cheek.

"I won't let your precious friend die," Immu told me in a
raspy smirk. "I'd never do anything so non-sentient. But I'll
let her pass out before I call off the nanites in her throat.
And," Immu continued, raising the sharp end of her tail
above Festina's head, "once she's unconscious, I won't have
trouble cutting off her ears . . . lopping a few fingers . . .
scooping out an eye . . . unless you put Esticus down. As
long as I don't actually kill this human, the League of Peoples won't stop me."

"Then the League will not stop *me*," I said, "from ripping
off parts of Esticus . . . which I shall certainly do if you hurt
Festina." I gave the Shaddill in my arms another fierce shake.

"Not so fast," Immu snapped. "You don't know a thing
about our anatomy. You don't know what's safe to rip off
and what could be lethal. For all you know, Esticus might
die from losing a single claw."

"I do not believe he could be so frail."

"But you don't *know*," Immu replied. "As for me, I'm thoroughly familiar with *Homo sapiens* physiology." She swung
her tail idly toward Festina; my friend grabbed at it weakly
but missed. "I know what will and won't cause fatal bleeding," Immu continued. "I know which human body parts are
expendable. But if you so much as break one of Esticus's

bones without knowing what you're doing, that's callous disregard for the possibility you might do lethal damage. Not a sentient attitude, Oar—the League will kill you on the spot."

"For breaking a finger? When you are threatening to pluck out Festina's eye?"

"I'm threatening to do something I know won't kill her. You, on the other hand, would be taking a blind risk with someone else's life. That is *definitely* non-sentient. Let my mate go before you get hurt."

Esticus whispered, "Yes, please, yes, please, yes, please . . ."

I stared at the whimpering beetle as he dangled in front of me . . . and suddenly I became furious. For five thousand years, these cowardly creatures had not hesitated to violate entire cultures, to kidnap and imprison individuals who interfered with their plans, to coerce whole species into insipid decadence, and *to give people Tired Brains*—yet Immu dared suggest I should be executed if I snapped off somebody's claw? My best friend was choking in front of me. My other friends were enveloped in gooey string, and who knew how well they could breathe inside those cocoons? The Shaddills wished to jelly me against my will, rather than take the slightest personal risk in pursuit of transcendence; yet *I* was the wicked one who might be punished?

Enough of this nonsense. I would command the Shaddill to remove the nanites from Festina's windpipe, to release my friends and leave us alone . . . or else I would grab Esticus's trembling mandibles and rip them right off his face. It was ridiculous for Immu to claim she could hurt my friends with impunity, but the League would not permit me to hit back.

Slowly, I lowered Esticus until his feet touched the ground. Perhaps Immu thought I was preparing to let her husband go . . . but in my mind's eye, I pictured punching the little brown Shaddill in the nose, smashing the mandibles all around his muzzle, hearing the crack of bones as they shattered under my fist.

And yet . . . and yet . . .

How did I know I would *not* kill the hateful fur-beetle? Perhaps smashing his mandibles *would* do lethal damage.

And for all that I was blazing with righteous indignation, I did not wish to murder shaky wee Esticus. The League would then murder me . . . and I did not care to die so stupidly.

Was there anything I could do to vent my wrath, yet not kill a weak Shaddill one?

Yes.

Changing my grip on Esticus's wrists, I whirled him around by the arms and slung him into the fountain.

Splash

I did not throw the furry alien, but swung him like an ax: holding his arms and sweeping him across the pool's surface so that he scooped up a great sloosh of honey that flew in a frothy tsunami. It was fortunate I did not get any splashes on me . . . but I was wearing my Explorer jacket, and the few drops of spatter that came my way hit fabric instead of skin.

Neither Immu nor Esticus fared so luckily. I had aimed the husband perfectly at the wife—the thick wave of crimson scooped up by Esticus hit Immu full in the face, drenching her head and all down her front. She squealed in terror and jumped backward, trying to wipe honey from her fur; she squealed again when she realized she now had the liquid on her hands. Her eyes bulged horrified as she stared at her fingers . . . for as she watched, one of her claws melted into soft purple and fell plop to the floor.

Esticus was no better. From the waist down, he was soaked in honey; and his pelt had begun to bubble, sloughing off fur as each little hair dissolved into goo. The skin underneath was already turning puffy. I let him fall to the floor and leapt back to make sure I did not get the honey on me. He staggered to his feet almost immediately . . . but the dirt where he had landed was covered with a glossy slick of purple and the part of his body that had touched the ground looked like its hair and skin had been shaved off clean.

Howling, "Help me!" he turned to Immu; but his wife was in no condition to help anyone. Her entire head was turning purple—all but those bulging eyes, because she had blinked them shut just before the Blood Honey struck her. Now her eyelids were gone, turned into goo that slid off her eyeballs and slurped into the general morass of her face. Her cheeks dripped onto her chest; her forehead was slumping into a great overhanging brow that would soon flop down and cover those raw exposed eyes.

A raspy laugh gurgled in her throat. "All right," she whispered to Esticus, "I'll help you."

She reached toward him and gave his hand a squeeze. Though her head had turned to slime, her arms and legs were still mostly intact; she let go of Esticus's hand, scooped him off the floor, and held him to her disintegrating chest. The motion shook dollops of jelly loose from Esticus's legs, laying bare the bone underneath. Then Immu flexed her powerful haunches for one last great leap.

Husband and wife plunged together into the pool.

The Cost Of Salvation

The Shaddill's jump did not take me completely by surprise—I had enough time to hurl myself backward out of range of their splash. Festina was far enough removed too, and protected by her uniform; patches of the gray cloth looked wet and glossy, but no splashing honey landed on her exposed head or hands.

There was only one problem: Festina was still choking. Even as I watched, her body went limp and tumbled clumsily into the dirt.

"Villains!" I screamed at the Shaddill, now decomposing in the fountain. They were totally immersed, and totally coated with purple, but I screamed at them anyway. "Call off your nanites, you poop-heads! Get them out of Festina's windpipe!"

No nano cloud emerged from my friend. I could see no sign of her breathing.

"Stick-ship!" I yelled in Shaddill-ese. "Tell the nanites to leave my friend! This is an order—obey me!"

No response. I ran to Festina and knelt beside her. When I opened her mouth, a gold nanite glow shone from the depths of her throat . . . but the actual blockage was too far down to see, let alone to reach with my finger. Anyway, how could I remove the obstruction if it was made of billions of tiny robots, all following orders to strangle my friend? If I did manage to sweep some away, they would simply rush back into place.

I needed a means to fight the nanites directly. I needed nanites of my own.

"Nimbus," I said aloud.

Leaping to my feet, I rushed to the webby blobs that held our companions. With so much honey splashing around, the blobs had been struck with spatters . . . and wherever the honey had touched, the webby surface had dissolved into jelly. *Praise to the Hallowed Ones!* I thought: the blobs must be made of living matter, susceptible to Blood Honey. Now all I needed was a tool . . .

Festina's stun-pistol lay on the floor a short distance behind me—she had dropped it when she saw it did not work on the Shaddill. I grabbed it and poked the metal muzzle into one of the purple patches on Nimbus's cocoon. With a twist of the wrist, I flicked the jelly off the gooey surface; the result was a small hole where the jelly had been. Even better, the gun's metal barrel did not seem affected by contact with honey . . . which meant I could use it to dig into the blob that held Nimbus prisoner.

For Festina's sake, I hoped I could do it quickly.

Wrapping my jacket around my hands and arms to avoid getting stuck on the blob's gluey surface, I pushed the cocoon holding Nimbus to the edge of the fountain. Once I had the cocoon in position, I dipped the pistol's mouth into the basin, got it wet with red liquid, then prodded it into the blob's exterior. The sheen of honey on the gun's barrel ate into goopy webbing, turning it to a gel which could then be flicked away. This was not a speedy process—the honey did not corrode the goo nearly as fast as I wished—but little by little I deepened a hole into the blob, telling myself all the while I would soon free Nimbus.

A part of me realized this might not be true. If Nimbus's little misty bits were all trapped separately, like millions of bubbles in a solid block of ice, I could never carve them loose in time to save Festina. But if there was one big chamber in the middle, a single holding area like an egg, and all I had to do was pierce the shell to let the cloud man out . . .

A great gust of mist shot out from the hole, straight into my face. It felt cool and kindly, a fog of salvation. "Nimbus!" I cried. "There are nanites down Festina's throat! You must clear them out and start her breathing again."

I expected the cloud man's mist to swoop immediately toward Festina; but it only wisped around and around, swirling close to me, then shying away again. "Clear them out?" Nimbus whispered. "How? I'm not designed for fighting other nanites. I couldn't *begin* to take on warrior nano . . ."

"These nanites are not warriors, you foolish cloud, they are just translator things. But they will kill Festina unless you take action."

"It's not that easy, Oar!" Mist was all around me, wreathing my head, brushing my cheek. "My only way to stop the nanites is smashing my particles against them. High-speed collisions that will hurt me just as much as the nano."

"Are you such a coward that you fear a little pain?"

"I'm not talking about pain; I'm talking about mutual destruction."

"And I am talking about the death of my friend!" I swept my hands at him viciously, trying to push him away from me. "You are a healer, are you not? Festina needs healing. That is all you have to think about."

"No, Oar. I also have to think about my daughter. And . . ." His mist shuddered. ". . . and my owner. My owner's wishes."

"Your owner? Uclod would wish you to help Festina!"

"I told you, Uclod isn't my owner—he's just ronting me. I'm the property of . . . of someone who doesn't know or care about your friend Festina, and who wouldn't want me to risk myself on her behalf." The mist-man shuddered again. "I'm a valuable investment," he said bitterly. "I have strict orders not to endanger myself on 'unprofitable moral whims.' "

"And you listen to such orders?"

"Oar," he said. "I told you when I met you, obedience is hard-wired into my genes. I despise it, but I don't have a choice. It's how I was built."

I stared at him a moment, then closed my eyes. "I will tell you a thing, Nimbus. We are all built in ways we would change if we could—we are flawed or damaged or broken by forces beyond our control. In the end, we are limited creatures who cannot exceed our boundaries." I opened my eyes again, seeing only mist. "But here is the other half of the truth: our boundaries are never where we think they are. Sometimes we think we are the most wonderful person in the world, then find we are nothing special; sometimes we think we are too weak to do a great deed, then find we are stronger than we believe." I took a deep breath. "Please save Festina, Nimbus. You do not have to be so hard-wired and obedient. Please save her, and prove you are more than you think."

For a moment, he did not answer. His mist shimmered . . . as if it were glistening in some light beyond the dimness of that dusky room. Then his voice murmured in my ear, "All right. I'll do what I can."

He swept around me one last time, brushing tenderly against my neck. "My daughter is still inside the web. Get her out and keep her safe."

"I will," I promised.

He swirled away, streaming across the room as fast as an eagle, not slowing down as he flew straight into Festina's face. The cloud man disappeared up Festina's nose as he had once before . . . only this time I was not scandalized by his effrontery, but overjoyed he was going to save her. He would fly down her throat to fight the gold nanites . . .

And who would win the battle? Who would survive?

I did not know.

Carefully, because I had nothing else to do, I widened the hole into the cocoon that had held Nimbus prisoner. The hole was only three fingers across, the breadth of the pistol's barrel. Smearing more and more honey into the gap, I increased the breach in the goo-ball until I could stick my arm through safely, with no risk of touching the damp jelly sides.

All that time, I forced myself not to look in Festina's direction. Nimbus would succeed; of course he would. There was no other way to save my friend, so the universe was *compelled* to let Nimbus triumph. I merely had to get Starbiter out of the blob; the moment I managed that, Nimbus would emerge from my friend's mouth and say, "Oar, everything is all right now."

Even before I reached into the blob, I had caught sight of Starbiter. She lay amongst the webbing so tranquilly, I wondered if perhaps she thought she had returned to her mother's womb. But she did not protest as I wrapped my fingers gently around her and drew her out into the world. I had long since discarded my jacket, for fear of the patches where honey had turned the cloth to gel . . . so I cradled the little Zarett tight to my chest, right where she could hear my heart beating.

"Now, Nimbus," I said. "Now you will come out."

For many long seconds, nothing happened. Then a vicious spasm shook Festina's body, and she gave a gagging cough. It was the sound of a human about to vomit; I sped across the room and rolled Festina onto her side just as she gagged again. A spew of yellow phlegm erupted from deep within her, spattering onto the ground. It poured out in streams, puddling on top of the soil. I put an arm around her to hold her steady . . . and I knelt there, supporting Festina with one hand and baby Starbiter with the other.

"Come out now, Nimbus," I whispered as Festina took a ragged breath. "Your job is done. You have vanquished the enemy. Come out."

But he did not come out. He did not appear and he did not appear and he did not appear . . . until I realized he had *already* come out and I just did not recognize him. The spew on the ground was comprised half of golden nanites and half of Nimbus.

Both halves were dead.

I stared at the puddle as it slowly seeped into the dirt. Then I lowered my face to my friend's shoulder and wept.

True Freedom

"Well, well, well," said a familiar nasal voice, "three cheers for the visiting team! At the closing whistle, the score is Oar 2, Shaddill nothing."

I lifted my head. The Pollisand stood perched on the rim of the basin, looking down at the purple lumps that had once been Immu and Esticus. A creature his size could not possibly balance on the narrow basin wall, but he was there anyway; he pranced a few steps in a rhinoceroid victory dance, then jumped to the floor. "How are you lovely ladies doing?"

"We are splendid," I answered, "no thanks to you. But Nimbus is doing most poorly; you must bring him back to life."

Deep in the Pollisand's throat, his eyes grew dim. "Can't do that," he said. "Sorry."

"You *can* do that," I replied. "You have told me repeatedly how clever you are. You could bring Nimbus back just as you did for me; you must do it *now*."

"No, I must not," the Pollisand said . . . and there was something steely in his voice, something much different from the grating tone he usually affected. "Your friend Nimbus made a *choice*, Oar: a conscious decision to be more than a slave to some absentee owner, even though he knew it might cost him his life. I do *not* tamper with the results of such decisions."

"But you saved *me* . . . when I consciously made a decision to fall eighty stories!"

"You didn't believe you would die. You didn't believe you *could* die. When you grabbed your enemy and jumped out that window, you thought *he* would die but you'd be just fine; hardly a deliberate sacrifice like Nimbus."

The Pollisand walked over to the slightly muddy patch beside Festina—all that was left of the cloud man. He put out his great clumsy foot and held it over the soil as if he intended to touch the wetness . . . but then he stepped back and planted his toes on solid ground.

"Nimbus knew he wasn't designed for battle," the Pollisand said. "As he told you, his only method of fighting was to smash his component cells into the nanites over and over again, until both sides were battered into oblivion. I refuse to trivialize Nimbus's sacrifice by 'fixing' things as if his decision never happened."

"But . . ."

Festina placed a weak hand on my arm. "You aren't going to win the argument," she said. With a thoughtful expression, she gazed at the Pollisand. "You care about decisions, don't you? Good decisions, bad decisions . . . you care about them a lot."

"Deliberate choices are the only sacred things in the universe. Everything else is just hydrogen." He turned to me. "By the way, kiddo, you finally made an honest-to-god life-or-death choice yourself: when you decided not to rough up Esticus. If you'd broken so much as the little bastard's finger, the League of Peoples would have put you down like a dog."

"Breaking his finger would have killed him?"

"Hell, no," the Pollisand answered with a snort. "The Shaddill are just as indestructible as you are—they'd probably survive if you crammed H-bombs down their throats. Furthermore, if you'd just gone ahead and smashed Esticus in the face as soon as you thought of it, the League wouldn't have minded that either . . . but then, Immu got to blathering that horseshit about, 'Hey, you never know,' and even worse, you got to thinking, 'What happens if she's right?' *That's* when you were in trouble: the only time you've truly been in danger since we first met. If you genuinely recognized the risks and decided to pummel Esticus anyway . . . well, as Immu said, that really *would* have been non-sentient. With the League, it's never the actual result that counts; it's what goes through your head."

His eyes glimmered in the hollows of his neck. As I gazed at him, a disturbing thought crossed my mind. "If I had made the wrong decision at that time— if the League slew me for non-sentience—you would have let me stay dead. Because then my death would have been a result of my own decision. Correct?"

"Correct." The Pollisand's voice sounded amused.

"But if I had died for any other reason—not as the consequence of a personal decision but through accident or someone else's malice—you would have been willing to heal me. That is correct too, yes?"

"To some extent." His eyes glimmered more brightly.

"So when you told me hours ago," I said, "there was a teeny-tiny-eensy-weensy chance I might get killed, you did not mean the Shaddill might slay me. You meant I might make a bad decision, and you would not save me from the results." I glared at him fiercely. "Did you foresee *everything*? Did you know it would come down to me deciding whether or not to punch Esticus in the nose?"

"Hey," he said, "I keep telling you: I'm a fucking alien mastermind."

"Or," said Festina, "a complete fraud who takes credit for being a lot more omniscient than he really is. You took damned good care to keep your leathery white ass out of sight till the Shaddill were gone. Could it be you were afraid to tangle with them directly?"

"Ah, yes," said the Pollisand in an even more nasal voice than usual. "A god or a fraud? Am I or ain't I?" He lifted his forefoot and patted Festina fondly on the cheek. "You don't know, my little chickadee, how hard I work to keep the answer ambiguous."

Another Career Step Upward

Festina struggled to her feet, barely managing to stay upright until I lent her my arm for support. "All right," she said to the Pollisand, "now that the Shaddill are out of the way, could you maybe deign to help us? Like finding some way to get our friends out of those . . ."

With a great gooey slurp, the blobs surrounding Uclod and the rest dissolved into runny gray liquid. It sloshed in sheets to the floor, leaving Lajoolie, Aarhus, and Uclod soaked to the skin but free of their sticky entanglements.

"Well, would you look at that," the Pollisand said in mock surprise. "The Shaddill must have been right about this ship starting to break down—those confinement chambers were in such bad shape, they could only hold together a few minutes." He gave a theatrical sigh. "It's a bitch when you live on a ship five thousand years old. Things just fall apart."

Festina stared at him. "You're scary."

"Babe, you don't know the half of it." Inside the alien's throat, one of his crimson eyes winked.

"And you couldn't have arranged for that to happen five minutes earlier?"

"Sorry," the Pollisand said. "Lesser species have to fight their own battles."

Festina grimaced. "Now that the battle's over, how about arranging for this old decrepit ship to have a breakdown in its master command module? A short circuit that screws up security protocols and makes it possible for us to issue commands without worrying about passwords or voice identification . . ."

The lights in the room flickered. A raspy voice spoke from the ceiling in my own tongue. "Reporting a major malfunction in security module 13953," the voice said. "Awaiting your orders, Captain."

I looked toward Festina expecting her to answer; but then I remembered she did not speak Shaddill and therefore could not understand what the raspy voice said. "Are you speaking to me?" I asked the ceiling. "You believe I am the captain?"

"Affirmative. Awaiting orders."

"Uhh . . . do not repair the security malfunction. I shall give further orders soon."

Festina looked quickly back and forth between the Pollisand and me. "Was that what I think it was?"

"I am now in command of this vessel," I announced. "It seems I am excellently well-suited for a career in the navy: I have gone from communications officer to Explorer to captain in just a few hours."

"Don't stop yet," Festina muttered. "If we get out of here and bring down the Admiralty, you may end up head of the new High Council."

"If I do," I told her, "I will not forget the little people who helped me along the way." I gave her arm a reassuring pat, but Festina did not look reassured *at all*.

I Become A True Explorer

Released from their bondage, Uclod and Lajoolie had
fallen into one another's arms . . . which is to say, Lajoolie
was hugging her husband so fiercely his orange skin had
darkened several shades. He did not object in the least.

Meanwhile, Sergeant Aarhus sloshed damply toward us,
his navy boots going squish-squish-squish. "So," he said,
"did we win?"

"The Shaddill no longer exist," the Pollisand answered.
"Not as Shaddill anyway."

"In which case," I said, "it is time for you to honor our
agreement."

"What agreement?" Festina asked.

"I will explain later," I told her. "It is time for Mr. Pollisand to cure my brain . . . and if you say the remedy is to
turn myself into purple goo, I shall punch you in a manner
you will find most painful."

"Yeah, well . . ." The Pollisand looked down at his
forefeet and shuffled in the dirt. "Suppose I told you the
remedy was to turn a *bit* of yourself into purple goo."

"Then I should still punch you very hard."

"Oh come on, darlin'," he said, "it's the cleanest solution
to your problem. Sure, I could toss you onto an operating
table and rewire your whole brain . . . but that'd leave you a
completely different person. Certainly not the warm and
generous bundle of joy we've all come to love."

I narrowed my eyes at him and balled up my fist in a
meaningful way.

"On the other hand," he said quickly, "if we just dab some
honey on your skin, a tiny patch of you will go transcendent—uplifting just enough of your consciousness to get
you past the Tiredness."

"Uplifting her consciousness?" Festina asked. "Sounds
like bullshit to me."

The Pollisand growled at her. "Give me a break, Ramos. If
you want, I can give a ten-hour lecture on how it'll release
certain hormones to overcome certain other hormones that
tend to suppress yet another group of hormones, and blah

blah blah. But the long and the short is if she accepts a teeny-tiny-eensy-weensy transformation, it'll be enough to offset the physiological processes that are gradually deadening her brain. And," he added, winking at me, "it'll kick in a long-overdue maturation process that the Shaddill artificially repressed. My little girl," sniffle, "will start growing up."

Festina glared at him. "Are you sure this isn't just a prank for your own amusement? Are you sure, for example, you might not have arranged for a delayed-action cure when you saved her life four years ago? Maybe you implanted a curative something in her brain while you were repairing her broken bones . . . and you just want to smear her with Blood Honey because you like the idea of making her purple?"

The Pollisand gave a soft chuckle. "I like you, Ramos; I like the way your paranoid mind works. But if I *did* foresee everything and set up Oar with a brain implant, I'd surely make certain the implant wouldn't activate until a patch of her glassy ass skin turned to goo. How else could I consolidate my position as the most annoying creature in the universe?" He turned to me. "I assure you this *is* necessary if you want to save your brain. A teeny-tiny-eensy-weensy bit of you has to become jelly."

"All right," I said, gritting my teeth. "If that is what I must do . . ."

"It is," the Pollisand said. He went to the fountain and dipped his toe into the honey. Of course the toe did not turn purple—no doubt Mr. Foul Annoyance had such evolutionarily advanced skin, it did not succumb to the honey in the same way as lesser beings.

"Where do you want it?" he asked, walking back to me on three feet to keep his damp toe from touching anything. "Bottom of your foot so it's hardly ever visible? The tail of your spine so it's covered by your jacket? Atop one breast like a purple tattoo?"

I turned to Festina, thinking I might ask her advice . . . but as soon as I looked at her, I knew what it had to be.

I lifted my finger and pointed to my right cheek. The Pollisand moved before Festina could stop him.

EPILOGUE: BECAUSE I HAVE ALWAYS WISHED TO COMPOSE ONE

Dealing With Tedious Details

Being the captain of a huge alien starship is not so much fun as you might think, because there are many fearsome burdens. The greatest burden turns out to be one's Faithful Sidekick, who is constantly worried one will speak carelessly to the ship's computer and thereby Precipitate A Tragic Incident. Festina dictated to me exactly what commands I should give the stick-ship, and forced me to recite the instructions several times in English before allowing me to say the same in Shaddill-ese. Even then, she required me to think and think and think about the proper Shaddill-ese translation for each word; she would not let me speak until I had pretended to ponder for at least ten seconds over each instruction.

Of course, I did not *really* think about the translations that much—I was more concerned with contemplating the new appearance of my face (which reflected quite nicely in the fountain's basin). The Pollisand had only brushed my cheek lightly with his toe, no more than a casual dab . . . yet he had created a precise duplicate of Festina's birthmark in both size and shape. Immediately thereafter, he had produced a strip of clear plastic bandage which he slapped over the jelly smear to prevent it from slopping off my face. The bandage instantly bonded with my skin and is (supposedly) permanent.

Festina, of course, was anguished at the change in my features—she is a very nice person, but she has a Deep Psychological Fixation about her appearance which renders her a bit crazed. In her heart of hearts, she believes her birthmark makes her very very ugly . . . whereas she is actually ugly because she is opaque, and the birthmark has little effect, pro or con.

I hasten to point out that the jelly now composing my cheek, while undeniably purple, is a *transparent* purple; if I wiggle my fingers behind my head, you can see the movement quite easily, staring straight through my cheek and my brains and all. So the blob on my face is not a disfigurement, but merely a Colored Highlight that adds an extra-special accent of beauty. I am even more ravishing than ever . . . which I know is hard to believe, but after all this time listening to my story, you must surely realize I would never tell you falsehoods.

Nor will I tell you all the finicky arrangements we made in the next few minutes. Of course, we ordered the stick-ship to stop swallowing the little Cashling vessels, and to put back everything it had captured. We also released the crew of the *Royal Hemlock* from the stick-ship's sinister holding cells. The cells contained many other individuals of various species, all of whom had been kidnapped by the Shaddill due to these individuals being too smart for their own good. Captain Kapoor promised he would transport the prisoners back to their homeworlds as soon as possible . . . or to any other world they wished to visit, as a pleasant consolation prize for being locked in Durance Vile by wicked fur-beetles.

Speaking of fur-beetles, their jellied remains disappeared from the fountain while we were busy with other matters. I hoped they had merely gone slurp down the drain, but Festina suspected they had used some newborn mental power to transport themselves to wherever the rest of their people lived: an alternate dimension (whatever that means), or perhaps a distant Jelly-Planet where all the furniture jiggles. It seemed most unfair that these monstrous villains should simply ascend to their own nirvana without suffering retribution; but then I realized it could not be a very *good* nirvana considering that everyone there was all googly . . . and perhaps it was not a nirvana at all, but a horrible awful hell, where the only entertainment was persuading others to join you. So I decided not to make myself glum over never punching a Shaddill, and I regarded this as a sign of my Growing Maturity.

I believe I shall be excellent at maturity.

An Annoying Au Revoir

The Pollisand disappeared about the same time as the jellied Shaddill—again while our attention was distracted by more pressing business. He left behind a slip of paper with words written in glowing letters exactly the color of his eyes: HEY KIDS, IT WAS TRULY SPLENDIFEROUS WORKING WITH YOU, I MEAN THAT IN THE SINCEREST POSSIBLE WAY. AND GUESS WHAT? MY CRYSTAL BALL SAYS I'LL BE SEEING ONE OR TWO OF YOU AGAIN REAL SOON. BET YOU'RE LOOKING FORWARD TO THAT. HUGS TO YOU ALL, AND BIG WET KISSES. OH WAIT, I FORGOT; I CAN'T KISS YOU BECAUSE I DON'T HAVE ANY GODDAMNED LIPS! COUNT YOUR BLESSINGS, SCHMUCK-HEADS.—THE P.

As soon as we had all read this, the letters on the message blazed brighter and set the paper on fire. No one made any effort to extinguish it.

"Do you think he really knows what's going to happen?" Lajoolie asked most fearfully, staring at the burning note.

Festina made a face. "He obviously gets a kick out of jerking our chains—and whether or not he's prescient, he's definitely a first-class schemer. If he wants us embroiled in his machinations, he'll manage it somehow."

"Ah, Admiral, ever the optimist," said Aarhus. "Some see the glass half full, some see it half empty, and some see it crawling with toxic alien parasites who want to devour your pancreas."

Festina shrugged modestly. "Hey . . . it's a gift."

Final Dispositions

So here is how we all ended up.

Lady Bell and Lord Rye never left *Unfettered Destiny*
while it remained in the hold of the stick-ship. They cowered
like cowards until we told them everything had been resolved in our favor. After that, Bell insisted we still must pay
the "ransom" we agreed to—so we recorded our testimony
as originally promised, and the result was broadcast to the
entire sector.

This caused much stir amongst the peoples of the galaxy.
It also caused a torrent of broadcast money to flood into the
Cashlings' pockets . . . whereupon Bell and Rye bade adieu
to their vocation as Prophets and set off to become producers of sensationalistic VR extravaganzas. Apparently, this
was not an uncommon career path for persons of their race.

Because of our broadcast, the admirals of the navy's High
Council found themselves the targets of Public Outrage, not
to mention repeatedly being invited by civilian police to "as-
sist in criminal inquiries." Each high admiral tried to shift
the blame for the reported atrocities onto his or her colleagues, while he or she claimed to have been kept "out of
the loop." A few of the villains also managed to disappear
before being apprehended by authorities. Despite such de-
velopments, Festina felt certain the majority of the council
could not possibly escape incarceration, even if a few managed to wriggle away from the clutches of the law.

It has not yet been determined who murdered Uclod's
Grandma Yulai; but as Festina predicted, that particular
crime garnered a strenuous reaction from the Technocracy's
civilian government. With the League of Peoples forever
watching, humans cannot allow a homicide to go uninvesti-
gated. If necessary, Festina says she will look into the matter
personally when she returns to New Earth.

As for the rest of the Unorr family, they had already gone
into hiding by the time Grandma Yulai was slain. They realized the High Council might commit drastic deeds in order
to conceal their crimes . . . so the Unorrs removed them-

selves to a place of safety until all was well. It was only the grandmama who voluntarily remained in the open so as to coordinate the Admiralty's ultimate exposure.

Therefore, Uclod and Lajoolie had a family to which they could return: a family who eagerly awaited the couple in order to congratulate them on a job well done. Apparently, Uclod's relatives were vociferously telling everyone how wise they had been to purchase Lajoolie as Uclod's wife—Lajoolie had "made the boy a man," had "helped him fly right," and had achieved many other goals expressed in hackneyed phrases. The Unorrs swore they would recommend the same Tye-Tye marriage broker to all of their friends . . . which was not a pleasant prospect to contemplate, but at least it ensured that the broker would not wreak vicious acts upon Lajoolie's brother.

It turned out that one of the vessels in the outreach crusade was a female Zarett with a male Zarett on board. Using monetary credit from his family, Uclod purchased the couple and put baby Starbiter into loving Zarett care . . . where I imagine she was tucked into a soft spherical crib each night and spoiled with hydrocarbons of excessive sweetness. Uclod also promised to erect a monument to Nimbus in the Unorr family cemetery on the Freep homeworld. Starbiter (the mother, not the daughter) will receive an even larger memorial in the same place—perhaps a life-size model with a special fungal coating to mimic a Zarett's gooey-ness. I think that sounds most icky indeed; therefore, I have resolved to visit it immediately if ever I find myself on that planet.

Before I go there, however, I shall have to visit New Earth. When all the navy villains are brought to trial, I shall be required to give testimony . . . which I shall do most prettily and with great condemning vigor.

Alas, Festina tells me it will take a long time for any admirals to wind up in court. First there must be an Extended Media Circus, then an Orgy Of Knee-Jerk Recrimination, then some Somber Universal Soul-Searching, followed by a Period Of Desensitization Due To Massive Overexposure, leading to a Backlash Of Cynical Indifference, then Collective Amnesia And Perversely Partisan Revisionism, finally culminating in Cattle-Call Jury Auditions wherein hundreds of out-of-work actors vie for "cushy all-expenses-paid gigs with a high exposure quotient and very few lines to memorize."[15]

So my presence will not be required on New Earth for months or even years. Festina will go there immediately, of course. Sergeant Aarhus will accompany her, for he intends to serve as her personal bodyguard. When he spoke of this to Festina, she contended she needed no bodyguard . . . but he said she did, since many powerful admirals now hate her and wish her harm. Anyway, Aarhus feels most guilty about Nimbus's death— the sergeant believes that if he (Aarhus) had only done a better job as a security mook, Festina would never have found herself choking and the cloud man would still be alive. This line of thinking does not make sense; but grief makes fools of us all, and even I sometimes catch myself wondering if there was something I could have done to save the cloud man's life.

Nimbus was my brother and my friend. I have not had so many friends in my life; I could tell you the exact number, but the count is so low I do not wish to reveal it for fear you will think there is something wrong with me. There is nothing wrong with me *at all*—except that at the moment I am sad Nimbus will not see his daughter grow up big and strong.

Even happy endings have little tears in their eyes.

And So . . .

Festina and I stood together in the receiving bay of *Unfettered Destiny*, staring out at the vastness of space. Cleaning robots from the stick-ship were beeping in disapproval as they fastidiously scrubbed the floors around us; the Cashling ship still smelled most disgusting, but the worst of the odors were fading. Moreover, the walls were all glass, so I felt

---

[15]It is possible Festina was making a joke when she gave me this list of events. Or not.

quite at home . . . and it *was* my home, for I had appointed myself the new Prophet of this crusade.

Outside in the blackness, the ships of my disciples jostled for positions close to my magnificence. More arrived every hour; the entire Cashling Reach apparently regarded me as a delightful novelty, and untold numbers of supplicants were on their way to join my congregation.

"It won't last, you know," Festina said as we watched another ship appear in its faster-than-light way: popping into existence, with a stream of afterimages trailing out behind, as light from where it had been caught up with where it *was*. "You aren't the first non-Cashling to set yourself up as a Prophet. People will flock in for a while, then lose interest as soon as something new comes along."

"But in the meantime," I said, "I will use them to accomplish great deeds."

Festina nodded and turned back to the starry expanse before us. I had ordered *Destiny* to turn in such a way that we could only see a tiny edge of the mammoth stick-ship . . . or, as it had recently been christened, *The Giant Vessel Propelled By A Single Oar*.

The name was my idea. It was an excellent joke.

A small communication device chirped on Festina's belt. Sergeant Aarhus's voice said, "Admiral . . . ready to leave at your convenience."

"I'll be there in a minute."

She glanced at the airlock. A borrowed Cashling yacht was docked there—supposedly the fastest vessel my followers could offer. A band of science persons from the *Hemlock*'s crew had adjusted the yacht's computers to make it possible for the ship to charge its FTL field inside the nearest sun. Festina and Aarhus would fly back to New Earth at speeds no human had ever reached before.

"Aarhus tells me," I said, "that when you reach New Earth you will become commander of the entire human fleet."

"Sergeant Aarhus has always had an exaggerated opinion of my importance," Festina replied with a rueful chuckle. "Even if the entire High Council is thrown in jail, there'll be plenty of admirals left, and they all outrank me. But Aarhus insists everyone else is tainted by association with the old guard; I'm the only one whose reputation is still squeaky clean. He thinks the second I walk into navy HQ, I'll be made the fucking council's president."

"You will make an excellent fucking president, Festina. Will they give you a bigger gun?"

"No," she said, "they'll give me a great load of headaches. Even if I don't get named to the council, I'll have a million things to do. First and foremost, I'll set my people to figuring out what the Shaddill did to make *Homo sapiens* stupider. If anything." She stopped. "Damn! I wish we'd had time to ask them about that."

"Do you think they would have told you?"

"I don't know. But I honestly believe our guesses were right—the Shaddill deliberately dumbed down the Cashlings and the same thing is happening to us. Just look at the High Council of Admirals, for God's sake; four hundred years ago, none of those corrupt bastards would have been put in charge of *anything*. But we've sunk so low, they qualified as the cream of the fleet. Shit, shit, shit, shit, shit."

"Do not whine, Festina. You will find out the truth and make everything better. If you are ever puzzled, ask yourself what I would do in a similar situation."

"Then I'll end up punching a lot of people in the nose."

"If that is what it takes."

Festina smiled. Leaning quickly toward me, she kissed me on the cheek. The left cheek. The one that was not purple.

She drew back abruptly as if struck by sudden shyness. Turning away from me, she looked through the glass hull at the Cashling vessels congregating around us. "You'll have to take it slow on your way back to Melaquin. Those small ships can't go very fast—you might take two weeks to get home."

"I am in no hurry," I told her. "During those two weeks, I can entertain everyone by telling my story and propounding my thoughts about the universe. I am a Prophet now, Festina; I have an obligation to share my wisdom."

She laughed. "If anyone has the kind of wisdom to catch

the Cashlings' attention, you're the one. Still, you've got a big job ahead—trying to undo the Shaddill's legacy." Her face grew sober. "You realize the Cashlings are all brain-damaged, right? Whatever the Shaddill did to them, the effects could be irreversible. The Shaddill had more than four thousand years to turn the Cashlings into self-absorbed ninnies . . . and it might not be something you can fix."

"If I cannot fix the Cashlings, I can still use them to fix my own people. That is a start."

I moved forward so I could see a bit more of the stickship; it would be traveling with us to Melaquin, bringing its Blood Honey fountain. No one could tell whether the honey would actually succeed in reviving the millions of Tired persons who lay dormant on my home planet—perhaps the honey had only worked on me because the Pollisand gave me special treatments four years ago. However, I had great hopes. I would lead my Cashling disciples down to the surface of Melaquin with bottles full of Blood Honey, and together we would seek out the cities, towns, and villages hidden all over the globe.

A dab of purple on each person's face might bring my world back to life.

Festina's thoughts must have turned in the same direction as mine, for when I glanced her way, she was staring at my cheek. "You're sure Blood Honey *is* a cure?" she asked softly.

"Dr. Havel has examined me. He says my brain is now undertaking a natural process of pruning: divesting itself of childish linkages to make me a full-fledged Adult. I am not so happy at losing what I have always been—I was an excellent person, Festina, even if you thought me juvenile—but the doctor believes this pruning is what I require to overcome mental stagnation. The same process may stir the rest of my people from their stupors."

"And all you have to do," Festina murmured, "is blemish your entire species—"

"It is not a blemish," I interrupted her. "It is a medicinal beauty mark."

"And you feel all right?" she asked. "You don't feel . . . I don't know. It's possible the purple guck is bad for you. Slowly possessing your brain or something."

"My brain is *just fine*," I told her. "I have not had a single incident of Tiredness since the Pollisand did this to me. In addition, I have become more worldly-wise since my transformation. For example, you will notice I am not making a scene about you leaving me again; I am now such a one as can handle cruel emotional abandonment."

Festina looked at me with a thoughtful look in her eye. "You're now such a one as can *joke* about cruel emotional abandonment." She smiled. "I think, Oar, you're going to become a very interesting woman."

I do not know which one of us started the hug; but I wanted it very much and it happened, so that is all that matters. This time I did not feel sheepish and self-conscious about embracing my dearest friend.

Not even a little bit.

We hope you've enjoyed this Eos book. As part of our mission to give readers the best science fiction and fantasy being written today, the following pages contain a glimpse into the fascinating worlds of a select group of Eos authors.

Join us as acclaimed editor David G. Hartwell brings you the best fantasy stories of the year and Juliet E. McKenna returns to the fascinating world of the Einarinn and the adventures of the thief Livak. As Dave Duncan sweeps you away to a land of swords, sorcery, intrigue, and the finest swordsmen ever. As Kristine Smith builds a suspenseful story of military secrets, interstellar politics, and alien intrigue, and James Alan Gardner returns to the fascinating world of Melaquin—and the deadly adventures of Explorer Festina Ramos. And as Martha Wells tells an epic story of endings, beginnings, and a malevolent plot to keep the world from being reborn.

Whether you like science fiction or fantasy (or both!), Eos has something for you in Fall 2001.

Year's Best Fantasy

Edited by David G. Hartwell

Coming July 2001

In the tradition of the popular YEAR'S BEST SF series, acclaimed editor David G. Hartwell now gathers together the best fantasy stories of the last year, in the inaugural volume of the YEAR'S BEST FANTASY. Travel to exotic worlds—far-off and just around the corner—with this dazzling collection of fantastic fiction.

Never before published in book form, the best fantasy stories of the last year (and the first year of the new millennium!) appear here in one volume—tales of adventure and possibility from both established masters of fantasy and rising new stars.

In "Debt of Bones" fantasy titan Terry Goodkind regales us with a long-ago adventure of the Wizard Zedd and the price of honor, in a story set in the dark times before Richard Cypher discovered his destiny to wield the *Sword of Truth.*

New York Times bestselling author George R.R. Martin returns to the *Song of Fire and Ice* with "Path of the Dragon," as Daenerys Stormborn crosses the ocean on a dangerous mission to build an army of vengeance.

In "Greedy Choke Puppy," critically acclaimed, award-winning author Nalo Hopkinson tells a tale of life and death, and the night-raids of the soucouyant, while reader favorite Charles de Lint weaves a story about injustice and making a stand—for honor and beauty and life—in "Making a Noise in this World."

The YEAR'S BEST FANTASY also includes stories of wonder and imagination from Storm Constantine, Nicola Griffith, Sherwood Smith, Michael Swanwick, Gene Wolfe, and many more.

The Gambler's Fortune
The Third Tale of Einarinn

Juliet E. McKenna

Coming August 2001

Sorgrad leaned closer to me.

"So what's the offer? No offense, Livak, but the last I heard you'd gone off with Halice to work for some wizards again. I can't say I fancy that. Charoleia told us she'd had a letter from Halice all the way from some new land clear across the ocean. The Archmage discovered it?" He gestured towards the stage where the heroine was now weeping alone. "People sleeping in a cave for thirty generations, heartless villains trying to steal their lands, wizards raising dragons to drive them off; Niello couldn't make a masquerade out of a story like that and expect people to swallow it!"

"I know it sounds incredible, but those people in the cave were the Tormalin colony that Nemith the Last lost track of just before the fall of the Old Empire," I explained.

Sorgrad looked more interested, despite himself. "We've all heard the stories about the lost colony, rivers running over golden gravel, diamonds loose in the grass. People have been trying to find it again ever since the Chaos."

"I don't know about any of that, the gold and the gems, I mean," I said hastily, 'but do you remember those islands out in the eastern ocean, the ones where I was taken when I was forced into thieving for that wizard?"

Sorgrad nodded warily and I strove to keep my voice level, ignoring memories of the ordeal. "Don't forget how much coin I brought back from that trip, Sorgrad. Say what you like about wizards, they certainly pay well." If you come back alive, I added silently to myself. "It was these Ice Islanders—well, their forefathers—who stamped the original settlers into the mud. The ones that managed to escape hid themselves in a cave, wrapped themselves up in enchantments and the Archmage sent an expedition to find them last summer. That's what Halice and me got ourselves mixed up in. These people had magic, 'Grad, old magic, not the flash tricks of the Archmage and his like, but lost enchantments that put them to sleep and kept them safe while all these generations passed. Truthfully, I saw it with my own eyes, saw them roused."

"I've heard no word of any such threat," interrupted Sorgrad skeptically.

"That's because Planir and Messire have put their heads together and decided to keep it all quiet until they've got some plan in place." Ryshad and I had argued ourselves breathless over that one, advocating instead the circulation of detailed descriptions of the Elietimm in their distinctive liveries, so that they'd stand out like the stones on a stag hound if they ever tried to make landfall again. I still thought our so-called leaders were wrong. "Some time soon, the Emperor and his cronies will be facing organized soldiery backed by enchanters who can pull the wits out through someone's nose from half a league away," I continued. "My master knows he'll need magic to fight back."

I held Sorgrad's gaze with my own. "Messire D'Olbriot wants to understand this old magic, ideally before anyone else thinks to start looking, to know what he might be up against. It gets better. The Archmage wants to learn all about this old magic as well. Artifice, that's what they're calling it now, or aetheric magic, take your pick. The point is, the wizards of Hadrumal can't use this old magic, don't ask me why. That's got Planir worried, so he's doing everything he can to find out what he might be facing."

"So your patron, if he has the information the Archmage

is so keen on finding, he can trade it for some mages to start throwing fire and lightning at any Ice Islander who wants to come ashore without paying his harbor dues?" Sorgrad was still looking thoughtful but less hostile. "That makes sense."

"I knew you'd see it," I grinned. Messire D'Olbriot hadn't, not until I put it to him, for all his years of shuffling the pieces around the games of Tormalin politics. The whole notion of getting involved with mages and wizardry was still about as welcome in Toremal as dancing with a pox-rotted whore. "As I say, this is a job that could pay very well indeed. We might even be able to play both ends against the middle and double our winnings."

Sky of Swords
A Tale of the King's Blades

Dave Duncan

Coming September 2001

"Malinda of Ranulf, you are summoned in the King's name to—"

"The Usurper's name!"

The Chancellor's dark eyes were filmy, as if he had spilled milk in them, and hair like white cobwebs fringed his red hat, but age had not softened him. "You are indicted of high treason, numerous murders, evil and illegal conjuration, fornication, misprision, conspiracy to—"

"Considering my youth, I must have been exceedingly busy! As rightful Queen of Chivial, I do not recognize the authority of this court to try me on these or any other charges."

His name had been Horatio Lambskin on the night he swore allegiance to her. Now, as Chancellor, he would be Lord Something-or-other. He posed always as a bloodless state servant, an altruistic tool serving only the common weal. He probably believed his own lie, so he would not view his change of allegiance as a crime, just a higher loyalty. At the moment his mission was to see her condemned to death, but if he failed and she ever won back the throne that was rightfully hers, he might well turn up for work the following morning in full expectation of carrying on as before.

"I will acknowledge nothing less than a jury of my peers," she said.

They had found a way around that argument, of course. "This is not a court, mistress. A bill of attainder has been laid before Parliament, condemning you to death for high treason, divers murders, evil—"

"You sound like a parrot."

Nothing changed on the skull face. "If this bill is passed by Parliament and signed into law by His Majesty, then your head will be struck off. Parliament has therefore appointed a committee to consider the evidence against you. If you do not wish to testify, you have the right to remain silent."

Strategy . . . she must think strategy. Somewhere beyond these gruesome walls, out in the world of smiles and sunshine, her supporters would be plotting on her behalf, although of course they dare do little while she was a prisoner. The Usurper could not rest easy on his ill-gotten throne as long as the rightful Queen of Chivial lived. Assassination was what she had expected: poison or pomard or the silken noose. Every new dawn had been a surprise. She had not seriously considered the possibility of a public execution, and a public trial she had never even dreamed of before the warrant for this inquiry was thrust in her hand the previous day. Perhaps Lord Chancellor Whatever-his-name-was-now did not have Parliament quite so much under control as he would like. Had an outcry forced the Usurper to stage this farce?

Dare she consider the faint possibility that she might not be going to die of it? Alas, when hope flickered, the rage that had sustained her waned and gave way to fear, so that the skin on her arms puckered in gooseflesh and her fingers began to shake. She was on trial for her life and the deck was stacked against her.

The clerk had stopped.

One of the peers jumped in with a question. ". . . that you conspired to effect the murder of your father, His Late Majesty Ambrose IV—"

"No!" she snapped. "I deny that charge utterly."

"How would you describe your relations with your father? Warm? Loyal? Dutiful?"

"It was no secret," Malinda said deliberately. "As a child I was taught to hate him, fear him, and despise him. When I was old enough to make up my own mind, I found no reason to alter those opinions. He drove his first two wives insane and murdered the third; his fourth was to be a girl a month younger than I. I sincerely believe that he was a strong and effective king of Chivial and the realm has suffered greatly from his untimely death. In his private life he was a tyrant, and I never loved him, but his death was not something I planned or desired."

She had never intended to kill him. That had been an oversight.

Law of Survival

Kristine Smith

Coming October 2001

Jani Kilian watched the roofless vehicle resume its slow-float toward the Ministry proper. Then she pressed her hand to the gatekeeper square; the device scanned her palm, and the gate swung open.

Colonel Niall Pierce stood near the entry, bent over a late-blooming hybrid rose. He wore dress blue-greys, but no fairy tale Jani could think of would have claimed him as its hero. In contrast to a prince's clean, broad brow and high cheekbones, this weathered pretender possessed a narrow visage, sun-battered and lined, the effect of length accentuated by the scar that cut the left side of his face from the edge of his nose to the corner of his mouth. Young blond was replaced by old bronze; springy fitness gave way to wary tension.

Only his eyes spoke to the humor in the man. The warm gold-brown of the richest honey, they hinted at depths of emotion.

Niall straightened when he heard the gate slam shut. "Jani." He touched his fingers to his forehead in a modest salute. "One brass-plated jackass at your service." His voice twanged, middle-pitch and sharp, lower-class Victorian blunted by years spent on other worlds.

Jani shoved her hands in her pockets to keep from saluting back. It was a private joke between them and she didn't feel like humoring him right now. "You scared the hell out of me."

"I doubt it." He grinned, the expression twisting his damaged lip into a sneer. "I wish I could have seen the look on Pull's face when you sneaked up behind him on the overpass."

The memory of the young man's cherry redness forced a smile from Jani. "It was fun."

"Pull's a good kid." Niall moved from the rose to an autumn hydrangea, lifting one of the bloom-heavy branches to his nose. "Unfortunately, these days, tailing means homing in on someone's ID chip and letting the equipment do the work. Next line of offense is an implant in clothing or a vehicle. Pretty Boy's chip is sheathed, you had yours removed after your discharge, and Pull never got close enough to plant anything."

"His hair's a problem." Jani wandered a wide semicircle until she stood alongside him. He pushed the branch toward her, and she bent to sniff the blooms. They were brilliant purple, with a heavy, spicy-sweet scent. "He might as well have been carrying a torch."

"He's a wizard with an instrument array." Niall released the branch and stepped away. Jani had flinched once when he accidentally touched her. Since then, he took care not to remain close to her for too long. "I wanted to give him some old-fashioned street work, show him all the things he didn't know that he didn't know."

Jani watched him straighten and lock his hands behind his back. For all his outward gallantry, he didn't seem the least concerned that he had alarmed her, that he had used her past against her to manufacture a training exercise for his green lieutenant. "You're nasty."

The full meaning of her remark settled over Niall gradually—his grin froze, then faded. "I was just trying to get your attention."

"Well, you have it."

Niall reached beneath his brimmed lid to scratch the top of the head, readjusted the braid-trimmed hat to its former dead-on level, then plucked a speck of nonexistent dirt from the front of his steel-blue tunic. "Ever been to Tsing Tao Station?" He tugged at a badge. "Biggest shuttle transfer station in the Pearl Way, last stop before you hit the GateWay and enter La Manche, the Channel Worlds—"

"I know what it is." Jani watched Niall take great care to look everywhere but at her. "A few years ago."

"Four and a half?"

"Yes. Four and a half."

"Did you just pass through, or did you work there for a time?"

"I did a few odd jobs to earn billet money. Same as I did at every other station I ever passed through. I think I stopped-over there for a total of six months."

"Five." Niall yanked a brown leaf from the branch of a late-blooming rose. "Kill anybody while you were there?"

Jani studied him for any sign he joked. The hints were always there to see—the narrowing of his eyes, the working of his jaw as he bit the inside of his cheek to keep from laughing. But she couldn't find them this time. Unfortunately. "No."

Wheel of the Infinite

Martha Wells

Coming December 2001

Maskelle paused at the dropped tailgate, looking into the dark. She could see the temple from here.

The massive domed spire was black against the lighter shade of the sky, the moon shape of the portal below it barely visible; male and female phallic symbols woven together. The detail of the terraced carvings were entirely lost in shadow. They had passed small sanctuaries along the way, but this was the first time in too many years that she had been so close to a true temple.

She moved away from the wagon, one of the oxen snuffling at her as she drifted past. The temple was calling to her, not the stone shell, but what it represented, and the power that likeness gave it.

She walked through the sodden grass until she came to the edge of the baray and stepped up onto the stone bank. The Koshan priests had the custody of the temples, but they were only static forms. It was the End of Year Rite that remade the universe in its own image, and that was only performed by the Voices of the Ancestors. The End of Decade rites were even more crucial.

This year would be the End of a Hundred Years rite.

Maskelle lifted her staff, holding it above her head. An echo whispered through her, a reflection from the Infinite through the structure of the temple. After all these years, it still knew her. "I helped another stranger tonight," she whispered. "I didn't kill anyone to do it. Not intentionally, at least. Is that enough for you?"

A slow wave of darkness climbed the temple wall, the lamps in the windows winking out one by one.

She lowered the staff and let out her breath. No, it wasn't enough. *And now they will all know you're back.* Oh, the delight in the power never died, that was the curse, and her true punishment, whatever the Adversary had decreed. She shook her head at her own folly and turned back to the camp.

She reached the wagon and climbed up the back steps, closing the panels that faced the campsite. She sat on the still damp wooden floor, looking out at the temple and the silver surface of the baray in the distance.

She was facing the right direction for an illusion of privacy, though voices from the other campsites, oddly distorted over the plain, came to her occasionally. The night breeze was chilly on her wet clothes, the drying mud itchy on her legs. And someone was watching her. She knew it by the way the oxen, caught in the firelight from behind the wagon, cocked their ears. She found his outline in the dark finally, about twenty feet away, sitting on his heels just out of reach of the light. She might have walked within ten feet of him on the way to the baray. Again, the shock of being so taken by surprise was like ice on her skin. She waited until it drained away, then quietly she said, "Come here."

The breeze moved the short grass. He stood up and came toward the wagon.

Her staff, as much a part of her as her hands or feet, lay on the wooden bench of the wagon. He stopped just out of arm's reach. Her arm's reach. She was within easy range of his sword.

JAMES ALAN GARDNER

From Festina Ramos:

I met Oar beside a moonlit lake, just after dusk on the day I had murdered my best friend. She was tall, sad, and impossibly beautiful: like an Art Deco figurine molded from purest crystal.

Yes—she was made of glass. Looking through her, I could see the beach, the moon, the world . . . focused through a woman-shaped lens.

When I think about her, I can't help perceiving her glass body as a metaphor. She was, for example, transparent as glass emotionally. When she was angry, she raged; when frightened, she trembled; when lonely, she wept. She was as open as a child . . . and people who didn't know her often dismissed her as childish, unintelligent, bratty. Oar was none of those things—she was a fully grown woman with an intelligence high off the scales (she learned fluent English in just a few weeks), and her constant claims of superiority to us "opaque persons" weren't arrogant but heartbreaking: an attempt to convince herself she had some value in the universe.

Like glass, she was fragile. Not physically, of course: she was damned near unbreakable, and immune to disease, drowning, even starvation (she could photosynthesize energy from the weakest light sources). She was strong too—fast and agile. But mentally, Oar was ready to shatter. Thousands of years ago, her kind was created by unknown aliens in mimicry of *Homo sapiens* . . . but due to a design flaw (accidental or deliberate), the glass race always suffered mental shutdown by age fifty. First, a tendency to boredom; then, a growing listlessness; finally, a descent into torpor, a sleep that could only be broken by the most extreme measures and then only for a few minutes before senility crept back in.

Oar was on the verge of that abyss. Her whole species was. They didn't die, they just grew Tired: turning into ageless glass statues, alive but dormant. As Oar approached the age when her brain would betray her, she fought her fate, she denied it, she raged; and in the end, it seemed as if she had found a way out. During a battle to save her world from extinction, she sacrificed herself by plunging from the top of an eighty-story tower, taking with her a madman who planned the destruction of her planet. I wept when I saw her body smashed on the pavement . . . but I told myself that by choosing death, Oar had avoided a more cruel destiny—the gradual loss of who she was, the dull fade-out to oblivion.

Her glass would have warped with age: the lens going dark, the mirror turning cloudy.

But I was wrong. Oar didn't die in that fall—she was tougher than I ever imagined. Bulletproof glass. And now that she's back, pursued by inhuman creatures with secrets to hide, the question is whether she can avoid mental oblivion long enough to save those of us who need her help.

Running from aliens, dodging the gunfire, trying to figure out what the hell's going on before we all get killed . . . hey, it's just like old times.